Mrs Normal Sa

Sheila Hayman

VariOUS books

First published in the UK and on the internet by
Various Books UK in 2008

ISBN 978-1-4092-4895-8

9 781409 248958

"One man with an idea in his head is in danger of being considered a madman, two men with the same idea in common may be foolish, but can hardly be mad; ten men sharing an idea begin to act, a hundred draw attention as fanatics, a thousand and society begins to tremble, a hundred thousand and there is war abroad, and the cause has victories tangible and real; and why only a hundred thousand? Why not a hundred million, and peace on earth?"

William Morris

...but William Morris was a man. And he didn't have childcare issues.

'Maid of Orleans or Millac Maid?' The voice found Iris and dragged her back to life.

'Excuse me?'

'Black or Millac Maid with your tea, the fridge is on the fritz again. You've missed supper and that's it until breakfast. I haven't got all night.'

Something was odd about this situation. How long was it since Iris had been offered tea in bed? People like her are not brought tea. They are the bringers of tea, as well as everything else. It's a rule. So who was this strange, fuzzy person looming over her with a mug? Iris shifted to get the person into focus, and a flight of daggers converged behind her eyeball. Her right knee was an aching hummock under the bedclothes, and her left hand, as far as she dared to look, was covered in meringue.

Then she remembered.

Normal life doesn't prepare you for becoming a murderess. Part of you – the habit-forming, reptile-brain part – carries on just as before, unaware that it's no longer appropriate to hum, read your horoscope, or pick your nose as you fall asleep. You don't stop wanting a cup of tea with proper milk, just because you've killed somebody.

But even as she opened her mouth to complain, the other part of her brain clamped it shut again. What was she doing even doing thinking about tea, when she had in one tiny, irreversible moment, destroyed not only her own life, not merely those of her own family, but no doubt a huge brood of her innocent victim's children, destined, in years to come, to unleash a chain reaction of violent revenge on the world?

She checked her wrist for handcuffs, but all she found was a plastic wristband saying 'Sedate as necessary', which seemed ominous enough. Nor were there any detectives ringing her bed; in fact she had no visitors at all, which was, on reflection, exactly what she expected. Who'd waste seedless grapes on a murderess like her?

Something bad had happened that day – well, she was beginning to realise, more than one thing. It had begun normally enough: Malcolm had waited until his breakfast was in front of him to tell her he'd be fine with just a cup of coffee. Ted had sprayed cereal like an epileptic hamster over his clothes, the floor, and somehow one earlobe, while reciting in ball-by-ball detail his latest download from ITV Sports Extra. And Molly had managed to snatch the essential building-blocks of adolescent genius from the fridge without interrupting her brooding passage from locked bedroom to front door with either a 'good morning' or 'goodbye'.

So, with the others gone, Ted safely crowbarred into Gordon Road Primary, and the collateral damage more or less repaired, it had seemed like a good day to attack the question of whether Aidan at Fly Away Home, one of her favourite accountancy clients, could charge his most recent ski trip as a legitimate business expense. Travel agents' holidays were always good for a prolonged, and profitable, argument with the Revenue. It was the last day she could file the tax return, but also the last query on it, and she got off the phone at lunch time with a pleasant sense of having shaken another bureaucrat out of his certainties. And there remained just enough time to sort out her summer clothes from the attic before the children returned from school; a job which ought to have taken only minutes, given that ninety per cent of it would be too young, too tight, or both.

But right next to the bag of garments stockpiled for the day when open-toed Granny boots might boomerang back into fashion, she came upon the box of Ted and Molly's things, hidden evidence of a shaming sentimentality. Molly's first ballet shoes, with three rows of elastic to keep them on her doughy, tiny feet. The Brio swing bridge that Ted always opened just in time to let the train crash to its doom on the dinosaur rug. And there was the Johnny Cash CD! Iris had looked everywhere for that, and had finally given up hope of ever seeing it again. Here was the soundtrack to a summer marooned with her babies, on a love-soaked island of maternal bliss.

At that moment Iris heard the front door bang downstairs. Molly, clumping, via the fridge, to her room. Molly's bag hurled to the floor, the door double-locked, the chair dragged over to her computer. Ted would be behind, shedding garments like autumn leaves. Iris waited for him to yell a greeting, excited at the prospect of sharing her discovery.

There was his schoolbag, hurled to the floor in turn. There were his implausibly huge school lace-ups galloping up the stairs. A second bedroom door slammed. Then – nothing.

Silence. He wasn't coming out. Iris waited another minute, puzzled and then distressed. Something terrible must have happened at school, something so bad that Ted couldn't bear to tell her. Still holding the CD, Iris ran downstairs and opened his door, poised to console. But the face looking up at her was as happy and candid as a buttercup. 'Hi Mum.'

'Oh hi, Ted – um – is something wrong?'

'Wrong? No Mum, look here, look at what the Chelsea strikers were wearing in 1972...'

'Only – it's just that you didn't say hello. When you came in.'

'Didn't I? Look Mum look here on eBay, you can get George Best's shirt he was wearing for the FA Cup...'

He forgot. He forgot I was here, waiting for him to get home. He forgot I even existed.

Iris stood there, the CD frozen in her hand, with the sense of an irreversible moment passing. In another mood she'd have scruffed his hair and feigned an interest in George Best, but sentimentality had stripped her defences. She thrust the CD towards him like a talisman, willing it to work its magic. 'Look Ted I found that CD, you know, the one you used to make me play all the time when you were four? "Just around the Corner, there's Heartbreak"...'

With a tiny sigh, Ted swing round from his computer and turned towards her a pale, quizzical face – not cruel, not intending any hurt, just blank, as though the passionate joy he had put into yelling Johnny Cash with his adored mother had simply been rationally erased to make space for something more age-appropriate, like Thierry Henry's goal average. A moment searching for the lost data, then: 'No, Mum, I don't remember. Actually I'm a bit busy right now...' and he swung back to OldFootballShirts.com.

Iris turned and stumbled out of the door. Just around the corner there's heartbreak, indeed. The diabolical genius of Johnny Cash, precisely skewering the transformation – no doubt mirroring his own – from adoring, inseparable soul-mate to grudgingly cooperative lodger, with prior loyalties to a Japanese game machine.

'Oh Mum could you make me tea Mum, not too hot and more milky and are there any crumpets left, can I have two?' The voice trailed her down the stairs.

His imperial majesty needs tea. Of course. Get back into your box, Iris. Know your place Iris, pick up their jumpers, earn your kisses, make the tea, get it right or else. And don't waste time yearning for what's gone.

She opened the freezer on autopilot, pulled out the crumpets, and banged them into the microwave, glancing at the clock as she slammed the door.

Tea's late today – that's what you get for wallowing in nostalgia. Late... The tax return! If it's not in the post tonight...

Iris cancelled the microwave, yelled up the stairs 'I'll just be a minute, Ted!' and raced for the door. She'd missed the last delivery to all the walkable post boxes. She'd have to take the car. She grabbed the keys, realising she was still clutching the CD, and arced it into the dustbin as she rushed down the path, sniffing back tears.

She banged out of the gate, narrowly sidestepping a neatly knotted bag of dog turds, sprinted to the car and squealed away from the curb, leaving a souvenir paint slick on Number 23's Golf. The matched pairs of London brick villas with their white-iced gables and variegated front doors, which usually gave her the comforting sense of inhabiting a densely-populated fairy tale, had suddenly become breeding grounds for self-deception and broken dreams.

She gunned by them, over the lumpy strip of new tarmac covering yet another giant broadband pipeline, bringing ninety-three more channels of junk to distract the residents of Hartland Gardens from the multiple anxieties and disappointments of their lives. Failing for the first time ever to wave at Mr Slobodka in the door of his corner shop, she spun the corner on two wheels, only to be confronted by a happy gang of Murphy men with jackhammers and striped barriers, busy installing yet another set of speed bumps furnished by a yet another European slush fund.

Iris reversed sharply. Damn. It would have to be the bloody High Street then, the route she'd been hoping to avoid, it being now peak hour for returning commuters, last-pickup UPS vans and packed bendy-busses. Sure enough, she ended up right on the tail of a Number 29, as it juddered to a halt exactly across the turning she needed to avoid the temporary traffic lights by Danny's cash machine.

She sat there, watching the pedestrians barge and nudge each other, taking their chances in the road to gain a few seconds. Rushing to make somebody's tea, load the washing machine, change another nappy. Just like her, thousands of them. Probably millions. Millions of women who'd put away their own private joys and desires, suppressed all thought of how it might have been, to raise a generation of children who think their lives will end if they don't have an iPod Nano, or a PS3, or a face like Beyonce or Hannah Montana, who go straight from school to Father Ted's with a £5 fake ID card to fortify themselves with lager and Mr Potato Heads for an evening dodging homework. Children like Ted and Molly. Not delinquent, aberrant or criminal, just...

For God's sake, how long can it take? Come on. Come ON!

The bus hadn't moved, a wavering line of pensioners shuffling sticks, shopping bags and travel cards at its open door. Suddenly, the traffic coming the other way opened up for a moment. Iris spun the wheel, jammed her foot down and curved out past the bus, just as a plastic Tesco bag wisped across her windshield, blinding it for a moment. It floated off, and suddenly, from nowhere

- A bike.

Laden with bags. Wobbling right at her, down the middle of the road.

Bloody get out of the way, you...

MOVE, YOU STUPID COW!!!!

Oh god. What happened then?

Something very, very bad.

Iris came back to the present, wanting only to die herself, as soon as possible. Unfortunately, that didn't seem to be an immediate option. The meringue on her left hand was a fat white bandage, the fuzzy vision came from another on her forehead, and the lump under the bedclothes throbbed periodically, but apart from that nothing major seemed broken.

'I don't think you ought to be taking in caffeine, you're probably still in shock. I've got plenty of this Bhutan chai, if you can reach it. And help yourself to arnica drops as well, you should put them under your tongue, for the bruising.'

Chai! Arnica! Why not snake venom, with a chaser of strychnine? But the voice from the next bed was soothing, like a Japanese pebble fountain. 'My name's Soren, by the way. Sorry I can't shake hands, I'm a bit banged up I'm afraid. Would you like a raw macaroon?'

Iris shifted awkwardly to take a closer look. Soren's head was turbaned with bandages, and both arms were swathed up to the hem of her hospital sleeves. Her face was kind, with eyes like big, deep pools of understanding. Iris' ravenous reptile brain had retreated in shame, and she couldn't imagine eating or drinking ever again. 'No, that's really sweet of you but I – somehow I've lost my appetite for – er – raw macaroons.'

Soren smiled kindly. 'I'm sure it's not so bad. You've had a nasty bang, your energies will still be quite depleted. It'll all look much better in a day or two. Think of your children, you have to be brave for them'.

How did she know Iris had children? Oh of course – the tabloids. There were none anywhere in sight, a sure sign that the nurses had taken them away for their break. Maybe that was the silver lining in all this? Max Clifford was bound to be interested in the story of a blameless housewife, mother and part-time book-keeper turned road rage maniac. She'd probably have to arrange for the proceeds to be left in trust for her motherless brood. But they'd be sure to turn up on visiting days, with a giant legacy in the balance. Wouldn't they?

Soren was eating her macaroon in tiny bites because of her bandages. She must have had a terrible accident. Iris was about to ask, when Soren swallowed the last crumb and asked: 'Is it something you'd like to share with me?'

The woman didn't look like a fellow-murderess, but neither

did Iris, so far as she knew. And there is, as Malcolm was apt to remind Iris whenever their joint bank account developed a mysterious deficit, something very comforting about confession. 'It was all my fault. Totally. I mean – I don't know what happened. Or I do, but what it did to me - I've never been angry like that before. It was like I was somebody else. Some insane, rage-fuelled maniac. And it happened just like that, just because...'

'Because what?' Soren leaned in to listen. Even through several layers of gauze, her skin was not a great advertisement for raw cuisine.

Iris pushed away the thought, and tried to focus. What was it, really? 'Well, I mean it's going to sound so silly. But you know – when they're tiny, I mean your children, they're part of you, aren't they? I mean, literally. And even when they're born, you're touching them and holding them, all the time. And then they start to walk, but even then you have to carry them and lift them up, they still need you for everything. And then...'

'Don't upset yourself, it breeds toxins. Just allow the feeling. It will flow though you more quickly. Just breathe deeply, and feel it flow.'

Iris tried, but all she could feel was the pain in her head, and her eye patch getting soggy. 'I'm so sorry – I wonder, do you have a tissue?'

'I'm afraid I don't do disposables. I've a hankie if you can reach it, look, there by the nori balls...'

A hankie? Iris leaned nervously towards Soren's bedside table, fearing the worst. But there it was; clean and folded, a soft, silky square with a rich Paisley pattern. 'Gosh, it's beautiful! I haven't used a proper hankie for ages...'

'Most people don't. Enough tissues are landfilled every year to cover Warwickshire, you know.'

Iris carefully unfolded the hankie and wiped her eyes with it. It smelled of hay and bluebells. She sniffed deeply before wiping her eyes, keeping it clenched in her hand as she continued: 'Where was I? Oh, yes, the children. And then, you know, they start to grow away. You lose touch. Literally. I mean they have to grow up, of course, I know that really, but... And then pretty soon they only kiss you as a ritual sort of thing, at bedtime or at school, so long as nobody else is watching... And then...'

Then, one day, you discover that their charm has become self-conscious, a currency to be bartered for treats and money, traded up in competition with each other. Molly only graces me with a kiss when she needs to shake me down for something. And Ted's hugs are just a ritualised way to check that I'm still here, in case he might possibly need feeding or putting to bed whenever the current Fantasy Football daydream loosens its grip.

'...And then you realise it's been fifteen years of your life. Gone. And for what?'

'Any more coffee cups? Tea cups?' The nurse was back, rattling her trolley like a spectre's chains. Iris sniffed into the hankie again. 'Well, I suppose that part of my life's over now. They'll be grown up and gone before I'm out.'

'I don't think you need to be quite so pessimistic. I heard the doctors tell your husband you'd be on your feet in a couple of days.'

'I didn't mean out of here! I meant...' Iris muttered, barely audibly, into her paper gown – 'I meant out of... Holloway'.

'Holloway! Goodness, I don't think you need worry about that, I've already told them I'm not going to press charges'.

'You?' Iris looked at Soren again. That face – she knew she'd seen it somewhere... 'You're not going to... it was you? On the bike? And you're alive? You're alive! Nurse! She's alive!' Suddenly Iris was ravenously hungry, and enormously cheerful. 'Nurse, I know you said we'd missed supper, but... could you possibly rustle something up, do you think?'

The nurse looked at Iris as though she was well overdue for her sedation break, muttered something about not being paid to rustle, and hurled a menu onto the bed as she banged out of the swing doors.

'Yes, it was a little miracle. The plastic bag slowed you down just enough to let me get out of your way. You went into the clothes bank, and I ended up by the cash point. HSBC I think it was.'

'Really? I bet Danny was shocked, that's been his pitch for ages.' Iris picked up the menu and scrutinised it eagerly. 'This food sounds okay actually, are you going to have anything? Look there's steak and mushroom pie... Oh, but I guess you probably don't eat meat, do you? I keep meaning to stop, the slaughterhouses and everything.'

'I'm afraid the slaughterhouses are the least of it. It's the land they occupy, which you know about, I'm sure. And of course the land used to grow their food. Then there's the nitrogen in the fertilisers.

Almost half of the world's cereal, I'm sure you know, is fed to intensively farmed animals. And then...'

Did I know? Maybe I did...

Soren had only paused to breathe '...Then there's the water. Nine thousand litres of it, for every kilo of beef. Third World countries are crippling themselves to import clean drinking water, just so people here can eat...' Soren's voice quivered with revulsion '...steak and mushroom pie. Not that I'd ever make a judgement on any particular individual, of course.'

Water! Should I be worried about water?

Iris looked out of the window. Being May, the rain wasn't just coming down, but bouncing energetically off every surface on its path. Water didn't seem to be too much of a problem in the immediate neighbourhood; but then, there weren't a lot of cattle farms in the inner suburbs of London. Soren leaned over and added: 'Of course, it's totally your choice. I can't remember when I last ate meat, so it's no hardship for me any more. It must be tough to stop when you're really hooked.'

I'm a junkie now, not just a murderess.

'Oh look, cauliflower cheese. That sounds very soothing, doesn't it?'

'I'm sure it's delicious...'

'Nurse! Nurse, could I please have the...'

'... so long as you don't think about where the rennet comes from. Still, there is a kind of twisted logic to it, isn't there? They have to do something with the calves, once they've torn them away from their mothers. I don't suppose you've ever been to a dairy farm, have you? They cry for weeks. Day and night. It's almost kinder to kill them. Though of course that doesn't help the mothers.'

Now I'm a murderess, a junkie and a bovine infanticide. Can I really have slept a full eight hours only days ago?

For some reason Iris' appetite for hospital food had vanished as suddenly as it had arrived. Soren smiled forgivingly. 'But go for it, honestly – Iris, isn't it? Of course, I'd never dream of imposing my views on anybody'.

'God, you didn't really think I was going to eat any of it, did you? I just wanted to see how bad things had got with the NHS these days.'

The nurse returned and loomed over the bed, daring Iris to

add to her workload. She took one last look at the menu. Jam roly poly. How cruel could that be?

'Could I just have the roly-poly please?'

Oh god. Suet.

'Come again?'

'No, that's fine, I'd better not overload my system just yet. Could I just have – a glass of water, perhaps?'

'You'll get water with your pills at ten.' And grabbing the menu before Iris could change her mind again, she vanished.

'Don't let them feed you any of those painkillers. Here, I'm sure if I just... Oh, golly. I really am a bit bashed up!' Slowly, wincing with the effort, Soren eased herself out of bed and hobbled towards Iris. She was obviously in a lot of pain – and it was all Iris' fault. Yet she hadn't uttered one word of reproach. How could Iris ever make it up to her? Something about this woman - so calm, thoughtful and forgiving - made Iris feel like a less evolved organism: a kind of moral grub. Still, Iris was slightly worried by the hands, lumpy with New Mexican silver, converging on her neck.

'I should be able to do this still, and my fingers could use the exercise. We just need to release the shock. Here. Relax.'

She was just going to give Iris a head massage. After everything! Iris felt more ashamed than ever. 'I'm really, really sorry. I was just so upset about the children, and then I was late delivering the tax return from Fly Away Home, and I'd have got into terrible trouble if I hadn't posted it... oh God. I didn't post it. Did I?'

'Don't worry. It was a miracle, and it was for a reason. You've been spared, and so have I. So now we need to think about what to do with this incredible second chance.'

Fresh from her near-miss with incarceration, Iris had been rather looking forward to a return to normal life, but clearly Soren had her gaze fixed on higher ground. The fingers grinding into Iris' neck at least distracted her from the pounding and aching elsewhere. The soothing voice murmured in her ear: 'I know how you feel about your little ones. And I only wish I could tell you you're wrong. But I'm sorry to say, I've got three grown up children, and I don't hear from them from one year to the next. One in Australia, one in Hong Kong, and one in Beaconsfield, but they all have their own lives, and of course I wouldn't be selfish enough to have them spew all that carbon into the atmosphere to visit me, just from a sense of duty. You wouldn't want your children coming to visit you out of guilt either, would you?'

She paused for a moment, to let the finer details of the picture imprint themselves on Iris' inner eye, before continuing: 'I'm afraid it's just Nature's way, once the cycle of childbirth and shelter is accomplished. You and I are just so much rotting vegetation on the compost heap of humanity... But do you know, I don't believe that's the real reason you're feeling depressed. Look out of the window. What do you see?'

Iris struggled a bit higher up in the bed, and peered between the plastic slats of the blinds. 'Well, there's the Peabody Buildings, it said in the paper they're going to be converted into luxury flats to pay for the new leisure centre, anything to keep the council tax down I guess... And oh look, they've finally taken the temporary traffic lights away. If they'd only done it last week, you and I would have...'

'Do you see beauty, wildness, nature - anything to lift the heart?'

'Well, um...'

'No, you don't. It's been torn up, crushed and destroyed, all of it. We've taken a gorgeous, vibrant planet, a breathtaking web of evolutionary miracles, and turned it into a wasteland of junk food, toxic landfills, internet pornography, and civil wars, where orphaned children are raped and drugged into shooting each other with Kalashnikovs they can barely lift. Even the glaciers of Mont Blanc are yellow with human urine!'

Put like that, it did seem rather grim. How had Iris managed to ignore all this up to now? Soren brushed one hand over her forehead. 'You're getting very tense again. Give away the tension. Just relax.'

Iris tried hard to relax into the knowledge that she had been spared a violent early death, only to awaken staring wide-eyed at the evils of a world of which she had previously been, no doubt irrationally, rather fond. Her relief at not having killed anybody was giving way to a terrible sense of generalised foreboding. Maybe she really was depressed. Now she thought about it, there was plenty to be depressed about.

'But it's all right.' The seaweed-scented breath wafted past her ear.

'It is?'

Soren moved round to sit on the side of Iris' bed, and rested one bandaged hand on her plaster. Moral righteousness appeared to be an energy source as infinite as the winds and tides. Iris, her resurgent cheerfulness utterly deflated by the litany of doom, clung like a drowning kitten to this hint of hope.

'Iris, what did you say to me just now?'

'I don't know – sorry? Did I say sorry yet? I mean, I owe you...'

'You don't owe me anything. You said you felt your life had been wasted. Do you remember, way back when you were young...'

It's not that long ago, Iris thought.

'...Do you remember what you thought your life would be?'

Iris looked back along the years, back before the children, before even Malcolm. She remembered jumping around in fields to the Happy Mondays with her first boyfriend. She remembered coming top in her maths exam and thinking she'd be running a FTSE 100 company in ten years. Then what happened? She went on her Gap year, and... 'I thought I'd be changing the world.'

'There you go.'

'I don't quite...'

Soren patted Iris' arm and gave her an encouraging little smile, like a kindly maths teacher waiting for the answer to pop into her pupil's head. 'You said your children didn't need you any more. Of course they don't need you to change their nappies, or blow their noses. They need you for something much, much more important. They need you to set an example; an example that that lifts, not impoverishes, the spirit. A life defined by values and ideals, not the things you pile up behind you. Then you'll feel good about yourself again.'

Iris wasn't sure that she had the energy, right now, to invent an entirely new blueprint for civilisation. On the other hand, she had to admit, however reluctantly, to a kind of nagging, low level guilt that it would be quite nice to lose. And it was true – she had somehow lost her ideals along the way. But didn't everybody? Wasn't that part of growing up, to realise your dreams were just - dreams?

'So there you are. It's a big task, but we are all capable of so much more than we realise. Your children are grown, your time is your own. Listen to that voice, the one that said you could change the world. Listen to it, Iris, and you'll find the answer.'

Suddenly, Iris got it. Soren wasn't just talking about hydrogenated fat in Jammy Dodgers. She was talking about Nelson

Mandela, Martin Luther King – Joan of Arc!

'I'll leave you to rest now. I do get a bit carried away, and then I forget I'm still pretty knocked about.' With a brave little smile, Soren slid off the bed, and nearly fell. Guilt stabbed anew at Iris' conscience. 'Oh dear, can I...'

'No, I'm fine. I'm just a bit wobbly. Try to get some sleep now. You've got exciting times ahead!'

Iris felt terribly tired herself. A lot seemed to have happened since she'd come round. She'd think about it all – later.

Joan lay in bed, her eyes closed, savouring a moment of peace before she got up to milk the goats. There was a pain in her knee and another in her head, but they hadn't woken her. What had woken her was a strange buzzing noise. It sounded like paper being scrunched up for recycling, except paper and recycling hadn't come to the village yet. Maybe it sounded more like radio interference? But radio hadn't been invented yet either. As she puzzled over all of this, the crackling steadied into a voice, whispering in her ear.

'Joan!' it said. Maybe it was Grandpa, needing his night bucket. Surely she put it out for him? She turned over. Ouch.

'Joan!' The voice was more irritated. 'JOAN! Wake up! I have a message for you!'

Ah. Toothless Gaston with an errand for his lordship. More love potions from the old witch at the crossroads, no doubt.

Joan opened her eyes and had a good scratch, which was how she usually greeted the day. Everything looked just the same as usual; the window shutter was still falling off its hinge, the cat had deposited another rat in her clog. But the voice, tetchier than ever, was still there.

'Joan! Pay attention. I need you to save France, which as you know is, in effect, saving the world.'

'Me? I don't know a thing about saving, you try saving with the oats market at an all-time low.'

'Nevertheless, I've chosen you. Hurry up and eat your unappetising dry crust and gruel, and get yourself down to the blacksmith, he's expecting you.'

'The blacksmith? What about the goats? And young Edouard hasn't finished his psalms for Sunday school, there's only me between him and thirty Hail Marys.'

'He's excused the psalms. Trust me on this one. And the goats can wait. Get up, you lazy thing. How are you going to do the work of a thousand men if you can't even shift your arse out of bed?'

'Why the blacksmith?'

'For your breastplate and sword, of course.'

'What, I have to kill people?'

'Or be killed. Your choice. Saving the world is not for the faint of heart. Now get on with it. Feeling better?'

'What?'

'Feeling better?'

'Oh. Oh, Malcolm! Yes, actually, I had this really weird – I think it was a dream...' Remarkably, Iris did feel considerably better, whether through Soren's ministrations or the big bag of Pringles, Penguins and mini Melton Mowbray pork pies dangling between Malcolm's russet-bristled face and her bed. He wasn't beaming with undiluted affection; but nor did he appear, to Iris' relief, to be clutching divorce papers. Life was definitely worth a second go.

Then she remembered Soren. But, swivelling her head painfully to check, she discovered Soren fast asleep. And after all, a person can't be expected to change the habits of a lifetime just like that, especially in the aftermath of a near-fatal accident. A doctor's opinion would be required, at the very least, and luckily the presence of a doctor in Ward H was about as likely as dolphin in the canal next to Sainsbury's. She'd just have a bit of everything, to wean herself off it, and then never eat anything but steamed vegetables and bulghur wheat, ever again.

'I'm ravenous. How clever you are.' Iris was about to reach for a pie and a kiss, when she noticed something else. 'I suppose the children aren't here because they're ashamed of me. And who can blame them?'

She paused dramatically, but Malcolm was switching off his mobile, so she carried on. 'Anyway, it doesn't matter. I'm surplus to requirements. It's not their fault I'm just a – a rotting pile of leaves on the great dungheap of human evolution...'

'I've no idea what you're yammering about, but he children aren't here because they're at school. Unless Molly's off doing more of what she's pleased to call 'feral learning'. It's ten o'clock in the morning.'

'Ten o'clock? Morning? I've missed breakfast!' Somewhat consoled, Iris took the pie and shoved it into her mouth in one bite. She was rather hoping it would taste of dust and ashes, but it was more delicious than any pie she could ever remember. Well, if this was the last junk food she was ever going to eat, she might as well make the most of it. 'Can you open the Pringles, do you think? This wrist...'

'You're lucky it's not worse. If I'd known you were going off-roading on the High Street I'd have bought a dodgem, not a Jeep. What on earth did you think you were up to?' But he reached for the tube and began to wrestle it open.

'Can't you do it more quietly?'

'Quietly? Why are you whispering suddenly?'

'It's – er – Soren there in the next bed, I don't want to disturb her sleep, and...'

Iris made a feeble grab for the bag. '...D'you have any silent food in here, by any chance?'

'Silent food?'

'You know, soggy sandwiches, boiled spinach – what was that? She's waking up, quick, put it all away!'

Malcolm put a hand to Iris' forehead. 'Should we have that head X-ray double checked, d'you think?'

'Head? No, my headache's totally gone. She really does have special powers. Ooh look, she's turned over, I'll just have a quick Penguin and then you can hide it all again.'

'I've just this minute bought it, why would I need to hide it?'

'Or better still, throw it all away, on your way out.' Looking into his bemused face, Iris realised, foggily, that the time had come to put her cards on the table. The shock that had driven her out that day, the accident, Soren's hint at a grander destiny, and then that curiously vivid dream... Her eyes had been opened, and, however painful the vision, she couldn't un-see it now. She unwrapped a Penguin, took a bite, and began. 'Malcolm – I've been meaning to talk to you.'

'You'd do better without a mouthful of chocolate, but talk

away.'

'Please. This is serious. Did you know the average Sunday lunch travels fifty thousand miles to reach us?'

'From my memory, it's been about four years since we had a Sunday lunch, so if it's been looking for Hartland Gardens all that time, you're probably right.'

'And do you know how much water it takes to produce a kilo of beef? Nine thousand litres! For one kilo! And yet global meat consumption is set to double in the next twenty years!'

'Aha! You've been reading the Guardian, haven't you? How on earth did you find it in here?'

'Malcolm! You're not listening!' How could he remain so ridiculously flippant in the face of these revelations? Like some schoolboy, hoping it would all go away if he laughed at it. Iris racked her memory for some more of Soren's horrifying statistics. 'The water tables of the world are sinking catastrophically because everybody is eating meat instead of tomatoes! Every time somebody in the West eats a burger, a little child in Africa - dies!'

'Fine by me, I'll just stick to chips. Presumably if there are all these cows around, there'll be plenty of milk for the children?'

'Only because the mother cows are brutally torn from their babies almost at the moment of birth. Imagine if every baby in that post-natal ward at St Mary's had gone off to be weighed, and just - never come back. Imagine little Ted... so tiny and helpless...'

'Now, now, don't upset yourself. Molly seems to prefer WKD Shooters these days anyway. I was shielding you from it, but you'd have found out some time. Where are you getting all this rubbish from, if it's not the Guardian?'

'Rubbish! It's not rubbish, it's...' In the next bed, Soren snuffled and shifted in her sleep. Iris tried to lean in front of the Permaculture Weekly by Soren's pillow, but he'd spotted it. That and the bottles of blue-green algae. And the macaroons. 'It's her, isn't it?'

'It's not what you think, she's wonderful. She's the woman on the bike! I nearly killed her and she forgave, me, just like that. She's really you know, a good person.'

Malcolm looked dubious. He'd always been suspicious of good people ever since being slammed into a dustbin full of burning newspaper at his Catholic primary school. But all he said now was: 'You're probably wise to humour her, she could still land you inside for a few years. Now get some rest, they said you can go home tomorrow with a bit of luck.

As it turned out, the next day there was a salmonella outbreak at the Parma Café and the hospital needed her bed, so Iris got to go home sooner than she'd expected. She wasn't entirely sorry, having eaten nothing since Malcolm's illicit supplies. On the other hand, it was rather pleasant being in the next bed to somebody with limitless faith in Iris' talents and potential, as well as an inexhaustible stream of shocking statistics to spur her on.

As Iris dressed to leave, Soren looked over, and smiled from under her bandages. 'Go home to your lovely family, and make the most of the life you've been given back for them.'

'I will – of course I will and – thank you, thank you so much. I'll come and see you, shall I? Tomorrow?'

'That would be very kind. But meanwhile – just promise me...'

'Anything!'

'Promise me from now on, you'll do the right thing. It'll change your life – and it might change the world!'

It was all of twelve hours later, in front of the kitchen cupboard back home, that Iris began to realise that the awakened life was not going to be the joyful stroll in the park it had seemed from the horizontal abstraction of a hospital bed. After a happy couple of hours unpacking her things and reacquainting herself with the modest delights of home, she had decided it was time to make good on her debt to Soren.

So she was standing there, with a can of CocaCola in one hand and a Muller Corners Fruits of the Forest in the other, when it hit her: if Coca Cola and Muller Lite are the devil's work, but waste and excess consumption are the origin of all our problems, is it good or bad to throw them away?

For some reason she was reluctant to call the mobile number Soren had scribbled down for advice, so she decided to compromise by just rearranging everything with the dubious items hidden away, so with luck they'd pass their sell-by dates before being discovered. That way they'd still have to be dumped, but it wouldn't count as wasting good food. With some effort, she climbed onto a chair, and was just shoving the last of the Penguins into the highest cupboard behind the rock sugar swizzle sticks, when something hit the chair like a small caterpillar truck. This time it wasn't an ethical dilemma, it was Ted home from school. Ted was only nine, but very solid, and the chair rocked perilously for a moment. 'Ow! My knee!'

'Sorry Mum, I was practising my skills. Look at this, look at this goal celebration, this is Frank Lampard's new goal celebration Mum.'

'Can I have a hug?'

Somehow, Iris had totally forgotten that only days before, he'd carelessly shattered her heart and thrown away the fragments. All she could think about was the familiar wet dog smell of his hair in her nostrils, and the idiocy of his football mania. She didn't even mind having to ask for the hug, especially as he obliged by almost suffocating her. How appalling to think that she'd been only microns away from losing this, for ever. And through her own fault.

As she looked down at him, a little, greyish cloud passed over the joy of reunion, trailing the memory of Soren's reminder. He was as adorable as ever – but one day, not far off, he'd be gone. And then...

She chased the cloud away, stroking his head with her uninjured hand. He pulled away to look up. 'Mum, Mum I did remember that song, after you said, only... you know sometimes you're a bit embarrassing, Mum...'

'You did remember! "Just around the corner, there's heartbreak! Down the road that losers use!" Come on, you can do the chorus ...'

'Oh Christ, singalong time on the geriatric ward...'

There, leaning on the frame of the door, not quite committing herself to joining in, but nevertheless addressing her mother directly, and with a detectable trace element of affection beneath the sarcasm – there was Molly. Iris kept one arm round Ted and waved her bandaged hand in greeting. 'Molly! Oh, I've missed you so much! Isn't your hair nice today, and how lovely you look in that er – thing...'

Molly's adolescent cocktail of defiant nerdiness and repelled fascination with her own physicality had found a number of different sartorial expressions, the most recent of which was slogan-decked Goth, like a walking news bulletin from the Dark Side. Today's said: 'Only the wise know the depth of their own foolishness'.

Molly sighed. 'It's a tee shirt Mum. Didn't you have them in your young days?' But she sloped across the kitchen floor to kiss the air behind her mother's left ear. Iris sized the chance of a quick hug. 'It's so wonderful to be back! Did you want something?'

'Why would I?... Just because I...'

'No, no, I didn't mean...'

'God, Mum, I just came to say welcome home, I'm allowed to do that aren't I?'

Iris shivered, her nostrils prickling with nori and chai.

Soren was right. This is what it's really like. But do we have to go back there quite so soon?

Ted turned from interrogating the cupboard that normally contained his after-school snacks. 'Mum! What's that in your hand, Mum in your hand is that a Penguin?'

Iris looked down. There, in plain sight, was the incriminating six-pack.

'Can we have Penguins for tea please can we? Hey – Molly! Give them back they're not yours! Mum make her give them back they'll give her spots!'

With the dexterity of long habit, Iris intercepted the biscuits and held them out of reach. 'Tea! What a lovely idea. We can share them, in fact, let's have two each and eat them all up. And then...' In a flash, the solution to her dilemma had presented itself. '... later on we're going to have the most enormous, delicious supper you've ever seen!'

Malcolm sat at his desk, carefully paperclipping a business card to this week's only invoice. The card said, 'Malcolm Richie, Technical Director'. Colin's said 'Colin Winterbottom, Technical Director.' Colin and Malcolm were, in fact, the only employees of Richie Winterbottom Engineering Consultancy, but the high ratio of chiefs to Indians was the least of their problems. When Malcolm had left WorkSpace Solutions two years ago, frustrated at their lack of vision and general reluctance to let him spend his time doing exactly what he wanted, he had been sure that all, or at least most of, his clients would feel the same way, and leave with him.

Alas, the cowardice and perfidy of the corporate world is hard to overestimate. The clients, reluctantly and after long and regretful consideration, stayed with Workspace, and with none of the big fat contracts he'd been expecting, Malcolm had been reduced to small one-off jobs, mostly re-configuring botched machine tool setups, and advising aggrieved plaintiffs in personal injury cases. These latter, though not hugely profitable, did at least take him along some interesting byways of human conflict; only last week he'd been called in to advise whether the hinge on the door of a telephone box in Farnham could be said to be too stiff for the average senior citizen to operate. And the invoice he was submitting now had involved travelling all the way to Dorset, where a pitchfork used to shovel manure from a herd of Highland cattle was alleged to have constituted sex discrimination against the female operative required to lift it, with its load.

But his carefully-worded advice on these matters (yes and no, respectively), wasn't going to pay the bills. And Colin wasn't likely to bail them out, either. Colin was his oldest friend, though, as Iris often point out, it would be more accurate to say that Malcolm was Colin's last toehold on human society. Even at university, Colin had spent more time in the lab than anywhere else, and the adult world had done nothing to shift his allegiances. Colin was supposed to be concentrating his efforts on building a portfolio of waste management contracts, waste being, in the modern world, no longer a problem but a profit centre. But waste management contracts were mostly dull affairs, requiring detailed knowledge of ISO standards and the reactive properties of landfill liner membranes. And Colin was a dreamer.

Malcolm looked over at Colin, absorbed as usual with his racks of tubes and his shelves of petrie dishes. Colin's shirt and beard were a log-book of the day's food and drink, his trousers had quite visibly been pulled on over his pyjamas, and on his feet was a pair of slippers apparently fashioned from an old hotel carpet. He was muttering to himself as he scrutinised each dish in turn, and then typed his observations into the computer. Colin was not somebody to send out on a blind date with a potential client, even in local government.

Malcolm looked at his watch. Nearly time to go home. He felt vaguely guilty not to have gone to fetch Iris back from hospital, but as he'd pointed out, it was hardly his fault that there wasn't a car to fetch her in. He thought he'd been pretty restrained, considering how lovingly he'd always tended the Jeep, and how financially ill-equipped they were to replace it. And he was needed here, to drum up work. Maybe Colin could do the drumming for the rest of the day. He swung his chair round to face Colin's as he folded the invoice into its envelope. 'How'd you get on with that incinerator in Woodford? Colin? How d'you get on with that...'

He was used to having to put every question two or three times; Colin reacted badly to paper pellets as a mode of attracting his attention. Slowly, like a diver surfacing from a deep ocean, Colin turned from the screen to face Malcolm. 'Woodford? Did I – oh, Woodford.'

'You know, Woodford. The incinerator.'

Colin thought for a moment, then pushed his chair back towards the screen. 'Local protest. Nimbies. Plans on hold. Probably cancelled, I should think.'

'Anything else come up this week?' Malcolm hated interrogating Col like this, but it made him feel efficient and managerial, a free man in charge of his own destiny, rather than a marginal might-have-been who'd jumped just at the wrong time. Thank God for Iris' work. Freelance book keeping wasn't exactly the high-powered career she'd imagined for herself either, but she seemed quite to enjoy its small challenges, and it had been a useful financial cushion this past year. Iris was reassuringly sensible, on the whole. She'd always been an almost excessively safe driver, entirely blind to the thrilling possibilities offered by continuously variable transmission. What could possibly have made her do something like that? And what was all that eco-babble she'd come out with in hospital afterwards? Just shock, with any luck. 'I'm off then.'

He slipped the invoice in his pocket to post on the way, and slid the chair in under the desk. Should he take this week's 'Ergonomics in Practice' to read on the Tube? He'd left it on top of the pile to remind himself. But somehow, his hand reached in under it and found MotoSport Italiano. Even the feel of it was rich with promise; six thick millimetres of pure inspiration. It would take more than 'Office Design Puzzlers of the Week' to anneal the pain of the Northern Line. 'Don't work too late, and don't forget to lock up.'

He always left with these words, but he had no evidence that Colin ever stopped working, or ever needed to lock up, for that matter. Less than a week after they'd moved in to what had been a relatively attractive, if bland, corner of the Kilburn Lane Science Park, Colin had arrived one morning with a rolled-up inflatable mattress, which he'd tucked surreptitiously into the corner behind his desk. The next morning Malcolm had arrived to find the mattress inflated and spread out in what was intended, eventually, to become the reception area, once the business picked up a bit. Colin had muttered apologetically and deflated the mattress, making sure Malcolm noticed that this manoeuvre took a good thirty minutes of valuable work time. After that, the mattress had stayed, though of course only until the next visitor. So far, there had been no visitors.

Malcolm stepped round it to the door, sliding the magazine into his briefcase and patting the Oyster card in his pocket. The next forty-seven minutes passed in the happy contemplation of the car that might replace the totalled Jeep. He was still mentally travelling through the rack-and-worm mechanism of the Honda FXS's valve timing as he swung open the gate of 26 Hartland Gardens, reminding himself in passing to re-point the brickwork by the new hinges. Superficially, 26 was identical to its neighbours up and down the street, but anybody who'd paused for a moment before entering would have noticed a subtle but definite difference. The tiles on the front path were the same Edwardian tiles, but they weren't broken, splodged with chewing gum or fringed with weeds. The wheelie bin was held in place with a neat galvanised hook Malcolm had fabricated one enjoyable Saturday morning. The gate itself swung more easily, and returned more silently, than any other gate on the street.

This was the home of a man who liked things to do their job; a man of modest, achievable ambitions, who loved his house and everything in it. Not a flashy home, but a happy one, where nothing much changed, and that was all to the good. Iris' strange outburst in the hospital was only to be expected in the aftermath of that accident. As for the cyclist, she was clearly just another of Iris' large flock of lame ducks, enlisted by guilt, not affection. Iris, who knew the homeless guy at the cash point by name, and sought out the rotting fruit at the greengrocer because she felt sorry for it, was bound to be a bit sentimental over a person she'd all but sent to the morgue.

He stooped to tidy the day's random litter off the path, and turned the key in the lock. A delicious smell gusted towards him. She was home.

The supper waiting on the table was not exactly what he was used to: Dairylea Dippers, three varieties of Pringles, stuffed crust pizza and the lone mini pie Iris had mysteriously failed to spot when she got home and polished off the others. Microwaving the pie had been an inspiration, and explained the delicious smell.

'And there's this Gu mousse and Oreo cookie cheesecake with Fresh Cornish Cream Custard for afterwards, Ted can have the Froobs. And look, I found some Cherry Coke left over in the picnic basket.' Iris wrapped her good arm round Malcolm for a kiss, before hobbling to the fridge to check that no mini Babybels had survived her pogrom. Poor thing, he thought, barely home and she's worrying about feeding us properly.

'I couldn't manage proper cooking, but I'll be back to normal tomorrow, don't worry. Go and wash, Ted, and could you possibly run and bang on Molly's door, it would take me a fortnight to get up there.'

Ted paused on his way out to survey the table. 'Can we have this tomorrow Mum, can we have it every day? Please?'

'Why not?'

For a moment, the spectre of Soren hovered over the table, tabulating the food miles, carbon audit and human exploitation represented by the spread. 'Oh God, Soren. I said I'd go and see her; I'll just have time, if we eat fast...'

'Don't go out Mum! Please, you've only just come back, you said you'd watch Kung Fu Panda after, you promised!'

Malcolm turned from the large pile of boxes and cartons he was folding to fit more neatly into the recycling bin. 'She'd hardly want you to neglect your own family for her sake, would she? If she's as saintly as you make out?'

The spectre, a little faded, turned to fix Iris with its sorrowful gaze. But being force-fed eight thousand calories of junk might be just the aversion therapy her family needed to change its ways. And surely Iris deserved one last evening of domestic harmony, to fortify her for the struggle to come? 'Well, I only said I might go, and too many visitors can be very exhausting. I'll go tomorrow. Come and eat Moll, isn't it lovely to be all together again?'

At one fifty-four the next morning, Iris was suddenly wide awake. Across her mind ran a banner headline: 'Fly Away Home Tax Return: DID YOU DELIVER IT BEFORE YOU CRASHED?'

Iris was too familiar with the psychological profile of the Inland Revenue to hope that something as trivial as a near-death experience would evoke a pardon. If that return wasn't in the mail, she might as well kiss good-bye to the modest but crucial income she still managed to sieve from the ocean of her maternal chores.

'You might as well kiss it good-bye anyhow.'

Sitting at her desk in the corner of the bedroom, Iris put a hand to her ear and scratched at it furiously, before realising the voice was familiar. Where had she heard it before? Oh! That dream, in hospital... But she wasn't asleep now, was she? So – what?...

She looked round to see if the voice had woken Malcolm, but the familiar rhythm of his snores, breaking over the duvet like waves on a beach, hadn't even paused. Then the voice continued: 'Just look at all these people you're working for. I can't have one of my chosen pocketing their tainted cash. You'll have to dump the lot of them. Anyhow, you won't have time now. You'll find you're quite busy enough, with an entire civilisation to turn around.'

'I thought you were just concussion...'

'That's the alibi. You'll be needing that; people don't like being told you've a hot line to an immutable authority. It's true the blow on the head didn't do much for your brain-cell count. Still, I've had plenty of idiots on my side before now. Too much intelligence can do as much harm as good.'

Iris turned her head. Beyond the wavering circle of the Ikea desk lamp, everything looked perfectly normal.

'You needn't bother trying to see me. I'm Ineffable. It means you have to use your imagination. It's what they had instead of DVDs, in the Olden Days.'

'But – I thought'...

'You thought what? That I'd give you a little talking to, and then just bugger back into the Old Testament, stroking my beard? Did all that interminable hectoring in Ward H leave no impression at all?'

'So - did you send Soren? Specially?'

'I told you I had all the idiots on my team. She means well, and she was the best I could find at short notice.'

Iris tried to make sense of a world where Soren and her bike had been manipulated into the path of her Jeep by a higher power. A higher power who'd chosen her, Iris Richie, possibly the least special person in the entire world, to fulfil its mission. 'But why me? I'm totally normal. Husband, two children, part-time job, semi-detached house in an inner suburb, average education, average outcome, average income. What's special about me?'

'Exactly. Not a thing. That's the whole point. You are, emphatically, the least special person I could find. And believe me, I looked. That way there are no excuses for anybody else. If you can change your ways, absolutely anybody can. Now, you'd better get out that list of clients, and I'll tell you if you can keep any of them. Well, go on, woman, what are you waiting for?'

Dazed, Iris pulled her address book out from under a pile of papers, and started to read out the names of her clients. There was Hairy Krishna, the spiritual barber shop...

'Too many toxic chemicals. I'll spare you the statistics. That's always where Soren goes wrong. Mugging her victims with figures.'

'Fantastic Plastic, Trade and Retail, all Office and Domestic needs catered for'...

'You've heard of petroleum by-products, I suppose. If you were in my place, facing the next ten thousand years staring at a giant pile of picnic cutlery and old Fisher Price, where you'd put a nice verdant planet, you wouldn't feel quite so positive about them, either.'

'Then there's Fly Away Home, if I can only find that tax return. If it's got scrunched up with the car I'm...'

'That little word "Fly" should tell you all you need to know about those people. I gave you lot an atmosphere, not an aerobatic playground to fill with dirt.'

'But how am I supposed to live?'

'There's a rather nice homily about the lilies of the field that I sometimes bring out on these occasions.'

Iris was becoming cross. 'It's all very well for you, being a deity and handing down orders, but the daily life of lilies obviously differs from ours in several crucial ways. Two of the most glaring being that they live on air and sunshine, and there aren't any laws against them going round naked.'

'Nobody's asking you to go around naked. Let me spell it out for you. Do you want to be a lily, or do you want to be a harassed, over-stressed bluebottle, banging off walls all day and drowning the pain in a bottle of Shiraz Creek every night? Try for one moment to imagine looking back on your deathbed - at what? All the bits of paper you've fiddled with. Is that how you want to spend what little time you've got left? You only get one chance, you know. Trust me on that. And this is yours.'

The voice was fading, possibly in self-defence. 'You'll work it out. The tax return is in a landfill in Pevensey, underneath a pile of dirty nappies, so it's probably as well you don't need their business any more. And don't forget to turn out the light. I won't be needing it'

From: Iris Richie   iris@btinternet.co.uk
To: service@hairykrishna.co.uk
Cc: info@flyawayhome.co.uk,mail@DecorYou.co.uk,
    admin@manandvan.co.uk, naomi@KleenMachine.com,
    info@murphybutcher.co.uk, admin@paradiseplastics.com

May 23rd 02 37 am

Dear All,

It is with great regret that I write to inform you that I cannot conscientiously continue to supply you with bookkeeping services. I have been re-evaluating my values, and realise that to continue in any way to support or encourage the further pollution of our fragile environment would be a betrayal of what I have (rather belatedly!) come to realise are my true and deep seated beliefs. It will entail some personal hardship for me and my family, but I am happy with my decision to put principle before self.

I am sorry if this inconveniences you, but I am sure that there are many other excellent companies that would be only too glad to fulfil your actuarial requirements.

And needless to say, should any of you, at any point, find yourselves unable to live with the conscientious burden of your current activities, I would be only too happy to work with you on any environmentally responsible business venture on which you might engage upon.

I have enjoyed our relationship and do this now only because I feel I must set an example.

Yours truly,

Iris Richie

The next morning, Iris staggered out of the minicab into the random human eddy outside the supermarket, wondering how she was going to tell Malcolm that she'd just abandoned a perfectly good living, for no reason other than that every one of her clients was wantonly hastening the end of the world. The supper last night had been a masterstroke in terms of family harmony, and though Malcolm had seemed a bit distant afterwards, it must, she supposed, be alarming to share a bed with somebody who yelps every time you turn over. In most respects, she couldn't have hoped for a happier return to normality.

Except it wasn't, and it couldn't be. Much as she might long not to have met Soren, it had happened, and it wasn't about to un-happen. In hospital, with the soothing voice, and the confident fingers kneading ineluctable realities into Iris' head and heart, it had sounded not just simple and obvious, but thrilling. So why was the prospect of sharing this new vision with her family now filling her with dread?

Maybe God would reappear and give her a few hints. After all, it was hardly the first time he'd charged somebody with delivering revealed truths to a potentially hostile audience. Surely a bit of preparatory coaching wasn't too much to ask?

She hobbled towards the automatic doors, and suddenly stopped dead, causing several hungry sandwich-hunters to crash into her.

Automatic doors! They use energy, don't they? But then, pushing the other kind uses my energy, and that has to be replaced by food. Maybe I ought to have used the escalator instead of the stairs, too. After all, the escalator is running anyway, isn't it? How many calories will I have to replace now?

She stood, pole-axed by her dilemma, until a weirdo alert in the eye of a passing security guard sent her scurrying through the automatic door in somebody else's slipstream.

Inside was the usual drift of stray plastic, doughnuts abandoned half-eaten before the checkout, and squashed grapes. There was the usual old lady at Customer Service, with a two for one voucher on wafer-thin ham. Normally this would have cheered Iris – the trivial exchange of ham for scraps of paper providing a little moment of human warmth in the lonely pensioner's day – but for some reason, today Iris only noticed that the checkout girl couldn't even be bothered to meet the old lady's eye, and the old lady had nothing else in her basket. Behind them stretched an endless line of blank-faced recruits from the remedial classes of the local failing comprehensives, marooned behind their electronic prison gates, longing to be anywhere else but here.

Oh dear. Iris pushed her trolley into Fruit and Veg, looked around for Organics, which had once again been moved in accordance with Head Office's latest computer model of local buying whims, and stopped in front of the strawberries.

Her hand reached for the nearest box – and froze. In tiny writing on the top she read: 'Country of Origin: Spain'. Beside them, with a big 'Eat Local!' banner, were some English ones. She picked them up instead and dropped them in the basket.

But – wait a minute – English strawberries, there's no way they can grow outdoors at this time of year. Which takes more energy, flying them from Spain, or growing them under heat right here? What had been the outcome of that wrangle about whether air freighted stuff could still be organic?

She couldn't remember, but the English ones were twice as expensive, a sure sign of worthiness. So she let that decide her, and moved on to the avocadoes.

Where are these from? Italy! That's all right. Except – oh look, there are some Fair Trade avocadoes right next to them.

But the fair trade ones were from South Africa. And how unfairly traded are those Italian ones anyway? If something isn't marked Fair, does that necessarily mean the farmer is being ground down into penury and an early death? Iris thought back to her last Tuscan mini-break, and the huge family parties in top-to-toe cashmere, piling into the restaurants for Sunday lunch. They hadn't looked especially oppressed.

On the other hand – it might still be better to put money in the pocket of a hungry baby in the townships, even if it did mean pumping carbon into the upper atmosphere...

'You all right there darling?'

Iris turned to meet the bemused eye of a shelf-stacker wheeling another vast load of Spanish strawberries. He thinks I can't afford them! He thinks I'm a sad person with nothing to do all day but wander the aisles of Sainsbury's! Oh no! He thinks I'm on the pull! And he's about fifteen!

Panicked, Iris left the fruit, threw a bag of organic carrots and another of potatoes into her basket and skidded off down the aisle. How, on the basis of her pathetically inadequate knowledge of combustion, physics, mechanics, machine tool production technologies, refrigeration indices, anaerobic digestion and the petrol consumption of delivery trucks – leaving aside the possibility that some of these trucks in fact run on biodiesel or LPG – how on earth was she supposed to decide?

'You seem to be making rather heavy weather of this.'

The itch in her ear was back. It was almost a relief, though Iris was still rather suspicious of all this special attention. 'Are you sure you can spare the time? What about all those kangaroos dying in Australia? I'd hate to keep you from them.'

'You can't be an effective deity without a bit of multitasking, you know. There are bags on those.'

'On what?'

'On the vegetables. More petroleum by-products. Put them back.'

Okay, back they go. Who needs fruit and veg? Ted doesn't eat them, Molly doesn't eat anything I put in front of her on principle, just because I'm her mother, and Malcolm only really likes sausages. Ah, Sausages. Well, I'll pick up a box of those veggie sausages. If they're good enough for Sir Macca, they'll have to be good enough for Malcolm.

She had been intending to buy fish for supper, but on being required to choose between trout, lake-farmed but not organic; sea-bass, organic but flown in from Chile; local cod, but from the endangered shoals of the North Sea, and sardines that Malcolm had vetoed on the grounds of smell, she was positively relieved to remember that none of them really liked fish.

It was not entirely relaxing, having to make choices that had previously been routine, in the knowledge that one wrong move might trigger divine retribution, or at least a telling-off to which she had no way of responding without attracting a lot of the wrong sort of attention. Warily, Iris moved on to Dairy, and reached for a cardboard litre of organic semi-skimmed. No evil plastic bottle for her. She could manage fine without an ineffable school prefect hanging out on her shoulder. 'I don't need you any more, look. You can go off and comfort an old man's last moments, or something.'

'Not so fast! You haven't read the small print, have you? Those cardboard thingies come all the way from Scotland. I watched those filthy old trucks all the way down the M1. That's a boring, stinky job for you. People think it's a piece of cake being God, but there's a lot of dreary, monotonous box-ticking in between the earthquakes and miracles, I can tell you.'

'And your point was?' Iris wasn't sure of the penalties for answering back to God, but her knee was hurting and there was still almost nothing in her basket. A faint, long-suffering sigh tickled her earlobe. 'You need to take a closer look at that other milk, it only comes from down the road. You can send the bottles for recycling, they're turning them into trousers these days. The uses to which you people put your intelligence never cease to amaze me.'

'Oh, and in any case...' Iris watched her own hand, weighed down by conscience, return the milk to its shelf. '...we can't have milk at all, because of the mother cows.'

And so it went on throughout the shop. Everywhere she went, God had some reason or another to stay her hand. Vast areas were out of bounds altogether, mostly those where Iris had previously lingered happily, toying between Wagon Wheels and Tunnocks Wafers, or wondering whether Ted would like freeze-dried strawberries or plump, juicy raisins in his cereal. Today, for some reason, all she saw were whiny children dragging on trolleys, and grey-faced office girls clutching Treat Yourself single serve dinners in nervous, scraggy hands. And there was the solitary old lady again, hovering over the chopped-up samples of Caramel Swirls at the bakery counter, as though anybody cared if she had three. Probably she was hoping to get arrested. That way at least somebody would have to talk to her.

By the time Iris reached Wines and Spirits, she was ready to break the neck of the nearest bottle against its metal shelf. She hovered experimentally, for a moment. European wine had to be all right, didn't it? Surely no killjoy deity could begrudge her a medicinal chug or two alongside the veggie sausages.

So far so good - no crackling. She reached out her hand...

'Not so fast.'

'I thought you'd gone.'

'Gone? I'm God. I don't go. You'll go, when I decide, but I'm here until the Knell of Doom. And sometimes, I'm telling you, it can't come soon enough.'

'So, what's the problem with the wine? It's... no, I give up, what is it?'

'Let me give you a little visual aid.'

The aisle in front of Iris went misty for a moment, and then cleared to reveal a gorgeous, mossy forest. Adorable baby wild boar snuffled among fallen acorns, and in the dappled shade in the distance... 'It's something to do with that wild cat thing, isn't it?'

'That animal is the European Lynx. It's one of my finest, I have to say, but extremely fussy about where it lives, and for some reason it's decided that cork oak forests are the only place it feels at home. Now look at that bottle.'

Iris did so. At that moment it looked liked her best friend in the world.

But it had a plastic cork.

'Remember those strawberries?'

'What about them?'

'All the Spanish cork oak forests are being dug up to grow them. You won't find anything with a proper cork that hasn't come thousands of miles.'

It was nearly tea time when Iris reeled back into the street, having wrestled from the grudging deity one packet of Veggie Bangers and four unpackaged baking potatoes, to feed her family for a week. All she could hope for was a modern version of the Loaves and Fishes, which seemed a high-risk housekeeping strategy. Still, at least, by stuffing the sausages into her handbag and the potatoes into her coat pockets, she'd avoided a lecture about plastic bags. She buried her face in her shoulder and muttered: 'I hope you're pleased with yourself.'

'That is my usual state, yes. As you may remember from the book of Genesis, sixth day – or was it the fourth? It's such a long time ago now.'

'Six thousand years or thereabouts, wasn't it?'

'Don't be a smartarse, it doesn't suit you.'

'So are you going to be around for the rest of my life, then?'

'I've always been around, as you well know. Only you never bothered to listen before. Always watching, always listening. No human act, however minor, ignored or forgotten. I've no idea why you people get in such a panic about surveillance cameras. As though they were something new.'

'And I'm stuck with you am I, for good?'

'That all depends. Given my current workload, I only intervene directly when you need a major steer. Most of the rest of the work I tend to delegate. As you've noticed. Oh dear. Major train wreck in Hyderabad. Byee!'

Iris shook her head to make sure the itching was gone. Quietly forgetting her promise to Soren was one thing, but this was clearly going to be harder to shrug off. The private thrill of being God's chosen vessel seemed somehow inadequate compensation for the material facts of her situation – various disfiguring injuries, nothing to feed her hungry family, no obvious prospect of future income - and the threat of a crippling lawsuit still hanging over her. Soren could always change her mind. She'd better keep at it for a bit longer.

But Soren was still in hospital, and safe in the knowledge that God was temporarily engaged elsewhere, Iris hobbled to the minicab booth. There was only one driver there, playing Street Racer on his mobile, between bites of a king size Mars bar.

'Is this your car?'

Even by local standards, it was an historic vehicle, but it was the only one there. Iris tried not to think about the jet stream of black smoke that exploded from the ancient exhaust as he turned the key and flooded the malodorous space with Heart 106.5. Before God had a chance to chip in, she muttered a silent promise. 'I'll get a bike, okay? When my knee's better. And when I have some money. And it's only a few blocks.'

They had gone about half of a few when the engine rasped,

banged, and fell silent. A car engine, like a child, is only really sick when it makes no sound at all.

'That was on the cards. I've been meaning to take her in', said the driver, without regret or surprise. 'That's four twenty-five. You okay from here yeah?' He grabbed the walkie talkie from its cradle. 'Hey! Mikey, I need a tow.'

He turned just far enough to take Iris' money, then went back to his call. She wrenched at the passenger door, which stuck, and then suddenly gave, sliding Iris onto the road, right on her injured knee. 'Ow! Shit! Bollocks.'

The potatoes rolled ignominiously around her. Meanwhile the sausages had somersaulted across the tarmac, to end up a moment later as sausage patties under the wheels of a Toyota. Iris made a feeble grab for the last potato as it headed for the gutter.

'You all right there?'

'Quick - it's going into that puddle - and it's all I've got for dinner.'

'Oh dear. I'm sure we can do something about that. Here we go.'

Iris looked up to see a girl of about twenty smiling down at her, with two pigtails sticking sideways from her head, dressed in what looked like an artful combination of a spider web and a giant's overalls. She put down her pile of folded cardboard, leaned down and gently helped Iris to her feet.

'My potatoes!'

'Don't worry, we've loads more inside.'

Iris looked up and realised she was right outside Buzzybees Wholefoods, a place she'd always shunned, on the basis that all its merchandise all seemed to be the same colour, and not one conducive to appetite. She'd imagined it a bit like the happy-clappy church by the bus garage: not something you could legitimately criticise, but also not a place you'd want to enter, in case you never got out again. But, suddenly, it was a haven from persecution. Nobody, human or ineffable, would nag her for going in here.

'I'm Sammy. Here you go. Jeez, you are banged up aren't you, d'you fall out of cars every day?'

Sammy was guiding her gently inside. It was bigger than Iris had expected, and lit, not by harsh rows of fizzing tubes, but sunlight filtered through a merciful layer of dust on the windows. Fruit and vegetables were piled in wooden crates; mud, not splattered Yakult, was splodged generously all over the floor, and a bag of ancient repurposed carrier bags jostled the bunches of herbs by the till. Iris could not help imagining Malcolm's reaction. He didn't consider himself fastidious, but when the tooth fairy arrived at 26 Hartland Gardens, she found her offerings scrubbed spotless, in tiny Ziploc bags.

'You hang on here, I'll get you something to sit on.' Sammy pattered off between half a dozen customers with cycling muscles and fresh-air skins, chatting breezily over the legume sacks. They looked a lot happier than the ghost-lit denizens of the supermarket. Best of all, the crackling in Iris' ear had gone. Did that mean she was safe?

Sammy came back with a chair. 'Here, I'll tuck you in the corner out of the way. Did you want anything while you're here, or d'you just want to sit and recover for a bit?'

Iris sat gratefully on her chair and peered at the vegetables. 'I suppose they need to eat something. My family. Are those carrots over there? It's hard to tell under all the mud.'

'Yeah, they're Cambridgeshire Old Fancies, they look like shit but they scrub up great.'

'Not the actual Cambridgeshire Old Fancies? They're famous! I read about them in the paper. They're about two thousand years old or something. Gosh, they look it too, don't they? Still, I bet they're delicious. I'd better have two kilos of them. And maybe one of those cabbages. Are they celebrities, too?'

'No, just vegetables. Watch out when you chop it up, Dave said he'd had slugs the size of cucumbers after that rain last week. Still, where you've got slugs, you haven't got pesticides, right?'

Sammy began shovelling carrots into a brown paper bag. Iris thought of all the new friends she was making, imagining the slug chatting to the lynx at her next birthday party over an elderflower cocktail, and wondering if it would make up for alienating her entire human family.

'Arlo, fetch us some more carrots from the back, would you?'

The boy behind the till stopped bundling watercress and padded, on delicate bare feet, across the floor. He passed a toddler stumbling behind its mum, and dropped an apple gently into its hand.

A shop where they give apples to babies! Why have I never been here before?

'Here's your water.' Sammy was back. 'You don't want any

bargain cut-price mint, do you? How about cheese, make a nice sauce for your carrots? Milk, any of that?'

'Oh yes, sure. Oh, no.'

'You intolerant?'

'Only in the moral sense, I'm afraid. It's the um, cruelty, you know. I've come to all this rather late.'

'Oh, you don't want to worry about that, we've got lovely sheep's cheese and goat's milk, the babies grow up with their Mums just like young wotsisname here. Oi, wotsisname, give me that if you've finished with it.'

Sammy took the apple core from the toddler, pitched it into a sack of cabbage leaves, and wiped her hand briefly on the spider-web tunic. 'I'll get you a bit to try, shall I?' She went off to the cheese counter at the back. Iris sat, feeling the stress of the supermarket trip fall away as she watched the toddler roll potatoes across the floor. Sammy rolled them back as she returned with three slivers of cheese on a piece of paper.

'Gosh, this one is lovely. What's it called?'

'Dorset Headwallop, I believe'

'Dorset Headwallop! Nigel Slater cooks with that! Give me a big lump of it.'

'I brought you a carton of goat's milk too. It does have what you might call a distinctive taste, but you get used to it. Or so I'm told. Better goat than camel, eh? Even the ponces in the Square didn't fall for that. Shall I ring you up then? Can you stagger as far as the till?'

She carried Iris' purchases over and started to ring them up, squeezing them in beside a huge pile of tea packets. 'Oh bollocks look, what're we going to do with all this short-dated green tea, Arlo? Nobody wants it since Gwynnie discovered white first bud.'

She looked up over the scales. 'D'you want thirty packets of slightly stale green tea, by any chance? No, thought not. But have one on me, just in case, yeah? That'll be twenty-four sixty. Grab yourself a bag.'

Iris riffled through the mound of slightly whiffy old plastic, pulling out the most chewed-up bag she could find. She was really getting to grips with this now. Who said doing the right thing would be a struggle?

'What's that?'

'Any cash back?'

'Yes please – oh – no thanks. Better not.'

Sammy could see right into her purse, which contained fifty-four pence and a Brilliant Work sticker off Ted's jumper that she'd been too soppy to throw away. Iris looked up into the friendly, bemused face. 'It's not that bad, only I've lost my job and I... Well I've lost my job. And my husband doesn't know. And if he did know, I don't think he'd be wildly sympathetic. So I don't actually have any money, to speak of.'

'That's not good, I grant you. But money's a curse, you know. Or so I'm told. I've never had any, or not for more than about two seconds.'

Arlo looked up from bagging camomile flowers. Wisps of red-gold hair feathered out from his knitted cap. 'Hey, how about LETS? She'd find something there, for sure.' His accent was faintly American. His teeth were American, too, pearly and even as sushi rice.

'You're a genius, Arlo. For a foreigner. Here, take this home, there's bound to be something on it you can do.' She held out to Iris a sheet of green paper that declaimed in cheery, chunky letters: 'LETS! The local trading scheme that keeps you away from the bank!'

It's keeping the bank away from me that's going to be tricky, thought Iris, as she pulled a Switch card from her purse. There ought to be enough on this to hold them off for a few days. She took the paper from Sammy and scanned it.

'It's like – a kind of barter thing. You do stuff for people, and they do stuff for you. A little Utopian dream, right here in your neighbourhood. They even had it on the Archers. You look a bit Radio 4? Peruse it at your leisure, and then come back and post your offer from here.'

'Oh. Thanks. Yes, I'll do that.'

Iris took the leaflet and the bag of food and made reluctantly for the door, self–pity adding a melodramatic frisson to her limp. She'd felt safe in here, for the first time since her accident. Sammy watched her sympathetically. 'That hurts, doesn't it? How far d'you have to get?'

'Oh, only to Hartland Gardens. Only I had this rather bad spill a few days ago, and then with today...'

'Arlo! Did you do that delivery yet to the gastropub up the hill? Thought not.' She took Iris' arm. 'The boy'll drop you off, it's on his way. Sort of. Here, I'll get the door. It's closing time anyhow.'

A moment later Arlo appeared, on the saddle of an imposing vintage tricycle. Between its rear wheels sat a large wicker basket. Sammy threw an old cushion into it.

'There you go, plenty of room for you and the purple salsify. Can you get in okay?'

Iris half-fell in with her bag of food, and Sammy waved as they set off at a gravid pace, angry taxis and homicidal vans speeding past on both sides.

'Iris!' Above her, a head shot out of a brand new Porsche Cayenne. 'Iris! I thought it was you. I heard about your little incident. So unlike you, we were all saying. Or maybe not! What a dear little courtesy vehicle. See you at school!'

Why was it, Iris wondered as Elaine's tyres spat mud all over her, that one's children always had to elect the most toxic child from the most toxic family in the class to be their best friend? Only a nature as sweet as Ted's could detect good intentions beneath Jack's playground terrorism. And only a lifetime's practice could have taught Elaine to compress so much venom and innuendo into barely twenty words.

Arlo disembarked Iris gently on the pavement outside her house, and trundled off. The elation she had felt at discovering Buzzybees had given way to the grim reality that she'd spent twenty-six pounds she couldn't afford on sheep's cheese and vegetables, and the children would be home any minute, clamouring for their tea. She remembered Soren's assurance that they'd be grateful later. Maybe. After she was dead. But there was no time to worry about that now, with a kilo of carrots to separate from two kilos of organic mud.

'How's the invalid this afternoon? Cup of tea? Why's it so dark in here?' Malcolm had the ability to enter or leave any room with the stealth of a cat burglar. He switched on the kitchen lights and gave Iris a hug.

'Ow, mind the hand... Gosh, is that the time already? Supper won't be long, it's quite – um – different from last night. You know, er - simple. I couldn't do a lot of shopping.'

'You spend far too much time worrying about food. I'm sure

it'll be delicious.'

He ran the tap. A thin stream trickled out, cutting an estuary through the sea of mud. He peered up the nozzle of the tap. 'There's something up here, hang on...What's this?' He stood there with a rubber bung in his hand. 'How did that get up there?' Still holding it, he reached with his other hand to where the PG Tips always stood. '...And where's the tea?'

'Right there, where it always is... Oh, have we run out? Never mind...'

'Run out? There was half a box here yesterday'

Iris wiped her hands on her apron and hobbled over, holding a packet out to him. '...Look, here's this organic green tea instead, I just had one, they're so much better for you... Actually here, have two, it seems to work better'...

As he took them, mystified, she turned away quickly, and yelled in the vague direction of upstairs. 'Supper time everybody! Wash your hands!'

A door banged, a pair of size five Doctor Martin's thundered down the stairs, and a voice shouted as it came: 'Hey Mum! Mum my PS2 was turned off, why d'you turn it off Mum, I hadn't saved my game and I had to go right back to the playoffs and I had to be Middlesbrough and everybody knows Middlesbrough are crap.'

Ted arrived in the kitchen, fell to his knees, and slid across the polished floor in a perfect slow-motion reconstruction of Didier Drogba's last-resort dive.

'Never mind darling, you're so brilliant I'm sure you'll be playing Barcelona again before you know it. But do you know what I discovered? I discovered that if everybody turned all their PS2s off at the mains all the time, there'd be enough energy to floodlight two hundred and fifty thousand Premiership matches!'

'Duh! They're already floodlit Mum, you don't know anything you're hopeless.'

He scrambled to his feet and trotted to the table. 'Mum what's for supper, I'm starving.'

A second pair of footsteps slouched into the downstairs bathroom. A plaintive voice called out: 'Mum! Where's the moisturiser? And the hand cream? There's – there's fuck all in this cupboard, Mum what's going on?'

She turned to reply and caught Malcolm looking at her. He

had given up trying to squish some flavour from the teabags in his mug, and the light of a terrible suspicion was in his eyes. 'Oh, I forgot to tell you, Moll...'

She felt Malcolm's baleful stare like a blade between the shoulder blades, as Molly's caught her head-on. She couldn't carry on like this. She just needed to explain it to them, like Soren had explained it to her, and then they'd understand, and everything would be all right again. But not on empty stomachs. '...Actually, sweetie, on second thoughts, I'll save it for later, okay? Now come and eat your supper.'

She pulled a casserole out of the oven. Malcolm hadn't moved. He was still staring at her. Possibly, by now, glaring. 'Have you been back to that woman in the hospital?'

'Which woman? Watch out, this is hot.' Iris banged past him, wielding the casserole like a riot shield, and set it down on the table. Ted waited eagerly for her to remove the lid, then slumped down his seat. 'Mum, I don't want this, I want what we had last night.'

'No you don't, darling, this is much nicer, you'll see. Anyhow, you can't have junk every night'

'Why not, Jack does.'

'And look at all his behavioural issues. Look it's lovely and crispy on top, and there are...'

Molly slid into her chair, twiddling a strand of inky hair round her ear. 'What is that? It looks like shit. Anyway, I don't care, I need to lose weight.'

Iris was beginning to feel beleaguered. 'Suit yourself.'

'What, so I do need to lose weight? Dad, she's saying I'm fat! No wonder I'm suicidal. I'll just have some strawberries.'

Ted stopped arranging his carrots in three-four-three formation. 'Strawberries, can I have strawberries too Mum, why can she have them and not me?'

'There aren't any strawberries Ted darling, the strawberries had flown a very, very long way from America, and so they had jet lag and they were feeling very ill and they wouldn't have tasted nice at all.'

Malcolm put down his untouched forkful. 'Funny that, I was in Sainsbury's picking up a sandwich for my lunch and they had great piles of Spanish strawberries right by the door. I'd have brought you home some if I'd...'

'It's quite all right Malcolm, in any case strawberries are full of water, which makes them much more prone to suck up heavy metal residues, and you wouldn't want Ted to eat mercury with his...'

'The earth is full of metals. What d'you think the Cairngorms are made of, Edinburgh rock?'

'AS I WAS SAYING, from now on, everything we eat is going to be local, so we can really be excited when the first raspberries arrive, or the first apricots, and then not get bored by eating them all year round, won't that be nice?'

'I never get bored of strawberries Mum, do I Dad?'

Molly shoved back her chair and made a dramatic dash for the cupboard. 'WHERE'S MY FUCKING PINEAPPLE?'

'What pineapple? Do come back to the table Molly, how can we teach Ted to sit properly if you keep jumping up like a ...'

'MY PINEAPPLE with the papayin in it, the fucking enzyme that I need to remember all the stuff I need to remember to pass my exams. That dried pineapple! Where is it?'

She banged the cupboard door, glared at Iris, burst into tears and dashed out of the room. Malcolm looked at her untouched plate and Ted's and pushed back his chair. 'How about I pop round for some fish and chips, eh Ted? Give your poor Mum a break until she's a bit better?'

'I'm FINE! And if any of you'd bothered to try it, you'd find out it's perfectly nice. Just eat it. Please!'

Iris suddenly felt very alone. Even the grumpy crackle in her ear would have been welcome at this point. But the only crackle she heard was the firewood igniting under her feet.

She took a deep breath, spiked a carrot on Ted's fork, and held it up to his mouth. 'Do you know, Ted, the farmer who grows these carrots has a son exactly the same age as you, and he's really into Chelsea too, and they live in a lovely place with hedgehogs in the barn, where we can go and visit to see all the vegetables growing if you like. And these carrots have a family tree, just like on 'Who Do You Think You Are?', that they can follow right back for six hundred years, imagine...'

'How can they Mum, they'd have to have names like Joe Carrot and Lord Carrot, carrots don't have names.'

'And d'you know, Iris, call me weird if you like, but if I'm going to be eating something, I'd as soon not have a mental image of its bereaved family staring up at me from the empty plate.'

But Malcolm had eaten his up, and was reaching over for Molly's plate. Iris was still trying to get Ted to taste it. 'Look Ted, your Dad likes it and you know how fussy he is. Just try this lovely crispy cheesy bit, it's called Dorset Headwallop, and the sheep come from a lovely place in the country, and they stay with their mums all their life, not like the poor baby cows who get taken away from their Mums when they're littler than you, even.'

'In cow years littler?'

'In cow years. And in this shop I went to today, there's a picture of the sheep, right by the counter. You can come with me next time, and see. Open up.'

Hypnotised by the stream of babble, Ted opened his mouth, and she shoved the fork in. Iris watched as Ted's face registered an unfamiliar taste. And wrinkled. And cleared. 'It's nice!'

'There. What did I tell you? Next time I hope you'll try it before making such a fuss.' Buoyed by this minor victory, Iris decided the moment was now. As Malcolm cleared the plates and Ted set off for his evening communion with Goalie Greats on YouTube, Iris headed him off at the kitchen door and called up the stairs, 'Molly! Serotonin fix!'

Then she turned to her wary family, with the smile she usually reserved for telling clients that once again, by some unfortunate accident, they seemed to have earned enough to owe several thousand pounds in tax, but not enough to pay it. 'Before you all disappear, I thought tonight, instead of all going off to separate corners of the house to microwave our brains, how about we spend a nice evening together?'

Molly appeared in the doorway. 'I hope you realise I'm only here because it's not humanly possible to memorise the periodic table of the elements with absolutely zero fuel intake. Did you say there was chocolate?'

Ted, in between bouncing a discarded sock on one foot, asked: 'Together doing what?'

'Well – talking. Talking about – how we might make our lives more enjoyable.'

Malcolm was in his element at the sink, which he'd defiantly filled with extra hot water and extreme bubbles. 'My life is perfectly enjoyable, thank you. So long as I'm left to enjoy it in my own way.'

'Well, it's just about to get a whole lot more enjoyable. Come on Malcolm, you can do the dishes later. And here's the chocolate.'

As she'd left Buzzybees, Sammy had thrown into Iris' bag several bars of expired Green and Blacks. Molly sloped reluctantly to the table. Iris sat down quickly herself, before Molly changed her mind again, and pulled out chairs for the others. 'Now. As you all know, I had a near-miss the other day...'

'Didn't miss your frontal lobes, from what I can see...'

Iris' hand swooped towards the chocolate. Molly fell silent as Iris steeled herself to continue, feeling totally unfit for the task. From what she'd heard, a gift for oratory was a basic prerequisite for successful proselytising, but the last person to call Iris 'persuasive' had been the headmistress in Year 11, after the incident with the fishnet tights. And even then she'd been kept in for detention.

Iris feared that worse than detention might be in store, very shortly. But she couldn't stop now. '... and it made me, you know, re-evaluate things. We all know about going green and carbon footprints and all that, but that's all just, you know...'

'Very MEGA dreary.'

'... moving the deckchairs on the Titanic. And yes, Molly, very dreary. And it's dreary, because..'

'...because we do about it EVERY DAY Mum, we barely don't do anything else in school any...'

'...BECAUSE Ted, the changes we need to make are bigger, more – more meaningful than that. Because all that stuff is about taking things away, it's all negative. And what I'm talking about is making things better. More creative. More fun.'

Fifty minutes scrubbing carrots had been a long time, and thinking about soothing, monotonous, activity, that had been normal, indeed inevitable, in the Olden Days, had reminded Iris of other lost pastimes; things that were probably much more satisfying than flicking through the Boden catalogue in front of Property Ladder. It was just a matter of sharing this revelation with the others.

Malcolm frowned and took the chocolate from Molly, folding the wrapper in a perfect blanket corner over the two remaining squares. 'What's all this "we"? So far as I know, you were the one who succumbed to an attack of unprovoked road rage, while the rest of us were blamelessly occupied elsewhere.'

'And because of that, I was privileged to – receive an insight –

that I'm now sharing with the rest of you. We...'

'How long are you going to go on talking Mum, I'm missing Match of the Day Two, it's not fair it's the only time I...'

'...WE NEED to make a total change in our value system, from things to activities, from products to processes. It's not about what we have, it's about...'

'Oh Christ, now she's channelling Al Gore. You really do have the worst taste, Mum.'

Iris looked at her daughter, her adored firstborn baby, wondering why she had never noticed before how routinely and casually her children insulted her, as though assuming that childbirth brought with it an extra layer of skin.

Molly took the chocolate back from Malcolm and finished it with an air of Proustian ennuie, before continuing: 'Ted, you might as well know, this is just a new arena for their boring marital squabbles. Don't bother about it. Would you like me to record that footie for you?'

In an uncharacteristic sibling moment, she took Ted's hand and started to lead him towards the door.

Iris sprang up to stop them, forgetting about her knee. 'OW! SHIT!' she yelled, and collapsed onto the floor. Pure surprise stopped the two children, as Malcolm helped her carefully back onto the chair. 'Easy does it. Come on Mol, your mother's had a nasty shock, she's not well yet, and here she's cooked you a lovely healthy supper. It won't kill you to hear her out'...

Iris beamed up at him in gratitude and surprise.

'...Especially with the economy going the way it is. If I were you two, I'd be grateful for tips about how to make do and mend. By the time you're thirty, ninety per cent of what you earn'll go straight to National Insurance. Sit down, the both of you.'

The children skulked reluctantly back to the table. Iris tried to ignore the zinging agony in her knee, summoned back the smile, and reached into her bag. 'Here, everybody, I've got a piece of paper and a pencil. We're going to make a list of things we can do, that don't consume lots of energy and materials, and will be creatively fulfilling and fun. Look, I've got one already, I'm going to write down "embroidery" '

'Embroidery! God Mum, you can't even do a zip!' Molly slumped across the table and tore into the second packet of Maya

Gold.

'Well, all the more reason to make up for lost time. I used to be quite good at sewing, I'd have you know. Which is sort of the point, isn't it? Anyhow, we don't all have to do the same things. Malcolm, your turn.'

'There's a few things round here that could do with a good clean-out. You could start with the welly boot cupboard; that should take a few evenings, if you're going to do it without benefit of modern technology.'

Somehow, exploring the darker recesses of a foetid cupboard on her hands and knees hadn't been quite the image of wholesome recreation in Iris' head. Meanwhile Ted had somehow wrested the second bar of chocolate from Molly before it all disappeared. 'Is it a game Mum? Can I get a prize? Is it my turn now?'

'No, Ted, the whole point is – we don't need prizes to have fun, do we? You remember what Miss Kilpatrick said, it's about taking part, not winning. You can put down 'playing music' and 'making up tunes', you sing beautifully...'

'So can I get an iPod then Mum? The music on an iPod just floats through the air, it doesn't give off carbon or...'

'You can have the music...'

'All right!'

'...but not the iPod, Ted, it costs money and it uses a lot of batteries.'

'She's wanting you to grow a pair of antennae, son. Come to think of it that's not a bad idea, you could probably do it with a couple of electrodes and...'

Malcolm's jokes had always seemed hilarious to Iris; but they'd never before been directed at her. Now, she determined to rise above it. 'Why not make a musical instrument yourself, Ted, out of driftwood and bits and pieces? We could do it together, that would be much more fun than just buying something wouldn't it?'

'And that'd be driftwood from the unspoiled beaches of Tufnell Park, would it?'

Iris had expected resistance from the children, but Malcolm taking their side was a shock. Maybe he didn't mind if they turned out greedy, small minded and materialistic. Or maybe he thought her efforts would backfire, and drive Molly and Ted into careers as arms dealers or opium smugglers.

Maybe they were just the wrong children. Maybe even Malcolm wasn't the noble-spirited, decent person she'd always assumed. She didn't like the implications of that, at all.

Or maybe the three of them were right, and Soren was wrong, and all her attempts to be a better person were sad and stupid, a puny finger in a dyke against the tidal wave of human history.

Iris looked at Molly, and found herself thinking of Sammy. Sammy, with her friendly openness, mad, home-made clothes, and casual affection for children and cabbages. Sammy wasn't sad, or stupid. Surely Molly would be happier with a bit of whatever Sammy had?

Don't give up yet, Iris. Where's that breastplate?

'Look, can we just lose the negativity and try this? I've got lots more. How about building an astronomical mobile for your room, Mol? It would look lovely, and if we put in all the planets and their moons it would take ages.'

Ted's face lit up with a sudden epiphany. 'Is it things that take ages Mum? I know I know, how about when you made those Chinese dumplings for when your friends came over for lunch, and they were too small and the filling was too big, and we had to start over, and then...'

Iris didn't enormously want to be reminded of the dumplings. 'It's not necessarily only that they take a long time, sweetie – there's no more chocolate Molly, you needn't bother looking - it's, well it's especially things that aren't screen-based, you know, computers and such.'

'Oh, so I'm supposed to do my mocks with a slate and an abacus am I? "I'm sorry I got like, zero percent but my Mum's a raving nutter and she threw away my computer and my calculator" '.

'Don't talk to your mother like that, Molly.'

'Well somebody has to. I've had it with this, if I'm going to be awake all night guarding my computer from my psycho mother, I might as well be lying down.'

She pushed out her chair so hard it banged onto the floor, and stomped upstairs on ten inch crepe wedges. Malcolm headed back to the sink. 'That went well.'

'No thanks to you. What happened to solidarity in front of the children?'

Ted was still there, furtively licking the chocolate wrapper, but she was too outraged to care. Malcolm turned on the hot tap. 'Any agreements between us on that front are rendered void by insanity. Next time you want support for a Luddite insurrection, you might want to consult me in advance.'

'You're the one who's always going on about them being addicted to their computers, and - I just thought we could return to happier times. You know, like the Victorians making their own entertainment round the fireside...'

'The Victorians sent nine year old children up chimneys filled with soot. Speaking of which, isn't it bath time?'

For the first time that evening, Ted was authentically enthusiastic. 'Hey, I've got one, not having baths! Mum can we stop having baths, that will save lots of energy won't it? Can we stop right now?'

Iris glanced nervously at Malcolm before whispering as she ushered him upstairs: 'You'd better have one tonight, but we'll see about tomorrow. Come on, we can make it a quick one, as it's so late.'

Molly moved the audio slider on Rage Against the Machine to max, and flew her mouse over the suburban malls of Second Life towards Altarica.

Things had seemed bad enough before: a porky engineer father, a mother obsessed with teeny trivia like some de-saturated Stepford wife, and an incredibly noisy, smelly brother who monologued about football every waking hour. Bad enough to be good at science, in a school where the girls all channelled Cheryl Cole, and the boys looked like tissue cultures from a medical research lab. Bad enough to have to pretend to be even fifty percent as dim, just to avoid daily crucifixion in the lunch queue.

But this was much, much worse. She'd read about people whose mums went mad. They had to hide it from the neighbours to keep Social Services at bay, and two minutes later they were full-time carers for their drooling progenitors. And when that happened, it was goodbye PhD in quantum cryptography, hello fifty years of shovelling FruGrains into them, while the neighbours talk about how wonderful you are, and cross the road to avoid passing your door.

Thank Christ for the Internet. If she was doomed to be walled in by bedpans from now on, she'd need her lifelines to sanity.

The blank grey of her screen swirled into blue-black darkness, like a sudden storm. Molly could never understand people going on about the beauty and mystery of made-up stuff like poems and art and shit; here, in basic maths and physics, was a world where the most amazing, unbelievably beautiful and mystical things were just like, normal. And it was all out there, waiting to be discovered.

But nobody had built it as a playground, before. Not until Altarica. Everything here was surprising and endlessly mutable. A tiny wormhole, one pixel wide, might suddenly open up into an unbounded infinity. A staircase might only ever go up and never down, but always take you where you wanted to go. And - major joy! You didn't have to make like a moron.

How cool must it have been, building it. And now Ubiquitur, the code god, had added superpowers. Last night she'd tried out invisibility, but it turned out that being invisible is only interesting when people are gossiping about you. Altarican conversations tended to run more along the lines of, 'Hey, your quarks are looking sticky tonight!'

She'd been working on the equations for the gravity of the planet Krypton; she rather liked the idea of leaping tall buildings at a single bound. But first, she wanted to find Ubiquitur. Even though he was like, the reification of pure wisdom, he always had time to listen, and he never tried to tell her what to do.

Aha! There was his avatar, an infinity sign, over by the ten-dimensional maze. Normally she'd have opened up the conversation with some light banter about writing code for leg muscles to resist G-forces of fifteen, but tonight she was in a hurry. She clicked on the dialogue box and wrote:

'Help me, oh powerful one. I am but young and ill-versed in the mighty arts, but a terrible calamity has befallen me.'

For some reason his conversational modalities seemed to come right from Dungeons and Dragons, but as he was the genius who'd come up with this whole world, she wasn't about to quarrel. She hit 'send' and waited, flicking through an old copy of 'The Physics of the Buffyverse'. The response was almost immediate.

'Tell me your woes, oh beleaguered one, and I will endeavour to assist.'

'It's my mother. She has suffered injuriously to the head region, and ever since she's been behaving really weirdly – that ist, she hath fallen into realms of weird behaviour. I need to undo the spell, like, with utmost speed, oh venerable one.'

'Ah. Mothers. It so happeneth that I have one of these myself. Do not act in haste, my child. This could be serious. Observe your ill-starred mother when she ist unawares. Draw her out to reveal the dimensions of her malady. Discover her weak spots, and turn them to your advantage. But above all, avoideth provoking her in any way that might arouse her demons...'

'Molly! Are you still awake? Can I come in?'

Molly slammed out of Altarica and opened 'Fascinating Topology'. She ripped off Iris' ancient mirrored kaftan that helped her get into character, and shoved it under the bed. Underneath she wore a tee shirt saying, 'Seen Enough?'

She flopped under the duvet, pulling it right up to her face.

'Molly?'

'I'm asleep, all right?'

The door opened a crack, and Iris' anxious face peered round it. Then a hand, waving a packet. Molly didn't move.

Iris opened the door and came in. Light from a purple bulb sparked off fossils from childhood holidays, neatly ranged on the window ledge, and luminous constellations glowed from the ceiling. Everything else was neatly shut away, most of it under lock and key. Iris addressed a motionless lump under the duvet. 'Molly, I'm so sorry. Look, I've found it.'

Molly was about to tell her to sod off, when she remembered Ubiquitur's advice.

('Draw her out'...)

The covers opened about an inch, just enough to reveal Iris, creeping towards her across the room, waving the packet like a white flag. 'Look, it's the dried pineapple, I found it in the cupboard. I remembered, I'd kept it because it's fair trade, from these people who...'

The crack slammed shut again.

'Okay, well if you're feeling like that, I'll just throw it away with the rest, shall I?' Iris turned to go.

'Mum...' The voice was muffled by the duvet, but it was a response. 'You threw away my stuff! All my Clinique, and my way pricey Origins scrub, and – what a bloody nerve, Mum, you didn't even bloody ASK!'

'I'm so sorry, sweetie, do come out and let me give you a hug!'

Iris sat down on the bed. The lump wriggled almost imperceptibly to make room. 'And you said I was fat!'

'No I didn't!'

'You so did. More or less. But anyway...'

(...'Discover her weak spots...')

The covers parted, and Molly's face appeared, chalk white under a Goth-black thatch, wearing an expression of sanctimonious disdain. 'I mean – all I was saying was like, it's not like you're the only one in the family who's bothered about all this ethical shit...'

'Aren't I?'

'Of course bloody not – like I was saying yeah, all those cosmetics you chucked out?'

'Did I? Ah. Well, maybe I did. Though I have to tell you, at the time it didn't really feel like me...'

Christ, Mum really has lost it. She's growing multiple personalities. Next thing there'll be voices in her head. Too bloody right about not provoking her demons.

Molly's face softened into a forgiving smile as she squeezed Iris' bandaged hand.

'Ow!'

'Ooh, sorry. No, anyway it's actually really good Mum as it turns out, because I was reading - in Ethical Consumer Magazine - that Clarins is really really like, the most responsible cosmetic company ever, even better than like Dr Hauschka, right?'

'Really? You read Ethical Consumer? Since when?'

('...and turn her weaknesses to your advantage')

'So like, you could buy me Clarins, to replace the stuff you threw away. Couldn't you?'

A winning softness seeped into her voice. 'Please Mum? It'll be like, really good for the planet won't it, you'll feel great about yourself? And you can, like, use it too. I mean, sometimes. You're so great Mum, I'm so proud of you.'

Iris sank onto the black duvet in her daughter's embrace, wondering if this was how a spider's victim felt in its last moments. And hoping that, as God's vessel, she had an allocation of miracles for emergencies. Obviously, she'd been totally wrong the other day to get so upset about Ted and Johnny Cash. Children's affection doesn't change as they get older. It just gets more expensive.

Colin, engrossed in a particularly gnarly bit of coding, had forgotten all about Morphea when his dialogue box lit up again.

'I am returned to report progress, infinite one'

'Tell me, maiden'

'Heeding your advice, I have challenged the Mother on her own terms, and won a victory.'

'Good – very good. What further help can I be to you?'

'I'll keep in - I will bideth my time and observe.'

'That is great wisdom in one so young. It may hap that greater spoils may yet come to you from this battle.'

'It may well hap er – thusly. Thank you, and good night. BTW remind me to tell you what I foundeth out about dragline webbing and Spiderman. It ist all in the strength to elasticity ratio, thou knowest.'

'Sounds great. Any time. Go in peace and wisdom, fair youngling.'

Colin hit 'send' and pushed his chair back. The Science Park server was supposed to be fire-walled, but luckily the IT junior was also an Altarican, and had enabled his access in exchange for three power levels and a 'God Doesn't Play Poker – Except with Me' tee shirt. Collin was wearing the same tee shirt, a faint shadow under the easy-care polyester mix of his short sleeved shirt. In Altarica he felt not just like God's chosen poker partner, but God himself. It wasn't just the joy of writing code for impossible shapes. It was feeling like the person he was meant to be, not the one squeezed painfully out of a baffling adolescence. In Altarica, the infinity symbol protected him like a magic robe, and there were no unmarked quicksands of small talk and pop culture. Here he was The Alchemist.

As he was, in a small way, with his tiny, resolute army of bugs. Colin was sweating into his polyester as he slid off the stool and padded over to the centrifuge where they hung in their tubes, quietly multiplying. It was hot in here, but they loved heat. He opened the lid and peered in. All the food had gone! They were even hungrier than he could have hoped. Speaking of hungry... He felt in his trouser pocket and pulled out a film-wrapped cylinder labelled 'Jumbo Sos Roll'. He read the small print before eating it, to make sure it'd been properly preserved, hydrogenated and emulsified. Colin didn't like to take risks with his diet. He spent his days, at least that fraction of them when Malcolm was about, appearing to busy himself with conventional waste disposal technologies, 'pay as you throw' regimes and his new favourite, CATNAP, or 'Cheapest Available Technology Narrowly Avoiding Prosecution', which had the extra attraction of appearing to endorse falling asleep on the job.

But behind the smokescreen of jargon and acronyms, his ambitions were much bolder. He was discovering a new kind of alchemy: turning dross into gold on the nano level. He got light-headed just thinking about it. Once you started re-engineering molecules, anything was possible.

He'd already tried it with the crumbs of a cheese-and-onion slice, with gratifying results, and was thinking of something more challenging next time. The major hurdle at the moment was making them hungry enough; making a chain reaction that would enable a very small number of his babies to eat a very large amount of something else. Some day soon, when he'd cracked that, he'd tell Malcolm about it. But not just yet.

He slid back onto his chair, pastry crumbs nestling in his beard, and checked to see how much traffic Altarica was getting. Not very much, as usual. His plan had been to use the virtual playground to finance his research, and he'd hoped that after moving it from the undifferentiated wastelands of the Web to a ruinously overpriced piece of real estate in Second Life, more people would have discovered it. But the sad truth appeared to be that mathematical magic had the same niche following in the virtual world as the real. For now, he'd have to stick with the day job, and the bugs would have to take second place to waste management.

There was a voicemail message from the H G Wells Pyrolisis Centre in Woking. Reluctantly, he logged out of Altarica and picked up the phone.

Still not entirely sure how Molly had manipulated her into a commitment to spend several hundred pounds she didn't have, on things neither of them needed, Iris arrived back downstairs to find Malcolm lolling innocently in front of 'Scrap Heap Challenge.' 'Look – recycling, on prime time. See, I'm doing my bit.'

For some reason, this evening Iris was not inclined to fall about in gales of helpless laughter. On the coffee table in front of Malcolm was a big pile of brochures of the latest cars, captured at rest and at play by the most exquisite photography, under the most expensive sunshine, in the world.

Iris realised for the first time that she was married to a man whose single greatest passion was, arguably, one of the prime movers of the imminent demise of human civilisation. It was a mildly alarming revelation, but she said nothing, just hobbled dramatically past to the washing machine and proceeded to empty it, as noisily as she could. After a minute or two, Malcolm gave up, and came over to help. He picked up a tee shirt, began to fold it, then bent over it, examining it minutely with a pained expression. 'Is there something up with the machine?'

'Not that I'm aware of.' She threw a pair of socks towards him.

'Thanks.' Now he was looking at the socks. 'Only, none of this stuff seems to be clean.'

'Well, that depends what you mean by clean, doesn't it?'

'Funny, I wasn't aware until now that clean was a relative condition.'

Iris snatched back the tee shirt. 'Isn't it meant to look like this? What's wrong with it?'

'It's supposed to be green.'

'Well it is – mostly – shades of green.'

'It's supposed to be one, uniform, unsullied shade of green, not an artist's impression of a deciduous woodland in early autumn.'

'They manage fine in India don't they, just banging things with rocks to clean them?'

'You're not banging my best shirt with rocks while Unilever's in business.'

'I'm not putting money in Unilever's pockets when there are non-toxic alternatives.'

'Like what?' Malcolm was now rifling in the laundry cupboard and came out waving a bottle labelled EcoClear Gentle Chamomile Laundry Solution. 'Is this it?'

He opened it, sniffed it, looked closely at the tiny print on the back. He hadn't done four science A-levels for nothing. 'I hate to stomp all over your newfound idealism, but homeopathy doesn't actually work on mud and sweat.'

'Did you know that one average load in a washing machine uses a hundred litres of water?'

'Have you looked out of the window lately? It hasn't stopped raining in weeks!'

'If you're saying you'd rather have your shirts hung out in the rain to wash, I'll go and buy a clothesline tomorrow, it'll certainly save a lot of work. And if it ever stops raining, we can save twenty-six trees' worth of carbon a week drying them outside too...'

'One more word, and I'm having you sectioned. Or exorcised. Your choice.' He stomped back to the TV, switched it on and cranked up the volume to a point that put an end to further dialogue.

It was occurring to Iris more and more forcefully that none of Soren's heartfelt rhetoric, or indeed the happy clappy Green propaganda that had been pouring from every channel of the media for the past couple of years, seemed to take into account the possibility that a heroic lead down the path of righteousness might not be followed with equal zeal by the rest of the household. Nor had God warned her about it. What else was He holding back? Iris resolved to try to have a quiet word later.

Meanwhile, it was time for a bit of conciliation. And she hated to end the day fighting; she never got any sleep confined to her own side of the bed. She pulled her top down an inch or two before going over to whisper in his ear. 'Well - we could maybe sort of adjust to wearing more dark-coloured clothes, and you know, patterns...'

'Why don't we go one better, and refit the entire bathroom in a tasteful shade of shit-brown, so we'll never have to clean it again?'

'Now you're being silly. Anyway, it's only because the light's so bright in here; if we changed all the bulbs to low voltage ones...'

'Or we could just stick pins in our eyes. You go first. Shall I fetch your sewing basket?'

He returned Iris' hug, but without much conviction. Ever since her sojourn in Ward H, the domestic harmony on which his own happiness rested had been shattered. Iris was a happy, positive person. Or she had been. Up until a week ago. Hadn't she?

The pile of half-folded laundry by the washing-machine was bothering him. Normally, any amount of housework was preferable to a conversation about the glutinous and imprecise world of feelings. But extreme times call for extreme measures. Instead of heading back to the laundry, he took her good hand and led her towards the sofa.

'What are you doing?' she demanded, as he sat her down and fetched a cushion.

'What do you mean, what am I doing?'

'There's an – untidiness situation over there. You never leave anything untidy.'

He picked up the remote and turned off the television. He rarely did that, either. 'It can wait. I want to know what this is all about.'

'What's what all about?'

He lifted her leg up and carefully slid the cushion under her knee, which, at close quarters, was not a pretty sight.

'Gosh, my bandage is getting a bit disgusting isn't it? You might as well change it, you'll only fret if you have to sit here watching it fester.'

Malcolm disappeared into the cloakroom and returned with a clean bandage. He sat back beside Iris, and began to unwrap the old dressing, as tenderly as a Cosworth engineer polishing a piston head. Malcolm's strong hands seemed to have their own confidence, quite irrespective of the sometimes erratic operation of his brain. Even when the babies were tiny, they'd stopped screaming the minute he picked them up, as though they realised that nobody yet born was better qualified to change a nappy, or un-twist a sleeve. It was like meditation, just watching him. Or maybe she was just very tired...

'So – tell me. Why it happened. Your prang.'

'Well it was Soren who...'

'No, I don't mean how. Why. Why you were so off your box in the first place.'

He pulled the new dressing out of its wrapper, in which he then placed the carefully-folded old one. Iris stared at the back of his head, wondering how much she dared explain. 'I wasn't off my box. Or at least, I didn't think I was. I was unhappy.'

'Unhappy? Why? You're never unhappy.'

'Well, not often, no. I wasn't, right up until that afternoon, or at least I didn't think I was. It was just'...The Johnny Cash story seemed ridiculous, in retrospect. It could have been anything. Why was it so hard to explain to Malcolm, and why was she so sure he wouldn't understand? '...it's just, you know, my life. It suddenly seemed so useless, and sort of, I don't know, petty.'

Malcolm carried on criss-crossing the gauze over her bruises. Would he think she meant their whole life together? She realised she had no idea what he was feeling. If anything. She rubbed a hand over his head, against the nap of his hair. She'd been doing that for sixteen years. Amazing.

'... I mean, I'm not sorry we had the children, or anything, but - well. They're going to go, aren't they? And quite soon, really. And then what will I do, with nothing on my CV apart from "eight thousand packed lunches" and "more patience with tax returns than the average idiot."? So it was all that, churning away, that upset me, I suppose. And then afterwards, in hospital, I just started to think about the way we live, just doing whatever we feel like, not thinking about the effects, because they're happening in places we don't go to, to people we don't know.'

'Well then, so long as we stay away, we're all right, aren't we?' He finished the job, tucked the end neatly under the perfect herringbone of the bandage, carefully removed her leg from his, and stood up. Iris was wondering whether she had the energy for another fight about unhelpful responses to serious issues, when she noticed him stuffing most of the clean laundry, including the garments she'd already folded, back into the machine. 'What are you doing now?'

'What does it look like I'm doing? I'm putting my clothes back to get clean.' He reached for the remnants of the Unilever extra-strength Agent Orange, challenging her with a look to stop him. Iris stayed where she sat, but couldn't help asking: 'What, you're going to do another whole cycle, just for that lot?'

'Or do it all four times as often with that hippie shite you bought. Anyhow, you ought to be pleased.'

'How so?'

'Well, presumably we'll be switching over to that green power company who just sent us thirty pages of introductory information on full-colour coated paper?'

'Well – yes – so what?'

'The ones who add a unit of green energy to the national grid for every unit we use?'

'So?'

'So, the more laundry we do, the more windmills they put up.

I'm doing the planet a favour here. D'you want me to do yours again, while I'm at it?'

It wasn't so much the deviousness of his arguments that she minded, or even that they usually turned out to be completely bogus. It was the unbearably smug face he wore to come out with them. He's wasted as an engineer, he ought to be a politician. Or possibly a car salesman. Speaking of which… 'Those brochures over there…'

He followed her gaze innocently, as though they'd been put there by the Car Fairy while his back was turned. 'What about them?'

'You're not really going to buy a Lamborghini instead of the Jeep, are you?'

'Why not? After all, there's at least one pandemic on the way, there's AIDS set to finish off most of Africa and India, there are millions of lunatic fundamentalists of all persuasions on the loose, thirty thousand unaccounted for nuclear warheads, bioterrorists with poisons that could eliminate entire nations, not to mention asteroids, earthquakes and volcanoes – what's the point of worrying about a motor car?'

Looked at like that, he had a point. On the other hand… Iris sat, visualising on the blank TV screen in front of her a man with whom she had always thought herself almost spookily in harmony, lounging behind the wheel of a throbbing chick magnet. Was this somehow her fault too?

He pressed the 'start' button on the machine, yawned, and made for the stairs. 'A Lamborghini? With whose cash? Come to bed, you daft lollop. But leave your broomstick outside.'

By next morning the drawbacks of the cash-free economy could no longer be ignored. A quick inspection of the fridge and pantry revealed that God had still not sent a miracle in the night, and the nutritive substances in the house consisted, as before, of two potatoes, half a kilo of carrots, a jar of pickles and one of crystallised violets, a rather small amount of goat's milk, a still sizeable mountain of Dorset Headwallop, and thirty-seven bags of undrinkable green tea. Unless Iris abandoned her sacred vow and crawled back to all her clients, LETS and Buzzybees seemed to offer the only way out.

Actually the prospect of Buzzybees was rather cheering to Iris; it seemed like the one place where she was reasonably safe from attack. Pouring the last drop of goat's milk into her tea with an all-or-nothing recklessness straight from the blackjack tables of Atlantic City, she sat down to peruse the LETS list.

The flyer was printed in jolly faux-handwriting type: 'A Brilliant Idea! Exchange Skills, not Money! Get things you need, do people favours, and make friends, all at the same time!'

Iris wondered uncharitably why people who were clearly totally confident of their own righteousness felt the need to emphasise it with quite so many exclamation marks. Maybe it was just an uncontrollable overflow of enthusiasm from the LETS experience. She turned to the list of things on offer: music lessons, batik hangings, reptile demonstrations, rug maintenance. Story tellers, baby feet sculptors, piano movers and chicken-house builders. There were people offering to choose birthday presents, return library books, paint a portrait of her house, sharpen her saws and chisels, and massage away her aches and pains. Iris' inner eye widened on a new universe of benign, creative activity, treading lightly over the earth and leaving only beauty and the odd bit of compostable waste behind.

Of course, this ignored the question of how she was going to lay her hands on the football kit, video games, High Street fashion items and late model mobile phones without which her family's life was apparently unsustainable, not to mention the entire Clarins cosmetic range. But still, there were organic fishmongers, egg sellers and market gardeners. She could put food on the table. It was a start.

The shop was much busier than before. A whole crowd of chic young mothers and artsy singletons milled around the salad fridge, and Sammy was barely visible behind the queue at the till. The pigtails had metastasised into cheery little spikes all over her head. 'How's the leg? Hang on, I'll get your chair.'

'Oh don't worry, I can see you're busy. What happened?'

'Bloody chickweed yuppies. That Food Foragers thing was on telly again last night. I keep telling 'em they'd be better off pulling it up from the pavement, but they will insist on coming here and paying three quid a bunch. Daylight robbery.' She turned her radiant smile on the woman in front of her, who'd just stowed four bunches of chickweed in her rush basket. 'That'll be thirty-four twenty. Enjoy! Hey, Arlo, help us out here would you?'

Sammy left Arlo to manage as best he could at the till, while she fetched a chair over to Iris, keeping her injuries away from the scrum.

'Oh thanks. Actually, I'm not buying anything today. It's about the...' Iris' voice dropped to a stage whisper. For some reason, being forced to abandon the sordid machinery of capitalism felt vaguely shaming, which was even more shaming in itself. Saints were supposed to be penniless, after all. It was ennobling. Maybe the nobility would grow over time. 'It's about the LETS thing. I thought I'd give it a try.'

'Oh yeah? Found something you want?'

'Well it's not so much that as – I wanted to offer my own services, you know.'

'Great! What do you do?' Sammy had pulled out another piece of green paper, and an old pencil with 'Healing Arts Zagreb 99' on it.

'Well, I used to – it's a bit dull but it's quite useful, I do book-keeping.'

'Fab!! I'll put it down here... What is book-keeping?'

'It's, you know, sorting out people's accounts. What they've earned, and what they've spent. Squaring it up with the Revenue. You'd be amazed how much people will pay, just to not have to deal with the Revenue.'

Sammy began to write. Then looked up at Iris. An adorable little crease appeared between her brows. 'That's like – totting up money, right? Money they've earned, and money they've spent?'

'That's it. Yes.' Then it dawned on Iris too. Who needs book-keeping in a cashless society? 'Don't any of these people use money at all?'

'Well – course they must, how else would they pay for their smokes? Give it a go, eh? Maybe we don't actually mention the tax word here on the form, keep it vague, yeah?'

'Tax?'

Arlo propped a 'No More Chickweed – Sorry!' sign against the till. As the crowd straggled sadly towards the door, he came over with a basket of samosas. 'Do not talk to me about tax!'

'Why not?' Sammy helped herself and offered one to Iris, who'd never knowingly eaten a samosa before, but had never had to manage on puffed kashi and goat's milk for breakfast before, either.

'That call from the Royal Philharmonic I told you about yeah? Seventy string zither needing a restring. One major deal.'

'Oh yeah, I remember. What happened about that?'

'Well, so in principle it's like a great connexion, okay, get it right and I'm in clover, hundreds more fucking instruments needing Arlo's famous TLC. So I say go for it, they zip it over, I do the job, they're thrilled. And then...'

He paused dramatically, a second samosa half way to his mouth. Sammy rolled her eyes. 'Then what? God Arlo, you're such a drama queen.'

'Then they send me their supplier invoice. Man, am I fucked! It's got like, VAT numbers, company names and addresses, all this shit, plus they've already contacted the Revenue and given them my name.'

'So you hadn't forewarned them about being paid in Black Tar and a wodge?'

Iris had just made the novel discovery that a cold potato samosa could be quite palatable if you were truly ravenous, which led her to speculate whether, if she delayed the meals at 26 Hartland Gardens from now on, she could feed her family whatever she liked without any resistance. At that moment she was slapped on the shoulder by Sammy, and nearly choked.

'Ooh, sorry, you okay? Looks like your lucky day, Iris, your first victim's right here. Iris'll sort you out, Arlo. You can pay her in store credit off your wages.'

'Outstanding! When could you...'

'Iris! I thought it was you, and then I heard your name. I had a little suspicion I might find you in here. Much more pleasant than the supermarket, isn't it? Though I have to say, rather busier than I'm used to.'

Iris watched Sammy's face change as the melodious, water-dripping voice cut through the hubbub of the shop. What was Soren doing out of hospital already? Iris was ashamed to discover that her own principal emotion at being found was not entirely positive. She felt, in fact, not unlike a baby rabbit being air-kissed by a weasel. 'Oh. Soren. How wonderful that you're out already. I'm sorry I never made it back to visit you, only...'

'You two know each other? How so?' Somehow, while Soren hobbled towards them, Sammy had managed to retreat almost as far as the till, where a patient queue had been building all this while.

Iris wondered how to distil 'I tried to kill her, and then she made me promise to dedicate my life to a higher purpose' into light conversational banter, and came up with, 'We met in hospital. In fact, Soren's the reason I'm er, downsizing. She made me you know, rethink things. Quite a bit.'

Sammy had now reached the till, and barricaded herself behind it again. 'Oh yes, Soren's ace at that, aren't you Soren? The conscience of the 'hood.'

'You will have your little joke, Sammy. But on that note, I did just want a quick word...'

Iris felt something touch her elbow. She turned to see Arlo. 'Would tomorrow work? For the tax stuff?'

'Oh. Yes, I'm sure it would.'

'You want to come to mine? It's close by.' His eyes were an extraordinary green, like dried grass, flecked with gold. 'I'll give you the directions before you go.'

Meanwhile Soren had hobbled on her crutches straight past the line of people waiting to pay, and was lecturing Sammy with unhurried conviction. '...Of course, I completely understand that the temptation to maximise your profits must be a very real one, but you know, they were bought out not long ago, and unfortunately the parent company are no longer the principled Quakers they once were.'

'Yeah, but you know, it's great chocolate and...'

'But that's not what you're here for, is it? I'm well aware that some of these people...' She surveyed the meekly waiting queue with a gaze that suggested they had all taken their morning baths in the freshly-drawn blood of enslaved cocoa pickers. '...many of them, indeed, don't concern themselves about the provenance of what they buy, but you know better than that, don't you?'

She was still talking as Iris backed out of the shop, wondering yet again how such an obviously virtuous person could inspire such uncharitable emotions.

Iris half-woke up the next day, and immediately wished she hadn't. Apart from being penniless, in pain, and further crippled by the weight of the world's conscience, she'd remembered this was the day Malcolm was taking the children to buy a car. A car that was no longer merely a car, but the actualisation of everything she had been trying to lead him and the others away from. Put like that, it was an act of war.

Still half-asleep, she buried her face in the pillow, wondering whether Joan of Arc minded losing all her friends. Or, indeed, whether she ever had any?

JOAN OF ARC: THE EARLY YEARS

SCENE: A HOVEL IN THE QUAINT VILLAGE OF DOMREMY.

Joan's mum, Joanna, is bent over the fire, trying to get it to burn up enough to cook the porridge. Enter Joan, aged five, rubbing her eyes.

JOAN:
'Maman! Maman! Didn't I tell you last night that smoke from wood fires is the leading cause of respiratory deaths? It kills more people than the Pox! Open the window, Maman!'

Joanna hobbles over to a small opening in the mud wall and pulls aside the scrabbly old piece of cloth that covers it.

JOAN:
'Maman! Maman! You're letting out all the heat! Last year the Foret de Doinville lost three rare species and fourteen per cent of the insects' ground cover, entirely because of our profligate use of its wood!'

JOANNA:
'Why not go out and play for a bit, love, until I can get the breakfast ready.'

JOAN:
'Just raw oatmeal and a soupcon of sugar beet treacle for me. My conscience is staying clear as God's voice in my head!'

Joanna bends over the cooking pot, wondering whether the priest might be induced, in exchange for her fattest broiler, to put a few well-chosen words into God's mouth.

SCENE: THE VILLAGE STREET

Joan skips down the village street, and stops at the well, where Vieux Paul is stooping over the handle as he draws up the water.

VIEUX PAUL:
'Give me a hand here Joan, my sciatica's killing me.'

JOAN:
'That's only because you don't take the right sort of exercise. I bet you haven't practised even one of those stretches I taught you lat week! And what about those dried sardines I told you to chew? You've only yourself to blame!'

She watches, hands on embryonic hips, as he finally succeeds in bringing the bucket to the surface. Joan dips the tin cup into the water and takes a sip.

JOAN:
'Ugh! The Ph balance of this water is way off! That naughty Jacques down at the smithy has been emptying his tempering buckets in the stream again! Jacques! Oh, Jacques!!'

She runs off down the street, yelling importantly. As she passes, doors slam shut and more sackcloth curtains are pulled tight.

ASSORTED VILLAGERS (O/S):
'That poor Joanna! That daughter of hers ought to have been left out for the wolves years ago. Mark my words, she'll rue the day she was born!'

Joan reaches the forge, whose door is bolted tight, and begins tugging energetically on the bell. Ring! Ring! Ring! She's not giving up...

Ring! Ring !

What kind of numbnuts calls at this time on a Saturday morning?

Iris sleepily followed the wire to Molly's door, slid it silently open, and salvaged the phone from under last month's Scientific American.

'Yes? Who? Oh – of course I remembered. Yup, I'll be there. Yup, I'll bring the supercomputer. See you soon!'

Oh well. She couldn't stop Malcolm spending a morning revving engines and ogling door trims, but she, Iris, was off to reinvent the basis of market capitalism.

And Spring had finally arrived, something Iris noticed for the first time walking down the canal towpath, with daffodils budding to one side and baby ducklings gamely paddling between floating bottles and sandwich wrappers on the other. Arlo's directions had led her unexpectedly to a little oasis between the arterial roads and clanking railways of her home patch. And now that her knee was beginning to heal, it was gratifying to walk beside the water listening to birdsong, as the others inched up a packed High Street in a seething line of cars.

The canal bank widened. To the right of the footpath itself, somebody had planted guerrilla allotments, with lavender, bean canes and even a little rose pergola. And here were the boats. This must be Arlo's, with the tomatoes on its roof and the vegetable patch alongside. There he was, digging in the damp earth.

Arlo turned as Iris approached. He was wearing a pair of cotton trousers, soft with wear, and pulled on an old tee shirt on as he stood. 'Hi. You made it. You know anything about weeds?'

'Not really. We don't have a proper garden, just a sort of paved rubbish display.'

'Only I'm like, boat-sitting for this guy who grows for Sammy, yeah? And she's been onto me to bring more chickweed. Only I didn't get a real good look at it yesterday, and... well, it's gotta be a weed, right? But...' He stood and contemplated the luxuriant green carpet around the onions, lettuces and carrot tops.

'I think it's this one'. Iris bent to pull up a plant and held it out to him, smelling the soil on her fingers. How nice it would be to get up in the morning and dig your lunch with your own hands. She resolved to go home and look up 'allotments' on the Council website. 'At least, this is what Sammy was selling in handfuls yesterday.'

'Wild. I'll take it down to her later. When I'm done with the zither. Come aboard.'

He held out a hand to Iris. It was warm, and muscled. She scrambled after him. Cushions were scattered over the boat's roof, and a large snake coiled round the chimney.

'Don't mind Pepita, she's just letting her breakfast go down.' He picked up an instrument lying near the snake, and folded himself neatly, patting the cushion next to him. 'Can you believe, I've been at it all morning and I'm only at string forty-three. What a bitch. Still, could've been a balalaika.'

'Is this where you live?'

'See, I don't really live any place much. I like – move around. You know. I'm kind of – virtualised? I go where the work is.'

'So this boat...'

'It's a LETS thing – this guy had it, he's like – off somewhere ...so this way he gets his vegetables like, watered, and his stuff looked after...'

'That's very trusting of him.'

'You think? Come on, I'll make tea, yeah?' He uncurled himself and stood up. A couple of inches of hard, brown stomach creased above his trousers. He shook out his arms like a small boy, and padded in front of her down the stairs. Iris had a sudden vision of Ted at twenty.

Inside, the boat was very clean, and almost empty. A pale, polished wooden floor, a sleeping platform with a mattress and a folded quilt. A laptop, a mobile, a roll of tools, and a pile of books. Iris sneaked a look at the titles: 'Alternative Irrigation: The Promise of Runoff Agriculture', 'Low Cost Pole Building', 'Step by Step to a Plastic Bottle Greenhouse' and 'The Chinese Biogas Manual'.

'They don't seem like very soothing bedtime reading.'

'Oh, they came with the boat. Most of what I need is, you know, digital. Everything's out there in the ether, right?'

How wonderfully liberating, to be able to live with so little. To be so free... Iris resolved to go home and throw everything away. 'Oh – hang on, I brought something'. She ran back upstairs and scrabbled in her bag. When she got downstairs again, he was sniffing at a handful of tea bags. 'I have no clue about these - you better pick one for yourself.'

'I don't mind, so long as it's not green. Would you like a scone?'

Carefully, she opened the lid of a biscuit tin on a pile of buttermilk scones which she'd proudly presented to her family at breakfast. Her first shot at baking for about twenty years, and they'd come out pretty well. 'Nobody wanted them. I just made them this morning, so they should still be warm, with a bit of luck.'

'You MADE - THESE?' He looked at Iris as though she'd just opened the tin on a pair of white tigers and a Stradivarius, then reached in and took one, broke it in half, sniffed ecstatically, and swallowed it. Iris couldn't help contrasting this with her family's reaction, which had been, essentially, that nothing produced by the disinterred skills of their mother could possibly come near to substituting for a Taste the Difference Pain au Chocolat or three, and anyhow there was bound to be a Starbucks on the way to the car showroom.

Arlo brushed the crumbs from his mouth and grinned at her.

'They didn't want them? How come? Can I have another?'

Iris decided it was too early in their acquaintance to hit him with the details of the civil war brewing at 26 Hartland Gardens, and luckily greed distracted him from pursuing the conversation.

An hour later, she was sitting on the deck in the sunlight, a light breeze playing shadows over the papers on her knee, as she tried to formulate, in the language of the Inland Revenue, the intelligence that a large part of Arlo's income came in the form of hand-reared vegetables, veterinary services, rent-free accommodation and bespoke sandals. The snake was still sleeping and Arlo was playing a sweet, if monotonous, tune on the re-strung zither.

'Done!' She waved the form at him triumphantly. 'Total taxable income, ninety-three pounds and forty-four pence. I don't think the Revenue will be bothering you this year.'

'Outstanding!' He smiled at her, stopped playing, and reached over for a velvet bag to stow the zither. The zither went in, and immediately reappeared out of the bottom. He caught it with one hand, and inspected the bag with the other. 'Guess that's history. Pity, it was my Mom's. I haven't much of her shit left.'

Iris folded the form neatly into its envelope, and went to

inspect the bag. 'It's just the seam, somebody could do this easily.'

'Like, who?'

'Well – I used to be able to sew. We did it at school, and my Mum taught me a bit too.'

'You can SEW too?' Iris felt a pleasing tingle of embarrassment at his tone. The longer she spent with Arlo, the more she realised how blind her family was to its amazing luck.

She threw a crumb to a passing duckling, thinking there was something very attractive about a home you could just move, if you didn't particularly feel like being there when the rest of them got back. 'I'm sure I've got my old sewing kit at home somewhere, I'll take it away and do it for you.'

Arlo was carrying a bulging sack over to the vegetables. 'You are a goddess, Iris.'

He paused, peering into the sack. 'Hey, what do you think, Sammy gave me these coffee grounds for the compost? She said just dump'em on the worms and watch'em go. But won't they be like, totally hyper?'

'It'd certainly speed up the composting. But I guess you'd want to steer clear of them when they crash.' Iris realised she had made her first joke since waking up in hospital.

Arlo carefully emptied the coffee over the compost heap. A couple of bikes were propped beside it. Iris dropped the velvet bag into hers. 'That reminds me. You don't happen to know anybody who might need some scones, or some mending, or even some accounting, in exchange for an old bike, do you?'

He looked over, then extricated one of the bikes and lifted it onto the towpath. 'Take this guy. I can put the saddle down for you...'

'Oh, but...'

'Hey, it's cool. Why would I need two? Plus, I've got a load more of those bags that probably need help? You could take them with you, yeah? No big hurry.'

Iris looked at her watch. Three o'clock! They'd be back any minute. 'Well – if you're sure...' What she meant was, 'If you're sure it's yours?', but that seemed a bit churlish. In the mysterious world of give and take that Arlo and his friends seemed to inhabit, the concept sounded almost grubby. Anyhow, if it wasn't his bike, that was his problem, not hers. 'That would be great. I'll just call you, shall I?

When I've finished the bags?'

'Now, whatever you do, don't provoke her, all right? She'll be in a terrible mood if she's spent the day cleaning wellie boots.' Malcolm and his son came giggling up the front path and opened the door. 'Hi!'

There was Iris, sunny and serene, humming a sweet, if monotonous, tune as she sat sewing, surrounded by a big pile of velvet bags.

'We're back.'

'So I see.' She smiled sweetly. Hmm! Hmmm! Hmm!

'So - er - What have you been up to? What's that you're doing?'

'Oh, just mending. I did the recycling too, all that stuff the bin men left because it violated regulations. It took a few journeys to the dump, on my bicycle.'

'Bicycle?'

Ted, unable to contain his excitement any longer, hurled himself on Iris, scattering the bags and missing the scissors by about two microns. 'Mum! Mum come and look at the car Mum it's got a place for me to plug in my PSP and a place for Molly's phone, and it's got tables and little pocket thingeys...' He grabbed Iris' hand and tugged, bursting with desire to share his joy. Malcolm followed, smiling at his son's delight. Iris unhooked her hand and stayed put, her mysterious serenity unwavering. 'I'm fine, thank you darling, I'm sure it's a lovely car. If you like cars.' She looked sweetly up at Malcolm on this last line.

'I seem to remember you liked the last one okay, until you drove it into the clothes bank and lobotomised yourself.'

'Come ON Mum.'

Reluctantly, she let Ted drag her out of the door. Malcolm followed. There, standing modestly at the kerb was an elegant, egg shaped, electric car.

'Look in the back, we get our own heating and music, with headphones, see?'

'What's Molly doing in there?'

'Uploading, or downloading. It's got Bluetooth built in. We

may have a problem getting her out.'

'It must have cost a fortune.'

'Well, the car you turned into a tin sandwich wasn't exactly cheap, you know. And given that, I thought you might like to contribute a bit. In your favourite cause. I can run a wire to charge it, and you can hold your head up in front of your new best friends.'

'I don't think so, thanks. I'm never going to drive it. Electricity still burns carbon, as you know. I'm very happy with my bicycle.'

'Just as well, you're probably still uninsurable after the last time. What bicycle would that be then?'

Iris pointed serenely at Arlo's bike, newly pumped up and polished, leaning against the wall. Malcolm moved over to it, and squatted down for a closer look. 'It's - hey, would you look at that, it's an old Jack Taylor. In good nick too. Somebody's put a lot of work into this. Where did you find it?'

'It's – a friend of mine gave it to me.'

'Oh yes? Any friend I might know?'

'I don't think so. He's a – new friend. He's young. He restores bikes. And musical instruments. He's very creative.'

'Is he, indeed? Well, you'll want the saddle lowering, I can...'

Malcolm was already reaching into his pocket for the LeatherMan, itching to get his hands on the bike. Iris climbed on, and straightened one leg on the pedal. 'It's all right, he did it for me. It's perfect, thank you. As I said, I've been out on it several times already. Gosh, it's so nice, being in the open air, with the wind in your hair.'

'And the grit in your eyes, and the particulates whooshing up your nostrils. You'd better get yourself one of those masks and a helmet; that way at least you won't have to worry about Elaine recognising you.'

Ted had drop-kicked his way as far as the recycling bin, and was standing over it, peering into its depths. 'Mum?'

Iris got off the bike and came over to hug him. 'There's nothing in there, your saintly mother did the whole lot today.'

'But Mum!'

'What?'

'My project?

'What project?'

'It's for tomorrow – it's my homework I TOLD you Mum I have to make a - a model of a geothermal volcanic system for our focus on Iceland. Miss Kilpatrick says it's the only place that'll be habitable in twenty years, and we've all got to spend our student loan money on flats in Rejkavik. But Mum you've got rid of all the junk modelling stuff, what am I supposed to do Mum?'

Iris watched the egg glide silently up the road, wondering at the complex chain of ironies that had sent Malcolm to the supermarket, by car, specifically to collect packaging. Her new friend – the ineffable one – clearly had a richly developed sense of humour. Anybody who could come up with the duck-billed platypus...

At least Malcolm hadn't taken the children, though he had waited to referee a long and bitter dispute between them over the relative merits, for geyser modelling purposes, of various brands of chocolate biscuit pack. Left alone, Iris returned to her blanket-stitch, remembering how easy things had all seemed a couple of hours ago; how calm, and happy, and appreciated she had felt, sitting in the sun on Arlo's borrowed boat.

'Who's for sausages then?' Malcolm marched cheerfully into the kitchen, carrying a cardboard box filled with enough supererogatory packaging to model the entire Icelandic land mass.

'Sausages?' Iris turned from the sink, where she was trimming asparagus.

'Yes, I thought I'd buy a few other things while I was there. We've not had sausages for a while, I thought we could have them for supper.'

'Sausages!' The remarkable auditory selectivity of the young, which makes them profoundly deaf to certain words and phrases like 'tidy your room' and 'bed time', makes them correspondingly hyper-sensitive to certain others. Ted had heard 'sausages' from thirty feet away and through two doors. He now yelled from his room: 'Sausages! Are they Porkinson's Dad? I love you Dad can I have loads, can I have seconds and thirds please Mum?'

Malcolm yelled back. 'As many as you like, son.'

Iris turned from the cooker to reveal, with a dramatic flourish of her arm, a meal that might have come straight from the Petit Trianon. Something about the sights and smells of Buzzybees inspired in her a culinary ambition that years of trudging the aisles of the supermarket had almost totally extinguished. 'It may have escaped your notice, but I've spent several hours making supper already.'

'Well, we can have both, can't we? I'm sure a few bangers will go fine with, with ...' He peered into a pan '...with whatever that is.'

'That's hardly the point. How can you expect me to cook Porkinsons, after all our recent conversations?'

'I'd have called them monologues, myself, but there you go. Clearly I'm naïve, but I had hoped that even under the new austerity of the environmental Taliban, I might still be allowed to spend my own money on my own supper, once in a while.'

'That's all very...'

He carried on unpacking, as though he hadn't heard her. 'But fair enough, if they offend your delicate sensibilities, I'll cook them myself.' He turned to call upstairs again. 'Moll? Porkinsons with your supper?'

His manner wasn't hostile; in fact, as he bustled past her to fetch the frying pan, he was the image of carefree cheer, which nothing, and especially not his wife, was going to sully.

Iris elbowed him aside. 'Don't be ridiculous. If poached duck eggs with asparagus hollandaise and fricassee printaniere isn't good enough for you, of course you can have sausages. I hope you bought ketchup and oven chips too, while you were about it.'

'As a matter of fact, I did.'

She slammed the frying pan down on the cooker and stalked past Malcolm towards the stairs, bellowing as she went: 'Ted, are you in the bath yet? If I get there and you're not, there won't be any sausages, or anything else!'

'What are you up to now?'

Iris turned furtively from the washing machine, as Malcolm came down from putting Ted to bed. 'Nothing.'

'You're taking things out of there, aren't you?'

'No – yes – well, only the ones that aren't dirty. She held Ted's England strip six inches from her nose, took a tentative sniff, made a face, and shoved it back in the machine.

Malcolm held a piece of paper out towards her. 'You wouldn't know anything about this, I suppose? I wondered why Ted suddenly didn't want sausages, after all.'

'I don't see why it should surprise you that your son's tastes should have become more discerning as he grew up.'

Once she'd overcome the insult implied by the addition of a big pile of sausages to the meal, it had been a great success. But Ted, after his initial jubilation, had mysteriously and resolutely refused to eat even one sausage. Now Malcolm was looking distinctly cross, and Iris had an idea why.

'So this isn't anything to do with you, then?' The paper was a photo of a large black and pink sow, immured in a very small farrowing crate. Half a dozen tiny black and pink piglets had been artfully arranged around her, snuffling pathetically at the bars of the crate. Across it was written, in fifties horror movie script: 'Imprisoned for Life! For the Crime of Being a Mother!'

Iris slammed the door of the washing machine. 'Well! It's true, isn't it? I just thought he had a right to make an informed decision.'

'He's nine! And this is the last thing you want him to see before he goes to sleep? What next? Throw out the sofa and make us all sit around on beds of nails?'

'Now you're being silly. You know we can't throw out the sofa, it'd just sit there on the pavement attracting all the happy hour casualties.' She moved to the window, where a dish sat piled with old vegetable peelings, eggshells, banana skins and teabags. She picked up the coffee pot and emptied the grounds on top of the pile. A huge mound of washing-up flowed out of the sink. Iris rolled up her sleeves and plunged her hands into the greasy, luke-warm water.

Malcolm took advantage of her leaving the washing machine unprotected to open the door again and shove it all back in. 'I can just about deal with this lunacy for now, but God knows what you're doing to the children.'

'The children! That's just it, isn't it? Because I'm a woman, I have to leave the big picture to the big hairy men-folk, and stay behind the picket fence, folding socks and fretting about supper. Well, not any more.'

'Off you go, then.' He slammed the washing machine shut with uncharacteristic force.

'Off I go where?'

'If you're determined to harangue people, go into politics, and harangue people who can harangue you back. I'm sure the local Greens could do with some new blood. Or whatever runs through their veins instead.'

'Me? Join the Greens?' Iris had never joined anything in her life, apart from an ill-considered dalliance with the English Traditional Dance Club in the wake of Freshers' Week, but he had a point. For one thing, it was another place, apart from Buzzybees, where her ideals and aspirations were likely to escape the hostility and derision they were attracting at home. 'I might just do that. What are you up to now?'

Malcolm had reached under the sink and brought out a bottle of hi-strength kitchen cleaner, which had bravely hidden itself in the shopping between the Porkinsons and a maxi-value box of PG Tips. Spraying it defiantly over every corner of the sink and work surface, he continued: 'Cleaning. Remember? That thing I do? Not yet illegal, so far as I know. Speaking of which'... Malcolm put a hand in the small of her back and pushed her gently towards the stairs...'There's one traditional recreation you forgot to put on your list that doesn't use scarce resources, or generate toxic waste. But it's a lot less fun when one of the participants smells of rotting cabbage. Go and have a bath, and I'll be up shortly.'

Malcolm was woken from a nightmare about dirty dishes by something crashing to the floor. He opened his eyes to see the alarm clock winking up at him from the carpet. He never had nightmares. And he'd never had a problem sleeping. Until now.

He leaned over to pick it up, trying not to wake Iris, who seemed to be enjoying her night's rest rather more than he was, judging by the smile on her face. Curled up in bed last night she'd seemed once again to be the woman he loved, with the same sense of humour and the same everything else. But now, instead of turning over and falling asleep again himself, he found his head full of worries, partly about what she'd get up to next, but also about the ever widening gap between the overheads at the Science Park and the work he and Colin were billing. They couldn't hide from it any longer. Whatever the worst might be, it had to be faced.

Malcolm carefully unpeeled his side of the duvet and padded over to the laptop sleeping in his home office, aka the corner of the bedroom.

FROM: mrichie@richiewinterbottom.co.uk
TO: cwinterbottom@richiewinterbottom.co.uk

01 34 am

Col

You may wonder why I am hunched over my keyboard while everybody but you and your troglodyte pals is sleeping sweetly, but the fact is that what A levels, student debt, bad prawn curry and newborn babies never achieved, Madam's new incarnation as Guardian of the Planet has brought about. We are talking nightmares and insomnia. Thanks to her efforts, the house has mutated into a one-stop shop for recycling a perfectly harmonious family life into a smelly battleground. All my patient explanations do not persuade her that days spent sorting rotting vegetables from rotting cardboard and rotting plastic film will not make a measurable impact on the fate of the Patagonian glaciers.

However, there is one positive side effect of being up at this hour, which is that it's the only time I can get away with laundering my own clothes, so I've a prayer of arriving at the office looking a few steps up the evolutionary ladder from Jerry Garcia.

Being wide awake, I have also been thinking about the business. I have to tell you, based on what I've been able to glean of your billings and what I know of mine, that I'm more than a bit concerned. Can we meet in the morning to chat about it? Nine thirty work for you?

M

FROM: cwinterbottom@richiewinterbottom.co.uk
TO: mrichie@richiewinterbottom.co.uk

01 40 am

Malcolm

Human females have always been an alien institution to me, as you know better than most. Though yrs always seemed some way abov the median in most respects. Cd it b the menopause? Or a brain tumour? Is she on a diet?

I'll be here 2morrow as ever. Don't worry, I'm right on the edge of a big brkthru wh' I can tell you abt v soon.

Gd luck on the home front

C

The hall was packed. Iris was rather disappointed to discover that the Green Party's national victory summit appeared to be unfolding in a standard conference centre, but at least the plastic chairs had been replaced with sustainable coconut fibre futon-style benches. Not that you could see them, packed as they were with row upon row of the party faithful, gazing up adoringly at – at her!

Squinting from her podium over the low-voltage spotlights, she allowed herself a moment's contemplation of her dizzying progress, from humble party member in Kentish Town little more than a year ago, to local councillor, MEP and now – Prime Minister! That sounded a bit too much like gloating, perhaps. Better to follow a more modest, collective line – something about being carried along on the wave of national passion for the cause. She had to hold her hand aloft a full ten seconds before the cheering died down enough for her voice to be heard. Soft, yet powerful, breaking a little with the emotion of the moment, it hovered over the hall, as she declaimed:

'Are you ever going to get up, Mum?'

Iris opened her eyes not on an adoring crowd, but Ted. He'd thrown a school polo shirt over the England strip he wore in bed, his hair was wetted into an endearing approximation of Joe Cole's razor cut, and he was clutching in both hands a rather wobbly assemblage of brown cardboard and Petit Filou pots. 'Only you said you'd carry this to school for me. It's the geyser? For my project? And I don't know what to have for breakfast, it all looks weird.'

Molly was dreaming she'd achieved the Superman leg muscles and stomped, very hard, on the school cafeteria, until it was a total flatpack, with all her worst enemies underneath. Why did Superman bother jumping over tall buildings, when it was obviously so much more satisfying, if you had all that extra force, to jump right on them, and turn them into rubble? Of course, you'd need some sort of giant snowshoe thing, to distribute the impact.

Damn. Before she could stop herself, Molly'd woken up. Downstairs she could hear Iris yelling something. Why did she have to yell all the time?

Oh shit. That green thing last night had been far too delicious to be low-fat. Molly slid out from under the duvet, pulled the scales out from beneath the bed, and balanced one foot carefully on the far edge of each side. She breathed in, despising herself for being just like the idiots at school, and peered down over the hideous lumps on her chest, waiting for the dial to steady.

No. How could it be? Almost – she rocked back as far as it could, but it made it worse – three hundred grammes more than yesterday. There was no way in the world she was going to eat any more of that snake's so-called healthy food.

Still in her night time tee shirt she sat in front of her computer, keyed in her fast-track code for Altarica and resumed the invisibility avatar from two days ago. She definitely did not feel like being seen by anybody right now, even as SuperGirl. If only she could spend all her time here. If only she could just live out her life in code...

She landed in the no-friction zone, just behind the seesaw, which was seesawing all by itself, as usual, and looked around for Ubiquitur. He had to be there. He was always there. Then she saw him, watching the non-stop action at the snooker table. Molly opened her dialogue box and typed frantically:

'My distress is great, oh powerful one, my Mum, who is now definitely insane, has embarkethed on an evil plan to force-feed us all super-calorie meals so we won't be able to get out the door away from

*her evil sphere of influence. I just want to like, vapourise, you
know?'*

Almost immediately, she got a response:

*'The physical body is a curse and a delusion, youthful pilgrim
on the Wisdom Way. I take very little notice of mine and it seems to
look after itself, more or less. Why not just ignore it?'*

This was not the advice Molly was looking for. How could you
ignore something that changed shape every three seconds, sprouted
zits like daisies, and sent totally irrelevant messages to your brain at
the exact moment you needed it at full rev for double maths?

*'Wise words indeed, master, but I have triedeth that, to no
avail, believeth me. Would that the excellent laws of Altarica could be
implemented in the real world. Do you know what I mean?'*

The zero-friction snooker ball was a blur on the virtual baize
in front of her. Molly watched its manic zigzags for a few seconds,
until his reply came back:

*'Perhaps you're talking about uploading? With all your
cognitive functioning stored on a chip the size of a Smartie, you couldst
implant into a surrogate body, become an android, or slough off the
pre-quantum world completely.'*

*'For real? What you mean like, store my brain on a chip and
dump the body?'*

*'If not today, in the not too distant future, verily thou couldst.
And if thou wert forced, for any sordid purpose, to mingle with human
kind, thou could just borroweth a form...'*

'This is well radical! Where do I goeth?'

*'Hold hard, youngling. Uploading is a perilous matter, and
those who can assist you are tricksters and malfeasants. Thou shouldst
probably read up on a few A.I. websites first, and do not on any account
offer thyself as an experimental subject without getting thy parents
written permission in advance'*

'A trillion zillion thanks, Master of all Powers.'

*'I will observe thy progress and protect thee all I can. Go in
peace and virtuality!'*

Uploading! Could it really work? And how? Molly stumbled
back under the black duvet for a few more minutes, trying to
remember what she'd read about artificial intelligence, and comforted
by knowing there was a place where nobody cared if she was a size
twelve, and her parents had weird fights at midnight about washing

powder.

Malcolm strode along the corridor to the lobby of G Building, trying to feel positive and purposeful. What was that line about abandoning the life you'd planned, to make room for the life you've been given? The problem with those books you read in college was that, at that age, you had no way of knowing they were about as useful as a lava lamp.

He waited for the lift, hoping that by some miracle Colin did, after all, have a world-changing, million-selling idea. He gazed vacantly round the dull, beige space. On the table using up dead zone by the ficus, somebody had scattered a pile of flyers. Malcolm picked one up and scanned it.

'ATTENTION ALL BUDDING ENTREPRENUERS!

SOUTH KILBURN SCIENCE PARK CELEBRATES ITS FIRST ANNIVERSARY WITH A MAJOR NETWORKING EVENT!

ON MONDAY, JUNE 10TH, WE WILL BE THROWING OPEN THE DOORS TO REPRESENTATIVES FROM MANY MAJOR PLAYERS IN THE WORLD OF APPLIED SCIENCES.

YOU AND YOUR BUSINESS ARE INVITED TO BE PART OF THIS EVENT, AND INVITE YOUR OWN CLIENTS TO SEE WHAT WE AT THE SCIENCE PARK ARE ACHEIVING.

DON'T MISS OUT ON THIS GREAT MARKETING OPPORTUNITY!

SOFT DRINKS AND LIMITED BAR COURTESY OF SCIENCE PARK. BYO NIBBLES AND SNACKS.'

The lift button pinged and Malcolm stepped out, re-reading the leaflet. This could be just what they needed. And if nothing else, it was the perfect opportunity to find out what the competition was up to. Who knew, some of them might have more work than they could handle, and might be just gagging to outsource the surplus to someone they could trust not to ruin their reputations.

All his natural optimism was restored by the time he pushed open the door of Suite G420, to find Colin pulling on his Wednesday Y-fronts. Today he'd actually discarded the pyjama bottoms, which were serving as a thermal blanket for the test tubes, against an unseasonable drop in the outside temperature.

'Seen this?' Malcolm waved the flyer like Long John Silver's treasure map. Colin peered towards him, blinked, and dived to rummage under a box of Frosties by the desk. Without his glasses, he could barely see that Malcolm was in the room. He came up wearing them, yawned, blinked some more, and said: 'No.'

Apparently assuming that was the end of the exchange, Colin turned back to his computer screen, which had clearly kept him up all night yet again. No wonder he was useless in daylight. Malcolm sighed, hung his jacket on the peg next to Colin's dressing gown, and said: 'I emailed you last night, remember? About the cash flow thing?'

Colin hunched lower over his keyboard, typing furiously. Clearly the great mystery idea was still a few notches away from knocking the world off its axis. Malcolm went to his own desk, put the piece of paper down, and sat backwards on his chair to face Colin's back. 'Well, this could be a way out. The Park's having an Open Evening, getting lots of big research institutes and corporates to send their reps. We could sign up for it. You could put together a little one-stop waste solutions package, and I could bring out some of my more successful feasibility studies.'

Colin stopped for a moment, but only to scratch himself. He brought a stray Frostie out from the crotch of his trousers, popped it into his mouth, and carried on typing. Malcolm was used to this. Colin's human interactions operated on an at-need basis, and he clearly felt there was no need, just yet.

'And then when we'd got them in here, we could hit them with the blue sky stuff. I could dust off PCP, and you could tell them about your bugs.'

He waited for the Colin comprehension lag to elapse. One second – two – three...

Colin stopped typing, sat still for a moment, swivelled round to face Malcolm, and said: 'I could?'

'It's the perfect showcase. A captive, self-selected audience, and once they're in here, you'll have their full attention. We could invest in a case of booze to keep 'em happy. I might even get Iris to rustle up a few canapés, she seems to have turned into a bit of a foodie of late, and she's always been a sucker for a hard luck story. If I say her cheese straws are all that stand between us and ruin, that'll do it. It's on June 10th, do you reckon you'll be ready by then?'

Colin pushed out his chair, padded over to the rack, and tenderly unwrapped his pyjamas. He bent over the racks of tubes, pulling them out one by one and peering at them lovingly. Malcolm swung back to his own desk. 'Now...' He opened the drawer where he filed his business cards. He put both hands in and scooped, until they were piled all over the desk top. '...we need to get onto the targeted marketing. I'll do up a letter, and we can send it out to all our current and past clients. Even if they don't make it, it'll be a good way to remind them we exist. Come on, Col, this is serious. Where's that list of councils the EU was taking to court? Surely you can scare a few of them into turning up?'

Colin was still surveying his brood. Malcolm switched on the computer. Normally he spent the first twenty minutes of his working day deleting junk emails and listening to phone messages from stationery discounters, but today he was a man with a purpose. 'Come on Col, you can make yourself useful here. You read these cards out, and I'll type them into the database, then we can just leave the letters to generate themselves over lunch. You can take the register later. Here.'

He handed a fistful of cards to Colin, who focused on the first one with some reluctance, before reading out: ' "Black and Blue Flame Grilled Burgers. Your meal, your way". 147, Kilburn...'

Malcolm stopped typing. 'You can miss that one out. And if there are any tyre fitters, dry cleaners or minicabs, you can probably miss them out, too. Next?'

Iris could hear 'Sleeps with Angels' from halfway down Hartland Gardens. Over the gate, she saw Malcolm, crouched on his hands and knees at the back of her bike.

'I knew you wouldn't be able to keep your hands off that. But, as you've no doubt discovered, it's perfectly maintained already. What have you got to be so pleased with yourself about?'

Malcolm stood up and moved away from the bike, revealing an elegant little trailer cantilevered out from the back wheel, supporting a large covered basket.

'Oh!' Iris stopped and gazed at it, entranced. He did care, after all!

'Norfolk rush basket, natural rubber lid – can't speak for the rubber plantation, but it's recycled from my old Ducati rain cover, so it's had a fair bit of use.'

'You came home early to do that – for me? After the sausages and everything?'

'I couldn't stand the sight of you wobbling around with that ridiculous pile of bags. This way the weight's all at the back, your steering's lighter, and you've a prayer of getting round corners in one piece.'

Iris wrapped her hands around his neck, scattering bits of paper, and gave him a passionate kiss. 'Look, I've got all my Green Party stuff, I'm going to a meeting tonight. You're so wise and kind!'

'If you're that grateful, you can make us a cup of PG Tips.' She opened the door and he followed her in. The post had been neatly arranged on the hall table. Underneath the bills and catalogues was a letter stamped: 'Metropolitan Police.'

Iris stopped dead, and picked it up, the smile wiped from herface. Somehow she had totally forgotten the matter of attempted manslaughter. But she nerved herself, to rip open the letter and scanned it quickly. 'Oh. Oh, thank God. No charges. D'you think I could have some PG Tips too, to celebrate?'

'Why not? If you're dedicating your life to politics, you can afford to ease up on the small stuff, don't you reckon?'

Iris rummaged in the packet and brought out two bags. 'It's so weird about Soren; she's so nice, in theory, but somehow in person she's sort of...'

'I refuse to incriminate myself by commenting. By the way, are you doing anything on the evening of June the tenth?'

Iris was rummaging for a chocolate HobNob, an unintended by-product of the packaging expedition. 'I don't expect so. Why?'

'Well, it's just that there's an open evening at the Science Park, and Col and I were thinking of taking part in it, you know - meet the neighbours, drum up some business, all that.'

'Oh Christ. Colin. And the Science Park. Well that sounds very good. Go ahead by all means, I'll stay here with the children and – unravel old jumpers, or something.'

Malcolm handed her a mug. 'Actually, I was really hoping

you'd come along to help us out. And maybe, who knows, rustle up some snacks. I wouldn't normally get you involved, but the fact of the matter is'...

Iris' attention had wandered to the trailer, visible through the window, but something in his voice brought her back to him. He looked, most uncharacteristically, almost worried.'...I've not wanted to alarm you, but things are not doing quite as swimmingly as I'd hoped on the work front. We really need to get some more business in. In fact, I was going to ask if you could manage to bung a bit more into the account this month, just until...'

Iris looked back at him. Oh god. What would he say if he knew? She'd been meaning to tell him about her job, just as soon as the right moment arrived. But this was about as wrong as a moment could get. There must be some way out of it. Maybe she could get one of those enticing lump sum loans the bank was always sneaking in with the junk mail. Meanwhile...

'Oh. Yes, I mean about the evening and the snacks. I'll have to look at my account about the money; I'm sure it'll be fine, only...'

At that moment the door banged open. Molly came through first, took one look at her parents, not only eating biscuits but actually embracing in public, and walked on by. As she vanished upstairs, Ted followed, balancing his schoolbag on his bent-over back as he zoomed across the kitchen. 'Hey! Chocolate biscuits! I love you Mum and Dad!'

Iris put down her mug and went to pour his milk. 'Oh and Mum I need new football boots can I have the ones Wayne Rooney was wearing against Benfica on Saturday?'

'I expect so, who makes them?'

'They're Nikes, you can get them at...'

Of course. Of course they'd be Nikes. 'Well, Ted, it's your choice of course, but as I'm sure you know, Nike have a very dodgy history, imagine Ted a boy not much older than you, getting up at'...

'I know Mum we did it in our Focus on Child Labour in Year 2, it's okay I'll just ask Dad. Dad can I...'

'NO!' She hadn't meant it to come out quite so loud. 'It's fine Ted. Of course you can have Nikes. So long as you've made your choice with full knowledge of the consequences. We'll go and look um – er next week, this week's a bit busy, is that okay?'

Busyness had nothing to do with it. The store credit from Arlo's taxes was down to pennies, she'd already promised Molly an entire beauty parlour's worth of top dollar cosmetics, Malcolm's business was in trouble, and now she was in hock to Ted for God knows how much in shiny plastic and swooshes. There must be somebody on the LETS register who paid tax, or was thinking of paying it, or could be strong-armed into it somehow. And once again, the rapidly-disappearing biscuits appeared to be the only actually edible item in the house. Maybe Sammy'd have some unfashionable vegetables looking for a home.

There was a fractious queue outside the door of Buzzybees, and shiny 4x4s double parked for fifty yards in each direction. Iris pushed her way in to find Sammy trying to discipline a large and noisy crowd at the till. 'One line only please and I'm afraid I've got to limit you to half a litre each, but it's highly potent so you wouldn't want to overdo it.'

She handed a grimy plastic bottle full of vile-smelling brownish solution to a woman in top-to-toe Stella McCartney Ethical. 'That'll be eighty-four ninety please, don't forget to bring the bottle back. Oh hi, Iris. Arlo, take over here will you? Come on Iris, I've got post traumatic stress from this lot.' She led Iris to the relative calm of the bakery counter, which seemed to be one area of the shop empty of customers. Iris noticed Soren clanging in through the door, and sidled behind the fridge. 'You're getting busy.'

'Yeah, it's insane. In fact we're being stalked.'

'Stalked?'

'Yeah, by that American mega-chain, what do they call themselves, Planet Plenty? Trying to buy us out. They're dead keen. I might take 'em up on it, I've always wanted to do that round the world in a Campervan thing. On chip fat. They eat chips everywhere don't they?'

'I should think you could go round the world in an Aston Martin from the look of it today. I'd miss you, though.'

A lot. Sammy had become the only sustaining element in Iris' newly-challenging world. Sammy, and... don't be silly, Iris. He's half your age.

'What's the magic potion then?'

'It's supercharged wheat grass. Extra nutrients in its water. Not sure how happy the wheat grass is about it.'

'What extra nutrients?'

'Oh you know, stuff that's past its sell-by date, old supplements, some of that green tea we couldn't shift... they're going mad for it. D'you want to try some? It might give you superpowers.'

'I don't need superpowers, I just need some work. And possibly a family transplant.'

'Work? What about the LETS thing, didn't that sort it? Here, you look a bit miserable, have a flapjack.'

She handed Iris one of the solid brown rectangles from the array on display. Iris took a bite and spoke through it. 'Well, it's a bit like Soviet Russia isn't it? You have to take what you can get and hope to swap it on later. Only unlike Soviet Russia, half of it's not tradeable. For instance, I got a call the other day from some aromatherapist...'

'Oh yeah, Mariella, she said you were a bit crabby.'

'Well, I may have been, but I can't exactly pass on a hot stone massage to the T Mobile people, can I? Those shoe things are nice, are they new?'

Sammy's look of the day was ornate even by her standards, starting with a plumed hat and progressing through several layers of mismatched vintage underwear, before terminating in a pair of dog-tooth check tweed trainers. She waved a foot, showing it off from all angles. 'Well, not totally, ReBorn they call 'emselves, some cooperative in Hoxton with a pile of car tyres and their grandad's old suits. I had to balance the hat.'

'You've done that all right.' Iris took another mouthful. The flapjack was nasty, even by the standards of square brown healthy snacks. 'Would you mind terribly if I ditched the rest of this?'

'They're not nice are they? We've got a real problem with our baker. I think she's a bit life-denying, to be honest.'

They both surveyed the dingy, solid cakes, slices and biscuits lying neglected in the window. They looked like trench rations from the Somme, or Bronze Age building components. They did not look like the cheering rewards for a day of honest toil that cakes are supposed to be.

'Hey!' Sammy slapped her brow theatrically. 'You bake, don't you? Arlo's been ranting on about whatever he ate of yours.'

'Well, I made some scones...'

'If you did our baking, you'd get loads of credit to feed your spawn. When can you start? I'll have to let Elfrieda down gently, so she doesn't get rejection issues'.

Engrossed in Elfrieda, they'd both failed to notice Soren creeping up on them. She'd lost the crutches, and with them the giveaway thump of her approach. 'Ah, Iris. You're looking well, didn't I tell you you'd be glad you made the change?'

Iris swivelled round to find herself looking into Soren's kind, yet somehow sorrowful eyes. 'Ooh yes, you were so right, and thank you SO MUCH for – I got the letter – from the police, saying...' Her voice tailed out as she realised that she'd never filled in for Sammy the exact contours of her debt to Soren. '... Actually I was just about to ask Sammy for some of that amazing goat mozzarella, Sammy d'you have a moment to...'

Sammy took the hint and set off past Soren towards the cheese counter. A tiny, disappointed frown puckered Soren's face. 'Goat mozzarella? Cheese?'

'Yes, my whole family are more or less totally veggie now, you'd be so proud of us.'

'But goats still fart and belch, you know. I mean, there's not much point in giving up your car and your Easyjet flights if you're still eating animal products, is there? I know you know that, really.'

She turned to make for the door, sorrow and disappointment trailing behind her like a witch's cloak. Sammy was still tossing squashed tomatoes in the approximate direction of the compost. 'She's a miserable old cow, Soren.'

'That's a bit harsh, isn't it? She's just let me off a long stretch in Holloway.'

'Is that so? You daredevil you. Pity you couldn't swap places.'

Iris contemplated the reaction she was likely to get at home to the news that from now on they'd be having Rice Dream in their newly-restored tea. Sammy finished with the tomatoes and picked up the compost bucket. 'Let's face it, she's not exactly a walking advertisement for her cause is she? Any more than Elfrieda's cakes. Make us something really gross and decadent. That sheep's cream is fine if you drown it with sugar.'

Iris had spent such an enjoyable day disinterring her recipe books and weighing the relative merits of cashew mocha loaf against orange, almond and polenta squares, that even the sight of the South Kilburn Science Park could not entirely dash her spirits. Throughout the eighteen months that Malcolm and Colin had been based there, Iris had mysteriously resisted the temptation to visit Malcolm's place of work. Now she toppled onto the damp pavement outside the sad, beige rectangle behind its token hedge of hardy perennials, eyeing the thin trickle of entrepreneurs and their patient spouses shouldering through the double doors. She carefully manoeuvred herself and her boxes through them, cheered by her own reflection. With all that cycling, she was back in clothes that hadn't fitted her for years. It was just a shame it had to be wasted on Colin and his incredible performing molecules.

'Welcome, Friends of SKSP!' The banner at the entrance was bracketed by floor plans of the presentations on offer, some promising live demonstrations. Iris followed Malcolm past the flashy real-world action of Mariner Undersea Robotics and OpChem Lasers, to the smaller, more modest homes of Genex Gene Targeting and ReNu BioMetallurgy. On the ground floor, in the expensive suites near the lobby, people were crowding in, and through the glass-paned doors researchers were visible, shyly hovering by their workstations. The journey of discovery was marked by islands of supermarket sushi and canapés, and a diminishing trail of abandoned plastic wine glasses.

'Through here. Let me have those.' Malcolm took half of the boxes and led her to G Block, ignoring the lift as though he'd never used it in his life. As they climbed the three flights of stairs to Suite 402, the noise and chatter dropped away; not even the snacks and drinks had made it this far, and the few people wandering the corridors seemed to be looking for the way out.

Iris looked over the boxes at Malcolm, who showed no hint of any disappointment. 'It's nice and quiet here, isn't it? I bet you get a lot done.'

'Yup. Yes, we don't get disturbed much, it's true. I fear that's the main attraction for Colin, to be honest.'

'You're not going to leave me alone with him, are you?'

'God no; I have to be here, manning my info packs and fighting off the mob.' He pushed open the door of Suite 402. It seemed unoccupied, until Iris caught her foot on something that nearly sent her boxes flying. Colin had taken advantage of the early lull to unroll his air mattress and was curled up under his knitted blanket, dreaming sweetly. Malcolm put down his load and leaned over to shake him. 'Wake up, Col, it's show time.' He went back to the door and propped it open with a copy of Metals Digest, peering hopefully up and down the corridor. 'Still, it's early days. And I did big up your cheese straws on the invite.'

Iris smiled bravely at Colin, dishevelled and faintly whiffy, as he uncurled himself and took up his position between a small grey monitor and a large whiteboard. A folding table in front of him was spread with lining paper, on which were scattered half a dozen petrie dishes containing what seemed to be yesterday's lunch. Or perhaps the lunch was just a random incursion into the experiment; hard to tell with Colin. Behind him was the rack of test tubes, over which he now bent, whispering encouragingly as he checked the thermometer buried in their midst.

She looked around for somewhere to unpack the boxes, hoping the visitors would not notice that the cheese straws tasted mostly of hot mustard, and that this was to disguise the fact that the cheese was not technically cheese, but tofu. Malcolm went over and switched on his computer, bringing up a detailed 3-d model of a production line. He took half a dozen identical folders from his briefcase and fanned them over the desk. That seemed to be the extent of his sales pitch.

'How's the family, Col?'

'It's a bit cooler than they like it ideally. I've had to improvise a bit, but they should be warming up now. Hello Iris. That's a very striking thing you're wearing, what do you call that?'

'Er – a dress?'

Malcolm was actually rubbing his hands together, as though hoping to strike from them a spark of energy to carry him through the hours ahead. 'So, not a lot of traffic yet, then?'

'Traffic?'

'Tell you what, I could use a drink. How about you, Iris? Oh, damn. What an idiot! I've left it in the car. I'll just pop down and...'

Iris wheeled round, panicking. A moment ago he'd promised not to leave her with Colin, and here he was, vanishing. Before she could stop him, he called over his shoulder: 'Won't be a mo. Try to hold back the mob, you two!' - and he was gone.   'So I'll give you the chat, shall I?'

Iris smiled again, more weakly than before. All that could save her now was Molly remembering her promise, on pain of forfeiting the impending Clarins, to call no later than 20 45 with a major emergency requiring Iris' immediate departure. Meanwhile Colin was looking positively animated. 'So I've got you to myself at last, ha ha! Only joking. The bugs are raring to do their stuff now, my little idea seems to have worked a treat, look.'

There was no escape. Leaning in to follow his pointing finger, Iris saw a polywrapped Cornish pasty, fresh from the microwave, sweating gently between the rows of tubes. 'So – test tube pasties! What a brilliant idea. How long does it take?'

Colin turned on her a look of mild reproach. 'That's just the thermal regulator. The interesting stuff if in these tubes.' He reached over, pulled one out, and held it tenderly towards her. Inside was about half an inch of viscous grey jelly. 'Meet my babies.'

'Really? Actually, I can sort of see the family resemblance, now you mention it'

'No no, what you're seeing in there isn't them, it's just the holding medium. There are far too many of them in there to be visible to the naked eye. Or even to most microscopes.'

'How many is that, then?'

Where on earth could Malcolm be? How long does it take to lug a case of Bigfoot Red through a half-empty office building?

'About sixty billion. Maybe a few more, they tend to breed a bit even when they're just sitting there.'

Sixty billion! Iris peered at the tube again, almost interested by this unfathomable concept. 'That's a lot of mouths to feed.'

'And on that very subject, that was an excellent lead in you just gave me Iris, because what we're about to do is feed them, and I think I can promise that you will be truly awestruck by what you're about to see! Now, let's go over here.'

He carried the tube from the rack over to the petrie dishes on the table. 'Now, if you look in here, what do you see?'

Now that Iris looked closely, she seemed to be seeing the dismembered fragments of a... 'A prawn sandwich?'

'That's exactly right! And prawn sandwich happens to be one

of the things my bugs like best of all!'

He shook the tube delicately over first one petrie dish, and then another. 'Here you go, now. Supper time!'

Iris leaned in too, trying to process the idea of pioneering science entirely fuelled by fast food. For what seemed like hours, nothing happened.

'Aha! See that?'

Iris couldn't see much at all through the haze of panic clouding her brain, but the sandwich fragments in the petrie dishes appeared to be turning into brown mush.

'There they go! And watch what happens, it gets even better!'

She'd never seen Colin so excited. The sandwiches had now all but dissolved into a greenish liquid.

'There! What did I tell you!'

'I'm – I'm just lost for words, Colin.' All she could think of was escape. 'D'you know, I'm a little bit worried about Malcolm, d'you think we ought to...'

Malcolm had made his way as far as the first floor atrium, where he couldn't resist an unscheduled stopover to see how his ex-WorkSpace colleagues, Tangible Product, Inc, were doing. Immediately he regretted it, seeing the mob at the entrance. He was just about to seek out the consolation locked in the boot of the car, when a hand fell on his shoulder. 'I don't believe it!'

Malcolm turned to a vaguely familiar face, round as a lollipop, smiling above a crumpled linen suit. He peered furtively at the name tag on the man's lapel, then suddenly remembered, just as the man said: 'Mikey Gordon! You remember...'

'Mikey! We were going to collaborate on that collapsible chair...'

Now it all came back. Mikey had had a daft, but briefly fashionable, idea for a range of floor-based office furniture that would have allowed everybody to work either kneeling or cross-legged, not only benefiting their posture and circulation but, more crucially, allowing landlords to fit twice as much square footage into their buildings. For a week or two Malcolm had been recruited onto the development team, until everybody else woke up, the funding collapsed, and Mikey took himself off, not a bit daunted, to pastures new.

'And you know, Malcolm, those petty-minded Luddites were the best thing that could have happened to me. And you know why? Because without them I'd never have made it to FreeFlow!'

Not that Malcolm hadn't liked Mikey, if only for his relentless optimism, but by now he was in severe want of that drink. 'Tell you what, I'd love to chat but'...

'In fact, Malcolm, I've just had a corker of an idea...'

Rude or not, Malcolm was heading for the door. What had he to gain from Mikey?

'... Person Centred Palletising!'

Malcolm stopped dead. Mikey had remembered. PCP had been Malcolm's big idea, his life's work. It had been going to revolutionise the working lives of countless thousands - millions - of people. And the idiots at Workspace had killed it, with barely a thought.

'You were always too smart for Workspace, Malcolm. But I happen to know that PCP is EXACTLY what they're looking for at my new gaff.'

Malcolm turned back, hardly able to believe that somebody not only remembered, but seemed to believe in, the idea that had cost him his job and led him to this doomed venture with Colin. Even if that person was Mikey. Who was now waving a business card in Malcolm's face. 'They're looking for somebody to design a whole slew of distribution centres. They want something radical and forward thinking, and they've got barrels of dosh. Give me a call and I'll get the spec to you.'

Iris had rarely been so glad to see a crate of wine. 'Malcolm! Fantastic! Colin's just finished showing me...'

'Oh no, it's not finished – don't you want to know how they do it?'

'Well, let's have a drink at least, call it the interval, shall we?'

For some reason Malcolm looked a lot more cheerful than when Iris had seen him last, in marked contrast to her own mood, which was approaching desperation. Molly had entirely failed to make good on her promise and, even with the door open, the combined odours of Colin, his bugs and their dinner was turning her empty stomach. She grabbed the glass Malcolm held out to her, and drained it in one swig.

Colin fumbled on the table and produced a piece of paper. 'I do have this handout that I can give you to take away, but the gist is, we take ordinary micro-organisms, like the ones you might find in your garden or your pond, and we genetically modify them to...'

'Genetically modify? These are GM bugs you're waving in my face?' Iris' grudging tolerance of Colin vanished like summer dew. 'Do you know what genetic modification has done to the cod in the North Atlantic? What about all those baby seals with two heads? And...'

Two visitors who'd been hovering by the door looked alarmed and fled. Iris' voice rose a notch as she struggled to retrieve everything she'd ever read about mutant life forms. '...it's just another evil conspiracy between the chemical companies and the World Bank, to...'

She was shouting, loudly. Colin backed away in shock, and thefew remaining onlookers fled. Malcolm took her elbow and dragged her towards the door, just as her phone rang. He grabbed it with his free hand. 'Oh look, it's young Molly. Better get home or there'll be hell to pay. Thanks again, Col.'

'Are you there?' Iris wasn't sure about the protocol of unsolicited calls on the Almighty, but she needed a bit of guidance. A large glass of BigFoot on an empty stomach, compounded by the stress of half an hour with Colin, had sent her much further off the deep end than she'd intended. Malcolm had had to smuggle her out via the service elevator, missing two hours of crucial marketing opportunity. He had made it clear that a couple of boxes of mysteriously spicy cheese straws was no compensation for her behaviour, and was now sleeping downstairs on the sofa.

She waited for a few moments, and then felt a reluctant, but distinct, tickle. 'I'm always here. That's the downside of the job. Weekends, Bank Holidays, Monday morning sickies – I don't get any of them.'

'What a terrible thought! You've never ever had a holiday?'

'No indeed. Anyway, where would I go? That's the trouble with being everywhere – there is nowhere else.'

'I suppose that's true. But what I meant is, can I talk to you? Just for a bit of advice?'

'You're feeling guilty, aren't you? I can sniff guilt at twenty miles. Mmm – delicious!'

'A bit. It's very difficult isn't it, this belief thing?'

'I really couldn't say. Being omniscient, I've never had much need of it.'

'I mean, if you really believe something, don't you have a duty to try to win other people over? Take the Inquisition. You'll remember no doubt, that strong smell of burning flesh wafting up from Spain and England a few hundred years ago. Those were your guys weren't they? They thought they were doing a kindness, saving the unbelievers from an eternity in the flames.'

'Of course I remember. The rate they were turning up here, the whole place smelled like a barbecue. I tried reminding the cardinals that free will can, on occasion, mean freedom to get it wrong. But did they listen?'

'Well, free will is all very well, if you're only getting it wrong for yourself. But this is different, isn't it? Elaine's freedom to jet round the world – to take a totally random example - is cancelling some Bangladeshi's freedom to survive at all. The people who are doing the most damage are going to suffer last. We all know it, only most people are just, you know, ignoring it. Because it doesn't suit them. Like the sugar barons and the slave trade.'

'What's your problem, then? You've got the high horse, jump on it and gallop off to battle.'

'The problem is – as you may have noticed – it's not making me very popular.'

'Popular? You think Martin Luther King worried about his ratings? You think Nelson Mandela had second thoughts when he discovered the Afrikaners didn't like him very much? I don't recall Edith Cavell popping home from the trenches to hobnob with the beau monde. You sign up for greatness, there's a price to pay.'

'And God knows what they're going to say when I hit them with the vegan thing.'

'I do know, of course, but I'll leave it as a delightful surprise.

Anyhow, that's not your real problem.'

'It's not?'

'Your problem, to put it in terms that even you might understand, is the way you go about it. Remember Cassandra? "Woe, woe and thrice woe?" She may have been right, but did anybody take a blind bit of notice?'

'Like last night...'

'Like last night. You're not going to get anywhere by haranguing people. Especially people who know a lot more about things than you do. Personally, I'm rather in favour of genetic modification of embryos with horrible congenital deformities and wasting illnesses. I'll admit it, there was a lot of detail in the Grand Design. I may have got some of it wrong. And I'm not too proud to accept help.'

'Well. That isn't what I expected you to say, at all.'

'That's me, full of surprises. Krakatoa 1883. That was a good one.'

'Anyway, I won't be making that mistake any more. I'm going to join the Greens and read all those leaflets cover to cover.'

'Good for you. Do your research, and think before you speak. And stop worrying about popularity. There's a reason saints rarely marry.'

Iris sat on the steps of the Community Centre, finishing an experimental apricot slice. She was quite looking forward to discovering new friends here – kindred spirits in the struggle to do right in the face of apathy and callous self-interest. As she swallowed the last crumbs, the trickle of early arrivals swelled to a stream, and comrades were folding in wholesome hugs all around her. It was time. She waved to Danny as he climbed into the Clothes Bank for the night, stuffed the leftovers into her string bag, and trotted up with them.

'So – everybody – let's get this started shall we? I've just got a couple of announcements and then we can crack on with it.'

The small meeting room was mostly filled with battered trestle tables, arranged on three sides like a low-budget Last Supper. Most of the Greens were sitting round them, while a woman and a man at the back made tea, and another man, in a chunky jumper and jeans, a mane of wild hair sliding away from his bald scalp, stood in Jesus' spot, waving a leaflet. Iris slid in next to a woman carrying a bulging backpack, who greeted her with a cheery Dunkirk smile and squeezed her hand silently.

'First, we need to thank the good folks at Buzzybees for generously donating a carton of green tea to keep us wide awake while we work. Hugh and Janet at the back there are just brewing up, so help yourselves, and of course, don't forget to wash up your cups before you leave. '

Everybody at the tables turned to Hugh and Janet, who gave an enthusiastic thumbs up as steam erupted from the urn.

'Next, I think we ought to pat ourselves on the back for a really remarkable result in the elections – our best yet. Finally, the message we've been promoting for, frankly, far too long, has got to the people who need to hear it – the British public. Thanks to Fern's tireless efforts and a great last-minute rally round by all of you, we managed to field candidates in all eight wards this time, which really made an impact on the ballot papers. For the first time ever, everybody who wanted to vote Green in the borough got a chance to do so!'

The woman next to Iris leaned over and whispered: 'I was a candidate this time. I'm Deborah by the way.'

'Really, how exciting! I'm Iris.'

'Of course, they had to promise me there was no chance I'd get elected.'

'Really? How disappointing.'

'No, it was a blessing; I'd never have had time to be a councillor anyhow. It was just for the ballot paper. Like John says. It's democracy, you see. It matters. Giving people the choice. I came dangerously close though – just as well the LibDems had that actress'.

John had heard them. He glanced reproachfully at Deborah, who blushed and sat back as he continued. 'And as a result, we now have two green councillors! That's a one hundred per cent increase on last time!'

Applause pattered round the room as he continued: 'It's particularly gratifying, because all three of the so-called major parties are now stealing many of our best lines, but I think the results prove that we remain the only party which actually tells the voters the truth, rather than what they want to hear.'

Puzzled looks fluttered between his listeners. John was positively beaming now. 'Somebody once said that nobody ever got elected by promising the public less jam tomorrow. Well, we're going to prove that person wrong! And here's how we're going to do it!'

He opened the piece of folded paper. Across the top was the bold slogan: 'GREEN CONSUMERS = OXYMORONS!'

Identical leaflets were piled in vast heaps on every table. John slammed his down and proclaimed: 'We need to stop pussyfooting round the truth and hit people with a really punchy slogan. Rather than sit on our laurels, we decided to get right back in there with Fern's brand new leaflet, to spread the good news, and energise our supporters at the grass roots. Two council seats down – three hundred and twenty to go! So - let's get stuffing!'

Iris tried hard not to feel let down that her introduction to political campaigning consisted in stuffing the sort of brown envelope that makes every heart sink, with a leaflet that appeared to be the product of an unexpected encounter between a lesser primate and a John Bull Printing Set. Somehow it didn't seem like the image of a party ahead of its time. Everybody around her, however, seemed happy enough, folding, stuffing and licking as the conversation bounced between them.

'...My friend who lives in Barnet can put supermarket trays in too – not the foam ones of course, but the plastic ones, even those black and brown ones, they don't need to be clear plastic.'

'Oh that reminds me, Marie...' Deborah briefly stopped licking and sticking to reach down between her legs and heave the backpack onto the table, '...I brought these for you to take to her, if you wouldn't mind.'

She tugged an old carrier bag from the backpack. Rancid tubs and trays rolled over the table to the other side, where Marie scooped them up. Iris looked along the table, trying to estimate how late into the night they'd all still be licking, sticking and folding, and decided, despite her novice status, to make a suggestion.

'Excuse me?'

Deborah looked up from her conversation, which had now moved on to debating whether the citizens of Newbury really did recycle bottle caps into green wellies. 'You all right there? More tea?'

'No, only I was wondering – if we divided up the jobs here, so one person folded and the next stuffed and the next stuck and the fourth stamped – wouldn't it all go a lot faster?'

The women looked at each other, nobody quite daring to pass judgement. Eventually, Deborah leaned over the table and began rearranging its contents, bellowing cheerfully up the room as she did so: 'John, I think we've got a treasure here!'

Things moved along much more efficiently after that, and by nine o'clock the table was cleared. All around them, people were stacking chairs and gathering up their bags. At the door, John and Fern, who turned out to be small, young and rather glamorous by local standards, were shaking hands, bathing the departing faithful in an enthusiastic glow.

'Thanks so much – you did a great job there – see you next week, yeah?'

Iris paused, torn between two ignoble emotions. Would it be worse to endure another evening like this, or to return home to Malcolm and admit she'd given up on her political career after three hours? She turned to Fern and asked: 'I was wondering – I'm new here as you know, but I'm quite good at sort of, meeting strangers and chatting to people – is there something else, maybe something a bit more you know – like outreach – that I could do?'

'How did it go?' Malcolm was standing between the kitchen sink and the door, screwing something to the wall. The house was quiet and immaculate, as it always was when he'd had it to himself for more than twenty minutes.

'It was pretty good, actually. I think I made a bit of an impact, in fact. Made a few suggestions about procedure, and so forth.'

'There you go. I knew you'd sort them out.'

'In fact, I've been put in charge of their next direct action.'

'That sounds dangerous. Do they know about your criminal record?'

'I don't have a criminal record, as you well know, and anyhow it's nothing illegal, it's just collecting signatures against the Third Runway next Saturday. I didn't think you'd mind, Ted could come with me if you need to go anywhere.'

'I think, to be honest, that young Ted doesn't need any more propaganda in his life right now.'

'Really? Well, you may be right... What's that, anyway?'

Malcolm moved away from the wall to reveal what looked like a cat flap mounted four feet off the ground. Iris peered at it. 'Don't tell me. Those Adopt-A-Wallaby people finally got to you.'

He put down the screwdriver carefully in its proper place, between the larger and smaller screwdrivers, and picked up the compost from the sink, which Iris now noticed was no longer sitting in Ted's chipped baby cereal bowl, but an immaculate stainless steel job, probably from Muji. As the bowl approached the flap, it swung magically open, allowing Malcolm to tip the contents straight through into a galvanised aluminium chute running outside. Iris went to the window to witness a stream of teabags and banana skins drop straight into the compost bin below, as the chute closed itself neatly off.

Malcolm took the bowl and washed it out fastidiously, before returning it to its place by the sink. 'Call me fussy, but something about the presence of rotting food in close proximity to my dinner wasmaking me uneasy. Of course, there is one problem still.'

'What's that?'

Iris came over to hug him. Clearly, though he wasn't saying anything, his actions made clear that he was coming round to her point of view. He sniffed her hair before hugging her back. Lemon juice and soap turned out to be a rather effective shampoo, with a slight disinfectant tang he found reassuring. 'We don't actually have a garden, and you're still ten years down the allotments waiting list . What were you planning to do with all this compost?'

'That's all right, we'll just give it away to people who do have gardens.'

'Who are all making their own compost mountains already. Pretty soon the whole country is going to be buried in the stuff.'

'Well then, we'll dig up the front yard.'

'And have nowhere to charge the car. How about asking your new friends for some ideas at the next meeting?'

As Iris passed Molly's door on her way to bed, it opened a

crack and a wild black head peered out. Molly's hair was always particularly deranged after an evening struggling with mock exam papers, but they seemed to have been manageable tonight, judging by the almost genial tone in which she called Iris' name.

'Mum, when are we...'

'Hello darling, did you have a lovely evening?'

'Do NOT mess with my hair, how many times? When are we going to get that Clarins Mum?'

The Clarins. Of course it was too much to hope that Iris could go to bed, even once, happy, beloved, and without worries swarming like bees in her head. She could stall no longer. The very next credit card application that plopped through the door would get her signature. With luck, she'd be dead before the first statement came in. 'How about after school tomorrow? I'll meet you with Ted, shall I?'

'Mum!'

'Hello sweetheart. Have you seen your sister? Oh, there she is, lurking.'

Molly was half-hidden on the doorstep of PoundStretcher over the road, hunched over so her hair and her hood met over her face. Resisting the temptation to wave and shout, Iris bent demurely to kiss Ted's cheek, which today was streaked with something brown and sticky.

'Don't tell me – pasta bolognaise!'

'No it was Pasta Surprise Mum.'

'Then I guess the surprise was that it was bolognaise, again.'

They set off down the road, Molly sidling in behind as they passed her.

'Hello Mol, I've brought a brand new credit-card, look!' Iris flashed the shiny plastic in Molly's direction and took Ted's schoolbag, as he asked: 'Mum can we go to Greggs? It wasn't a very nice surprise, and I'm hungry.'

Molly pulled a headphone from her ear and spoke for the first time. 'You'll never get the Queen of Green in there Ted, don't waste your breath.'

Some dormant spirit of defiance stirred in Iris, who had indeed been on the point of proposing an alternative detour to the fruit stall, where if you didn't ask, you technically didn't know your apple was from an apple factory in Argentina.

'Of course we can; here we go.' She took Ted's hand and marched him in through the door.

There is no concentration to match that of a child choosing cake. Finally: 'I'll have one of those apple caramel doughnuts please. Or - can I have two?'

'Three for the price of two love, looks like your lucky day.' The woman behind the till took a plastic bubble pack, each of its three doughnuts individually nestled in an inner bubble, and slid it into a plastic bag. Without thinking, Iris said: 'Oh, I've got my bag here, look, I don't need one. And actually....' She took the plastic pack, removed the bubbles, removed the doughnuts from the bubbles, and handed the pack and the bubbles back to the woman.'...We don't need all this packaging either. I know it says the bag is biodegradable but really, you know, they're just as bad because they make methane when they degrade. And doughnuts never came in bullet-proof vests when I was young. Thanks a lot. Here you go Ted, here are your two. Molly, do you want...'

But Molly had disappeared. Iris paid, took Ted's hand, and went to find her. There she stood, her back to the shop, shaking with fury. Iris opened her mouth to speak. Molly made a face and pointed sarcastically at her headphones, a force field of bangs and zizzes bursting from them to keep her mother at bay.

It may have been the credit card application, stamped and ready to post – Iris had spent too much of her life sorting out other people's debt to risk this lightly – or it may have been her protracted soak in the acid bath of Molly's negativity, but this gesture, only routinely insulting, had a dramatic effect. The turning of a worm is probably not something often witnessed by outsiders, but it was happening now, in full view of the whole High Street.

'Did you have a problem, Mol?' Iris asked, all sweet reason. She felt something a bit like vertigo. But she could get used to it. In time. 'I said...' and she reached over, very quickly, and pulled the headphones from Molly's ears. 'I asked, Molly, if there was a problem, at all?'

Molly snatched back, but too late. Ted took his doughnuts a judicious few yards away and bent his whole attention on them. Molly opened her mouth, closed it again, opened it again, and hissed: 'A problem? You want to know if there's a problem? No, of course there's not a fucking problem, why should I have a problem having a mother who's turned into Mrs Mao, and who can't even do the simplest teensy little trip to the shop that for any ordinary person would just be a trip to the shop, without turning it into a four-hour fucking struggle meeting about the politics and ideology and semiotics of doughnuts. Of course there's not a problem, why do you even bother asking?'

In all her fourteen years as a mother, it had never even occurred to Iris that there was anything even faintly unfair about the deal she'd struck at the moment of conception. A month ago, she'd have bitten her lip, waited for Molly to calm down, and then tried to corner her for a sympathetic chat later. A month ago, this conversation wouldn't even have happened.

But now: 'I ask, because it doesn't seem to have occurred to you, or any of your ungrateful little friends, that it's people your age, young people, who are supposed to be idealistic, who're supposed to want to change the world and save it from the bloody mess it's in! And if you're not going to do that, if you're just going to retreat into your iPods and computers and virtual whatevers like - like molluscs, somebody else is going to have to go out and change things instead. Because they – they fucking well can't carry on the way they're going.'

Ted quivered, nearly choking on his apple puree. Mum had said – Mum had never, ever used that word. Was there a teacher somewhere to whom he should report her?

Iris hadn't even noticed. 'And if you can't put up with being embarrassed by parents who are trying to rediscover their ideals, I suggest you go home and have a think about the alternatives. So there.'

That last 'so there' had a definite ring of the Junior Playground about it, but on the whole Iris was exhilarated by her own eloquence. Anyhow, it had impressed Molly. She stood there, mouth open, headphones dangling round her neck, music leaking down her hoodie. Iris went over to Ted, who was just finishing up, took his hand, and turned back to Molly, who turned away.

'So. I suppose, in light of what you just said, that you'd die rather than take my money for your Clarins. Shall we go home?'

'Mum, I forgot you have to read this!'

As she marched him, rather fast, down the High Street, Ted

dragged the schoolbag from her hand and pulled out a sheet of orange paper covered with enthusiastic black type. 'It's our class play, it's in two weeks and you have to read my lines with me Mum, it's your favourite, it's all about saving the planet.'

Iris turned to see if Molly was still following them. Molly immediately stopped dead and stared into a shop window. Iris turned back to Ted, and looked down the cast of characters.

'How brilliant, who are you being, are you the baby polar bear?'

'No Jack's the bear, he only has to stomp about and roar a lot. Miss Kilpatrick said it would play to his Issues. Mum, why does Jack always get the good parts?'

'I've no idea. Though it could be to do with his tendency to stomp about and roar when he doesn't get them, d'you think? Anyhow I'm sure your part is fine, what are you being?'

'I'm just the phytoplankton. Miss Kilpatrick said I was the only one in the class who had a prayer of pronouncing it right. I don't mind.'

Iris discovered that she'd been holding the third doughnut throughout her diatribe, and was holding it still. She tore it in half and offered half to Ted, who swallowed it in one bite, mumbling: 'Anyway, it's a very important part and I get lots of good lines.'

'Well let's get you home, and I can test you on them before supper.'

Molly went straight up to her room, feeling very cold and weird, like her body had been chopped away from her head, or something. It reminded her of that stuff about uploading. If there really was a way of just losing the whole body thing, just doing some sort of neural transfer, that would be...

She googled 'uploading' and waited.

If anybody'd bet her a month ago that there'd be a time she was nostalgic for the good old days, when Iris just nagged about shit like homework and tidying up: normal parent nagging, nagging by the rules, that you could predict... Now it wasn't even safe to be seen in public with her. Even when she'd washed. And there'd been something in her face and voice just now. Like she'd really meant it. Like she'd really been looking at Molly, and meaning all that stuff. Really seriously pissed off. Iris was never like that.

Of course, it could have been a shitty little trick to get out of buying the Clarins. But that would have been mega shitty, and Iris wasn't normally like that, either. But what was normal these days?

Molly scanned down the long list of entries on the screen. For a totally theoretical procedure, involving the simulation of several trillion brain molecules and therefore, inevitably, the building of a computer several trillion times the size of any in existence today, there seemed to be a lot of big money behind it. If IBM and Intel were throwing wads of cash at this, they must believe it's possible. But then, you could probably model the brain of the average IBM employee with a tennis ball and a razor blade.

Molly tried to focus on the strings of words on the screen: neural nets and neocortex, infomorphs and quantum computers. But she was tired, and she was hungry.

If I was a chip, she thought, I'd never get hungry. I'd never get tired. I wouldn't worry. Everything would be clear: one or zero, yes or no, me or not-me. I wouldn't have to change, or try to stop changing. I wouldn't have to go to school, or come home. I wouldn't have to be seen with Mum, or have Ted kicking footballs at me. I wouldn't have to worry about being blown up by a bomb, or stalked by a psycho, or even the creeps in the dinner queue.

I wouldn't have to go anywhere, or do anything.

In fact, I wouldn't be able to go anywhere, or do anything. Even if I wanted.

What could I do, without this body? I could listen to my music and watch videos. Or, like, upload them. I guess you wouldn't do it with ears or eyes. I could do all the stuff I like doing now, pretty much.

That was what Mum said though, wasn't it? That everything I do is virtual.

So? Like there's anything else worth doing. Like there's any point. Like anything's going to get any better, whatever I did.

I didn't make this shitty mess, did I? Why should I care about sorting it out?

I'm really hungry.

There's no way in the fucking world I'm going down there to ask her for food.

Downstairs in the kitchen, Iris was standing at the sink, washing spinach for supper and trying not to get water on Ted's script, balanced on the worktop. The play was one of Miss Kilpatrick's finest works, a testimony not only to a guilty passion for Gilbert and Sullivan, but also that ability, innate in all primary school teachers, to offer every member of every class, however unappealing or unsuitable, the chance to be included.

THE GREAT CHAIN OF LIFE

SCENE 1: The Arctic Shelf. In front of a big mass of ice, many ICEBERGS float on a blue blue sea.

THE SUN: (sings)	I'm shining down on the blue blue sea
	Everything in Nature depends on me!
	But if my heat should get too strong
	Everything in Nature will go all wrong!
ICEBERGS (CHOR)	We can see already that it's going wrong!
	Stay with us and you will hear a sorry song!

Enter BABY POLAR BEAR. He looks thin and unhappy.

BABY BEAR:	Roar! Roar! I'm so hungry! My Mum spent the whole winter looking after me, and we're both STARVING MARVIN (Roar!!!) Now she's left me all alone to go hunting for seals, and she's been gone ages and I'm hungry and lonely. I do hope she finds something for us to eat!

Exit BABY POLAR BEAR, still roaring.

Iris stopped picking spinach and wiped her hands before turning the page. 'You didn't have any lines in that bit, Ted. Shall I skip through until you come in? Oh look, there's a whale in this scene, I bet I can guess who's playing him, it'll be that boy who turns up every morning with a bottle of Lucozade and a bag of square crisps, isn't it?'

Ted was eating bread and jam at the kitchen table, a copy of 'FourFourTwo' hidden on his knee. 'That's very fattist of you Mum, JoAnne's being the whale. Miss Kilpatrick said her chair could be a WhaleChair, cause she can glide about in it. Go on Mum, it's nearly my bit now.'

SCENE 2 – THE OCEAN OFF THE COAST OF PERU

The sun shines down on a beautiful blue ocean. Flying fish and cormorants (no final numbers yet) are playing 'It', chasing after each other and squealing happily.

THE SUN: (sings)   Now here is the ocean just near Peru
It looks so beautiful, all clear and blue
But beneath the surface it's a different tale
Listen to the story of the Minkie Whale!

CORMORANTS/FLYING FISH: (CHORUS)
If the yearly algae bloom should ever fail
Then it will be curtains for the Minkie Whale!

Enter the MINKIE WHALE. She is pale and thin (for a whale). She is looking around her, very upset, as if she has lost something.

MINKIE WHALE: Where are they? I'm so hungry! One day they were everywhere, and the next they'd just disappeared! Has anybody seen my algae? I'm an algae farmer, and I need to eat fifteen thousand gallons of algae every day, or I'll die!

Ted looked up smugly from his magazine. 'All those bits Mum where she says 'algae' she was supposed to say 'phytoplankton' but she couldn't say it, so Miss Kilpatrick had to change them all to 'algae'. Nobody except me can say it. Phytoplankton! Phytoplankton! Phytoplankton!'

'You're a star, Ted. I think we've nearly got to your bit, are you ready?

As the MINKIE WHALE glides about the stage, the POLAR BEAR, the SEAL, the TUNA, the SARDINE and the ZOO PLANKTON all come on to join her.

All together, they shout out:

CHORUS OF ANIMALS: WHERE ARE THEY?

'That is well tragic Mum, silly voices at your age. I think I'd almost rather the ranting.' Molly stood in the doorway, wearing black jeans and a black tee shirt with 'The Statement on the Other Side is True' printed across the front. Iris dropped the script in the sink full of spinach water, but somehow mustered a smile for her daughter. 'Feeling better?'

Molly slouched across to the fridge and opened it. 'I haven't eaten anything orange today Mum. I need something orange to help with convergent thinking on my endocrinology essay.'

Ted, who had finally abandoned his magazine and climbed upon the chair to launch himself into his big moment, glared at her. Iris pointed at the fruit bowl, overflowing with oranges, as Ted jumped up, sending the bread and jam flying, and shouted out:

PHYTOPLANKTON: I'm the phytoplankton, you don't
know me
I spend my life at the bottom of the
sea
But I rise each year as an algal bloom
And if I ever didn't, all life would
suffer DOOM!

'Well I nevuh. Pam Ayres, writer-in-residence at Gordon Road Primary' muttered Molly through her orange. But she was eating it here at the kitchen table, not upstairs.

'Rise above it Ted, she's just being Molly. That was really good, what's next – oh it's just the last bit and then the final chorus, let's just finish it off shall we?'

ZOOPLANKTON: Oh good, now I can eat, I'm so hungry
(chases PHYTOPLANKTON off stage)
SARDINE: Oh, there goes my dinner, there'll be

lots more now

(chases ZOOPLANKTON off stage)

TUNA: Oooh, yum, lots and lots of sardines for my dinner!

(chases SARDINE off stage)

SEAL: That big fat tuna will be just perfect for my babies' lunch!

(chases TUNA off stage)

POLAR BEAR: FOOD! FOOD! ROAR!

(chases SEAL off stage)

(APPLAUSE)

'Go on Molly you're not doing anything useful, give us a bit of applause.'

Molly raised thin white hands in a single sardonic clap. Iris looked at her sharply. 'Adolescence is such fun, isn't it?' She put a supportive hand round Ted's shoulder. 'Come on Ted, let's hit them with the final chorus'

FINAL CHORUS (TO AUDIENCE)

Dear Humans, we know you don't mean any harm

But thanks to your actions, our planet is too warm

The penguin and the polar bear may both be sweet

But this guy here suffers most from the heat

Even though he's tiny, and almost invisible

The Great Chain of life is just not divisible...

'Can Jack really manage 'divisible' do you think Ted?'...'

So please, spare a thought for the great and the small

Before Global Warming destroys us, one and all

(MORE APPLAUSE)

'Hi, Malcolm, can you give Ted some applause please, Molly seems to have run out again.'

Malcolm was watching from the doorway. Obligingly, he put his hands together. 'No problem. Bravo! Speaking of being hungry, did you have any intention of producing supper at some future stage, or are we now on such intimate terms with all life forms that it would be rude to ingest them?'

'Oh my, is that the time? Sorry, how about some nice sustainable sardines on toast and spinach, that'll be quick.'

Ted looked worried. 'I don't think I can eat a fellow cast member Mum. Specially one higher up the food chain.'

'Nonsense, it's perfect Method, metabolising your part. Here, you can set the table. Molly, are you going to grace us with your presence for Omega-3, iron and vitamin B12, all wrapped in a luscious feuillete of domestic comfort and banal chat?'

Molly glowered, but stayed where she was. Ted stopped, knives and forks splayed from his hands. 'So Mum, if we're all family, does that mean the worms are family too? In the compost? If it's our compost? Shall we give them names?'

Molly's chair banged over as she made a dash for the door, one hand dramatically over her mouth. On the back of her tee shirt was written, 'The Statement on the Other Side is False'.

Malcolm righted the chair and sat down himself. Ted came to perch on his knee for a hug. 'That was pretty fine, old lad, but you left out the end.'

Iris brought the plates to the table. 'What end would that be? D'you want lemon on your classmate, Ted?'

'Well, when the Gulf Stream disappears, as anybody who watched that masterpiece of scientific research 'The Day After Tomorrow' knows it inevitably will, the oceans will cool down again and the phytoplankton will be fine. It'll just be us, living in Northern Canada without central heating, who'll be having a hard time. If I were you Ted, I'd not bother saving that polar bear, I'd go skin him, and make yourself a coat.'

The next morning as Iris dropped Ted off at school, Miss Kilpatrick caught her eye. Iris stopped dead. When a teacher indicates, even fleetingly, that she wants your attention, it's an absolute rule that you stay rooted to the spot for however long it takes her to finish distributing the literacy test results, before setting the children off on yet another fascinating treasure-hunt down the byways of the national curriculum.

Finally, she came over. 'Iris, just the person I wanted to see. You know Ted has a little part in the play? Well, it's little but it's crucial, I wouldn't want you to think...'

'No, yes, we're learning it already. I can see he's pivotal.'

'So he'll be needing a costume, of course. Are you okay with that?'

'A costume? As a phytoplankton? That sounds quite challenging. D'you know, I've very little idea what a phytoplankton looks like. But yes of course, I'm sure I can manage something. I've got a bit more time these days and actually I have been doing a bit of sewing, it's rather nice in some ways...'

'Ted did tell us.' Miss Kilpatrick's face was all human sympathy, and her voice dropped to a tactful whisper. '...About you losing your job, and everything, after your accident. If there's anything we can do...Post traumatic stress, is it? Oh hi Elaine!'

'No, actually, I...' Iris turned to see Jack's mother, hovering fragrantly about two inches from her shoulder '...I've moved into consultancy, which is, as you know, MUCH more highly paid, so I can afford to work much less and still earn plenty of money. How's it going Elaine? Jack coping with the challenges of his part all right, is he?'

That night, Iris sat hunched over the computer in the corner of the bedroom, while Malcolm lounged on the bed with the latest issue of Autocar.

On the screen in front of her gleamed the hidden population of the vast oceans; a magical array of gossamer creatures, geometric shapes with wispy tendrils, gorgeous spherical spider webs, spiky wheels and elegant threads encrusted with tiny, glowing beads. Every one different, like billions of aquatic snowflakes. Nature's unthanked work.

And nothing at all with arms or legs, still less a tangle of dirty blond hair. This was clearly going to be quite a challenge.

She typed in another search, for 'phytoplankton' and 'body'. A minute later the screen filled with dancing, neon-coloured lettering. At the top of the page, a banner pulsed to a disco beat: 'INCREASE YOUR SEXUAL POTENCY BY EIGHT THOUSAND PER CENT!'

And below: 'It's at the bottom of the sea's food chain – but it should be right at the top of your shopping list! Marine Phytoplankton has so much goodness the whole of life on earth depends on it! According to NASA, marine algae produce up to 90% of the Earth's oxygen supply – and the creatures who feed on it are living testimonials to its potency! Now, thanks to a process patented by GreenDreamTM, these benefits can be YOURS EXCLUSIVELY. GreenDreamTM Marine Algae contains at least SIXTY naturally occurring Sea Minerals, including pure GOLD, TITANIUM and ZIRCONIUM, plus nutrients, enzymes and twenty-two vital amino acids. Each and every one of these is in every drop of GreenDreamTM, now available exclusively to YOU in convenient hygienic living encapsulation. Change your life today!'

Queasy with exclamation overload, Iris called over her shoulder: 'Hey! I think I've solved the problem of the collapsing food chain.'

Malcolm grunted just enough to indicate that he'd heard her, so she needn't bother telling him any more, and relapsed into his magazine. She carried on anyway: 'And I've found something that enables people who eat it to live to 150 years old with full sexual potency!'

Malcolm put down the magazine. 'Which people are those then?'

'Listen to this: "May live for a hundred and fifty years, grows up to fifteen metres long, and is sexually active until it dies!" '

'What was that bit about fifteen metres long?'

'Well... it's a whale. But still...'

Malcolm picked up the magazine again. 'If you want to be married to a whale, just say the word. Those griddled goat cheese avocado-burgers at the Dog and Darner are pretty damn fine. I could probably manage two a day, if I forced myself.'

Iris shut down her computer and went over to the bed. Malcolm's hostility had abated somewhat, since she'd been focussing her evangelism on the Greens, but their comfortable intimacy had not returned, and she was missing it. 'It has to be a sexually active whale, remember. Full potency.'

Malcolm put the magazine carefully on the bedside table, reached out an arm and pulled her towards him. 'And just how potent is that, do we know?'

'I don't think there's any marine mammal porn on the site, unfortunately. There is a video, but it just seems to be people talking about their sinus problems. Mmm... This inter-species sex is very under-rated isn't it? Who knew?'

Malcolm was busy with a particularly tricky ribbon-and-button combination on her blouse. She pulled away, and raised herself on one elbow. 'But thinking about it, if you can breed the stuff and just chug it directly or use it to make oxygen, why does it matter about the polar bears and the seals?'

'What, you mean, sacrifice the whole biosphere apart from the top and bottom? Is this official Green Party policy now?'

'I'm just being practical. I thought you liked it when I was practical – ooh, that's nice... I mean, we could still keep enough of the ornamental life forms to decorate the places people expect to find them: lions and zebras in the Serengeti, bears and seals at the Poles, a few jaguars and camels for the inhabited bits of the Amazon and the Sahara. Like the sheep in the Lake District, just there for the tourists. D'you think we should sign up as agents for Green Dream? It could be the answer to the cash flow situation. We could probably do it through LETS and trouser all the proceeds.'

'There speaks the accountant. You'd better get that panto costume out of the way before you launch any more business empires. And anyhow, I had a lead about some work the other day that sounds pretty hopeful. Now, for God's sake, shut up.'

On Saturday morning, Iris arrived five minutes early at the William Cobbett statue at the bottom of the High Street. Almost nobody was around yet; Danny was still inside the clothes bank, and the girl in the Oxfam shop was scooping piles of dirty shoes and broken toys off the pavement, before swapping a sign saying 'ASIAN EARTHQUAKE DISASTER – DONATE HERE' for one saying 'PHILIPPINES FLOOD DISASTER – DONATE HERE'.

At nine on the button, Fern from the Greens appeared, looking tinier than ever under the weight of a huge brown cardboard box. Iris peered out at her from beside the statue, as Fern called out,

'There's another in the trailer, could you get it d'you think?'

Iris stepped reluctantly away from the statue, into full view. Somehow, all these years she'd been doing their books, it had escaped her notice that the Cobbett statue was right outside the premises of Fly Away Home. Luckily, there was no any sign of anybody in there yet, so she sprinted in the direction from which Fern had come. The box, half the size of the one Fern had carried with no apparent effort, nearly broke her back lifting it, and she staggered back wondering whether Fern was mainlining phytoplankton, and if not, whether pure righteousness could increase muscle strength by 100 per cent. Fern looked over apologetically. 'Oh, that's the heavy one with the leaflets, sorry. Just put it anywhere.'

'So what's in the other one?'

Fern was pulling apart the top of the big box and rifling inside it. She turned to Iris, with what looked like a five foot long inflatable dildo in one hand. 'Costumes – aren't they fab?'

The one good thing about standing around in the by now

heaving High Street on a busy Saturday, dressed as a Boeing 777 and assailing passers by with unsolicited propaganda, was that it made it somewhat less likely that Aidan would recognise her when he came to open up the shop. Fern obviously thought that getting a pitch for their protest directly outside the area's only remaining shop-front travel agent was a terrific coup, and said so several times. When Aidan duly appeared at about nine-forty, Fern flapped her wings and hopped cheerily over to introduce herself, just to let him know there were no hard feelings, and it wasn't personal, just a fundamental difference of principle affecting almost every area of human existence.

'Fair enough' said Aidan. 'They'll probably think you're an ad anyhow. I ought to be paying you.' He turned to his keys.

'And this is my colleague'... Fern tried to introduce Iris, but Iris was suddenly very busy explaining to a confused pensioner that the Greens were trying to bring back the Good Old Days, and that if he'd just sign on the dotted line, very soon there'd not only be no more nasty planes, but there'd be horse trams and proper jam for tea again, too.

She managed, in fact, to spend most of the morning out of sight of Fly Away Home, but, after several hours meeting only apathy and ridicule in equal proportions, she suddenly encountered a hugely enthusiastic group of Norwegian EFL students, who had been looking in vain for kindred souls, and demanded immediately not just to sign the petition but to join the party, and take a blood vow, if appropriate. Inevitably, Fern had disappeared for a toilet-break, which given the complexity of her outfit might well last half an hour. Iris crept round the other side of the statue to look for the membership information, which was somewhere under the leaflets, badges and corn fibre clip-on nosecones which the passing punters had been mysteriously reluctant to accept.

With only a two-by-three-inch slit in her mask to peer through, it was impossible to find anything. The Norwegians were beginning to look restless; there were six of them. How could she live with losing six new Green Party members, purely through fear of being recognised? Iris nerved herself and removed her cockpit. As she bent to look for the membership forms, a voice trilled in her ear: 'Iris! It had to be you! I was just thinking, "Who could be bohemian enough to dress themselves up like that, in full view of people they know they're going to have to face every day, for a lost cause like abolishing airtravel?" '

How did Elaine manage to be everywhere Iris went? Surely the whole point of people having Porsche Cayennes is that they spend every spare minute ostentatiously driving around, not stomping the gum-stuck pavements in search of acquaintances to humiliate?

'Elaine! How lovely to see you, you know I'm a teeny bit busy right now with these people...'

'I won't keep you. I was just popping in to see Aidan about our flights to Vietnam, we thought we'd take Jack somewhere a bit different for half term. Hi Aidan – you know Iris, don't you, didn't she use to...?'

But Iris was back behind the statue, jamming on her cockpit so she could swear silently and at length until Elaine finally left. Needless to say, the Norwegians had left too, and everybody else she approached seemed inexplicably indifferent to the manifest perils of binge flying. Fern came jogging back to find Iris crumpled at the statue's foot, looking like an emergency landing in mountainous terrain.

'Knackering isn't it, all this standing around? Don't worry, you'll get used to it. I've collected almost eight pounds already. John'll be thrilled. How many signatures have we got now? Ooh, nearly fifty. Well done. What's that brilliant line again? "One signature is a crank, two is a movement, three is the overwhelming force of public opinion?" I think we deserve another biscuit, don't you?'

'What are you doing, Ted?'

On Monday afternoon, Ted was standing at the washbasin in the bathroom, the £25 bottle of GreenDreamTM beside the tap, along with the kitchen salt canister. Iris came up behind to discover he had emptied the GreenDreamTM into a basin full of water, along with most of the salt.

'I'm giving them a bit of exercise. I thought they were looking peaky.'

'I think green is their natural complexion, sweetheart. And how were you going to get them back into their bottle afterwards?'

'Do they have to go back? I mean, if they're family, they didn't

ought to be caged up, did they? By the way Mum, I don't want you at the play, is that okay?'

The last sentence had come out as casually as the rest. He looked up at her, all blue-eyed candour. Iris felt a creeping chill in her heart. 'You don't? Why not?'

The candour misted for a moment, and he turned back to the basin. 'Just – I just don't. And would it be all right if you didn't pick me up from school any more either?'

'Why not, Ted? What happened?'

He turned to the towel rail, carefully avoiding catching Iris' eye en route, and wiped his hands with unnatural attentiveness. 'Maybe Dad can come, when Molly's got stuff to do? I'm going to leave these here, I think they need the sun for a bit anyway. See you later Mum bye!'

'It's that cow! It's that she devil! She told her horrible little boy and her horrible little boy told all the other little boys, and now Ted's being teased about having a loony Mum, and he's ashamed of me. My own son's ashamed of me, and he's only nine!'

Iris had pushed the pain away until everybody was safely in

bed. She'd discovered that she didn't need to address the Deity out loud, so she could chat away without waking Malcolm.

'I think you're making a bit of a fuss about this. You've got me away from a mass AIDS burial in a grotty township in Mali, you know.'

'I'm sorry. But you probably don't understand. After all, it never happened to you. You only had the one child, and he was a model son, spent his whole life telling everybody how wonderful you were and that they ought to give up everything to worship you. You'd have felt a bit different if he'd gone round telling his disciples, "That minging freak with the big white beard, I feel sick just looking at him, he's a total pain in the tits!" '

'I've had my share of rejection, as you'll be aware if you think for a moment.'

'I mean, Molly I'm used to, I can sort of deal with it. But Ted – sweet, adorable, huggy Ted. It's too cruel, I can't bear it. Look, I won't keep you from your AIDS orphans, I just wanted to say, this is all too much for me. Take the cup from my lips, etc. To use a line you'll recognise.'

'I'm afraid I can't do that. It's ordained.'

'Well then, unordain it. I'm resigning. Surely I can't be the only person who's fallen by the wayside?'

'Well. There have been one or two. For instance...'

'There you go, just sign me off and resume the search. How about Tibet? All those little lamas in waiting, you could easily hijack one of them, I bet nobody'd even notice.'

'...for instance, there was Judas Iscariot.'

'That's a bit harsh!'

'He may have been in a better position to grab the headlines, but he wasn't unlike you, from what I remember; loved it when he was making new friends and feeling smug, didn't like it so much when things heated up. And then of course, there's the "I do my bit, but family comes first" brigade...'

Iris looked over at Malcolm, sleeping like an old dog in a basket. Was he one of them? Surely he was a model husband, parent and citizen.

'...model spouses, parents and citizens, who never raise their eyes above their own front gates.'

Ordinary, decent people, thought Iris. People who manage to

build a wall of comfort, distractions and busyness just about high enough, most of the time, to stop them from wondering what it's all for.

'But by all means. Go ahead, give up, and you'll never hear from me again. It'll all be just the way it used to be.'

'Really?'

In her excitement, she'd said this aloud. Malcolm grunted, shifted, and patted her soothingly in his sleep.

'Of course. You can go on slogging up to the school gates for a couple more years, until Ted reaches the age when he wants a bit of freedom too, and you've got two of them doing everything they can to let you know they can't wait to leave for ever.'

'By the way, I've always wondered – did Jesus have a troubled adolescence?'

'I'll let you peruse the written record for an answer to that. But broadly speaking, it's a universal phenomenon. Call it nature's way of easing the pain of their departure. So, as I was saying, you can grab yourself a couple more years, until you're right back here again, wondering why your life is so empty, and why you didn't seize the moment and run with it, when you had the chance. You can stop rocking the cosy little boat at 26 Hartland Gardens. Or you can have your best shot at changing things for the better.'

'Well, to be frank, that's the problem, isn't it? If it felt even slightly like a grand and glorious adventure, it might be worth it. But stuffing envelopes and composting carrot peelings doesn't seem to have quite the kick I was looking for.'

'On that subject, I'll give you a little tip. You're not going to do it with those poxy little leaflets you've been politely mailing out. Not while catastrophe is snowballing at its current rate.'

'So...'

'So asking people if they might possibly lend a hand, like you're running a garden fete, is not the answer. On the subject of that written record, I think you'll find a few ingenious ways to draw people's attention to their shortcomings.'

'There was a phone call for you earlier. While you were

sleeping it off, whatever it was. And while I was giving the children their breakfast, and making their lunches, and listening to Ted's spirited rendering of "Blue is the Colour" on his recorder. Are you sure that's what he's meant to be practising?'

Malcolm was at the door, all ready to leave, when Iris made it downstairs next morning. Spending half the night wrestling with demons turned out not to combine especially well with getting up at 07 00 in order to be dressed by 07 13, have breakfast on the table at 07 31, make packed lunch by 08 10, supervise teeth cleaning and shoelace tying by 08 24 and wave cheerily from the gate at, or around, 08 32. But Malcolm had coped, apparently without mishap, and she'd had an extra hour of much-needed sleep. Why shouldn't he do it, for that matter? Why shouldn't she be the one with more important things to think about, for a change? Especially as both of her children now seemed happiest when she was as far away as possible.

'Oh. Sorry. I didn't sleep very well. Ted didn't say anything, did he? About me, I mean? Before he left?'

'Only that you always give him four chocolate biscuits in his lunch. Don't worry, he just got an apple, as usual. Anyway, she said her name was Mariella and she had some work for you. I wrote the number down.'

'She did? Oh, damn. Mariella.'

'I'd have thought it was good news. I couldn't help noticing you don't seem to have been wildly busy since you came out of hospital. Not that I'm wanting to put any pressure on you or anything, but given that you managed very efficiently to stop any potential clients coming near us on the Open Evening...'

'Look, I said I was sorry about that, okay? I mean – I really am sorry, and I am doing my best too...'

Malcolm hadn't mentioned her outburst since that night, which made Iris feel even worse now. This was clearly not the moment to reveal that Mariella's likely contribution to the family wealth came in the form of exotic massages and toe manipulation. 'I guess I'd better call her back then. In a minute. After you've gone, I mean.'

Malcolm gave her a suspicious look.

'Well, I mean, I've made you late haven't I? So you'd better go. Bye!' She waited for the gate to be carefully latched behind him, before dialling the number.

'Mariella? This is Iris Richie, look, sorry I was short, but the thing is I don't really need any massages or...'

'Oh dear, I'm in a bit of a pickle and I did hope... But I do other things, I've got a lovely natural cosmetics range I'm just launching, all herbal essences and wild flower oils, it's...'

'Cosmetics?'

In an instant, the solution not just to her fractured relations with Molly but a large element of her financial problems had presented itself. 'They sound totally perfect! As it happens I could squeeze you in, possibly even this morning, I've had a last minute cancellation. Could you give me your address?'

The day passed very satisfactorily after that. Mariella, whose actuarial problems conveniently turned out to be severe and complex, had been easily persuaded to offer a voucher for a skin-clearing facial as well as the entire range of her cosmetics, in exchange for help. So Iris had spent the morning making sure her cash income was just below the tax radar, and drafting a letter to the Inland Revenue much like the one that had worked for Arlo.

In it, she proved unequivocally that LETS was in fact fiscally identical to the mutual exchange of gifts at Christmas or birthdays between adults not necessarily related by blood, and the fact that a particular sub-section of the population had decided to extend this time-honoured practice throughout the year, should not in any way affect its exemption from tax liability.

Pleased with her efforts, Iris had left for home with the happy consciousness of having cornered a niche market in the early stages of a growth spurt. Clearly, the LETS demographic was not the natural playground of the chartered accountant; equally clearly, somebody who wasn't afraid of compound interest was exactly what most of them needed. And once the mass of the population, still suffering under the old regime of wages and taxes, discovered that she was the gatekeeper to a giant and previously undiscovered loophole in which they could call their labours 'gifts' and nobody would pay any tax any more, they'd be queuing all the way to Mr Slobodka's corner shop.

Iris had also come away with a large bag of surprisingly attractive creams and lotions, which she happened to have dangling from her hand as she knocked on Molly's door that evening. She was rewarded with a neutral mumble, which she took as an encouraging sign.

She was feeling rather lonely, since being marginalised by Ted.

And meanwhile downstairs Malcolm was guffawing wildly to Jeremy Clarkson's hilarious digs at women and tree-huggers, which had always made her uneasily aware of a gulf between them. Before her accident, most of it had been left unspoken, on the sound principle of 'don't ask, don't tell'; now, all too often, she felt as though an unbridgeable chasm separated them, and there'd been moments recently when she had no idea why they'd ever married, at all. It seemed that once again God was right, and she might as well give up on the happy home, since it seemed poised to self-destruct at any moment. Opening the door, she poked her head round it. 'Hi, sweetie.'

Very slowly, with a gesture borrowed from a thousand American political TV dramas, Molly swung away from her desk. One black foot tapped on the floor. The Secretary of State was not amused by this interruption to her mission-critical activities.

Iris' bravado vapourised in the frosty air, and she found herself feebly asking: 'Um - I think I've really upset Ted. He says nobody's talking to him at school, and it's all my fault.'

'It'll do him good. Nobody's talked to me since Dad and I made that egg-mobile in Year 7 that ran over all the others. They're all cretins anyway.'

She was about to turn away again, dismissing the intruder, when she saw the bag. Dignity and avarice struggled in her face. Helpfully, Iris waved it a bit closer. 'Oh, gosh, I'd forgotten I was carrying this. I was taking it to the bathroom, I thought I'd give myself a treat.'

'What sort of treat?'

'Well, it wouldn't be of any interest to you, they're not big brand name cosmetics or anything. More of a signature boutique line. Hand-mixed to individual prescription, from rare flower essences and essential oils. Somebody gave them to me today, I think she said these ones were made for – who's that actress, I'm so hopeless with names – Saffron – Rabbit, is it? Lettuce? Something like that'

Iris reached innocently into the bag as Molly whispered hoarsely: 'Saffron Burrows? These were made for Saffron Burrows?'

'Yes, have you heard of her?'

But Molly had already pounced on the bag like a hawk on a kitten. 'They wouldn't be any good for you then, they'll only work on, like, young complexions yeah?'

'Oh. Well, in that case I suppose you'd better have them. Do you think they might do instead of the Clarins, perhaps?'

She looked over at Molly. Molly looked back at her, cornered. Finally she conceded: 'I guess.'

Iris stood up to leave, barely able to contain her triumph at the total success of her master plan, but to her amazement, Molly muttered: 'Hey. Wait.'

Iris turned. Molly bit her lip, took a deep breath and said: 'I'm sorry I called you Mrs Mao, okay?'

'Oh, Mol!' Forgetting herself for a moment, Iris tried to hug her daughter. Molly jammed her chair towards the desk.

'Leave it out Mum, I've got my homework, right?'

'Oh, sorry, I thought it was just random surfing'

'Mum. Duh. It's not about content any more. What you used to call 'knowledge', yeah?'

'In the olden days, yes I know.'

'You can store the info wherever, you don't need to memorise it. All that matters is knowing where to access it, and how to move it around, okay? Navigating the datasphere? Are you with me?' Molly was typing the same sentence over and over on different web screens. 'Googlebombing, yeah?'

'Oh yes, of course. So, remind me...'

Iris sat on the edge of the bed, from where she could see the screen. Molly was rarely happier than when proving that her intellect and knowledge were way ahead of an adult's. If that adult were a parent or a teacher, so much the better. 'So, it's about getting your rating up in Google, yeah? But also a way to really really embarrass people who are creeps or morons. Without them knowing who did it. Look here, if I type in...' She typed 'lying piece of shit' in the search window. A moment later, a list of links appeared, the first of which was the home page of a Cabinet minister. In fact, Iris was amazed to discover, the first twenty were all either ministers, US Senators or columnists on the Daily Mail. According to the engine, there were 557,432 references to 'lying piece of shit' on the Internet. Truly, office culture had spawned some many-headed children.

'So Mr O'Leary set us who could get a page to come first when he types in "whiny adolescent dweebs". I mapped it onto Belle and Sebastian's home page. I had to set up eighty double-blind Facebook groups to do it, but it so was worth it.'

'So – you can use particular words as triggers, to take people somewhere else?'

'Give the woman a Nobel prize. Ted's right, you are majorly embarrassing Mum, you know.'

'Don't worry, I got my come-uppance. Whoever harnesses the power of embarrassment could probably rule the world.'

'So what I'm gonna do next is figure out how to make it work on mobiles. Only there's a software hack I'd have to do...'

Somewhere in the lower cortex of Iris' brain, almost beyond the range of her consciousness, an idea began to form, a potent stew of 'embarrassment' 'mobiles' and 'without them knowing who did it'. With God's last injunction in mind, she'd spent the last couple of hours scouring the Bible for punishments and curses, but plagues of locusts and frogs, though environmentally appropriate, didn't seem like propaganda tools she could very easily deploy on behalf of the Greens. She perched on the edge of the bed where she could see the screen over Molly's shoulder. 'Mobiles – you mean embarrass people, via their phone numbers...? D'you have a minute, Mol?'

By the time Iris had woven the last pale-green pipe cleaner into the fringes of Ted's costume, she had a newfound respect for the Theory of Evolution, and a total contempt for that of Intelligent Design. Even the lowest form of intelligence, let alone a Supreme Being, given a choice between individually hand-crafting every individual creature on the planet, and setting off an automatic self-replicating system to do it for them, would go for the latter option. And given the amount of time and effort it had cost her to create a single phytoplankton (two visits to separate charity shops for three gauze petticoats, two pillows, a baby's lacey blanket, and – a stroke of luck – half a roll of fine-gauge green garden netting, not to mention The Works for pipe cleaners and bobbles) it seemed clear that manufacturing every one of several thousand varieties just of these tiny life forms would have taken a lot more than a week.

Suddenly realising that she was uniquely placed to settle the question, via her personal hot line to divinity, she went to switch off Radio 2. But an item on the news stayed her hand.

'And finally – here's a wacky one. Seems like somebody in the

Green Party has been playing silly berks with'...

Iris quickly switched to Radio 4. '....an outbreak of a new and potentially alarming variety of mobile phone spamming. Technical experts have suggested that similar 'software hacks' could have the potential totally to disrupt mobile phone traffic, with extremely serious security implications. This particular outbreak appears to be limited to owners of four-by-four cars, indoor swimming pools, and private planes, and frequent travellers on budget airlines. Here's our technology correspondent, Greg Pankritias, to explain.'

'Thanks John well yes, this is a totally new phenomenon. What happens, as far as the caller is concerned, is that placing a call on his or her mobile automatically triggers a simultaneous text message. It's not unlike the technology that texts a phone number to your phone when you call Directory Enquiries. Only in this case, it's the person receiving the call who gets the message.'

Iris turned the radio up. Molly might be rude, uncooperative, sarcastic and useless around the house, but all parents of fourteen-year-olds had that to put up with. Iris, at least, had the compensation of knowing that long after those unpleasant transitional symptoms had vanished, her daughter would still be a genius. And Elaine would have had at least one day – or one hour – of knowing the exquisite torture of the embarrassment she'd been dishing out to other people all these years.

'And what does the message say?'

'Well, there are two elements to it. The first is annoying and embarrassing to the caller, but relatively innocuous in its effects...'

It was a simple idea, but like many simple ideas, touched with genius. Anybody who called Easyjet Frequent Flyers, Range Rover, Swarovski, and a few others would trigger a shocking little Green factoid on the recipient's screen, together with a touching picture of an endangered animal downloaded from the WWF web site.

'The Green Party has denied all knowledge...'

Iris, smugly confident that she and her daughter had between them finally put the Green Party - willing or not - at the top table of the political banquet, had begun to re-position the stuffing in the phytoplankton's mid section.

'...And when you hear about the second part of the message, you'll understand why.'

Iris froze. There was a second part? What second part?

'The next part is rather more serious. By an extraordinarily devious and complex piece of computer hacking, which for obvious reasons I can't detail here, the next thing that happens is that a considerable sum of money – in three figures, I understand – is deducted from the caller's bank account, and transferred to the Green Party.'

The costume dropped, forgotten, to the floor. Molly wasn't a genius, she was criminally insane. And she was Iris' daughter. And Iris had put her up to it.

'I think we can all see that this is very serious indeed. And what do the Greens say about that?'

'Well of course the Green Party's statement of innocence seems pretty plausible, given, as they say, that such action is pretty much guaranteed to be, to put it politely, counterproductive. The Special Branch are investigating...'

At that point, the phone rang. Iris switched off the radio, unable to bear any more, and eyed the phone as Socrates might have eyed his phial of hemlock. She let it ring three or four times, then crept quietly towards it, as though to take it by surprise. She nerved herself, grabbed it, and picked it up. 'Hello?'

Presumably the call was being taped. She'd better say as little as possible.

Calm down, Iris. How could they possibly know who's done it? Molly's world class at covering her tracks. Look at that time she spent a week wearing my best boots, and all the while convincing me they were being re-soled at some artisan workshop in the Netherlands.

Perhaps I ought to hang up, and call her? She may not know, it may not be too late. I could smuggle her out of the country. Or at least to Grandma's.

But no, that could make more trouble – what if they're already bugging her phone? Or ours. Anything is possible in the home of free speech and democracy. What if, by making the call to her phone, I unwittingly slip the last piece into the jigsaw of incrimination? How bad would I feel then?

At this point, there was an urgent banging on the door.

God, that was quick, I only picked up the phone two seconds ago. 'I'm terribly sorry, could you possibly call back in five minutes? Thanks!' She slammed down the phone and ran to the door, wondering if being gunned down by armed police on her own front porch would count as martyrdom. But it was only Ted, looking slightly peeved. 'Mum, I had to brung myself all the way home, I waited and waited but Molly never came. Hey what's this Mum is it my costume? Wow, this is sick!'

Iris deduced from his manner that 'sick' had followed 'ill' and 'wicked' into the lexicon of approbation. Automatically, she got up to help him put it on, while she computed what Molly's non-appearance might mean. Nothing good, that was certain.

He was half-way into it when the phone rang again.

'Hello, Iris Richie – oh yes...Yes – yes of course I'll come – yes right away.' She put down the phone, and hurried towards the door. What might they be doing to Molly up there? And it was all her fault...

'Mum!...' The phytoplankton waved plaintive feelers at her. She tugged the costume off, and he emerged with a beaming smile and wrapped her in his fondest hug. 'Mum, if you promise not to be embarrassing you can come to the play.'

Five minutes ago, that would have been the best news in the world. 'Oh – Ted – that's so sweet. But, I have to go out for a bit now, you'll be okay won't you? Have whatever you like for tea. But don't, on any account, answer the door.'

When Iris arrived at the school, the convoy of squad cars outside seemed about normal for the end of the day at an inner-city comprehensive. But children were bunched at the gates, no doubt hoping the press might turn up to immortalise them, as a shocked classmate or unwitting collaborator. Iris wondered, too late, if she ought to have brought a blanket to put over Molly's head on the way out? But, on reflection, it seemed safe to assume the cops would have one, if required.

There was another crowd around the office of Miss Okimeija, the head teacher, mostly consisting of the admin staff, whose chairs had evidently been requisitioned, leaving them hanging around unable to do anything except pretend not to be eavesdropping, in any way, at all.

Inside, Miss Okimeija sat in state, flanked by Mr O'Leary, Head of Science, and Ms Allardyce, Head of Year 10, who'd never much liked Molly and was having difficulty restraining her triumph. Two unfamiliar men leaned casually against the A-level artwork on the walls, ignoring the chairs. One was inputting notes into a Blackberry, and the other was idly flicking through Molly's school reports.

Molly sat facing Miss Okimeija, an entirely unfamiliar expression of utter contrition on her face. Today her tee shirt said:

-h2/2m a2psi/ax 2 + v(x,b)psi = 1hapsi/at

'I'm glad you're finally here, Mrs Richie,' said the head. 'We were wondering why we hadn't seen you lately. This is Detective Sergeant Bathurst and Detective Inspector Malachy, from the Special Branch.'

Iris decided this might not be the moment to reveal that both children had banned her from the school premises, and kept silent. The older Special Branch man tossed Molly's Year 8 PE report onto the desk and said: 'You do understand the gravity of the situation, Mrs Richie. I assume you're going to tell me you had no idea about any of...'

'On the contrary, in fact I...'

A furious coughing fit erupted from Molly. Bent double, face hidden, she was violently shaking curtains of inky hair in Iris' direction.

'...Which is exactly what I expected. As you know, an adult caught in this sort of activity would face an automatic gaol term of several years. But as your daughter is still a minor'...

'I know she is, and that's why it couldn't possibly'... She was about to explain that the chances of an average disaffected fourteen-year-old choosing to express their grievance against the world by promoting the Green Party were approximately nil, and it was all her fault, and adult or no she was determined not to hide behind her child – when her phone rang. She went to switch it off, then noticed it was the home number calling. Ted! What new catastrophe could this be?

'I'm so sorry, this is my son, would you mind?...' She held it to her ear. A small voice on the other end said, 'Hi Mum! How are you? I'm fine. This is fun. You can leave me alone again any time.'

'Ted, sweetie – was there anything in particular'...

'Oh yes I forgot. Mum, where's the other peanut butter, you know the one with no lumps in it, I don't like the...'

'The peanut butter?' Suddenly Molly swooped on the phone and held it to her own ear. 'Ted? Mum's a bit busy just now, but I think you'll find the peanut butter just on the top shelf – no, behind there – if you just climb up on a chair, be careful getting up..?'

Two police officers, three teachers and her mother listened, as a loving older sister helped her little brother to make himself a nourishing snack. As she leaned over to return the phone, Molly whispered 'Fucking leave this to me, Mum, okay?' Then she turned to smile sweetly at the Detective Sergeant. 'I'm so, so sorry about this, you know, like Mr O'Leary said, I just enjoy my homework so much I like get totally sucked into it, and he did say we could take the you know, the exercise as far as we liked. Didn't you Mr O?'

She smiled again, this time right at Mr O'Leary, and casually tossed back her hair. Iris reeled at this totally unforeseen display of sexual guile. Mr O'Leary was not unruffled either. Little pink specks appeared among the stubble on his bald head, as he looked down and tucked in his shirt.

'Anyway', Molly continued, and now a note of passionate idealism crept into her sweet, breathy voice: 'I just do feel so totally about you know, the planet and you know, and it makes me so mad when people just don't care, so I thought this is like a mega giant crisis, there are all these billions of people in the world whose countries are going to be flooded and stuff, and they can't help themselves can they, I mean they can't come here and protest because I mean we won't let them in will we, so I was like, hey, they need our help and...'

Miss Okimeija was beginning to look uncomfortable, and the younger Special Branch operative had stowed his Blackberry, presumably because Year 8 PE had yielded no incriminating data. The older one looked at his watch. 'That's all very impressive, young lady, but the law's the law. You can't just go around defaming decent citizens and hacking into confidential computer systems. But...'

Iris put an arm around Molly. Molly managed not to flinch. Mother and daughter silently begged for clemency from the stern but righteous arbiter of justice. '...As this is a first offence, and on the understanding that from now on you will stay well away from the computers at the school, or anywhere else, except when closely supervised by a responsible adult...'

Mr O'Leary tried not to look too obviously delighted.

'...On that written undertaking – which I have drafted here for you all to sign – I am prepared to consider letting you off with a caution.'

'I'm so, SO sorry Mr O'Leary', Molly said, lightly touching his sleeve as they walked down the corridor towards the outside door.

'Well, now, it was a bit foolish of me...'

'No I mean, not securing my double blind cyphers properly. I could easily've done it so they'd never've found me. Dumb or what?'

'I think, to be honest Molly, we'd better scale back on the software engineering just now, don't you? You've a way to go in your physics if you're to have a shot at that internship. All very well wearing the equation', he smiled shyly, 'but how far can you take it?'

The back of her tee shirt said, 'cherchez le chat'. He peeled off down a corridor with a cheery wave, and Iris and Molly pushed out through the swing doors to a deserted street. The Special Branch had vanished, taking the drama with them.

'God Mum I thought you'd never shut up, you know?'

'I was only trying to help. After all, it was my fault. What does that mean anyway, on your shirt?'

'It's Schrodinger's energy equation. Duh. It's what makes lasers and atomic fission and transistors work. What did you do all those years you were in school, you did go to school didn't you?'

'I'll rise above that one, if you don't mind. What you did was a bit silly, but I have to say you did an amazing job on them.'

'Clever though, wasn't I?'

'Very, very clever. I'm sorry I led you into it, anyhow.'

'Sorry? You're insane. The sad old cows were pissed off of course, but Mr O'Leary said it was the most creative piece of lateral thinking he'd ever seen and he's going to help me put in for this post-GCSE internship next year. At the European Space Agency! In Paris!'

The next day, when Iris came to pick Ted up from school, Miss Kilpatrick hurried up to her, buzzing with the peculiar pleasure teachers take in setting parents against one another. 'Oh, Mrs Richie, we've got a bit of a problem with Jack's costume. Just between you and I, Elaine's one of those people, if she can't just go in a shop and buy it, it's not going to happen. So I thought, seeing as how you'd done such a great job on Ted's, maybe you could be persuaded to help out with Jack's too.'

'There's nothing I'd enjoy more, to be honest. I presume I'd better not give him any teeth or claws he could do any actual damage with?'

As she and Ted passed the Big School, Iris noticed that Molly, who had always come out of school defiantly alone, was surrounded by an admiring posse of girls and, indeed, boys. Molly seemed very cool about this celebrity, and shook them all off with a casual wave, before amazing Iris even more by hurrying up to join her and Ted.

'You seem very popular all of a sudden, Mol. I'm not even going to ask why, but maybe you could consult me before you actually commit any more felonies, do you think?'

From: janos@planetcool.com
To: molly666@hotmail.com

Hi

That was a rare prank. I'm in awe. And in Year 11. The one with too much red hair. You up for helping on Planet Cool? Coffee? After school? Tomorrow?

J

From: molly666@hotmail.com
To: janos@planetcool.com

Thanks but I've got tons of work at the mome...

But...

From: molly666@hotmail.com
To: janos@planetcool.com

Could be. Planet Cool? Is that the new ninth planet then?

'Politics are for the present, but an equation is something for eternity' Albert Einstein

M

Trying too hard...

From: molly666@hotmail.com
To: janos@planetcool.com

could be.

'politics are for the present, but an equation is something for eternity' albert einstein

M

That'll do.

The next afternoon, Iris discovered why the joyless Elfrieda's baking had been geometrical and solid. Her own first batch of cakes, as airy, fluffy and decadent as Sammy could possibly have hoped for, went into the bike trailer immaculate and intact, and emerged from it, after an experimental turn round the block, an impacted, sticky mass. She rang Sammy to apologise. 'I don't think she had a death wish. I think it was the laws of mechanics. And geometry. If you make things square and solid, they don't move around and they can't get squashed. I'm so sorry.'

'Don't worry... Oh Christ, fucking shit. I'll see you later, okay Iris?'

'Sammy? What's...' but the line was dead. Maybe Pepita'd got into the cheese fridge. Looking up from the ravaged cakes, and wondering how anything robust enough to survive the journey could possibly earn her enough to feed the family, Iris found herself staring through the window at the car. The silent, smooth and relatively spacious little egg, which she had never even entered. Had, indeed, rashly sworn never to do so. But the financial situation was becoming critical; and, looked at from one point of view, it was more of a waste of resources to have manufactured it and then leave it unused, than to amortise the energy budget of its manufacture by – well, for example, by using it for deliveries. Iris set about converting the crumbs into a trifle, and began to plan her campaign.

After supper, she found Malcolm watching the news, an organic beer in one hand and - purely in the interests of fair play - a tube of Pringles Supremes at his elbow. Normally she avoided television, since it was one good example she could set the children without any personal sacrifice, but tonight she sat beside him on the sofa, sidling up so her thigh rested alongside his.

Malcolm turned to her, looked at the leg, and back at her. 'Can it be that an adult human female has re-entered the local ecosystem?'

'Don't be so sarky. I just came to keep you company.'

She snuggled a little closer and looked up at the screen. Malcolm looked at her suspiciously, and went to the fridge. 'You look like you need a drink. Here'

He came back with another beer for himself and a large glass of screw-top Italian verdicchio for Iris.

She took a sip, and was about to ruffle Malcolm's hair as a preliminary to asking a small favour, when the commercials started. She knew better than to interrupt him now.

'Look, it's the new Saab – look at that...' A happy smile played on his lips as, on the screen, a gleaming silver beast careened through a pristine forest, swerving with surreal precision to avoid every tiny flower and grass blade, before gliding to a stop right in front of an adorable baby squirrel.

'Oh, for God's sake!' Just in time, she'd managed to turn away and yell into a sofa cushion. Luckily, Malcolm was now watching the Daily Mail announce its bonanza giveaway of five hundred pairs of air tickets to Walt Disney World. 'Ted'd like it there. We should take him before he's too big.'

Before she had time to formulate a response, the news came back. Binge drinking up again, another pop star caught with child pornography, and three new oil wars in Africa. Malcolm switched off the television, yawned, stretched, and looked at Iris. 'Feeling better?'

Iris decided this was technically a rhetorical question, removed the sofa cushion from her ear, and smiled up at him brightly. 'Why wouldn't I be?'

'Gorgeous thing that Saab, isn't it? Clever sales pitch too.'

'I don't think it's as nice as ours. Yours.'

'You don't?' He looked at her suspiciously, and put down his beer. Iris pulled him down beside her again. 'Well – I mean, there are circumstances, you know, where driving is the only practicable solution. And in those circumstances - whatever they happened to be...'

'So you're wanting to be put on the insurance, then.'

'Only occasionally. Just for, um, deliveries. I promise. I'm sort of diversifying, you know, to get extra household income? Like you wanted? I tried using the bike, but even with your lovely trailer...'

'Well, there's a limit to how much suspension you can get out of the offcuts of a rubber sheet and a few bits of hosepipe. I could have told you that.'

'I'm sorry, I'm so pig headed, and you're always so clever and patient with me...'

Iris began to undo his shirt buttons, wondering, not for the first time, how somebody so acute to the vested interests in any business transaction could have such a vast blind spot for personal flattery. He smiled down at her, but warily. 'You're on then, but on one condition. Actually, two.'

'Anything!' Iris was far too busy congratulating herself on another successful deployment of her feminine wiles to remember the last time she'd said this.

'I'd like us to have Colin over for supper. If we've a chance of making this business work, he needs the odd airing in human society. And he is supposed to be my friend.'

Why on earth had it not occurred to her to say, 'Anything, provided it doesn't involve Colin'? She managed a non-committal grunt, followed by: 'And the other thing?'

'You're to stop dragging the children into all of this. It's just not fair on poor Ted to make him the laughing stock of the playground, twice. If he wants Nikes, let the boy have Nikes. It's bad enough foisting your experiments on him at home, but give him a chance of a normal adulthood in the outside world.'

Thank God, it didn't sound as though he'd heard about Molly and the Special Branch. Iris had spent some time impressing on her daughter the unlikelihood of her being allowed off on her own in Paris if her father got even a whiff of that. And Ted's reaction to the inflatable jumbo affair had been upsetting enough. 'Of course, I totally promise, I won't do anything that affects the children in any way. And Ted's absolutely fine. I bet he's forgotten all about the Nikes by now.'

Iris went to put Ted to bed, and found him at his computer, headphones clamped to his ears. His pocket money purse was open beside him.

'Ted? What are you up to now? It's bed time.'

Before Ted heard her over Fifty Cent at full volume, Iris got to the mouse. He pulled off the headphones and looked up. 'It's a surprise. For you.'

Iris looked over his shoulder at the screen.

'CARBON CREDITS INTERNATIONAL. CLICK HERE TO REVIEW ORDER'

Iris clicked. Ted watched.

'You have chosen to purchase   3   tonnes   of carbon credits

Your purchase price is (choose currency)   £35 UK
                                                   $50 US

Please select payment method....

Iris put down the mouse. Ted grabbed it. 'It was a surprise – for you. It's all I had in my pocket money. Well, it's a bit more than I have just yet but I thought you could, I could have my next month's early? It's so you can go back to being normal, Mum! It's enough for six months, I worked it out with my footprint calculator we made at school. It would be nice if you were normal again, wouldn't it?'

A rush of shame overwhelmed Iris, totally obliterating the question of how he was planning to feed a rumpled ten pound note and some coins into the CD drive of his computer. Poor Ted. How desperate must he be, when she knew he'd been saving every penny since Christmas for Brian Lara Cricket 2009. She knelt beside him and wrapped him in a hug. 'Oh Ted! Is this about the football boots?'

'Only a bit. Well yes, a bit. But look, I bought credits for them too. You can get credits for anything and it makes it all right!'

Iris looked on the menu and saw that Carbon Credit Inc was indeed offering – for a range of charges - absolution for every imaginable environmental lapse. Instead of confession, Hail Marys and scrambling up mountains on your knees, they'd substituted a quick vacuum of whatever bank card you offered up to them, on the promise of converting its contents into low voltage bulbs, charcoal stoves, trees, solar panels or turf-roofed homes for the indigenous peoples of places too faraway to check up on. Thereby offloading the responsibility, without actually annulling the offence.

'It's amazing how you people fall for that one, over and over again. Talk about wishful thinking.' Over the monotonous thump and clatter of Ted's PS2, stuck in a match-saving penalty since eight thirty-four this morning, the tetchy voice filled her head. Today it sounded as though his false teeth weren't in quite right. But presumably, if God's timeless...

'False teeth? I made the entire universe, I think I could probably replace my own teeth. I knew it was a mistake to waste the power of imagination on you lot. Anyhow, that's not what we're concerned with here. This offsetting business. It's as bogus as absolution, as you'd realise immediately if you hadn't had that second glass downstairs.'

'Absolution? Bogus?'

'Of course it's bogus. Just a cheap sales pitch a couple of desperate bishops came up with in the eighth century, when recruitment was flagging a bit. They certainly never had my blessing for it. And I'm the only one with a licence to bless. So far as I'm aware.'

'What, you mean they don't get to be excused their sins if they confess them?'

'Think about it. Tell somebody, and all the harm you did just goes away. Does that sound likely to you?'

'So – they die, all calm and happy in the confident expectation of eternal bliss, and then...'

'I told you I liked a joke. Anyhow, that's not the matter at hand here. What d'you think would happen if everybody decided to buy their way out of doing whatever they feel like doing? There's not enough space on the planet for all those trees. Even if they plant them. And speaking as one who's literally seen it all, it looks to me like just one more way to turn an easy profit.'

The itch vanished, and with it the voice. God's argument seemed all too plausible. But there was Ted, still smiling up at her. This was not the moment to puncture the shiny balloon of his idealism with the steely hatpin of logic. Especially given the promise she'd just made to Malcolm.

Iris turned back to Ted. 'If it means that much to you...'

'Can I have them Mum, the Nikes, can I?'

'We'll see – but...' Suddenly, she remembered Sammy's trainers. It was worth a try. It wasn't Ted's fault he was too young properly to evaluate the relative importance of preserving the only habitable planet in the solar system, against a few weeks on a higher rung of the social ladder at Gordon Road school. But, as an adult in full view of the big picture, she could at least try to win him over. 'Look – before we decide, how about I show you some others I saw the other day?'

She hit a few keys, found the ReBorn site, and skimmed swiftly past the tweedy pinks and mottled oranges, to a page labelled: 'Modern Classics – brand new, no brand!'

There were running shoes, basketball shoes, and – yes – football boots, in tasteful grey and black. 'Look Ted, look at the lovely place they're made in – look what it says: *"Deep in the forgotten mountains of the Portuguese Asturias, we discovered a village where the art of shoemaking has survived for four hundred years..."* Imagine Ted! That's older than Grandma! Blah blah, what else *"...then we sourced the highest quality rubber from mature Malaysian plantations, grown by workers who share cooperatively the profits from their sales...alternatively you can choose rubber from repurposed car tyres and feel even better about yourself"* Wow, you could be running around on Ferrari tyres Ted. Think how fast that would make you. Look, here's the picture, they're nice, aren't they? I'm sure nobody else in your class has those.'

She watched Ted anxiously as he zoomed into the image and scrutinised the shoes from all angles. 'Well – they're okay I guess'....

'There, I knew you'd like them!'

'...but they're not Nikes. I think I'll have the Nikes Mum. Shall I ask Dad?'

'No!' It came out much louder than she'd intended. The thought of Malcolm permanently identified with the provision of treats, and herself with gloom and duty, was more than she could bear.

Ted looked up at her, like a kitten wondering if it's safe to approach the milk saucer. She dropped a reassuring kiss on his head. 'I meant – don't bother him, it's fine. I can get Nikes for you. You're what, a five these days?'

The question was, how? Iris' rash promise to supply Jack's costume had finally drained her cash reserves. There was the option of waiting until Malcolm was embroiled in the inner recesses of a major domestic appliance, and rifling his wallet, but it didn't sound as though Malcolm's wallet was especially well-stuffed either, right now. And technically, he'd still have bought the boots, which she was absolutely determined not to let happen. Somewhat to her own amazement, she was beginning to enjoy her new life a lot more than the old one, but until it could make an equivalent contribution to the household expenses, she could hardly present it to Malcolm as a valid alternative.

Obviously, she couldn't go back to her old clients. The pool of potential work through the LETS scheme was barely more than a puddle, as most of the batik-printers and foot-modellers seemed to be struggling along well below the tax threshold. As for her revolutionary loophole, the unfortunate catch was that it was a loophole, and not a shop window. Advertising it in any way could have only one result. Or possibly two, if the prosecution for incitement to avoid tax was included. Either way, the more people knew about it, the sooner it would be pounced on and closed.

Meanwhile, if she didn't have cash, at least she still had the promise of Buzzybees credit. Having got her name on the car insurance, Iris spent most of the following morning working out that things incorporating lots of air and/or chocolate were likely to yield the highest profit margin, and baking accordingly. She was standing beside the open boot of the car, making a complex mental calculation of how many meringues and brownies it would hold, when her phone rang. 'Hello – Oh, Fern! What a – nice surprise.'

After their brush with the Special Branch, she'd stayed away from Green meetings. She hadn't heard anything directly, and Sergeant Bathurst had promised that Molly's name, as a minor, would be protected, but she wasn't taking any unnecessary risks.

It was starting to drizzle, so she shut the boot – very quietly, just in case Fern heard it – and made for the house. Fern's voice on the other end didn't sound especially angry, but then anger was probably not an emotion of which she, or any other Green, was capable. 'Iris, I'm so glad I've got hold of you, we thought it must be you but you know, we had to invoke the Freedom of Information act in the end. It was a huge hassle, but so worth it. You've done an amazing job for the Party!'

'I have?'

'Golly yes, haven't you heard, I mean of course it was pretty embarrassing at the time and we couldn't possibly have endorsed it officially, but since that phone stunt thing, our numbers have gone through the roof!'

'They have?' If this were really the case, surely it would have been all over the News, or at least tucked into a modest corner of some bulletin. But even if it were slightly true - if she'd actually helped the Green party towards its goals...

'So what I'm calling about, I'm sure you're dying to know, I'm calling to ask if you might consider standing, you know, as a candidate. Just for the council, at first, but with your talents...'

'A councillor? Me?'

Then she remembered Deborah's story. Maybe they just wanted her as a decoy councillor, a name on a piece of paper. 'So what, in an actual election, where I might actually win?'

'Oh yes. Totally.'

Councillor Iris Richie! Mayor Richie, perhaps, in due course. Mayor Richie, blazing a trail of community participation and publicly-acclaimed restrictions on - to take a random example - people dropping their children off at school in Porsche Cayennes. Mayor Richie introducing mandatory food preserving, dressmaking and maypole-dancing for boys and girls alike in all local schools, and turning out a generation re-connected with the past, yet prepared for the future. Mayor...

'...there'd be a certain amount of work, of course. You know, the weekly ward meetings, and you'd have your clinics every week as well, then there's the regular local party stuff that you know about. Maybe three days of committees a week, max. But...'

But - hang on, this was a full-time job. And between baking, costume making and the extra time entailed in doing all her errands on a bicycle, Iris didn't have much time as it was. What she needed was money. 'So would I get paid for this? I mean, of course, in the unlikely - I mean sorry, no, when I win?'

'Paid? Oh dear, no. I mean, none of us gets paid. That's not what we're about, is it? Financial gain?'

Embarrassment made Iris cross. It was all very well for Fern to float ethereally above the murk of material need, pursuing, like Arlo, an existence of singleton improvisation, but most wives and mothers who devote their time to charity turn out, when examined at close quarters, to have husbands in the City. The last thing Iris needed was a load more unpaid work. 'You know Fern, I'd have loved to, but unfortunately I have a family to support, and...'

'Yup, that's great isn't it? I mean in a way that's the best bit of all! A mother, a wife, and yet somebody who manages to find the time to make a difference on a bigger stage. They'd be a terrific asset, wouldn't they? And you'd be welcome to get them involved, bring them along to meetings... Iris?'

Iris was back inside, leaning against the fridge in the kitchen, one fist stuffed in her mouth to stifle a sudden fit of hysteria at the mental picture of the family joining her on the campaign trail. She briefly contemplated revealing to Fern that barely twelve hours earlier, she'd made a solemn promise not to get any of them involved in anything like this, ever again. What she said was: 'You know, Fern, I couldn't be more flattered, but just at the moment I really think I'd be better off you know, consulting in the background? Brainstorming ideas? But I'm so glad about the membership surge, that's really exciting. Thanks for letting me know – I'll see you very soon, yes?'

Iris put down the phone on Fern, impressed, despite herself, at

Fern's endless capacity for optimism in the face of self-evidently overwhelming odds.

But how else did ordinary people ever achieve anything great? Nobody'd have given Gandhi any kind of odds when he started out. And hadn't Joan of Arc achieved some rather amazing victories, before they turned her into a human torch? Perhaps she had also been tipped off by God that modelling herself on Cassandra was not going to achieve the desired result. Just look at Soren. You couldn't argue with a word she said, but she didn't exactly set an appealing example.

Something must have happened to Joan as she grew up, to fuel her unquenchable optimism. Maybe she had a political awakening, too...

JOAN OF ARC: THE TRIUMPHANT YEARS (or WEEKS)

SCENE: inside a castle on the road to Orleans. Several ANCIENT FRENCH DUKES are sitting around while their SQUIRES polish their armour. In one corner a MINSTREL is droning away to his lyre. Enter JOAN, aged seventeen but looking about twelve, dressed as a boy.

JOAN: (slapping her thigh)
'Come on then! What are we waiting for? Let's go and finish off those godless thugs. Oh, and can somebody lend me a sword?'

The DUKE OF ARRAS' SQUIRE picks up a sword and hands it to her. Her knees buckle under the weight, and she nearly chops off her leg as she collapses.

JOAN (brightly, as she scrambles to her feet)
'I expect you get used to it pretty quickly, don't you, once you're in the thick of it? Let's get going, I've just had St Catherine telling me today was the day!'

(the DUKES exchange looks, while the SQUIRES cross themselves)

DUKE OF POITIERS (peering out of the arrow slit)
'You've got to be joking1 There are thousands of them out there, and about ten of us. And thousands more arriving by the minute.'

JOAN

'All the more reason for setting off now, then. Before it gets any worse. Who's with me?'

Thick silence, but for the MINSTREL'S 'Lament for a Mad Dauphin', as everybody stares down at their greaves.

DUKE OF CLUGNY (trying to mend fences)

'How about a spot of lunch first? We're not going to get much grub in Orleans, if it's been under siege all these months. Might as well fill up now, what? Two or three courses, a quick coffee and a drop of cognac, perhaps? Then before you know it the reinforcements will have turned up, and we can just stroll in without any fuss or, ahem, bloodshed.'

JOAN (hands on hips, like a gym mistress on a chilly hockey pitch)

'If I didn't know you boys better, I'd think you were frightened! Frightened of a few lantern-jawed Anglo-Saxons with their knuckles dragging on the ground? This isn't the attitude of God's chosen army, is it?'

More silence, during which the DUKE OF PROVENCE vainly attempts to send his lunch order, in the form of a paper dart, through the ramparts. The MINSTREL finishes his Lament, and goes into a Dirge for the Fallen of Fair France, until a SQUIRE fires a catapult at his lyre, breaking the remaining strings.

Joan stands there, the smile wilting slightly on her fair unclouded brow. Then she turns to the SQUIRE of CLUGNY.

JOAN:

'Well, how about you brave lads then? Just because these old tosspots prefer to sit about clogging their arteries on foie gras, that's no reason ordinary chaps like you and I can't make a difference! This isn't about waiting for corrupt governments and their vested interests to act on our behalf. This is about empowerment, taking things in to our own hands! You can do it! Come on, it'll be a hoot!'
(raising her fist above her head, as though lofting an invisible banner)
'For God, and for France!'

To his own surprise, the SQUIRE finds himself raising a fist too, as do all the other SQUIRES. Joan, beaming, leads them towards the door, a spring in her step and the light of victory, or possibly insanity, in her eye.

DUKES (variously)
'What's going on? Hang on a minute, you can't just leave! Hey, that's my squire you've got there!' (etc)

JOAN (ignoring them, to the SQUIRES)
'Now, there's just one teensy problem – I don't have any armour. Or a horse. Can somebody lend me something? Oh, here we go.'

As they pass the KITCHEN, she picks up a large saucepan and slams it on her head, while grabbing a rolling pin with the other hand.

JOAN (cheerily, as they exit)
'Mum always said my place was with the pots and pans. There's bound to be a horse somewhere. Now, who knows the way?'

From: janos@planetcool.com
To: molly666@hotmail.com

hey. after school tomorrow? caff by the bank?

J

From: molly666@hotmail.com
To: janos@planetcool.com

should be okay for a bit

M

Molly sent the email and then realised what she'd done. She'd accepted a date. From a boy. A much older boy. She wasn't in the habit of looking at members of the opposite sex directly as in, face to face, but from what she'd observed through her hair, he was scary; a bit like that Green Wing actor, only better looking, and of course dressed with extreme artless chic, not a flappy white overall, which only added to the scariness.

Shit. What'll I wear?

She went to her wardrobe, unlocked it, and dragged its contents out into the light. Not that she needed to. She knew beforehand that it contained nothing but about eighty black tee shirts and half a dozen pairs of jeans, with a couple of pairs of baggy leggings for really dire days. There was no way in the galaxy she was meeting a boy in any of that. On the other hand, there was even less way in the universe she was spending her money on new threads just to gratify some spotty fuck's vanity.

And anyhow, was this such a good idea? Suddenly she felt the need for reassurance, or at least the sanction of an older, wiser male. That would not be Dad, then. Who else? There was only one other person with whom she communicated on a regular basis, and though he was obviously massively smart, she wasn't entirely sure he was even human. Still, it was worth a try. She sat down at her computer and logged on to Altarica.

After an entertaining detour on the Escher infinite staircase, she emerged into the Mobius racetrack, where half a dozen virtual racing cars were chasing each other. Ubiquitur was always more of a spectator than a participant. He was leaning on the crash barrier, dropping space-time wrinkles in the cars' path.

'Hail, master of majestic majesty. I come to you in need of guidance and advice. Shouldest I accept an invitation from a boy I've never spoken to? On the alternate hand, if I never speaketh to him, how will I get to know him? I prithee, who art so wise and all-knowing, to help me out on this one.'

Ubiquitur turned to face her. She'd forgotten to make herself invisible today, and her avatar was the default female, with a blank face and a slightly loopy glide. Which was how she often felt. He, on the other hand, was in chameleon mode, and barely visible. Maybe that was how he felt, too. Clearly, fashion advice was not going to be his bag.

'Greetings, fair maiden. Your question poseth a riddle in truth, *but not one to which I can aid you with much of a solution. The world and its ways are, to be frankest, a closed volume to me. Trust in your heart, keep your phone handy, and...'*

Colin was struggling a bit with this one; he wasn't often asked for advice on social etiquette, so it was almost a relief when Malcolm hove towards his end of the office, and he had to slam out of Altarica and into the e-newsletter of WRAP, the Waste Resources Action Programme. Malcolm leaned over Colin and rested a manly hand on his shoulder. Colin had never worked out why his business partner felt the need to behave towards him like a scout-master on a recruitment drive, but he had to assume it was a personal tic. Malcolm looked a lot more cheerful lately, whatever the reason. 'Okay, I'm off then Col. Dropping off the pitch at FreeFlow, and then might or might not come back. Don't forget about tonight will you? They're all looking forward to seeing you.'

As Malcolm left the building, his hopes and dreams neatly packaged under one arm, his phone rang. 'Malcolm Richie? ...Mol? Hi love, are you okay? ...Really? That's very sweet... Yup, as a matter of fact, I could - in about an hour? See you then...'

'D'you think Mum's all right? I mean, obviously not right now, but d'you reckon her personality is like, salvageable?'

Molly had emerged from the cubicle in the Top Shop changing zone to try out a new combination of garments on Malcolm. Nobody seemed to be especially concerned at his presence there; indeed, a couple of girls had asked for advice, which had almost had his pulse racing, until the younger one explained that her Dad was extremely strict, and seeing as how she was up from Cheltenham there was no way she'd get back for a refund on anything he wasn't having.

Molly was wearing a skirt, which was novel in itself, but the real bombshell was that it wasn't black. In fact it wasn't anything like black, it was hot tangerine, and short, and flared; and with the navy blue top skimming her navel, and the long legs, he was struggling to repress his feelings at the thought that his daughter had become, after all – and sometimes the cliché really is the right word – a swan.

She'd already piled up a dress and two more tops, and there

was a small mountain still in the cubicle, but that was fine by him. He had a strong sense that FreeFlow had bought his idea, and there was only one more meeting left to finalise the technology share deal. An ongoing royalty stream from Person-Centred Palletising was exactly what his business needed, and he felt optimistic enough to splash out on a few bits and pieces for his only daughter. After all, if he couldn't do that, what was the point of it all?

As for Iris – wherever she was today...

'I think your Mum's having what we experts call a mid-life crisis, precipitated by a trauma to the right frontal lobe, which may or may not have resulted in a permanent rearrangement of the reasoning faculties. That's good, we'll have all those. Next!'

Molly returned to the cubicle. Malcolm remembered something. 'What's this I've been hearing about you going to Paris on your own?'

Inside the cubicle, Molly froze. She quickly dragged on a gingham sun-dress, and peered round the curtain. He didn't look angry, or even suspicious.

'It's not till next year. At you know, like the European Space Agency. It's not NASA, but...' She emerged fully, and stood in front of the mirror, where she could watch his face. Still nothing but innocent pride in his daughter's brains and beauty.

'So how did that come about?'

'Oh...'

She looked right back at him in the mirror. 'I just, you know, wrote this cool bit of code for Mr O'Leary. He thinks I'm some sort of adolescent genius or something. Weird or what?'

'I'm sure you deserved it. Well done that girl.'

He scrutinised her reflection carefully, as though she were a blueprint for a new life form. 'You might have to make some minor mods to the overall formula if you're planning to wear that, d'you think?'

Molly looked at herself. Short, frilly red and white check between black Goth hair and torn black fishnets. 'It's perfect. There's like, pretentious up-itself Goth you know Dad, and there's ironic Goth.'

She disappeared again, shouting back through the curtain: 'D'you think she's banging somebody else?'

Malcolm winced, then felt foolish. Intimate conversations

about private matters were bouncing round the changing room like squash balls. 'Well – the thought had crossed my mind. Between you and me, in some ways I'd rather be discreetly cuckolded offstage for a few months than suffocated by self-righteousness in my own home for the rest of my life. But I'm afraid it's more serious than that.'

'Yeah, anyhow who'd go for her, looking they way she does these days? I think that's it Dad, can we go and eat now, I'm starving?'

Iris finished packing the cakes into the car, and set off in the pouring rain. Once she'd relaxed into it, the car was a delight to drive; smooth and silent, more than an exotic insect than a machine. And it was, undeniably, a lot more comfortable than the bike, especially in this weather.

After a few minutes, and realising that she had plenty of time in hand, it occurred to her that she might as well make the most of this opportunity to polish off a few errands that had been too hilly, too far, or too cumbersome to manage even with her trailer.

A little while later, it occurred to her that there could well be other, future occasions on which it might be useful to drive somewhere, and there was no reason why, on those occasions, she might not happen to bake an extra cake or two, which would of course necessitate borrowing the car.

By the time she finally pulled up and parked smugly on a yellow line right outside the shop, she was toying, in the crocodilian corner of her brain, with the idea of keeping a meringue or two permanently hidden behind the back seat. That way, according to the terms of her agreement with Malcolm, she could use the car more or less for whatever she liked, the Cake Defence providing at least technical immunity. Not to mention a useful emergency snack.

She opened the boot. There they sat, in perfect glossy rows and stacks. Once again the door was locked, so Iris banged on it, and Sammy came out to help her unload. They staggered in to find Arlo sitting cross-legged among the legumes, massaging Pepita's stomach and singing serenading her with one of his monotonous tunes. 'Hey Iris. Poor old Pepita, there was, like, a rat in the yurt this morning. I guess she's having issues with the claws. Hey Dad, this is Iris. Iris, this is my Dad, Troy.'

His sweet face looked up, brimming with hero-worship, to a tall man sitting on the counter, with knotted muscles and sun-bleached hair, swinging his legs and speaking into a late-model iPhone. 'Yeah... sure, you got it, Bob. Or should that be Saint Bob? Just kidding... see you later!' He looked like Arlo, only somehow filled in, solid where Arlo was ethereal; and his voice was the same, an octave down.

He pocketed the phone and saw Iris behind her boxes. 'Hey. You look like you could use a hand.' He jumped down and followed Iris out to the car. Iris opened the boot and handed Troy a box of meringues. They went back through the door, which Sammy had framed with a seasonal garland of nasturtiums and purple chicory.

'Cute little setup they have here.'

'Isn't it?' Iris could see how Buzzybees could just seem like that; cute, whimsical, scruffy, a bit shambolic.

'It's more than that, though. I mean, to me at least.'

'That right?'

They went in, and Troy handed the meringues to Sammy, who began setting them out. 'Oh dear, look, this one's had a prang on the way down. I suppose somebody'd better put it out of its misery.'

She picked it up and took a bite. 'Oh my lord Iris, you are a goddess. Or a sorceress. We can charge a mint for these. Where's the pen?'

Iris could not remember having been described as either of the above in the recent past, and certainly not outside these walls. How had she lived without this place? Sammy continued: 'Come to that, we could use an evil spell or two right now.' She sounded worried, which was not a condition Iris would ever have associated with her.

'A spell? Oh, was that why you hung up on me the other day?'

Sammy looked up from doubling the price on the meringues. 'Show her the letter, Arlo. It's from those Planet Plenty scumbags. They found out the lease is coming up and they've bought out the freehold. So any moment now, I have to sell out to them or lose the shop.'

Iris peered at the letter over Arlo's shoulder. 'God, that's a bit ruthless for Buddhists, or whatever they are. But, I mean if they did take it over, would that be so awful? Couldn't you carry on running it?'

Arlo stowed the letter and laid Pepita in a patch of sunlight near the salad greens, where she braided herself elegantly like a rug. 'Have you seen the way they operate? It's like fucking Walmart with greenwashing. Central supply depots, giant trucks...'

Sammy stopped tidying crumbs into her mouth to interrupt. 'That's nothing! How about the CCTV cameras in their shops! Spying on the customers. Can you imagine?'

The three of them stared into the looming future, contemplating the horror of this idea. Troy, who had been fielding calls from Mick, Madge and Jude, finally turned off his phone and turned a wry smile on Sammy. 'These guys with too much time on their hands – what can you do?!' For some reason Sammy just rolled her eyes, so Troy wandered over to the box of brownies, helped himself to one, took a bite, tasted it, and helped himself to two more.

Arlo, following like a puppy, took a brownie and reached for a meringue as well. Sammy slapped his hand away, almost irritably. 'They'd be spying on me too. And on my stock. No more snakes behind the lettuces, that's for sure. No more deformed Cambridgeshire Old Fancies. I'd torch the place with my own doobie first.'

'Planet Plenty?' Troy stopped dramatically in the middle of the shop, a brownie half way to his mouth. 'Of course. They did it in the States, why wouldn't they do it here? The scumbags! Wait up now...'

He stood there, cogs visibly whirring in his head. 'This could just be perfect – remember the protest tomorrow? Over Clean Tech? Okay, well now Clean Tech and the Planet are both part of Zoom International. Bad guys. Clean Tech fuels the Planet's trucks, from sugar cane where the rainforest used to be. So...'

Iris barely heard the rest of it; she only saw her next week's grocery allowance rapidly vanishing down the respective throats of father and son. Somehow they were both capable of talking and eating simultaneously, at turbo speed, and her cakes were almost gone. How was it possible for two slim, healthy-looking men to wolf three trays of cake in the space of about ten minutes? She had been hoping to ask Sammy how much credit she'd earned, but by now there was nothing left for anybody to buy.

She tried to position herself protectively between the few remaining brownies and the two of them, but they simply reached round her, eating and gesticulating with more and more fervour as the sugar took hold.

She'd just have to ask for credit against the next batch. Iris went over to Sammy, who was now trimming the outside leaves from a pile of ageing cabbages. Iris began to whisper: 'I don't want to be rude, or anything, but...'

'Good morning Sammy. The front door still seems to be locked, for some reason, but I found my own way in; I knew you wouldn't mind.'

Soren had materialised beside the grain sacks, like a tie-dyed fairy godmother. 'I'm glad I've caught you at last, the shop's been so busy lately I've barely recognised it. Only I've been thinking, it's really about time you put carbon prices on your stock alongside the cash prices. I think you'll find most of your regular customers are ready for it. Of course I couldn't speak for...' She stared suspiciously at the unfamiliar, and criminally tanned, cake-eating intruder '...for some of the ... I ... ' Then her face changed, and her voice faltered. '...It is - isn't it? Oh, my - it really is...'

Iris forgot all about the disappearing credit in her amazement, as Soren drifted helplessly up to Troy, holding out her hand. 'Troy Hauser...'

Troy Hauser! Even Iris had heard of him. Troy Hauser had stroked Rachel Carson's head as she lay dying. Troy had spoken at Bobby Kennedy's funeral, and visited Nelson Mandela on Robben Island. Troy had chained himself to mighty redwoods, and buried himself in concrete before advancing bulldozers. He must be Soren's Elvis. And he was Arlo's Dad. Right here in Buzzybees, just like a regular guy. So modest! So very nearly normal! Even his gluttonous raid on Iris' baking seemed, in this light, like a benediction.

He looked kindly back at Soren, taking her hand in both of his; very much as Elvis probably looked at his anonymous fans, with a smile almost worse than no smile at all. 'Guilty as charged. And you are...?'

Soren just stood there, her lips parted, breathing heavily. After a moment, Sammy took her elbow and led her gently away. 'Hey, Soren, I'll definitely think about it, yeah? Actually I had another idea, how about if we arranged the stuff by how far it's had to come? So like, you can be sure of being truly green and sustainable, if you never go more than five feet from the till? D'you fancy having a mosey round, see if it could work?'

She left Soren recovering in Ethiopia, and went back to her

cabbages. Meanwhile, Troy returned to his plan with even more dynamism than before, fuelled by two pounds of high-octane chocolate. 'So ...we hold our protest against CleanTech just like we planned, but we join the dots, we draw a line right from your little store here, to the millions of acres of rain forest torn down to grow the fuel, to fill the trucks, to move the produce around – and shazamm, finally people get that everything they do matters, because everything's connected!'

He and Arlo exchanged man-and-boy high-fives over the crumbs. Iris, on the other hand, recovered from her initial awe, was once again depressed at the prospect of explaining to her starving family that their supper had been inadvertently re-allocated to the cause of global enlightenment, and would they like stale rice cakes instead?

Meanwhile Sammy had returned to the carnage on the cake counter. 'Christ, you pigs, I hope you're intending to pay for that little lot.'

'Boy, did we do that?' Troy ruffled one hand through his hair, delighted with the enormity of his own appetites. 'Sure I'll pay. Hey, Ihave a better idea!'

He bathed Iris in a megawatt smile. Despite herself, her knees softened like ice-cream. 'How about we throw a party after the gig tomorrow? And you bake us a cake?'

'Oh, yes, of course - I mean, I would, but...' How could she say, 'But I can't afford the ingredients', to somebody whose entire life has been dedicated to fighting impossible odds on behalf of others? Troy probably wouldn't be above hijacking a lorry, in her situation. 'It's just...'

Sammy held out an expectant hand to Troy. 'It's okay, he'll front the cash, won't you Troy? Come on, I've got to open up or they'll be calling the riot cops on me.'

'Cash!' Cash for Ted's football boots! Iris looked at Arlo and Troy, transformed in an instant from gluttonous pigs to personal saviours, and grabbed Troy's hand in her own. 'I'd love to. Oh, thank you. This is so great!'

Troy smiled back, clearly assuming she was thrilling to his charm, rather than to the prospect of folding money, after weeks of marginally useful credit. He gently extricated his hand from Iris', and reached into the tee shirt sleeve of his other arm, rolled up to reveal a gleaming bicep. He pulled out a slab of brand new fifty pound notes and unpeeled five. 'This do you for now?'

Sammy caught Iris' expression. 'Oh, he's loaded. Fighting the good fight's a high-cost business. Ain't that so, Troy?'

Troy attempted to cuff Sammy playfully about the head. She ducked away sharply. It was impossible to imagine Sammy angry, but Iris caught a look that was something close to irritation. Troy, oblivious, checked his watch: a Rolex, which seemed a bit ostentatious for the scourge of consumer capitalism. Maybe it had been a present. and he was just wearing it not to hurt somebody's feelings. He pulled out his iPhone and looked at the screen. 'Hey. Wagons roll. So you'll bring the cake down to the InterContinental tomorrow, huh Iris? Leave it with the bell captain, he's a good guy.'

As Troy and Arlo left the shop, Arlo ducked back in, holding out to Iris a soggy package wrapped in newspaper. 'Hey. Could you use this for, like, your family? My Dad got it with his slingshot, outside the yurt this morning. He's got this, like, deal that if everybody only ate meat they killed themselves, there'd be...'

Troy, already striding down the road, looked back over hisshoulder. '...No more land wasted for livestock, no more slaughterhouses, and no more fat kids! With all the running they'd have to do, just to get a burger...Think about it. C'mon son, we gotta get going.'

Arlo dropped the package into Iris' shopping bag and followed Troy. 'Don't worry, we skinned it and everything! See you tomorrow!'

And they were gone, blotted out by the hordes finally admitted into the shop. Iris barely heard Arlo's last sentence, already pondering what sort of cake would be special enough to exchange for a pair of Nike Mercury Vapours. Suddenly, she realised she still had the shopping to do, and now the cake as well, before picking up Ted.

Luckily she now had the circuit of Buzzybees down to about fifteen minutes. The fact that there were only ever about four vegetables in season had turned out to be yet another unexpected bonus of abandoning the supermarket. What joy, not having to agonise between twenty sorts of butter and a dozen subtly nuanced baby tomatoes. She could practically feel the airy acres freed up in her brain by the elimination of all those trivial decisions. No wonder Joan of Arc had time to be heroic, when it was always cabbage, onions and beans for supper.

Even so, by the time Iris had established that Soren was safely out of range, there was no chance at all of a trip to Niketown today. She was longing to see Ted's face when she handed him the shoes. But she could tell him about them, anyhow. She had the means to obtain them, right here in her bag.

Iris and Ted banged happily through the door to find Malcolm in the kitchen, lolling about in an attitude of uncharacteristic idleness, and chatting to somebody who sat swinging long legs from the table, with her back to Iris – somebody he clearly liked a lot. This could have been to do with what she was wearing, which was short, tight, and brightly coloured. Iris stopped dead in surprise, as Ted cluttered upstairs to change.

'Hey Malc, you're home early...' Iris was suddenly aware that, by contrast, she herself was once again wearing whatever had seemed easiest at two minutes to seven this morning, and no makeup apart from a light scattering of self-raising flour, and whatever sticky residue Ted's kiss had left on her cheek. She was cross with herself for minding this, and crosser with Malcolm for not warning her about the mystery guest, nor bothering to introduce them.

'Hey Mum, you look like you've been mugged with a hedge!'

Malcolm chortled, rocking in his chair. The mystery visitor swivelled round to face Iris, who found herself face to face with somebody she barely recognised as her daughter.

Her body prickled with the shock of an irreversible moment. And then with indignation that it had come upon her unprepared. She'd walked up the path expecting the grumpy adolescent who'd failed to return her kiss as she left for school this morning; not a pleasant prospect, but perfectly manageable.

Instead, here, not two feet away, was herself at eighteen, with a better chin and the crucial advantage of tastes formed in central London, not Stevenage. Seismic shifts like this ought to come with several weeks' notice, and probably the phone number of a trauma counselling hotline.

'Well.' She really did want to say something positive and thrilled about having produced a daughter this gorgeous, and was about to do so, when Malcolm stood up and gently moved Molly's hair away from her eyes. 'Scrubs up well doesn't she? And she knew exactly what to go for, too. We were in an out in under an hour. You should get her to take you shopping, I bet she'd have some ideas to buff you up at the edges.'

He might as well have said, 'Don't worry; it's true that she has, in the space of a couple of hours, supplanted you as alpha female of the household. But don't worry! If you make enough of an effort, there might yet be a role for you as occasional chaperone.'

Soren's words about the genetic garbage heap had become real. For a terrible moment, Iris thought she might weep. Then she remembered Troy, and Sammy, and all their campaigning allies. There was a whole world out there of people with ideals and moral courage, with big souls and a grander vision of life than afternoons at TopShop. Who cared if she had to come home to these others, these - ethical pygmies? It was a pity, but in the end, it was the pygmies' loss. 'Some of us have our minds on slightly less superficial goals than endless consumerism, actually. Now if you don't mind, I need to get on with....'

'Dad! Mum's buying me the Nikes! Tomorrow!'

'Oh really. That can't be consumerism, then. She must have found a new name for it.'

'Oh, that's great, Malcolm. Who was the one telling me I was ruining his chance of a normal life? And the minute I...'

Ted jammed his hands over his ears and ran to Malcolm for a hug. Molly slid off the table, kissed the top of her father's head, turned her back on Iris, and shimmied up to her room.

Ted's voice had acquired a heart-breaking little tremor. 'I just said, Dad, it was Mum said she was, just now when she...'

'You're fine son, don't worry, your Mum's had one too many organic martinis with her tofu wrap down at the commune'

'And I'm starving, Mum what's for supper?'

'AS I WAS ABOUT TO SAY I'm just making supper now, so I need to clear a bit of space, if you don't mind.'

Malcolm stood up and ruffled Ted's hair. 'Come on, I'll give you some goalie practice. Oh, and Iris, you've not forgotten it's tonight Col's coming over?'

Colin. More like an arsenic martini, with him as the olive. How was it possible for everything to go so bad, so fast? The phone rang as Malcolm and Ted disappeared through the front door. Iris grabbed it, furious. 'Yes? Who is this?'

'Hey - Iris - you sound weird, man - is this a bad time?'

'Oh. Arlo. Sorry.'

There was a pause at the other end. Iris wondered what was coming next, and whether she had the stamina to deal with it. 'Hey. Sorry. That was like a - another rabbit kinda thing. Just ran right into the yurt. I got it out though.'

'Another rabbit? Is that what's in that...'

She looked over to the kitchen table, where her shopping bag was gently oozing pink.

'Yeah. It died you know, fast? He's a good shot, Troy. Anyhow, I remembered. Sammy said you had a car now? Like electric or...?'

'I do. Well, actually, I don't, but my husband...'

'Great. That's so great. Could we like borrow it tomorrow morning d'you think, for an hour? Sammy and me've made this bunch of banners for the protest, and we need to get them to the site? Can't exactly take them on the bus, you know?'

'Borrow it? I don't...'

'I guess I thought, seeing as how you're coming down anyways...'

Me? Iris hadn't even thought about it. She'd imagined herself baking the cake, delivering it to the Inter-Continental, whizzing round to NikeTown, possibly even parking right outside, and returning home in triumph with her spoils for Ted. But that would just expose her to more of Malcolm's ridicule, and that was suddenly not bearable. Her great mission was to change the world, not buy Nikes for her son; her safe, comfortable, already over-indulged son.

Arlo continued: 'I guess you didn't really get to hear what the protest's about? These guys are tearing down forests in Borneo, and in Brazil and wherever, to grow sugar cane and palm oil, and all the local tribes just you know, get thrown off the land, their kids get diseases, their old folks just die...'

Iris remembered what she'd felt standing around with the Greens, politely asking people in her nice, non-threatening, middle class voice to sign a little bit of paper that some junior bureaucrat in Whitehall might or might not ever see.

What's the point in petitioning a government that bangs on about low voltage light bulbs, but won't stop building airports? That spends trillions on weapons systems that can't ever be used, but won't give a child a break from caring for its sick parents? What's the point of putting your faith in leaders too spineless to outlaw plastic bags? What good do feeble, law-abiding gestures do, in the face of all this?

'Well... It's not going to be, you know, violent, is it? I'm not going to get arrested or anything?'

'Violent? No way, man. You don't fight fire with fire. D'you think your old man would be okay with it, then?'

What Iris thought was that she would rather engrave her own eyeballs with a rusty screwdriver than ask a favour of Malcolm.

Then she remembered the cake.

She'd need the car anyhow, to drop it off. So technically she didn't even have to ask Malcolm, who she somehow suspected might not be 100% behind it being used to transport anti-capitalist propaganda. 'Well, maybe - but I couldn't hang about or anything. Would that be okay? If I just came for a bit?'

'Sure it would. Whatever works for you, Iris. You're the best.'

Iris put down the phone, trying to persuade herself that this was no more than a fair exchange for a whole evening of Colin. Gingerly, she unwrapped the soggy paper from the rabbit and tumbled it into the sink.

'So. Col's been doing quite well with the local government work, haven't you, mate?' Malcolm never called anybody 'mate', but with Colin under his own roof, and in the presence of his resentful wife and two suspicious children, the nervous scoutmaster had resurfaced. He opened a beer for himself and another for Colin, as Iris asked: 'Can I hang that up for you?'

Colin shied away, hugging his ancient jacket closer to him. Body heat was just about enough to keep the bugs happy, at least those few he'd brought with him. He always carried a stockpile whenever he had to leave the lab, in case of disaster in his absence.

He stood there, in the middle of the kitchen, looking nervously up at Iris. It was some time since he'd been in a family home, and he was unsure about the protocol. Even Iris felt sorry for him. She pulled out a chair and he sat in it, gratefully.

Unusually, Molly was watching Meerkat Manor with Ted, having apparently decided that her new babelicious image obviated the need for further learning. Iris couldn't help sneaking looks as she laid the table, amazed that such a transformation could have happened so fast, and still hurting from Malcolm's joke about her own need for an upgrade. Faced with the prospect of a beauty contest against her own child, she thought she might prefer to adopt the Continental tradition. It might be rather soothing to wear the same baggy black dress every day.

She came round to find herself standing with a fistful of cutlery, being stared at through thick lenses by Colin's vast, cloudy eyes. She began to distribute the cutlery round the table.

'Supper won't be a mo. What work is that, then?'

'Well you know Iris, it's pretty mundane, but Malcolm here's been shoving me into rubbish lately ha ha, and what with all these initiatives to reprocess food waste, it seems to have become rather er – er – sexy...'

Molly, switching off the TV in the next room, caught the last word, looked over at the visitor, then down at her own exposed flesh, and rushed for the stairs. Colin stared after her, bemused but not apparently offended, and accepted his manly ale from Malcolm.

'Dad?' Ted was pulling at Malcolm's sleeve. 'Dad, my new FourFourTwo came and I haven't read it yet, can I be excused from the visitor? Molly's gone Dad?'

'Why not get it and bring it back here, Ted, there's a good lad. Sorry, Col, carry on.'

Ted dived for the door before Iris could countermand the permission. Colin, who had meanwhile been timing the decay rate of the head on his beer, wrote a note on his sleeve and continued: 'I think, Iris, it was you who witnessed the impressive results of my little experiment with the prawn sandwich, and I'm happy to say that I've been able to scale it up and add other elements. This time I fed them the wrapper as well. Worked, if you can imagine, even better!'

Iris pulled the stew out of the oven, drained the carrots, and shouted up the stairs for the children. Eventually, Molly appeared, wearing the baggiest tee shirt in her wardrobe with 'Entropy – Nature's Anarchist Collective' across her chest. Ted slid into the other empty chair, the magazine on his knee. Malcolm fetched some more beers and a large glass of wine for Iris. 'We should have you round more often Col, we don't eat like this every night, I can tell you.'

Iris smiled sweetly and ladled out the stew. Molly speared a tiny piece on her fork, hunched low over the table so she didn't have to watch Colin eat. Everybody else tucked in to their wild rabbit fricassee, its mahogany jus enriched by the pureed liver and heart. Colin continued as he ate, dribbling slightly:

'So it appears we can use more or less anything that'll rot: old sandwiches, mouldy pies...'

Ted stopped reading the magazine under the table. Suddenly the conversation had possibilities. 'Maggoty meat? Stinky milk?'

Molly made a retching noise and pushed her plate away. Colin was too delighted by Ted's enthusiasm to notice. 'The stinkier the better! Any old rubbish that's been lurking at the back of your fridge, or indeed your supermarket shelf. Food waste is no longer a problem – it's a valuable resource! In fact....'

Colin leaned over his plate to Ted, shirt cuffs trailing in the gravy. Ted backed haplessly away from the appalling waft of Colin's breath, and the meat and soggy breadcrumbs macerating in his beard. '...In fact, you know Ted, there's a train in Sweden that actually runs on gas from slaughterhouse waste and human faeces – what I suspect you normally call poo!'

At this, Molly disappeared again. Even Iris couldn't blame her. Ted meanwhile was bouncing delightedly in his seat. 'A poo train? A poo train!'

'A poo train indeed. Nothing wrong with poo. In fact it has some very interesting...'

'More stew for anybody?' Iris had resorted to singing old nursery rhymes in her head, a long-established, undetectable distraction from intolerable stress. Colin wiped his mouth on his sleeve. 'Well, I certainly will, if it's going begging. Were you always such a fine cook, Iris? What is it, anyway?'

Iris refilled his plate and Malcolm's before replying: 'Wild rabbit. From the Heath, actually. Fresh killed today.'

Ted stopped chanting, very suddenly, and stared up at her. 'You killed a bunny rabbit, Mum?'

'No, actually Ted, somebody else killed the bunny rabbit, but you've been happily eating Porkinsons and bacon sandwiches all your life haven't you? And those pigs don't just go off into a quiet corner and turn their eyes to heaven every time you feel a rumbly tummy coming on, you know. It died very quickly, and I bet it had a much happier life than...'

She caught Malcolm looking at her, clearly remembering the farrowing crate incident. He had also stopped eating, and Colin appeared finally to have run out of fascinating food facts. In the sudden silence, Iris stood and began to scrape the half-empty plates. Colin patted his pocket and produced a plastic bag. 'In fact, just to prove the point, if you're going to empty that lot in the bin, Iris, I can put it to good use.'

Molly locked her door and sat at her computer. She didn't have time to go looking all over Altarica, and anyhow, she couldn't bear the idea of being seen any more today, even virtually. Everything was too confusing. A few hours ago she'd stared into the mirror at Top Shop, imagined herself meeting up with Janos, and fizzed to her toes and fingers with excitement. Then she'd sat two feet from Colin, and the terrible thought had hit her that Janos might look like that in about fifty or sixty years, or whatever. How could you know? Did it mean that by the time she was Mum's age, she'd be subjected to – oh shit, it didn't even bear thinking about. And what was the fizzing, anyway?

She went right to the dialogue box; he'd pick up a message, wherever he was on the site.

'Ubiquitur, great master of arts and wisdom, thou who can bendest the laws of science and of nature to thy will and make the impossible real – pleaseth thee, I really need to talk!!!'

She hit 'send' and waited, trying to breathe slowly and deeply, and taking big gulps of the Diet Coke she'd ordered Iris to buy as a mandatory study aid.

She waited. Nothing happened. For the first time ever, he wasn't there. In any case, she wasn't sure that this was a problem for which the virtual world had any answers. The virtual world wasn't where she had to meet Janos.

Malcolm dropped Colin off at the Science Park for another thrilling night of anaerobic magic with his two bulging bags, one of stew and the other of soymilk semolina pudding, which had unaccountably remained untouched by the family, though Colin had eaten two large bowls of it without noticing, as he sketched out for them a new world of benign, reconfigured molecules. Iris had done quite a lot of staring into the distance, but had refrained from actual violence. And the rabbit had really tasted pretty good, though it might have been wiser to pretend it was chicken, at least to Ted. Maybe there was some sub-clause of the New Puritanism that forbade drawing even the gauziest protective veil over the wide eyes of childhood.

But she probably hadn't even thought about it. She was probably still upset about Molly. Poor Iris, it must have been a bit of a shock - it had shocked him, and he'd watched happening.

He pulled into the forecourt of the local petrol station, where a few bunches of roses waited to expire under the strip lights. Maybe Iris needed a bit of reassurance. Mothers and daughters, and so forth. The flowers looked a bit sad, but she'd appreciate the gesture.

He held his offering out to Iris as he came in through the door. She turned from the compost chute and stared at them suspiciously. 'Where are they from?'

'From the Esso at the roundabout, it was the only place open at this hour.'

'No, I mean - where on the planet? They're probably from Kenya, that's where they grow all the roses. They're poisoning Lake Naivasha with the fertilisers, and all the locals are getting cancer. Still, you wouldn't...'

Malcolm just looked at her. Then he walked to the bin in two strides, and shoved them in, smashing their stalks.

Iris watched in shock, as much at herself as at him. What sort of monster was she becoming, to react like that?

'Oh God. Was that me? I'm so sorry. So, so sorry.'

'I should bloody well think so, you harpy.'

'They're lovely - or they probably were - and anyway it's lovely of you.'

'You could have fooled me. What do you think it's like, living in this minefield? I try to thank you for putting up with Colin, and this is your response.'

He was tugging his coat off, almost roughly, as he made for the stairs. Iris ran after him. 'Oh, don't. Please. I really am sorry. Mol said you were celebrating something today, what was it?'

'Oh. That. Nothing, probably. You wouldn't be interested.' But he let her pull him back to the sofa, where she sat him down and gently kissed the wrinkles from his shiny forehead. 'Tell me.'

'Oh, well, I've got a meeting tomorrow. But with quite a big time operation. Might lead to all sorts of things. I'm pretty sure this first deal is going to happen, anyway.'

'That's great. What's it about?... oh hang on, the cake.'

'Cake?'

Iris jumped up, pulled open the oven door and peered in. 'Perfect!' If this one went down well, who knew what extra business it might bring in? In fact, now was probably as good a time as ever to tell Malcolm about her career change. She put the cake tin on the side to cool, came back and sat on his knee. 'There's something I've been meaning to tell you about for a bit.'

'Oh, yes?' In Malcolm's experience, Iris' nature was not one of those that habitually mulled things over at length before sharing them, unless there was good reason to hold back. A piece of news that had hung around for 'a bit' was unlikely to be good.

Iris caught his look and her nerve wavered. Somehow, now that the moment had arrived, it was easier to say it with her face buried in the curly hair at his neck. 'It's only that – it's just that – well, I gave up all my book keeping clients after the accident.'

'WHAT? You did what? ' He pulled away to look her in the eye, banging her sharply on the nose.

'Ow, shit... No, really, you don't need to worry, I've been doing pretty well on the baking, in fact the Greens wanted me to be a councillor, and I had to tell them I didn't have time... Anyway, like he said, I'm going to spend a bit of it on Ted's Nike's, he's been so patient - is that okay?'

She waited for him to say something else. Silence. She pulled away and faced him. She could read nothing from his expression.

'Well.' He stood up, unloading her, not especially gently, from his knee, and made for the stairs. 'Let's hope I do get this contract, then, eh?'

By the time they'd packed all fifty-five 'STOP BIOFUEL GENOCIDE NOW!' posters into the back of the egg, there was no room for Sammy. Arlo had gone ahead to pick up Troy from the InterContinental, and the boot was entirely occupied by the cake, a marvel of caramel frosting adorned with a cornucopia of kirsch-soaked raisins and walnuts. Iris, taking no chances, had fenced it in with cardboard and scrunched-up paper. Sammy closed the passenger door, waved cheerfully, and set off on the tricycle.

Iris parked and made her way to the start of the route, pushing through a considerable throng, leaving the banners and cake in the car, for now. She was amazed and impressed that Arlo and Troy had mustered such numbers so quickly for a relatively obscure cause. Then she noticed that the banners and placards seemed to be promoting and protesting a range of interests that didn't all seem to have much in common with illegal rainforest clearances. An angry huddle of SWPers were trying to give away flyers saying, 'Kill the fascist agents of the rogue imperialist powers!' but unfortunately there seemed to be nobody to take them but a woman selling Rasta hats and whistles. Meanwhile a posse from Free Palestine Now were attempting to unload their own imprecations against the illegal so-called State of Israel onto a rather reluctant, peace-loving posse from Wiccans for Polymorphic Perversity.

But most of the people Iris slipped past, looking for Troy and the others, could have been any crowd at any student party, chatting on their mobiles, trying to find each other, swigging from cans of 1664 and wisecracking with the police, whose benign cordon seemed there more to give directions and stop the traffic than to oppress the voices of diversity and dissent.

Finally she found Sammy, handing out yesterday's samosas, and Arlo and Troy, deep in discussion. Beside them stood a man with long, thick hair and a dark complexion, holding two big-eyed children by the hand. Troy's tee shirt was even whiter today than before, and even more perfectly cut to define his sculpted muscles and set off his tan. Iris couldn't help remembering, by contrast, the incipient muffin top

Malcolm had discovered on attempting to put on his good suit for the first time in months.

Arlo turned and saw her. 'Hey. Iris, You made it! Good job! Iris, meet Ignacio and his kids, Elena and Alejandro. Ignacio is from Baratoria? He's travelling with Troy on this like, protest tour? Representing the Government of Baratoria?'

Iris offered Ignacio her hand, which he ignored, instead putting one hand on each shoulder and kissing her warmly on both cheeks. She smiled at the children, who turned and buried their faces in their father's flowing shirt. He smiled back at her over their heads.

'What lovely children. And how exciting for them to be able to be here with you!'

He nodded, and hugged the children to him, ruffling Alejandro's hair. Iris tried to imagine what Malcolm would have said if she'd brought Ted along. Then Troy, who seemed not to have noticed Iris, looked out over the crowd, turned and said something to Arlo. Arlo grabbed the megaphone and shouted: 'Okay people, here we go!'

Troy raised his two fists, and a cheer rang out. Flanked by a group of musicians with drums and solar-powered rain sticks, he led the procession off. The sound flooded the street and juddered off the buildings, conveniently drowning out the battle cries of the feuding Marxists, and setting the procession dancing like the Pied Piper's tail.

Sammy turned and smiled a welcome at Iris. Arlo padded behind Troy and Ignacio, eager as a spaniel. The children ran alongside, blowing their whistles and giggling. The sun was out, and as the joyous, energetic crowd surged along around her, Iris felt a long-forgotten elation. Here she was, literally shoulder to shoulder with people who'd given up their day to defend a cause they believed in. Unarmed and outside any political structure, rallied in their thousands by mobile and internet, they were taking over the streets of London, dancing and laughing where vans and taxis normally churned. Many of the besieged van drivers seemed amazingly cool about it, especially the ones working for large companies, who presumably wouldn't be so personally compromised by a bit of a delay. Not all the taxi drivers were so positive, but still, they were stopping – the police were seeing to that. It was a heady thought that just a few hundred people could bring the great engine of the city to a stop.

Democracy works! Direct action is the real power! Why haven't I been doing this for years?

Malcolm arrived for his meeting at the corporate HQ, only to be directed round to the back. He felt stressed, and anxious. There were police officers and metal barriers all round the square, and his bus had got mired in traffic, which was why he was a few minutes late. He hated being late.

All his dealings with the company so far had been in the dingy lab at the minor subsidiary where Mikey was based, or via email. This huge glass tower was a different order of institutional might. His suit was tight and hot; he was wearing it for the first time since the inauguration of the lunchtime burger and fat chips routine, and he'd have been more comfortable in something more forgiving, but at this point in the negotiations he wasn't taking any risks. And deep inside - in that gravitational core where English men bury their emotions - he was quietly elated. The contract in his briefcase might look like a long, boring exposition of non-linear product flows and semi-proven technologies, but to him it was up there with General Relativity: nothing less than a manifesto for a revolution in thinking about what distribution, indeed the entire world of work, might become. Infinitely mutable, personalised, yet...

'Here for the meeting, sir?' The man at security, whose suit looked considerably more expensive than Malcolm's, passed a pad across for him to sign. 'Very good. The young lady will be down to collect you any minute, Sir.'

A moment later the lift door pinged and swooshed open and a tall girl with gleaming chestnut hair, rose-pale skin and a lean, elastic body strode towards him on rackety heels. 'Hi, I'm Katariina. You're Malcolm Richie, right?'

Her voice had a husky Nordic edge; her smile dimmed every light in the atrium. Malcolm couldn't help pulling at his tie to loosen it, as he followed her into the lift.

As she threw open to doors for him, the view from the twenty-third floor boardroom was spectacular. A long table, oval enough to welcome all contributions, but rectangular enough to offer no doubt who was boss, was ringed by immaculately tailored men and a couple of women. There were only two seats still empty; the girl ushered

Malcolm into one by the window, and strolled up to seat herself at the head. Oh my god. She's...

'So. Mr Richie. I am Katariina Toivonen, Vice President of Technology here at FreeFlow. We have heard exciting things about your concept for the design for our distribution centres here. As you all know, today is a big day for our parent company, and thus for all of us. Today is the day we commit our future here in London. And we are all clear that this future is with person-centred products and technologies, balancing responsibility to investors with respect for our people; not just our customers, but our stakeholders and partners, who must always be front and centre of everything we do.'

There was a moment's silence as everybody looked at the table and respected the humble toilers on the payroll, and Malcolm composed himself for his presentation. Then Katariina flashed a smile and everybody looked relieved. 'But we around this table are just FreeFlow, and our business is moving things from one place to another as efficiently and cost-effectively as possible. Before we proceed to the formal part of the agenda, I would be grateful if you could share with us the broad outlines of your proposed project.'

When they got to the square outside Zoom International, a platform was waiting for Troy. The crowd broke and surged around it. The police shifted slightly, herding them away from the building. Troy mounted the podium, followed by Ignacio and the children. A distant, disgruntled tail was still chanting: '...When do we want it? NOW!!'

Troy looked around for a moment, waiting for the crowd to register his presence. Taking control. Then he began to speak. The platform had been wired up; his voice carried right to the back of the crowd.

'People. We are here today to expose a lie – a nasty, dirty little lie that the governments of the world are spreading, in your name. A lie that somehow raping virgin forest, destroying endangered species, and wiping out entire populations, is okay if it's done in the name of "green technology." '

Angry mutters rippled through the crowd, accompanied by a Mexican wave of assorted banners. Troy let the moment pass, then raised his hand. 'But it's not all hi-tech miracles. Who cuts the sugar cane once they've planted it? Shall I tell you? Slaves. In the twenty-first century. Corporate-owned slaves, that's who.'

He paused, gratified by the shock rippling through the crowd. 'Yeah. Your clean green machine is powered by the sweat of native Indian slaves, working in prison camps, round the clock, for a couple of dollars a month. Many of them just little kids.'

While his audience absorbed this, he looked over at Ignacio, then bent and lifted Elena onto his shoulder, while Ignacio did the same with Alejandro. 'Kids like these. These two, until only a few months ago, lived happily in a village in the rain forests of Baratoria. They played in the sunshine, they had their own village school, they lived like they'd always lived, with their families, in Nature and with her.'

Iris looked up at the children, trying to work out how old they were. The little one was probably about Ted's age, but half the size; delicate and elfin, where Ted was thunderous and solid. You'd have a job hefting Ted onto your shoulders like that...

'Today, these children have no home. Because CleanTech Fuels have sent in bulldozers, and mercenaries with AK47s, and taken their lives away from them.' He looked up at Elena, who looked back, shy and baffled. 'This sweet, innocent little kid, and God knows how many others. And it's happening, with the connivance of your government, and mine, in more and more places every day. And through them, we – that's you and I, folks! – WE, are abandoning these blameless kids to die from fever, or be gunned down in the favelas of some big city, just for what? So you and I can drive our cars to the mall! Is that right? Is that what you want?'

'No!!!'

No! Iris looked up at Troy, aflame with righteous anger. She looked at the children, and imagined Ted or Molly, fleeing from guns and bulldozers, terrified and alone in some hellhole of noise and destruction. How could it be happening, and nobody step in and stop it? How could humanity breed such monsters, to do such things?

And what would the world be, without people like Troy to bring these horrors into the light?

All around her, the crowd erupted with cheers for Troy, and boos for CleanTech. Arlo was staring up at his father, like a bug at a lamp bulb.

The children began to squirm. Troy and Ignacio gently lifted them down and their Dad gave them a hug.

The crowd didn't look so happy now. And the police were looking distinctly less cheery, too. Some just looked bored, some unsure whether regulations permitted them to listen to subversive propaganda, and half a dozen or so were talking quietly into handsets. The power of numbers, which had seemed so benign a minute ago, suddenly began to scare Iris.

And Troy wasn't done yet. 'And the last piece of the puzzle? This same outfit owns Planet Plenty. Yeah, that temple to purity and wholesomeness that's busy invading your high streets, where you get a halo going in, and your wallet flattened going out. It's just another money-spinning scam, feeding on greed and vanity. And all their trucks are fuelled by CleanTech.'

Anger in the faces around Iris was temporarily supplanted by confusion. Surely Planet Plenty, the all-organic supermarkets, had to be good guys? Troy carried on, savouring their discomfiture. 'Yeah. And it's all working out so well, they're relocating to London. This very day, they're gonna turn millions of dollars of profit on their stock. And why London? Because this city is like the Wild West. There's so little regulation here, they can get away with shit that would be illegal most anywhere else.'

The police began, very gradually, to move inwards, tightening the cordon around the demonstrators. Scattered cries of 'Kill the bastards!' and 'Capitalist scum!' popped from the crowd. Even from Arlo, still at Iris' side but red-faced and breathing hard, his fists clenched.

Troy raised his own hands, in a final, climactic appeal to the crowd. 'So I ask you, how many more lives have to be lost to feed our greed? How much more of our precious earth has to be raped and ruined, before the world takes notice? And how about us, here, today? Are we just going to stand by and let them get away with it? Are we? Or are we going to help Ignacio and his children to live their lives in freedom?'

The police began to look at each other. One or two reached for their batons. Suddenly Iris noticed the time. 'Christ. Ted. Come on Arlo, I can't be late, it's the first time he's let me pick him up since he stopped being ashamed of me. Here, you need to unload those placards.'

She tugged at Arlo's arm. He didn't move. Tears were streaming down his face as he gazed up at his father, still in the full flood of oratorical frenzy.

Iris shouted into his ear. 'Look, I'm not turning up at the school gates with a bunch of anti-corporate propaganda sticking out of my back window.' She wasn't going to tell him about the trip to Niketown. 'The car's just here, you can dump them on the pavement if you like, it'll only take a minute.'

She yanked hard at his backpack. Finally, reluctantly, he came with her. They pushed through the crowd to where the little egg sat just outside the barricades.

As she unlocked it, a roar erupted behind them. Arlo and Iris turned to see the huge black glass doors swing open, and a phalanx of sleek, dark-suited men stride out towards a convoy of waiting limousines. Smiling defiantly, they paused only yards from the demonstrators, and the man at the centre, the tallest and sleekest of all, turned to his neighbour and shook hands, before bringing out a sheet of paper with '£18.74' printed on it, in big letters. He held it out, right at the crowd. They knew all about the protest. And they didn't care.

Arlo gasped, and yelled: 'I don't believe it! That's the stock price - they're shoving it in our faces! The bastards!'

'Come on, I'm going to be late!'

She dragged Arlo back towards the car. As he reached for the placards, he saw something in the back. Big, squidgy and creamy. Too late, Iris read his mind.

'No!' She tried to grab it from him, but he already had the cake in both hands, as he turned and rushed back into the crowd. She shouted after him: 'Stop it! That's Troy's! Stop that boy, somebody!'

But Arlo was unstoppable. The crowd parted in front of him like the Red Sea as he ran, the huge shining cake in front of him. Iris had no choice but to run behind, trying somehow to grab his arm and get it back. She was right by him as he got within range - and within sight of his father.

As Iris made one last desperate grab for the cake, Arlo shoved her back with one hand, and lobbed the cake on its silver board with the other, straight at the alpha male. For a bizarre second the Zoom boss seemed to have grown a giant silver head. A gasp whooshed through the crowd. Then a cheer. Then the cake board dropped away, leaving the boss, and most of his colleagues, covered in praline buttercream and caramel fudge.

Thank God there were no news crews here, thought Iris. No incriminating footage. Nobody had expected a company flotation to attract this sort of thing.

But it was all the excuse the police needed. No more cheery banter now. They squared up, tightened in, got out their truncheons, and charged. Iris grabbed Arlo by the sleeve. 'Come on, idiot! This way!'

They got to the egg, jumped in and roared away, as the melee erupted behind them. Iris' fury erupted. 'For God's sake, why did you have to do that? That cake was for your dad's celebration tonight! What's he going to do now? What a damn stupid idiot infantile...'

And what am I going to do for Ted's boots? I'll have to give the money back now. I knew I should have gone to get them yesterday. Damn. Damn.

Not to mention a waste of a good cake. I might as well have bought a pie at Tesco.

Arlo meanwhile seemed to have relapsed into some kind of reactive shock. He'd thrown his backpack onto the back seat and was rocking back and forward, tugging at his ears and wailing. 'Fuck, I really did it this time. Man, what a fucking idiot! What'll I do now?'

'Oh for God's sake. Get a grip. You should have thought of that before, you bloody fool.'

Until now she'd been driving more or less at random, just to get away. Judging that they'd come far enough, she pulled in at the corner of a leafy square, and stopped the car. 'Get out.'

'I can't! You don't get it, Iris, they'll be looking for me everywhere!'

It seemed a bit of an overreaction. Inflicting public humiliation was no doubt emotionally scarring, but not, so far as Iris knew, a criminal offence. It seemed unlikely that a major police operation would be centred on its perpetrator.

'Just get out for one minute and help me dump your bloody placards.'

Still whimpering, he pulled his hood over his face and handed her the placards to throw into an overgrown corner of the square. Then he turned to get back into the car.

'I gotta go underground. It's my only chance.'

'Well, that's not a problem. You can go underground right now, right over there where that sign says Warren Street'. And before he could protest, she opened the door, shoved him out, and urged the egg at top speed towards Gordon Road Primary.

Of course, Ted was already waiting for her outside the school, and of course Elaine was hovering over him. 'At last! We had no idea where you were, and I didn't know what to do. Poor little Ted's always welcome to come home with us you know, Iris, if things are getting on top of you with the – consultancy, was it?'

Elaine peered into the car at her, and for the first time Iris noticed there were dobs of praline back-splatter all over her tee shirt. Also that Arlo had left his backpack in the back seat. Elaine appraised the car. 'Nice to see you driving again Iris. That bicycle was a noble gesture, but it's hardly practical with the children, is it?'

'Come on Ted, let's get you some tea. Thanks Elaine, see you soon I'm sure'. And almost before Ted had time to climb in, Iris whoomphed away at a speed no egg had ever achieved before.

'That was a long day for one delivery. Where were you taking your cake – the Isle of Wight? Here you go Ted. I got you these. I don't think your Mum'll mind, when she sees them.'

'Sees what? What's in that box?' Iris noticed that Malcolm, still wearing his suit, looked very like the men she'd just been yelling at. Worse, the box he was holding out to Ted could only contain shoes. He turned to Iris. 'That meeting I told you about. Went well. Come on, let's have a look.'

He pulled off his tie and waited as Ted tugged at the lid. They watched his face, wildly elated, as he opened it. Then it fell, just a little, as he saw what was inside.

There, nestling in the tissue, were the football boots Iris had found for Ted on the ReBorn site. The rubber-tyre soles, the artisan hemp uppers - the swoosh?

Ted saw it at the same moment. 'AwRight! Thanks Dad! Nobody's got these yet!'

Malcolm looked over the box at Iris, and handed her the other shoe. 'Same traditional happy peasants, same quaint artisanal village, making the same shoes from the same materials in the same way – only they're making them for Nike. Just another niche, after all. Everybody happy now?'

The one thing she'd been looking forward to. The proof that she could live virtuously, and still be a loving parent. And Malcolm had beaten her to it. Iris took one look at Ted ecstatically clamped to his father, muttered something about changing, and fled upstairs, still clutching Arlo's backpack.

Half way up, her phone beeped. A video message from a number she didn't recognise. She opened it. A fuzzy but perfectly recognisable image of her, Arlo, and the cake, as it hurtled towards its target. Shit! Who'd done that? Who had her number? She hit 'reply' but it just said 'no number'. She ran into her room, closed the door and threw the backpack onto the bed.

The backpack squirmed.

Wriggling out of her tee shirt, Iris stared at it. She wasn't mistaken. It was moving. Bulges appeared and disappeared around its seams, and the buckles creaked. She pulled on a clean shirt, delicately approached one buckle, and edged it open. A beady eye looked out at her, and a red tongue flickered through the opening.

That's all I need...

'Mum! Mum look what they look like on, can I show you Mum?' Ted was already thundering up the stairs.

'I'll be right down - just hang on...' Somehow, she'd got away with today so far. Nobody within these walls knew that she hadn't spent it in the kitchen, baking. She just needed to hang on to her sanity for a couple more hours. And hide a snake.

She picked up the backpack, keeping as much of Pepita inside as she could, darted across the landing to the airing cupboard, and hurled it in.

Snakes like warm places. She'll be fine there until I can get her home. I just need to make sure that's soon.

She trotted back downstairs, once more the perfect wife and mother. Ted's delight in his boots melted her resentment. As she cooked, Malcolm switched on the News. 'And finally...'

Iris gave the sauce a final stir. 'Here we go, perfect timing, I'll just drain the pasta.'

'...and finally, something not often seen at a City share flotation...'

Iris gagged on her wine and slammed down the pan. She heard Troy's unmistakable battle-cry, the roar of the crowd, the threatening murmur of the police... How had this happened? How had it got onto the national news?

'Supper time!' She dashed over, grabbed the remote and stood between Malcolm and the screen. No TV crews had turned up for the protest, but then thousand phone cameras were charged and ready. By a pure fluke, in the shot they had only her arm was visible, desperately struggling to restrain Arlo. The video played back in slow motion, every ghastly moment reviving itself in her memory.

'Come on everybody, nothing nastier than cold pasta!' She tried to switch it off, but Malcolm grabbed back the remote, unaccountably fascinated. 'Christ. No wonder it was all cordoned off.' He peered in for a closer look. Iris was too rattled even to wonder how he'd known about the cordons. She wrestled the remote back from him. Calm down, Iris. It could have been anybody's arm. And anybody's cake. Just keep your head, and nobody will ever know.

Iris waited until Malcolm was deeply asleep before venturing downstairs to the fridge. The Porkinsons were more or less thawed out, but she gave a couple of them a blast in the microwave, on the basis that a warmed-up raw sausage would probably taste more freshly-killed to a boa constrictor. If Pepita was hungry, she'd eat it.

She opened the cupboard door a crack. The backpack was empty. Her heart jumped, until she saw that Pepita had wrapped herself round the hot water outlet from the boiler. Iris held a sausage out in the direction of the head. A tentative flicker, and it was gone. As she waited to make sure it didn't come up again, she got out her phone. She needed to get rid of the bloody snake, before it decided the setup at 26 Hartland Gardens was too cushy to leave.

She checked the time - not yet midnight. Let's hope Sammy hadn't gone underground, too.

'Hello?'

Thank God. 'Sammy – it's Iris.'

'What? Who?'

Iris crept over to shut the bedroom door, and raised her voice from a whisper to a hiss. 'It's IRIS'.

'Oh. Hi. Hey wasn't it fab today?' Sammy's yell seemed to come from the production floor of a pre-war machine tool factory. Behind her were deafening thumps and whoops, punctuated by the odd scream.

'I don't know. Was it? Where are you?'

'Yeah well – you know, we showed the buggers didn't we? Didn't you see it all over the news? And all thanks to you. If it hadn't been for your cake...'

'To be honest, if I'd known it was going to end up there, I'd have...'

'What? It's a bit loud here, sorry.'

'Where? Where are you?'

'Troy and Ignacio's party, yeah? Ace caipirinhas. Why aren't you here? Come on down.'

'Didn't they get arrested?'

'What? Oh. Nah. Ignacio's a diplomat, yeah? They couldn't touch him.'

'Sammy, is Arlo there? I really need to speak to him.'

'Arlo? Hey! It's Iris! Can you... What? Slow down... you what?...'

Iris held the phone away from her ear for a moment's respite and massaged Pepita's throat, down which the sausage was slowly progressing.

'Iris? You there? Can you hear me? Sorry - no, he's being a bit weird to be honest (you what? Okay, got it.) Iris, you still there? He says the entire CIA will be looking for him, they've got access to every CCTV camera and every mobile phone circuit in the country, and he can't be seen in daylight. I think that's about it. Oh, and he can't talk to you, and you must forget you ever knew him.'

'That's ridiculous. Anyway, even if he won't talk to me, I've got his snake.'

'His what? Really? How come?'

'He left his bloody backpack in the car. I can't keep her here, nobody knows where I was today. Look, how about I bring her round to the shop in the morning? She's had her supper, I expect she'll live till then, and you can get her to Arlo, wherever he is.'

'What's that? (Oh, why not bugger it, go on then, cheers guys) Sorry, hang on, I'm moving...'

The background noise faded enough for Iris to make out the rest. 'Iris? Yeah, so we had the Health and Safety people round today, Planet Plenty got the Council to send round the inspectors. INSPECTORS!! Y'know like, the Stasi? They nearly shut us down, apparently we were infringing thirty-two EU directives without even trying. Look, I'll talk to him okay? I'm sure in a day or two he'll have you know, chilled a bit and we can do something. Okay? Sure you can't...?'

The phone cut out. Iris stared at it, too tired to think. Then, with Pepita wrapped around the boiler-pipe, contemplating a luxurious future of pre-digested meals, she staggered back to bed.

Unfortunately, although Iris had remembered to get rid of the evidence smeared all over her tee shirt, she had forgotten that Malcolm, unlike most people, regarded his car as an extension of his pristine and well-ordered domestic environment, and not as the core of a mysterious time warp where you're still fifteen, or in other word, a pigsty.

At six-forty-five the next morning, which seemed to Iris about one minute after she'd finally fallen asleep, she was vaguely conscious of somebody getting up, and responded in the only rational way, by pulling all of the liberated duvet over her head.

At seven o'clock Malcolm, washed, dressed and humming happily, removed the vacuum cleaner from the airing cupboard and took it down to the car. It was a bit heavy, but as nobody else ever emptied it, he assumed this was just several weeks of Ted and Molly's lives, compacted into a sticky grey mass.

At seven-ten he connected the extension cord from the socket by the front door, plugged it in, switched it on, and watched it spring into surreal, furious life, and hurl itself out of his hands onto the pavement. Being a calm and rational soul, he switched it off at the mains and waited until it had writhed and hissed itself into calm, before he disconnected the hose and peered warily inside.

'MUM can you make my toast stripey and not all the butter melted in?' Ted yelled the same breakfast order down the stairs every morning.

'Ted, you know, I bet if we wired you up to the mains you could cook your own toast just by shouting at it.' Iris was aware, as she smothered the offensively melted butter in raw sugar marmalade, that somebody seemed to have come in through the front door behind her, and was standing there, looming. She felt him looming, way before she heard him say: 'Were you intending at some point to inform the rest of the household that there was a dangerous reptile in the vacuum cleaner?'

Iris managed to drop the toast onto Ted's plate, rather than the floor, before turning round, nerving herself to stay calm. 'Dangerous? In the vacuum cleaner? Oh, the snake. How did she get in there? How smart of her, I suppose it is a bit like a cave, with, you know, a tunnel leading into it.'

Malcolm stood there, the vacuum in one hand and the other holding, warily and at arm's length, an undulating and rather dusty snake.

Iris glanced at them and turned her attention to the coffee and hot chocolate. 'You didn't switch it on, did you? She wouldn't have liked that, not after she'd crept in to feel safe.'

'Of course I bloody switched it on, it doesn't work by auto-suggestion. The snake is fine. I just want to know what it's doing in my house?'

'Ted, your toast is ready, and there's a lovely surprise for you here.' Iris had had a few moments to come up with something plausible. 'I'm just, you know, snake-sitting it. It's a LETS thing. Like the cakes. I look after the snake for a few days, and in exchange...'

'...in exchange, your husband dies a natural death at a conveniently early age so you can collect on the life insurance.'

'You don't have life insurance.'

'I'm beginning to think I should.'

'Mum, I don't like soy milk, I told you last night.... DAD! DON'T MOVE! It's all right but there's a...'

'Don't worry, Ted, your mother's finally found a use for the vacuum cleaner.'

'Hey! Cool! Can I feed it Mum? If it's a Boa Boa it'll need fish and birds, but I think that's a Boa Amaralis from Bolivia, we might have to get some guinea fowl chicks...'

'The snake's only here for a day or two, and so far she seems very happy with Porkinson's. Come here, Pepita, Malcolm can't drink his coffee and wear you at the same time. Ted, you just try this new soy milk, it's utterly different I promise, and anyhow I've made it into hot chocolate, just for a treat.'

Iris uncoiled the snake from Malcolm and made for the stairs. He picked up his coffee, looked at it warily, and took a sip. Apparently it was acceptable. 'Before we get too comfortable, is the rest of your family allowed to know what other predatory life-forms are sharing the local eco-system? Any piranhas in the toilet cistern? Tarantulas in the bathtub?'

'Don't be silly. MOLLY, triple chemistry this morning, another chance to blow up the school!'

'That wasn't soy milk, was it?'

Iris was still wearing the snake round her neck, and at first she thought the hissing was Pepita making conversation. 'Well − strictly speaking, no. But you saw how they reacted to the semolina pudding. At least, I have to assume you saw. Being ubiquitous and all.'

'So you're still hoping to save your entire species from self-destruction, but you can't muster the nerve to wean your own family off milk?'

'Look, I don't like to make a point of this, but it's not as though you've ever had much experience of eating and drinking, is it? I mean, anybody who can think wine and wafer biscuits are the same as blood and raw human flesh...'

'If you know enough to know that, you'll also no doubt remember that I took carnal form for a number of years. I seem to remember the meze were rather good in Old Jerusalem... and there was that delicious bread and fish beside the Red Sea...'

'Yes, well, if I could work miracles, I'd make soy taste like something actually intended for human consumption. But unfortunately, not having been given miraculous powers to go with my rather heavy calling, I have to rely on a bit of ethical gymnastics. If I tell them this Extra Creamy Organic Guernsey milk is soy, and they like it, then they'll go round telling everybody else how delicious soy milk is, and the vegan cause will have a whole lot of new converts, won't it?'

'I see. That's a new one. Tell me, I've forgotten – were you raised by Jesuits?'

Bearing in mind Pepita's change in diet, and the unpredictable effects it might have on her digestion, Iris removed all but the oldest towels from the airing cupboard before putting her back by the warm pipe. She was just removing the vacuum cleaner, which was clearly too tempting a sanctuary, when her phone rang.

'Hello? Iris?'

'Arlo, thank God, don't go anywhere, you're not going anywhere are you?'

'I just spent the last twelve hours looking for a public phone, and I'm not planning on staying in Enfield longer than I need. Can you call me right back?'

He gave her the number and she dialled it. 'Why do you need a public phone? Nobody uses them but crack dealers, do they? And English Heritage members, making a stand, of course. But they only use the red ones.'

'I told you, Iris, things are tricky for us now. Those bastards from Zoom International complained to the Home Office and they're rushing in a whole bunch more anti-protest laws. Even Uncle Joe never took socialism this far. There's still over a hundred people locked up, just for being on the demo.'

'That's not good.'

'Yeah, so we're mounting a protest against it. A protest against the infringement of our right to protest. You can still protest against not being allowed to protest, if you do it like, individually. So we're gonna test that. Hundreds of us, all protesting individually, but like, randomly happening to be in the same place.'

'What, so like an anti-anti-protest protest?'

'Yeah – I guess. Next week. But don't tell anybody, at all, right?'

Iris paused to wait for the front door to close behind Malcolm. A terrible thought had struck her. 'So – this new law, and these guys in prison. Is it - kind of - our fault?'

'No, jeez, not at all, you were amazing, look at all that publicity it got us. Anyways, it was me who threw it, right?'

'It was my fault. I made the bloody cake.'

'Well you know man, water under the bridge.'

'Yes. Thanks. Anyhow, the thing is you've probably missed Pepita by now, you left her in the car. Can I bring her to you? Are you still in the yurt?'

'The yurt? No, I'm, like I said, kinda virtualised you know? Just till it all dies down?'

'So if you're virtual, how do I get the snake to you?'

'It's a problem.'

They sat in silence for a few seconds, on the virtual and concrete ends of the phone. 'Hey. I got it. We've got a non-violent resistance training before the protest. One day next week.'

'Which day?' She knew the answer before she heard it 'Tuesday? Yeah, Tuesday. You could meet us there and get your training in at the same time. If you're still up for it, that is. Like you said, I mean I guess you are kinda – implicated. In a way.'

'Oh, shit... I do have something on next Tuesday...'

Iris stood there with the phone, contemplating yet again the mysterious conjunctions of human stupidity and blind chance. If only Ted hadn't wanted new football boots - if only she hadn't been so determined not to let Malcolm get them. If Troy hadn't been such a gut-bucket, and if Arlo hadn't been so desperate to impress his Dad... Now, it appeared, she faced an indefinite future of criminal activity, in the cause of a distant country she'd barely thought about until yesterday.

Tuesday was, of course, Ted's show. But it was happening at three-fifteen, at the end of the school day, in order to hijack the maximum possible audience. This thing of Arlo's was only a training day, and she hadn't committed to the protest, so she didn't really need to do the training. She could just meet him there, do the swap, and flee. She could be over to Hackney and back in plenty of time, so long as she got everything finished first. And then the bloody snake would be gone.

'Iris? You still there?'

'What? Oh, yes. Yes, okay, I'll make it work. I'll have to. I'll be there.'

On Tuesday morning Iris waved goodbye to Ted at the school gates, confident that, with both the polar bear and the phytoplankton packed and ready alongside Pepita, she'd be back from her errand in plenty of time to sit in the front row, weeping enjoyably with maternal pride.

'You'll be there right, Mum? Not late or embarrassing or anything?'

Blithely, she looked Ted in the eye and smiled. 'Nothing would keep me away, my sweet.'

'Promise?'

'Promise!'

Iris finally located the non-violent resistance workshop via a grubby piece of paper blu-tacked to the door of a disused dairy, which also housed a disability arts centre and a cross-cultural counselling practice. Mysterious groans and cries issued from several of the doors she passed, but the one she pushed open revealed nothing more menacing than a small group of people, unwinding scarves and unpeeling dayglo cycle vests. More sad blobs of blu-tak stained the walls, and a couple of plants were expiring silently by the window.

'Right. Let's all start by sitting in a circle, shall we, and find out who we all are and why we're here?' The man speaking had a Hapsburg beard and an oddly bulging bottom, but otherwise seemed fairly sane. No sign of Arlo as yet. He'd phoned again that morning to confirm the rendezvous, but still sounding panicky, and making a great thing about how they'd have to be fast, which suited Iris fine. Meanwhile there was nothing for it but to park Pepita, on whom Parmesan cheese had turned out to have a useful opiate effect, in her backpack on a chair by the wall, and join in.

'My name is Wayne, and I'm here to make sure that all of you know exactly what you're getting yourselves into tomorrow.' Wayne turned his head and smiled encouragingly at the girl next to him, who carefully made eye contact with everybody else in the circle before whispering: 'I'm Liz. I'm here because I've been reading prison diaries since I was about fifteen, so it's sort of, you know, a bit of a long-held dream. Getting arrested. And of course, I thought I might as well do it in a good cause.'

'Very good. Chas?'

Chas was in a wheelchair, decorated with a novelty number plate, a pair of Y-fronts saying 'Make Tea not War' and a clown's scarlet rubber klaxon. His response to Wayne's question was to squeeze his klaxon right into Iris' ear, before slithering, with astonishing speed, out of his chair, and into the tiny cavity between the wheels.

'I think Chas just showed us his new strategy for resisting arrest. Right, Chas?'

Two squirts on the klaxon from Chas, whose grinning face was now looking up Iris' skirt, not making it any easier to formulate an excuse for her presence that wouldn't involve live snakes and callous fellow-travelling. But all eyes were on her, so she had to say something. 'Well, I was at the Zoom International thing the other day and...'

'Ooh, so was I, bastards aren't they?'

'Strictly speaking, Sonja, that was an interruption. But I think we can all excuse you, given what's got us here today.' If you ignored what he said, Wayne had a very nice voice. Relaxed, but sure of itself. He looked around the circle. 'I don't need to remind anybody here that this so-called government of ours – no, Chas, I know you don't buy into the notion, so I'm just using it as a shorthand here, all right? – they've spent the last ten years eroding our civil rights., with three thousand new criminal offences, plus two hundred and sixty-six excuses to kick your door in, including "checking for foreign bees", "inspection of high hedges", "offences related to stage hypnotism", and "surveying the seal population" '

A giggle went round the circle. Wayne looked at them gravely, and the giggling stopped. 'Sounds like a joke, yeah? But it's no bloody joke at four a.m., I can tell you. Who here's been raided?'

Sonja's hand went up, and Chas blasted his klaxon, twice, which Iris suspected of being pure bravado. What police officer in her right mind would want to deal with him at four in the morning?

'So you know what I'm talking about, yeah? But what all this new legislation says to me, it says this government is scared. And what's scared them? They've realised that a few guys, ordinary guy...' he caught Sonja's reproachful look and corrected himself '...persons like us here, determined and sticking together, can be a formidable force. Think about all the great advances in civil rights in this country. Who can think of one?' He looked encouragingly around the circle. Liz ventured: 'Votes for women?'

'Very good.'

Other voices chimed in: 'Abolition of Slavery!' 'Universal education?' 'Free Speech' 'Er, would bus passes count?'

Wayne held up a long, tapered hand, like a saint on an icon. 'Right on. And you know guys, none of that started with government. Ministers don't wake up in the morning and think, "I know, we'll just give the poor and dispossessed a helping hand". Trade unions, workers rights, freeing the slaves – none of it would have happened if people hadn't got together and said, "Enough! No more!" And kept on saying it, until they won.'

He looked around the circle, charged with calm determination. Iris, in a dawning sense of shame, had almost forgotten about Arlo. Here she was, in a circle of twenty strangers whom, only half an hour ago, purely on the frivolous basis of their clothes and personal grooming, she'd dismissed as pathetic saddos. Yet surely this was what Soren's message had really been about. Not the trivia of grocery shopping, or switching from one form of personal transportation to another. These people were way above all of that. They were out to change history.

Iris rummaged back to her history GCSEs. How many Tolpuddle Martyrs were there? Not more than the people sitting round her now. Would they have shopped at Abercrombie and Fitch, or spent hours every day tweezing their nose hair? Unlikely. Nor had the Pankhursts worried much about gentility when they were being force-fed in prison. If it hadn't been for civil disobedience, she, Iris Richie, wouldn't be able to vote, to own the half of 26 Hartland Gardens that contained the nice pillows and the toasted sandwich-maker, or even to drive the car that had brought her here. What was that quote about 'all it takes for evil to take over the world is for the good people to do nothing'?

Was she going to be one of those good people, doing nothing?

After her vow, and after getting this far?

By one-fifteen, Iris was tightly entwined between Liz and the saintly Sonja in a non-violent circle of support, while Wayne tutored them from the sidelines.

'Okay. Now we're going to practise being carried off by the arresting officers. And before you begin, here's a little tip. '

He turned round, and for one terrible moment Iris thought he was about to take his trousers down. But all he did was reach round and pull two inches of corrugated cardboard out from the waistband of his sweat pants. 'You might want to consider stuffing something down here, for when you're being dragged off. Animals at the abattoir get better handling, I can tell you. Now, who wants to be carried off first?'

At the mention of 'animals', Iris' other life suddenly flashed back, with an image of Ted, waiting for his costume. At the same moment, the door opened and Arlo appeared, looking distinctly jumpy. Wayne smiled a welcome. 'Better late than never. You can be our arresting officer. Who wants to be arrested first?'

'Me! Me!'

Arlo saw Iris, looked relieved and padded over to her. She nodded at the backpack and muttered at him. 'Quick, we're being arrested. Arrest me and drag me over there, the snake's on that chair, see? You can arrest me out of the door, nobody'll notice.'

To Liz and Sonja's evident disappointment, Arlo had no difficulty in separating Iris from them. He grabbed the backpack, and they were making for the door when a mighty crash splintered it inwards, and twenty men in black suits and Balaclavas burst in, wearing helmets and riot shields, and strung with about ten tonnes of precision-made annihilation technology. 'Police! Freeze! Who's in charge here?'

As any pianist climbing the stage for her first live performance of a Rachmaninov concerto will attest, there is a vast chasm between rehearsal and reality, which only the latter reveals. All the careful groundwork of the last three hours melted into chaos, as Chas tried to dive under his chair backwards, and Liz and Sonja struggled furiously to work out whether their hands were supposed to be crossed in front or behind. Somebody yelled, 'Is it stiff or floppy that makes you heavier?' and somebody else yelled, 'Don't struggle, you'll be resisting arrest!'

None of them seemed to have noticed that, with the arsenal of a small African nation on their persons, the police didn't actually need to do anything but stand around and watch the turmoil around them.

But behind Wayne's handy flip-chart of do's and don'ts for successful direct actions, Iris spotted the back door. It didn't look locked. It wasn't apparently guarded. It was worth a try. Anything was worth it, to keep her promise to Ted.

Arlo had picked up the backpack and slung it over her shoulder. Iris grabbed his hand and made a run for it. They wrenched the door open. They were out! No, they were almost out, when a hand landed on her shoulder and wheeled her forcefully around. 'What have we here? Aha! I thought so. We've met before haven't we?'

'Don't be ridiculous, why on earth would I... and her voice tailed off, as she found herself looking up into the sardonic face of the Special Branch's own Detective Sergeant Bathurst.

The holding pen of the police station had all the charm of a chiropodist's waiting room, and all the distractions of a blank envelope. It was already two fifty-three when the avuncular constable checked Iris in. 'I'm going to need that phone, if you don't mind, madam.'

'You can have it just as soon as I've...'

'Now, please.' Not so avuncular after all. Iris miserably handed it over.

'Can you make a phone call for me, then? Please? Only it's my son, it's his class show and I promised absolutely I'd be there, and...'

'Not right now I'm afraid. I'll see about it later. If I get the time.' He began writing her details down, very slowly. Eventually, he looked up, and Iris flashed her most innocent, 'There's been a silly mistake here' smile. 'It's really important. How long do you think this will take?'

'Well, first I have to check you in, and then you have to wait to be processed, and there are currently...' He squinted over to the number screen suspended from the ceiling. '...thirty-five people ahead of you. Another busy day, I'm afraid. The criminal fraternity are an industrious little lot. Four hours maybe? Five?'

'Oh no! It can't! I've got to...'

'You should have thought of that, madam, before you engaged in acts of an illegal and subversive nature. Now if you'd just go and take a seat over there for me; I'm afraid you're going to be here for some time.'

Iris sat as far away as she could from the rest of the Resisters. All the passionate conviction she had felt for their principled idealism had melted into nothing beside the reality that she'd deceived her family, abandoned her responsibilities and broken at least one solemn promise, to end up here. There were no magazines to read; not even a fish tank. Lacking even the mindless distraction of clearing old messages off her mobile, she had nothing to stem the flood of self-reproach. All she could do was watch the time pass, and imagine...

3.20

Even now Ted would be standing, a little way off from the others, an expression of bewilderment, still faintly tinged with hope, on his face. His Mum wouldn't break her promise to him, would she? Not in front of the whole school? And there would be Jack, talking loudly to the whole cast about Ted's loony Mum who always let everyone down...

4.20

After an hour going over the play, line-by-line, in her head, it would all be over. Ted would have missed his chance, his faith in his mother gone for ever. Never again, as long as they both lived, would he trust Iris, believe anything she said, run to her for safety and reassurance. Jack would be rubbing it in, taking out his own disappointment on Ted, and Elaine would be beside him, seething – or worse, gloating. Oh, horror; Elaine would probably take pity on Ted and sweep him off for an orgy of junk food, plasma TV and humiliation. After all the effort she'd put into those bloody claws!

5.20

By now Elaine would have called Malcolm, who'd probably

have had to leave a vital meeting with his new partners...

6.20

...and now she'd compounded her selfishness not only by letting down the boys, but making the whole family sick with worry. They had no idea where she'd gone; they wouldn't know where to start looking for her. Instead of giving Ted his tea in triumph and listening to a final iteration of his lines, she'd taken away his glory, stolen his day, ruined his life.

7.20

The constable would probably never call. And if he did, Malcolm would probably refuse to come and get her. Why should he? Come to that, how could he? Oh Christ, the car...

8 20

...given where the car was parked, by now it was undoubtedly stripped to the chassis, and quite possibly torched as well. Unless some enterprising youth had found a way to hot-wire the electric motor and was even now ghost-riding round the council estates, spraying expletives over the pristine upholstery and urinating in the Bluetooth cradle.

9 20

God, I'm hungry. Forget corrugated cardboard, if I ever get out of this place I'm texting Wayne to advise edible trouser padding from now on. Twenty or thirty of Elfrieda's life-denying muesli bars down my trousers would have been a lot more use...

At ten fifteen, the next shift of desk officers finally booked Irene, with the joyful news that she might, or might not, be allowed out, assuming somebody could be found to stand bail for her, and she might, or might not, be fined up to a thousand pounds for resisting arrest, not to mention whatever she turned out to know about the dangerous international terrorist accompanying her at the time of her arrest..

By eleven, she was in a cell, trying to eat a cold, naked baked potato, under the scrutiny of a female duty officer hunched over a particularly delicious looking plate of Chicken Tikka Masala.

She had just got to sleep at two-forty-seven when the lights snapped on, and the officer returned to report that, as requested, they'd phoned her husband, who was not best pleased and told her he'd come and bail her out after he'd got the children up, fed and off to school, and re-rescheduled the meetings he'd had to miss yesterday and had already re-scheduled for this morning.

'Those were his words' she finished, reading from her pad. 'Now be a good girl and get some sleep. This is no place for the likes of you.'

The last sentence, in a more robust form, was more or less what Malcolm said when he turned up to collect her next day. The relief of being free and outside was only slightly dulled by the humiliating intelligence that they hadn't taken her seriously enough to press charges.

'It turns out they were after some American terrorist who was also in that place where you were doing whatever you were doing.' Malcolm had moved away from her, quite explicitly, when she'd leaned over for a kiss. He was speaking to her in the voice he normally deployed on the water company when they'd once again failed to turn up to read the meter. Calm, reasonable, but horribly, unmistakably cold.

It seemed fair enough to Iris, huddled miserably in her seat. 'Terrorist?'

'That's what they said; animal liberation, food contamination, that sort of thing. One of these direct action lunatics. Don't suppose you even knew who he was.'

'No. Well. I can't have done, can I?'

I thought I did. Can all that really be Arlo? So, how many other 'terrorists' are just sweet, dopey boys trying to live up to their Dad? 'I'm so sorry. And there's something else I have to tell you...it's about the... The car!'

There it was, shiny as the day it was hatched, parked on the yellow line right outside the cop shop.

'How did you...'

'Molly Googlemashed it, weeks ago. In case. There's a GPS sensor in the roof. She found it for me in about two minutes. But not in a part of town I'd ever want to visit again, if it can be helped. Could I request you maybe to move your future criminal activities a few rungs up the social scale, just for everybody's peace of mind?'

'I tried to call you right away but they took my phone. Oh god, my phone...'

Malcolm took it out of his pocket and threw it into her lap. 'It's probably bugged. You might want Molly to take a look at that, too.'

'You must have been worried sick...'

'On the contrary, I knew exactly where you were. Any time I need to locate you now, I just switch on BBC News 24.' He wasn't smiling. And there'd be worse facing her at home.

'Oh god, poor Ted. He'll never forgive me. Nor should he. But I'll make it up to him. I'll go and collect him from school and take him straight to - to Soccer World in Carnaby Street.' It was the worst sacrifice she could think of; worse than two tickets to a touring production of Les Mis. But no self-laceration, at this point, seemed too great.

'I don't think he'll be up to that. The poor thing's been in bed since lunchtime yesterday, with a raging temperature. He missed the show, and he's pretty miserable; I had to get Molly to stay back with him so I could pick you up.'

Suddenly the temperature in the car seemed to drop thirty degrees. Iris had imagined her son bewildered, publicly humiliated, frightened, shamed, and abandoned, but - ill? Feverish and delirious in his Chelsea-blue bed, tossing and turning, calling out in a feeble whisper to a mother who never answered, who had run off and forgotten he even existed...

Malcolm checked the rear view mirror, turned into Hartland Gardens, and continued in the same even tone. 'He said to tell you to leave him alone, and he never wants to see you again.'

from: Kateriina Toivonen, ktoivonen@freeflow.org
to: Malcolm Richie, mrichie@richiewinterbottom.co.uk

Good morning Mr Richie!

I am sorry you were not able to come to the meeting today. Please give a big hug to your little one. You are very lucky to have a beautiful family. I would give a lot of my so-called glamorous life for that!

Anyway, we have good news. The big bosses have given their official thumb-up for your visionary person-centred plan for our distribution centres. So the President has asked me to arrange a little treat to celebrate, where it will be a chance to meet some of my colleagues from our sister companies, and for us to have a little fun together. Because if life is all work and no celebration, we might as well be all dead, I guess you'd agree.

My office will send you the official notification, it will be next week, and please bring your wife. You have never told me much of her, but she must be a most remarkable person if she is married to you.

Many many congratulations, and I look forward to next week, VERY much. Please do make sure you can be there, this time.

K

Iris crept downstairs from Ted's room, which appeared to be barricaded from the inside. No amount of banging, pleading, apologising or cajoling had had any effect, except to elicit the muffled complaint that she was giving him a migraine, and had ChildLine called back yet?

If only she could talk to him and explain. Or even give him a hug. But she hadn't even seen his face. She could only torment herself by imagining the expression in his eyes; the wary, stony gaze of innocent trust destroyed.

The next time she went up, a sign was jammed in the door frame, on which was written, in Ted's half-formed scrawl, the single word 'FOOD'. Iris felt a flicker of relief. At least he was still prepared to accept nourishment from her. She went back upstairs with a plate of freshly-baked drop scones oozing jam and real butter, to find a new sign, 'DRINK'. So it continued all day, like the shrine of some especially finicky deity, with Iris as the votive pilgrim. At one stage she contemplated climbing the stairs on her knees, but there seemed little point unless Ted came out to witness it. By the time Malcolm got home, she was exhausted and beginning to be rather cross.

'Well, what did you expect?' Iris had sat down on the sofa beside him, but he shifted away and carried on watching 'Never Mind the Buzzcocks' over her head.

'What do you mean, what did I expect? It's not my fault that the police have turned into a bunch of goose-stepping thugs with no respect for the basic freedoms of the people they're supposed to be protecting.'

'They were protecting people. From you, or at least your dubious associates.'

'So, just because I care enough actually to try to do something to make the world better, that makes me a worse person than certain other people who spend their lives watching rubbish on TV?'

She felt his anger, but all he did was switch the TV off. In the sudden silence, Iris felt very tired, and very alone. 'I'm sorry.'

'I should think so.'

'Not for doing what I did, but for letting it interfere with Ted. And you.'

Except, how could it not? How are you supposed to achieve anything if you always have to stop to make tea?

But she didn't want another argument, about that or anything else. She snuggled into his shoulder, hoping he'd put an arm around her. He didn't, but this time at least he didn't move away. 'Anyway, if you're really sorry, there is one thing you can do for me.'

'Anything!'

'No, this time I mean it.'

'All right. What?'

'There's this do I have to go to, it's a work thing. You'll hate it, you have to be a corporate wifey, but it's with the new partners. I had to cancel a meeting with them this morning at short notice, and they've made it pretty clear that it's a three line whip this time, so...'

'So I don't have a choice. Okay.'

'And – don't be cross but...'

'But I'm not to say a word either. That goes with the corporate wifey territory, doesn't it? Shall I get a perm and a facelift while I'm about it?'

He put down the remote, carefully setting it perfectly parallel to the neat pile of magazines on the table, and sat back to scrutinise her. 'Now there's an idea. You could have done a plea bargain, and got a new face for nothing on witness protection.'

Thank God. A joke. Even if it was on her.

'It's a pity, you could have chosen anybody. Liz Hurley, say. I wouldn't mind her as a corporate wifey.'

He's always said he couldn't imagine fancying anybody more than me. I've really pissed him off now.

After another day of leaving offerings outside Ted's closed door, Iris calculated that he was eating about fifty percent more than when he was officially well, and it was time to stage an intervention. Exactly fifteen minutes after the large plate of scrambled egg and toast fingers had vanished into his room, Iris was able to ambush him in the bathroom. It wasn't the pleasantest place to negotiate a truce, but at least while he was actually sitting there, she knew she had his attention.

'I'm never going back to school again! You've ruined my life! I hate you!'

'Okay, well I guess I deserve that. But leaving aside your feelings for me, what are we going to do about your education? Or were you planning to spend your adult life sitting under a cashpoint, like Danny?'

'I can get a job. I can get a job at Game!'

'I think you'll find you need at least one degree from a good university for that. And probably a postgraduate diploma in transactional retailology as well.'

'Then I can do home schooling. Dad can teach me, he knows everything.'

'But Dad has to go to work. You'd end up being home schooled by me. I don't know anything about anything. Plus, you hate me.'

'Well then – then you can send me to a different school. A boarding school. With a football pitch and a rugby pitch and a cricket pitch and a swimming pool.'

'It would probably be cheaper to send me to live in a luxury hotel. But I wouldn't like that. Because I'd miss you.'

Ted screwed up his face for one final push, and glared at her. The bathroom, which was small, filled with an overpowering miasma.

Iris tried to speak without inhaling more than she absolutely had to. 'But, you know what? Why don't we spend some of that money on something more fun instead?'

'Like?'

'Like - if you go back to school tomorrow, I'll collect you afterwards, and we take you to Soccer World.'

'For real? In Carnaby Street?'

'In Carnaby Street. Careful!'

In his excitement he'd fallen over his trousers. Iris went to help him up, and found herself hugging him tightly. 'Oh Ted!'

'Oh Mum!'

'God, I'm so, so sorry, and I'll never let you down like that, ever again. Promise.'

'Can we stay as long as I like?'

'What, in here?'

'No at Soccer World, stupid.'

Ted's forgiveness being, by definition, only partial until the retailology had worked its magic, Iris was required to wait for him the next day, not at the school gates, but round the corner by the back entrance to Subway. But, to her amazement, the minute the gates clanged open he rushed up, arms open, schoolbag flapping, and dragged her back towards Gordon Road.

'Where are we going?'

'This way. It's quicker.'

Iris found herself escorted all the way through the playground, past the milling crowds of parents and children, through the hall, past Lost Property, and out again. Then he took her back through the playground, in by the kitchen, past the open door of the staff room, and through the Infants and the Nature Garden before emerging once again into the playground. She noticed that a lot of the children were staring, and whispering. And, more surprisingly, that Ted didn't seem to mind this one bit. He was about to embark on another circuit when she put a hand on his arm. 'I think, if we're to get any time at Soccer World, maybe we ought to set off fairly soon.'

'Oh. Okay. Bye Jack! Laters, yeah bruv?'

Iris waited until they were beyond range of Elaine's sonar. 'So am I forgiven then?'

'Maybe...' He couldn't contain it any longer. '...Everybody knows you were inside, for a whole night. Nobody's Mum's been inside. Jack's Dad was inside lots, before they got rich. But not his Mum.'

'Yes, that would be a surprise.'

'They think you're like Bad Girls.'

'Wow. Does that mean I can carry on doing it after all? What shall I do next, shall I rob a bank?'

His smile wavered. She squeezed his hand. 'It's okay. I think once is probably enough. It wasn't very nice. Oh look, isn't that Molly outside Costa's? It's so much harder to recognise her, now she wears all these different colours'.

Something about the way Molly swivelled away and hunched even lower over her phone made it clear that she didn't want their company. 'Come on Ted, we'd better hurry. It'll be closing in four hours.'

Molly was on the point of giving up and buying a double chocolate muffin to go, when Janos finally slung his frame over the chair beside her. From one moment to the next, her skirt suddenly seemed way too short, and her top totally the wrong green. The excited fizz she'd felt before had become a gross sweaty prickling all over.

Oh christ, I bet I stink.

She shuffled her chair a couple of inches away from his, and casually put down her phone. He looked at her, unhurried and in detail, before he spoke. 'Nice green. Sorry I'm late. Been here long?'

'God no. Just sat down like, this minute. D'you want, like, something?'

'Sure. I'll have one of those smoothie things. Yellow.'

How come boys get not to care how they look? And sprawl around with their legs open? Christ, I bet my bottom is huge in this skirt, I never checked. DON'T pull at it, DON'T! How did this ever seem like any kind of good idea? Just get it over and go.

'This smoothie, and an Orangina please. And...' Does he want a straw? Do I want a straw? Does a straw make me look cute and sassy, or like a baby with a dummy? Have I ever seen a boy drinking out of a straw? Why can't I remember?

Why is this Mcperson staring? Shit, you can see like, all my boobs in this. Quick, hold the drinks in front of it.

'Here you go. And a couple of straws.'

Molly breathed deeply and carried the drinks over, carefully handing Janos his without bending over. He looked up at her over it. 'A straw! Great! Like being a kid again. Did you blow bubbles when you were little?'

Oh, but those eyes, they're amazing. And his hair, it's like a million colours of gold, like a corn field or something. Oh, no, now he's smiling, I'm gonna lose it...

'Thanks. Hey, was it your Mum got nicked with that activist?'

Molly choked on her Orangina. 'Sorry, that didn't go on you did it? I am so beyond embarrassed by her. All that dreary ranting about the planet, like she's going to make any difference...'

'You kidding? It rocked. My old lady's idea of radical is a new haircut. She always been like that?'

'Oh. Well – I guess it's been a while, yeah. She got into all this way ahead of the herd. I got her into it, in a way. And I help her out, like with the technology. ID stuff, anti-surveillance ...'

'Oh yeah, you and the Special Branch. That's so wild. It was what I first noticed about you. Well...'

He's staring right at me! How can he DO that?

'...almost the first...'

So what's that all about? My tits? He's into tits? Is that like, weird? Just hold it right there. This I can just about deal with. Oh God, his foot, it's like, practically touching my leg on the chair. No more. Please.

'Yeah, so, I'm involved in GlobalCool. It's totally not gonna be like Live Earth. Like, can you believe they were gonna play Antarctica? How irresponsible is that, man? We're playing Darfur and maybe Afghanistan, to show it's all connected, yeah? Resources and war and climate? We're gonna power it all with these like giant solar arrays, which we leave behind afterwards for the people?'

'Cool. Who's the line up?'

'We've got the BareNaked Ladies, they've been neutral for like, four albums now.'

'Wow!'

'...and the Chilis, they funded an entire pineapple forest with their last CD. And you heard of Nick Cave? He was massive once. It's good to have a couple of old guys for you know, the press, cause they are too. So long as they're ex-junkies. So they can relate.'

A week, even a day - face it, half an hour ago – I'd have perforated my own eardrums rather than listen to the BareNaked Ladies or the Red Hot Chili Peppers. So why...

'So we've got like these ecoSWAT teams going round, collecting batteries and broken strings to like, recycle into jewellery? You could be in one of those? Or maybe even in charge of it? How about it – Molly?'

That's my name. Is it my name? It never sounded like that before. I should be so creeped out at this point. But...

'We could hang. You - and me. There's a meeting tomorrow. Hey, I gotta split. Just mail me, okay?'

Malcolm waited until the actual day to spring on Iris the news that the corporate event was an evening in a grim industrial park marooned between the goods yards behind Vauxhall, driving racing cards round a test track. 'I suspect you'll find it's mostly men.'

'Mostly?'

The image of the hell into which she was about to be plunged focussed on a new threat.

'Well, there is this Finnish woman. The one who sewed up the deal for me. Pretty high powered, in fact.'

Malcolm was pulling on a pair of aged khakis dating from the pre-Dog and Darner lunches, which extruded half a kilo of abdomen over his waistband. 'But she said dress casual, so I wouldn't worry, just wear something - casual.'

Iris scrutinised him, feeling that he might be interpreting 'casual' a little too liberally. Still, he was making reassuringly little effort for the Finn, whoever she might be. In that sense, the worse he looked, the better.

'The trousers are good. I'm not so sure about the socks – d'you remember, Ted gave you those? It was an offer on a Frosties pack.

Those squiggles are teeny tiny Tony the Tigers. Still, they're definitely casual.'

'I'm doing my best with the limited resources available. Had I not had to shell out the last vestiges of my savings on a new car, no doubt I'd be in top to toe Armani.'

I walked - or drove - right into that, thought Iris. She went to her half of the wardrobe and riffled the hangers. 'What should I wear d'you think? If she's a corporate type, "casual" will mean navy tailoring and trousers with flesh-toned pop socks, won't it?'

'I wouldn't be so sure'. He pulled on a baggy polo shirt, which more or less hid the bulge. Iris turned back from rummaging to watch him. What did that mean, 'I wouldn't be so sure?' Who was this Finn, and how come she hadn't been mentioned until – twenty-four minutes before they were due to meet? She moved over and casually adjusted his collar, as though expecting it to reek of Chanel. He looked at her. 'You are going to behave yourself today aren't you?'

'Like a Trappist postulant at her final vows. You won't even know I'm there.'

Malcolm's hints turned the interpretation of that one word 'casual' into a riddle as intractable as pineapple on pizza. A skirt seemed a good beginning, since there was no way she was going to be climbing in or out of cars, and people other than Malcolm had frequently observed that her legs, finally clear of bruises and toned by all those potato-lugging errands, were her best feature.

The problem arose with the top. 'Casual' clearly meant a simple, perfectly cut tee shirt, a staple in every properly-assembled wardrobe. The problem was that Iris' wardrobe had apparently been stirred together by a malevolent and colour-blind witch, into a soup of the too plain, too frilly, and too bright, and all blighted by at least one, not always large or obvious, stain. All of Molly's tee shirts were black and confrontational, and Ted's were – ah, hang on. There was that pack of plain white school ones she'd been going to take back because somehow she'd picked up the Age 14, while brooding on a particularly depressing news item. One of those would do.

So it was dressed thus, in a boy's round-necked tee shirt and her girly flats, that Iris was introduced to a Nordic goddess in custom-tailored white racing overalls, cut to show off every detail of a supermodel's body.

She loomed down at Iris, all dazzling hair, eyes and teeth, as a leopard might at a deer that had somehow strayed from the herd. 'At last we meet! Malcolm, you never told me she was so cute! I'm Katariina from FreeFlow. Come, I'm so excited, I can't wait for you to see the cars!'

'Oh, I love cars. Almost as much as Malcolm does.'

They set off down a long passage. Iris heard the growing roar of jostling engines and felt Malcolm's excitement building with it. He was just about keeping up with Katariina's loping stride, but Iris was forced to trot beside them, as Malcolm shouted over her head: 'Brilliant idea this – yours, I bet.'

'Yes, it was quite a stroke of luck. Our sister company is hoping to sponsor maybe a Formula 3 team next year. So they could offer us this little treat. I just adore driving these machines.'

Iris had expected this evening to be dull. But already it was shadowed by little clouds of foreboding. Less than five minutes in, Malcolm seemed like somebody else – hearty, jocular, ingratiating. Maybe it was just nerves; after all, this was at least partly about securing this job he obviously really wanted. Still, he seemed to Iris to be lavishing Kateriina with more enthusiasm than professional interest required, as he added: 'Well, you certainly look the part.'

'Yes, isn't this outfit fun? You know, Kimi Raikkonnen made me a present of it. Wasn't that sweet of him?'

'Kimi RAIKKONEN??!!' Malcolm stopped dead. Kateriina laughed, tossing her gleaming hair, and put an arm round him. Iris finally caught up with them, just as they set off again.

'Well of course, Kimi's an old family friend, all Finns more or less know each other. But he's really a sweetheart you know, celebrity just has not touched him one bit. Hey, you must come by when he's next over, wouldn't that be fun?'

'Just try to keep me away!' He looked round at Iris, apparently expecting her to share his joy at the prospect.

Kateriina looked round too. And down. And smiled kindly. 'And bring Iris, of course.'

Malcolm replied before Iris had a chance. 'Of course, we'd love that wouldn't we Iris? I read something really interesting he said once, about how the Finns make such good F1 drivers because they start skiing so young, d'you reckon it's true?'

As Kateriina launched into a lengthy and detailed analysis of the question, they pushed through a swinging double curtain of heavy rubber, emerging into the slanting glare of evening sunlight, and the deafening rev of the cars. The track was right ahead of them. Malcolm longed to jump right into the nearest cockpit, but Kateriina led them over to a complex of marquees just distant enough for shouted conversation. She ducked into the nearest one, where food and drinks were laid out on a table, below a giant plasma screen displaying the names and numbers of the drivers enrolled so far. At Kateriina's appearance, several waiters rushed up.

'Well, here we are. Soft drinks for the drivers, and whatever for everybody else. The schnapps is rather delish, we had a most enjoyable tasting last week. Oh look, how marvellous, here are blinis and our special Finnish caviar.'

She took one from the tray, opening her mouth to reveal more teeth than any human could possibly need, and chewed appreciatively on it, with a lot of action from a lithe pink tongue that somehow left her perfect lipstick unscathed. 'Mmm! You must try this Iris, this is something special. And also tell me a little about your children. I want to hear everything!'

Iris happened to be in the middle of deciding that there was such a thing as too special, and Finnish caviar was it, so Malcolm answered for her. 'Oh, I don't think I told you, one of them's grown a conscience, hasn't she, Iris? Our oldest, Molly. Signed up for some kind of celebrity green movement – of course it's not going to change anything, we know those showbiz events never do...'

Iris seemed to be in difficulties with her blini, which the others tactfully ignored.

'...but I'm rather proud of her idealism, I have to say.'

What now? Molly's 'grown a conscience' right under my nose, but it's her new pal Malcolm - Malcolm, the world's biggest cynic - she chooses to tell. And what's his response? Does he tell her she's wasting her time, remind her of her responsibilities, or advise her to hop down to the Greens and do her 'ranting' there? Apparently not.

Kateriina finished her blini, drained an espresso, and clapped Malcolm on the shoulder. 'So – shall we begin? I think there are people here from all our three divisions. Unfortunately the CEO got delayed, but he'll be along for dinner in an hour or so. We should commence with the test lap, it's a safety requirement, I'm afraid, such a bore but hey, what can you do! Iris, are you racing today?'

Am I interested in being strapped horizontally into a lethal, barely controllable machine that inhales oil by the barrel, solely for the purpose of careening round a track while half a dozen testosterone-charged strangers do their best to kill me?

Iris smiled sweetly back at Kateriina. 'Do you know, I think I'll pass for now, thanks all the same.'

Over in the pits, cars were being revved up by a posse of mechanics in navy overalls. Katariina put a hand on Malcolm's arm and squeezed it lightly. 'Well then, would you mind terribly if I borrowed your gorgeous husband? I have a suspicion he can give me a run for our money – or should I say his money, Malcolm? We'll be right back Iris, make yourself comfortable. You can keep an eye on him on the TV here. I have a feeling he'll turn out to be quite a goer!'

She took Malcolm's hand and set off. He kissed Iris briefly on the cheek, and headed happily towards the cars. Iris was left lurking below the plasma screen, which now showed a diagram of the track, with all the hot spots and danger zones marked in red. She wondered how much she'd mind Malcolm topping himself on a hairpin, and decided actually, not that much.

'Nasty double chicane over by the trees, I nearly lost it there last time.'

'That why you're not racing?'

'Nah, I'm leaving the kids to get over the excitement first.'

Two men had wandered up to the table and were helping themselves. The blinis had been replaced by fjord prawns the size of lobsters, and elegantly coiled herrings. They seemed to provoke the men into some sort of hierarchical eating contest, an impression reinforced by the volume at which they were shouting.

'So what's new and special with you?'

'Same old same old, cherchez le dosh. I've been looking at some of these green tech stocks, but the market's still a bit frothy for my tastes.'

'Oh, I dunno...'

Iris sidled closer. She shouldn't dismiss them out of hand. There must be City types who use their wealth for good. Maybe she could put in a word for Troy, and one of them would just reach into his pocket and...

'...I just look at it like everything else. You look which way the wind is blowing and follow it, yuh? Take a fr'instance...' He opened his mouth and shoved in two more prawns. '...the whole Third world is running out of water, yuh? So I'm going with Monsanto and their drought-resistant seeds. So long as they limit the supply, the price just keeps going up, yuh? Same thing with epidemics, cholera and typhoid are on the up all over Africa, so vaccine shares'll be thermonuclear in the next few years. Every cloud has a silver lining, yuh?'

The other man took the last three prawns and shoved them in, chewing messily as he raised the bid. 'Tell you what, the carbon market's come through this last wobble with a smile on its face. I've been making trading profits in the high twenties, low thirties all this year. No overhead of course. Money for old rope,.'

Using their wealth for good? These scumbags were worse than cockroaches. They weren't even worthy to clean the whiskers of a giant prawn, let alone shovel it down their throats.

Iris turned away, clenching her fists, as she thought of Ted - sweet, trusting Ted - consigning every penny he'd saved for months to bloodsuckers like this, laughing at his naivete even as they trousered his precious pennies.

The first man leaned across and finally noticed Iris, if only because she was between him and the mustard mayonnaise. 'Somebody's looking a bit queasy. One too many shots, yuh? Easily done.' He took about half a second to evaluate her, and decide there was no possible advantage, sexual or commercial, to be mined here. Iris swivelled round and looked him right in his fish-stinking face.

'Actually, I haven't drunk a thing.'

'Fair enough. So which division are you with?'

'Which what?'

There was a sudden roar and cheer, as a new phalanx of drivers approached the grid. Kateriina was in pole position, Malcolm third. They were both clearly set for the day. The camera caught Malcolm's face as he pulled the helmet over his head. Iris hadn't seen him look so blissful for years. At least, not with her.

She'd missed the answer to her question, and the men had turned away. She was feeling sick, and her head ached. Maybe there'd be an aspirin in the cloakroom.

There was no sign of an attendant, but a woman standing by the mirror looked friendly.

'Excuse me, you wouldn't have an aspirin or something, by any chance?'

The woman looked at Iris in the mirror and looked puzzled. Iris tried again. 'Sorry, do you speak English? Only...'

The woman reached up to her ears and pulled a foam plug from each of them. 'That's better. Golly, it's loud, isn't it? I can't stand this kinda thing. I'm more of a spiritual person, to me it's just more male hormones sprayed all over. Like we need that, huh? I had to be here for the Planet. I'm Suki.'

She shook Iris' hand. Hers was soft, cared-for, with perfect, unvarnished nails. Iris almost wept with relief. 'Really?'

'Yeah, I'm like their Awareness Auditor? We run checks on the health of every line in every store, every thirty minutes. I was at the flagship just yesterday and you know there was like, zero microbial flow over the greens, they were totally pure.'

'The Planet? Planet...'

A voice broke in, booming over the tannoy above the distant engine noise. 'Good afternoon, ladies and gentlemen. If you would like to take your seats for dinner, it will be served momentarily next to the pit lane.'

A silence descended, sudden and refreshing as rain, as the cars pulled in and the drivers clambered out, shaking out their legs and clapping each other's backs. Iris followed Suki, her brain racing now. 'The Planet', in the context of the purity of salad greens, could only mean Planet Plenty. What was Planet Plenty doing here?

Suki led the way to another marquee, where a big round table was spread with a chequered cloth. Iris found her place, next to Malcolm's. The place card on his other side said 'Kateriina Toivonen, FreeFlow Distribution'. That sounded harmless enough. Iris was moving to investigate the card on Kateriina's other side when she looked up to see Malcolm and Kateriina coming back, laughing, heads close together. As she watched, the two investors converged from the TV tent. Iris watched Kateriina introduce them to Malcolm, and Malcolm smile and shake their hands, swapping jokes.

He likes them, she thought. This is where he belongs. These people are the kinds of people he wants to spend his time with. I just never knew.

So what would he make of Sammy, or Arlo? He'd hate them. No, it's worse. He'd laugh at them.

As Malcolm and Kateriina approached the table, a tall figure in a dark suit intercepted them, putting a comradely arm around

Kateriina. Iris was too far away to hear what he said. She saw Malcolm shake this stranger's hand, too, apparently accepting congratulations. And then they turned, and came towards the table.

Iris felt the shock in her guts before she registered why. That perfect suit. That casual, arrogant gaze. That wing of raven hair, last seen clotted with crème patissiere.

It was the pie man. And he, and Malcolm, and Kateriina, were coming right towards her.

Iris jumped up and made for an empty place at the opposite side of the table. The card staring up at her as she sat, keeping her head down and her face hidden, said: 'CleanTech Energy Solutions: a division of Zoom International Ltd.'

Planet Plenty and CleanTech were part of the same operation. Troy had said so. Planet was the produce, CleanTech fuelled the trucks - so FreeFlow must be...

In the time it took to work this out, the others reached the table. Kateriina registered Iris' empty place, but hadn't yet seen Iris. There was still time; she could run, right now. She could – No, she couldn't. Kateriina had spotted her. She put a hand on the pie man's sleeve, and in that husky, unforced but surprisingly carrying voice, Iris heard her say: 'And over there is his wife, Iris.'

He looked across. He saw her. For a moment, the world stopped, as his memory worked. Then he smiled, held her gaze for an interminable moment, and turned to Malcolm. 'Well, Mr Richie, your wife and I have met before. I think I can say I would know her anywhere.'

His voice was like a surgeon's scalpel. 'And I would certainly know her baking.'

Malcolm groped for a response that would buy him time to figure out what was going on. 'Oh. Thanks. Really?...'

'Perhaps it would be best, for our future relations, if she stayed a little closer to the kitchen.'

The table was ringed with the baffled faces of men regretting the last schnapps, and Malcolm was beginning to realise that this might not just be about fairy cakes, when Kateriina put a hand on his arm, and began to whisper very fast in his ear. He gaped. 'Iris? You? That was... You bloody...'

He reeled back, as though she'd slapped him. Iris jumped up from her chair and faced them across the table. Suddenly, in a moment, it came to her. Everything she thought about all of this, everything she wanted to say. Every synapse pinged, every follicle prickled. She opened her mouth to make the speech of her lifetime. About greed and cynicism, the death of conscience and the unstoppable tyranny of economic growth, the lost children and the ravaged wildernesses. Everything that was wrong with everything Zoom International embodied.

Then she saw Malcolm. She saw his face, appalled by her, dreading what she was about to do. She remembered how jubilant he'd been at the prospect of getting away from the Science Park. And she remembered how happy he'd looked all this evening. Until now.

That was it, really. She had no place here, but apparently it was where Malcolm should have been, all along. She'd been married to a totally different man from the one she thought she knew. Nothing she said would change anything. She should just leave him here. For ever. Right now.

But meanwhile the whole table was looking at her, waiting for her to speak.

'You know what? I don't belong here. I'm going before I go deaf and - stupid, like – like the rest of you!' It wasn't the speech of her lifetime, but it was all she could manage before her voice gave out. She stumbled round the silent circle of faces towards the exit. On her way, she passed Suki. She had a sudden image of Buzzybees with microbial monitors, security cameras, and no Sammy. She paused for a moment, leaned down and whispered into Suki's ear: 'And lay off Buzzybees. They have some VERY powerful friends!'

She paused for long enough to fix Suki with what she hoped was a chilling smile, then fled, without a word or a look at Malcolm.

The pie man waited till the marquee flapped shut behind her, then leaned over to Kateriina. 'You know, if anything, I rather suspect it helped the share price. It's all publicity, as they say!'

All around the table, the tension was exhaled in a whoosh of laughter. Whatever the moment had been, it was over, and they were still here. Malcolm had half-turned to go after Iris, but Kateriina put a long, polished hand on his arm for a moment, and whispered into his ear: 'I think you had better stay.'

Malcolm couldn't read her face; the jokey intimacy had gone. Whatever she personally might think of his work, it seemed pretty unlikely that FreeFlow would want to put a huge contract in the hands of a man married to a lunatic activist. Of all the idiotic, infantile...

All the work he'd done. All the bloody time and thought and effort he'd put in, when nobody was listening at WorkSpace, nobody gave a damn. The insane risk he'd taken in leaving, just for the sake of keeping it alive. All the tedium of those dreary expert witness appearances, those meetings with lawyers who couldn't say one thing without saying ten, and wanted everything sent to ten different arbitrators before they'd write him some measly cheque. All his hopes of getting away from the Science Park, the endless days memorising HSE memoranda and British Standard guidance notes on workplace safety. All gone, finished, history. Just because he'd been silly enough to let Iris out in public.

Beside him, Kateriina's phone rang. She picked it up, listened. Her face became even more grave, and she looked over at the CEO as she whispered into it. After a bit, she put down the phone, thought for a moment, then said something into the CEO's ear as she stood up. She smiled at the faces round the table, waved, and left.

Malcolm now had Iris' empty place on one side, and Kateriina's on the other. It was going to be a long evening.

Iris' dramatic departure called for a stormy, windswept, rain-lashed night, but in fact it was rather nice - unseasonably warm for late May, and the trees luminous in the evening light, as Iris stumbled, still in shock, onto the broken pavement of the industrial park. Clearly, she had, by total, random, infuriating accident, ruined Malcolm's big project. There seemed little chance, even if she managed to explain that her cake had a totally innocent purpose and her presence at the demo was barely more than coincidence, that she'd be forgiven, or the deal salvaged.

But what kind of deal could it be that had him involved with Zoom International and that rapacious woman? Now she remembered, he had been suspiciously monosyllabic about the whole thing. What else was he hiding?

She set off on foot, with no idea where she was, only knowing she could neither go back nor home – at least, not yet.

I ought to have said it. I had them all, right there, all those horrible smarmy fat-cats with their eight-figure bonuses. Sloshing down their hundred-pound bottles of wine, and congratulating themselves for stomping over the rest of us to the top of the heap. Thinking it's only they who see things clearly, and that everybody else, everybody who gives a damn, who values anything that can't be measured in money, is some kind of pathetic fool, blinded by sentimentality and doomed to imminent extinction.

'Sounds rather stirring, why didn't you come out with it?'

Iris took a moment to recognise the voice. Something was different about it.

'You've swapped ears.'

'The other one's blocked. Not at all pleasant in there, I can tell you. You should get it seen to. Anyway, as I was saying, you should have let 'em have it in there. Can't beat a captive audience, I've always found. That's why they make church doors squeaky.'

'Yeah, I suppose you'd be really pleased if I totally and irrevocably ruined my life in one big, empty gesture.'

'On the contrary. I want to see you get on with your life, and stop banging about like a hysterical insect, trapped in a prison you won't see. If you refer back to the place where we began, I think you'll find that Joan of Arc's tag was "The Maid of Orleans". Not "The wife, mother, part-time baker, fancy dress costume maker, taxi service, homework supervisor, cook and PE kit packer of Orleans". When she rode into battle, she rode into battle. She didn't feed the cat, leave a note for the milkman, have supper in the oven and arrange for childcare cover, check her watch, and decide she just had time to do her eyebrows before she rode into battle. She rode.'

'So I just chuck it all in, my marriage, my family, my last fifteen years, just like that?'

'Well, something's got to give. It doesn't seem to be working particularly well any more, does it?'

'But how can anybody make that choice? It's all right for you, you got to have your son in two places at once, down here sorting out the sheep and the goats, and up there at your right hand on high, keeping you company. If I could be in two places at once, none of this would have happened.'

'Did I say it would be easy?'

There was a long silence, during which Iris noticed a large stain down the front of her tee shirt. Presumably when she'd jumped up, she'd knocked her plate over.

Great. Not only did I make a total fool of myself, I made it with mustard mayonnaise all over my chest.

'You see, that's exactly what I'm talking about. Do I bother about the odd fleck of angel dust on my robes? I do not.'

'And how do we know there hasn't been a Mrs God in the background all this time, washing and ironing twenty white robes every week, putting plasters on the cherubs' grazes and making sure Peter's got a ready supply of nice sharp pencils?... Well?'

But no reply came, and her ear no longer itched. Now even God wasn't talking to her. She marched on, in shock, trying to keep the horror of what had just happened at bay. Trying to be rational about it all.

Keep a clear head. Stay calm.

I suppose it happens all the time, doesn't it? People finding they're married to somebody they no longer know, or never really did know. People 'outgrowing' their marriages, or seeing through them. It just feels different when you're reading it in a magazine. It doesn't feel like suddenly finding yourself on a tightrope over the abyss.

Don't think about that now. Whatever's going to happen, there's no way I'm sharing a roof with Malcolm tonight. Better find a hotel.

But how will I pay for it? Bother these evening bags, what's in here? Lipstick, keys, phone, grimy old tissues and a scrunched-up fiver, just in case. That won't get me far. And anyway...

Anyway. How can I not go home, after the last time? After breaking my promise to Ted?

What would it be like never to go home to them again? Oh no. Unbearable. I'd miss them so much! I won't leave. I can't.

Why can't he go? I could manage Ted and Molly, I'm much more used to it than he is.

Yeah, right. On what? You think he'd cheerfully leave you his beloved, immaculate home and his adored children, and pop a cheque through the door every week?

Iris had reached a tube station. She had just about enough cash to get her home. If she hurried, assuming he was staying to patch up her gaffe, she could be upstairs before Malcolm got back.

Just so long as I don't have to see him, or speak to him. Just so long as I can see the children, drink in their sleeping breath, kiss them again. That's all I need, for now.

The familiar aroma of wet dog in Ted's room was mixed with a distinct whiff of stale fish, from some long-past phytoplankton spill. To Iris, it smelled like damask roses. There he lay, one pale leg sprawled out, faintly snoring, a simple spirit wide open to the world. Maybe it was best after all that she leave. Rather than scar him still further with these awful fights. It was just a matter of she, Iris, and Malcolm, being grownup and mature, rising above their difficulties in common concern for their offspring.

She sank a kiss deep in the hollow of Ted's chin, and another on his cheek. How often had she kissed him like this as he slept? Storing up love, arming him against whatever life threw at him. She tangled a hand in his damp hair. Ted would survive. But Molly?

She knocked on the locked door, then felt for the spare key she'd hidden under the carpet in case of fire.

For once, Molly's head was outside the covers, turned to the light from the window. She looked so peaceful, her sleeping face not clouded with anxiety or hatched with rage. Poor Molly, struggling through the ghastly pupation of adolescence, compounded by the pointless sadism of the National Curriculum. No wonder she was grumpy and difficult. But look at her now. She was beautiful. And she was brilliant, and brave. And now, apparently, she even had a conscience.

Maybe some of that is down to me. That time at Greggs? And now this pop thing. Maybe she'll understand.

Suddenly Iris was very tired. She needed to be in bed. Tomorrow, if the worst happened, if Malcolm forced her to leave, she'd show them how to use the washing machine and the dishwasher, and write out a meal planner for two weeks, with all their favourite recipes. She probably had just about enough credit left to fill the freezer with cooked stuff, to keep them going. So they'd know she was still thinking about them.

But for now, she was going to have one last night in her own bed.

Iris had meant to wake early and be up, brave and cheerful and bustling about the kitchen by the time anybody else stirred, but in the event it was Malcolm whom she found bustling at seven-fifteen, with Ted already seated at the table, fully dressed in pristine school clothes. Even Molly had laid a place for herself and was rummaging in the cereal cupboard.

They both looked perfectly normal. Clearly, nothing had been said. Maybe Malcolm was going to forget the whole thing. After all, it had been partly his fault. The way he'd been behaving with that – troll. It was he who'd done the deal with the devil, whatever it was. And he hadn't even bothered to hear her side of the pie thing. Clearly, Malcolm had seen that he had provoked events by his behaviour, and this was his way of saying 'sorry'.

Maybe she should listen to his side, too. It was wrong to condemn him without at least giving him a hearing. There was, she supposed, a distant possibility that once she knew the whole story, she could find a way to forgive him, too.

'Molly, could you ask your mother if she wants a coffee, please?'

Molly looked surprised and was about to speak, when he continued: 'You could add that she looks as rough as I've ever seen her, so she could probably do with one, given the explaining she's got to do.'

Not quite forgiven, then.

'I'll tell her for three quid. That and the answer for a fiver, yeah?'

Iris walked past and helped herself from the coffee pot. 'Don't be daft Molly; you know, and he knows, I can hear him perfectly well. Tell him he's being very childish, and if he's got anything to say to me, he can say it after you've gone to school.'

Molly opened her mouth again, but Iris continued: 'And you could also tell him that it's going to take more than a cup of coffee to make him look fit to go to wherever his "work commitments" are taking him today.'

At this point Ted looked up from the sports pages. 'Is it a

game? Can I join in?'

'No, Ted, it's not a game. Your father and I have had a – a disagreement, and I'm...' Iris felt a little catch in her throat that she couldn't quite suppress... '...I'm not sure what's going to happen.'

There. It was out. Wasn't it the worst thing you could do to your children, pretend everything was all right, when they had razor sharp instincts telling them it wasn't? But looking at Ted's face, she wasn't so sure. He got up, took hold of her arm, and pulled her towards Malcolm. 'I think Mum and Dad, after supper tonight we all ought to sit down and watch The Lion King on DVD, and then everybody will feel better.'

'That's very sweet of you, Ted, but I'm not sure it's going to work.'

'It did last time. When you locked us out of that holiday cottage.'

'Anyhow'... Iris was aware that even Molly was listening now. She wanted to say, 'It'll be all right! I promise!' but frankly, she was no longer sure that it would. Instead, she kneeled down beside Ted, smiled bravely over at Molly, and said: 'Anyhow, tonight we're all going to be quite busy, because I may be – going away – just for a bit. So I have to teach you to use the vacuum cleaner and the washing machine, and how to cook...'

'Ted, since you're close enough that it might actually sink in if you shout it right in her ear, I'd be grateful if you'd remind your mother that it was I who taught her what little she knows about housework, when I rescued her from the putrefying stinkhole she was calling home. And as her subsequent aptitude has been amply demonstrated by the fact that she appears to have no use for the vacuum except as a holding pen for borrowed reptiles, she can be fairly confident that - if it comes to that - the domestic environment is at least as safe in my hands as in hers.'

'I don't think I can remember all of that Dad. Can you say it again, in bits?'

At that moment Malcolm's phone rang. 'Yes?' he barked into it, and then almost immediately: 'Oh – sorry. Yes... A bit early, yes... No, I haven't checked my emails this morning... Yes, I'll do that right now. I'm sure it will be fine... See you later.'

He snapped the phone shut and swung a jacket off his chair. 'However, since your mother has suddenly acquired a taste for domesticity, I'll leave you in her eager hands, and go to do the only thing she seems still to need me for. We can talk about it later.' And pointedly bypassing Iris, he kissed Molly and Ted, and was gone.

from: Kateriina Toivonen, ktoivonen@freeflow.org
to: Malcolm Richie, mrichie@richiewinterbottom.co.uk

Malcolm!

Well, that was quite a night. I'm sorry I had to run out on you. Corporate politics, you know what I'm saying? Do not be worried or concerned for our project. It is true that right now Carlos is a little aggrieved, but between ourselves, I think we do not have to worry too much about him.

But I am more excited by other possibilities. Thinking about what your wife did and why gave me many many ideas, and truly, I am too excited to sleep, which is why I am emailing at this godless hour.

I think if we are to save our project and maybe even move on to the others I am speculating about, we should meet very soon. How about breakfast at eight-thirty tomorrow? I will have the address texted to you.

Sleep well, hang tight, and I will see you again, in a few hours.
K XXXXX
Kateriina Toivonen
VicePresident, Technology and Vision
FreeFlow Distribution, Inc

As he prepared to get off the bus, Malcolm closed his laptop and pulled out his phone. On one level, it was a relief. On another, it was unnerving. To have FreeFlow behind his project was a coup. But to have Kateriina's hot breath in his ear at every step would be... He remembered how he had felt last night at the race track, at least until the Iris revelation. It wasn't that Kateriina wasn't attractive. Far from it. It was just – the only word that seemed to work was 'disproportionate'. It was like having Scarlett Johannsen for a project manager. Of course, Scarlett Johanssen was all very well, but in the proper context, which was seventy feet high, and on a screen. Kateriina seemed to be about seventy feet high in the flesh.

Still, the main thing was that his project wasn't dead yet. He'd do whatever he had to do to keep it alive. And the one thing he mustn't be, was late.

He pushed bit further through the crowd of shoppers, and checked the address on Kateriina's text message. Could this be right? It seemed to be the flagship outlet of Planet Plenty: what he used to think of as a shop. He approached the door which slid open to admit him into a vast, air-chilled hangar, which seemed an excessive precaution against the feeble onslaught of an English spring. It was packed with sleek women, cluttered with handbags and babies, ogling the displays and conversing earnestly with open-faced young customer associates.

He was wondering what to do next, when he saw a sign saying: 'Nothing But Treatment Spa'

That was the name in Kateriina's text. He followed the signs past undulating hills of soft fruit, dewy salads, and pearly archipelagoes of line-caught fish and hand-made cheese. Just short of panic, he wandered round a pyramid of hand-pulled loaves to find himself in a pale, scented cocoon, misted with the whispers of votive beauticians. Marble basins lined the walls, reclining chairs clustered in the middle, while around them solemn teenagers dipped tapered fingers in airy tubs of cream.

Half-dressed women padded casually between treatment rooms, sipping smoothies and chatting on tiny phones. There were no other men, as far as he could see, and certainly none in a suit from Debenhams.

Malcolm was just deciding to check the address from the safe neutrality of the nearest Starbucks, when he spotted Kateriina reclining on an Alvar Aalto chaise longue, Blackberry on her lap, headset round her neck, sending emails and taking phone calls while a very young girl painted her toenails with focussed dedication. Kateriina looked up, and smiled. That seemed like a reassuring sign.

She gestured Malcolm to sit on the chaise next to her. As he did so, disarmed all over again by finding himself semi-horizontal next to several yards of her bare, pale leg, he was suddenly glad of the suit. It felt like a coat of armour, adopted for a boardroom clash, but now offering another kind of defence.

Kateriina paused in her multitasking to lean over, her robe

parting as she kissed the air beside his cheek. Malcolm was no longer sure which mode he preferred. She'd mentioned breakfast in her email. He began to wonder if perhaps she meant him.

'Have whatever you like, Malcolm. It's all fabulous here.'

He looked up at the crop-haired girl poised to write. 'I'll just have a coffee, thanks'

'With?'

'Sorry?'

'Syrup, ginseng, goji, chai spice, cinnamon, extra shot, protein, or a twist?'

'I think a dash of milk, thank you very much. Any old milk. Except soy.'

The girl's face blanked professionally as she pocketed the pad and glided off. Kateriina switched her Blackberry to divert. 'Well. Your wife is quite a woman of surprises.'

'Isn't she just?'

'But, as I said, to me she was also a great inspiration last night.'

She leaned towards him again, and he fought the urge to lean away. 'When I first met her, I thought - and I'm sure you'll take this the right way - I was a little - disappointed? She looked - how can I say - almost ordinary.'

Yes, he thought. That was what I always liked about her. 'I suppose I can see that.'

'But now I see that's just because she is British. We continentals make a big noise, we talk loudly about politics and philosophy. But you British, when you care about something with a passion, you...'

'...throw pies.'

She laughed. He was looking straight at her perfect tonsils. The coffee came, and with it a basket piled with pastries. Kateriina blew on a fingernail, decided it was dry, and tore the throat from a muffin. 'The pie was, maybe, a little childish. But the feeling behind it... It made me really understand that we at Zoom International have seriously misjudged our public. The world is in crisis, Malcolm. I think we must all recognise that. And in a crisis, the public will no longer be bought off by a little green branding. They want the real deal. They want new ideas, new thinking. They want - integrity!'

The kneeling vestal finished on the first foot and looked up, cradling it reverentially. 'Is this good for you?'

Katariina twirled the foot languorously towards Malcolm. 'What do you think, Malcolm? Is this a good colour for me?'

Malcolm splashed coffee over his tie.

'I think that's a yes? Okay, you can do the other one.'

The vestal bent to her work. Kateriina finished her muffin, shook out her fingers, and began to speak, once more reassuringly brisk. 'That phone call last night, I was called to an extraordinary board meeting. I can tell you in confidence now that Carlos is no longer in post. Maybe even in somewhat as a result of what happened the other day, at the demonstration.'

'Really?' Malcolm felt a tremor of shock, realising that his officially dull wife appeared to have toppled the CEO of a major global powerhouse.

'Well, among other factors that have been building for some time. What do you call it, a straw in the wind? And so now, I have some of his responsibilities. Including oversight of research and development structures for Europe and the Middle East. And I believe'... Five perfect nails landed on his sleeve; perfect nude-glossed lips whispered close to his ear...'that you can help me. Us. To change.'

'Me?'

She drew back and nodded solemnly, big eyes meeting his. 'The first time I saw your ideas I knew it. The seats that recognise who is sitting on them, the cybernetic robots that place the goods exactly where that particular operator can reach them, the sensors to adjust speed of flow to the speed of work. The newest technology, but with the human at the heart, and in control. Is that not what you said?'

It was exactly what he'd said. But he'd thought he was just designing a distribution centre. She carried on, her excitement apparently real. 'It's inspired. And that is what modern corporations must find. We can buy all the automation, all the computing power, all the human labour we need. But!' ...The long fingers gripped his sleeve. The luscious lips breathed inches from his... 'What we need is more than that. What we need is - vision!'

The second foot was done. Kateriina, suddenly brisk again, sat back and checked the time. 'Oh, wouldn't you just know it, my conference call. So, Malcolm, can I share with you my little plan? Before we embark on the distribution centre, which I'm sure you must admit is a rather tedious use of your gifts, let me put to you something I believe you will find rather more inspiring... and for both of us, I hope, more fun.'

The fresh air, lightly drizzling, cleared Malcolm's head a little as he turned towards the office. Walking would take longer, but he needed to think. The deal on the distribution centre had been fine; more than fine, in fact. He'd worried about abandoning Colin in the Science Park, except that Colin seemed almost to be enjoying his new career as waste alchemist.

But this idea of a Genius Farm was the kind of thing that sprouts in the overheated foothills of Silicon Valley. 'Whatever it takes to make the ideas come!' she'd breathed, apparently convinced that if Malcolm could transform the working experience of warehouse operators, he could also uncork the vat of inspiration in other scientists. The motivation made sense – Dubai had the money, and they wanted to spend it on intellectual property, for when the oil finally ran dry. It was the next bit of her plan that had rattled him.

But whatever he felt about a 'just the two of us' fact-finding trip, he wasn't in a position to say no. He'd spent ten years of his life keeping Person Centred Palletising alive. He wasn't about to give up on it now.

Oddly, the more he thought about Kateriina, the more he found himself missing Iris. Dull, maybe, possibly even drab, yet honest, heartfelt Iris. Kateriina's reaction, and her news, had made him almost proud of his wife. For once, it seemed Iris' erratic activities had backfired into a positive result.

Maybe he'd been a bit hard on her this morning. She was bound to be feeling terrible about it by now. That was Iris all over, acting on these crazy, if well-meant impulses, then agonised with regret at the totally foreseeable consequences. What would she do without him to keep her steady? She didn't mean half of what she said, he knew that.

He'd better go home and have a proper chat with her. Just as soon as he'd figured out what to do about the trip to Dubai.

How dare he? How dare he swan out like that, without a word, and leave me here, hanging around, praying for the moment when he finally deigns to return home to pronounce my fate, and that of our two poor blameless children?

Iris had spent the entire ten-minute walk up to school in a raging internal monologue, with the result that she not only failed to interpellate the usual friendly listening signals into Ted's customary riff on the highlights of this morning's Match of the Day 2, but ignored every one of the street-sweepers, homeless people, and other mainstays of the urban village with whom she normally exchanged neighbourly greetings.

And why should it be he who decides anyway? What an idiot I was to tell the children I was leaving. Why shouldn't he leave? He's the one who's been cuddling up with that – that Valkyrie. If I didn't have to spend half my life keeping the house ready-buffed for the photographers from Architectural Digest, I'd have plenty of time for the children, and a meaningful life of my own as well.

Anyhow, whatever happens, they're all way overdue for a domestic reality check. No more coddling! They'll thank me in the end!

She arrived home in a tornado of righteousness powerful enough to blow the front door off its hinges. Sadly, it was a metaphorical tornado. Even as her hand flapped open the bag to scroffle for her keys, she saw them, just where she'd left them last night: inside her right shoe, by the bed, upstairs.

And the spare, normally attached to a magnet behind the drainpipe, had been redeployed for the window-cleaner, and never replaced.

Iris stood there, hungry, dazed and finally out of ideas. At that moment, she'd rather have walked away from her entire life than call Malcolm to rescue her. Even if he would.

But she couldn't just leave. Not now. It was one thing to make a theoretical decision, knowing there was all the packing up and arguing to do before it actually became final, and another to find you'd done it by accident, in your nastiest old clothes, and without even saying goodbye.

And then her phone rang. She stared at it, not recognising the number. Was it safe to answer? It could have been anybody – that lovely Sergeant Bathurst, Childline finally returning Ted's cry for help, or perhaps Elaine with yet another fancy phone, calling to congratulate her on yet another humiliation. She couldn't think of a person in the world she actually wanted to talk to at that moment, but she answered it anyway. 'Yes? Who is this?'

There was a short pause, as whoever it was recoiled in shock. 'Iris? Is that you?'

'Sammy! I didn't recognise the number.'

'Yeah, sorry, we had to change it, cos of you know, Arlo.'

'Arlo! what's happened to him?'

'He got deported. He was gonna leave anyhow, and this way Troy had to front the fare to the Home Office, so it was like, a result.'

'Is he really a terrorist?'

'Nah. Well, not really. There was that research centre he torched.'

'No!'

'After he'd liberated the animals, bien sur. And some stuff disabling bombers. And I think there was a do at the Israel Import-Export bureau... nothing major. I just wondered if you were bringing any like, stuff in today?'

'Oh, Sammy. Oh, it's so nice to hear your voice. No, I can't...' Iris found herself wondering how many white chocolate bagels she'd have to bake every day to keep herself and two children in a council flat in Kensal Green. '...I can't actually make anything today.'

'No worries, I'll just tell the guys. But...' The voice moved away from the phone for a minute, as Sammy whispered inaudibly to somebody else. 'Well – how about coming over anyway? Just to – er – hang out. Try the new Hebridean raspberries, yeah?'

'Oh yes! Could I? Please?' To her amazement, Iris found herself in tears. She stuffed a fist into her mouth to hold them back, just long enough to croak. 'I'll see you in ten, okay?'

By the time she got to Buzzybees, ten minutes of hysterical sobbing had made Iris feel much better. But the shop was dark; the sign on it said 'Sorry! Try again!' and in the little light that fought through the dusty window, it appeared deserted. Iris suddenly realised how much she'd been relying on seeing Sammy; she was fighting back the tears all over again, wondering what to do now, when a gleaming Prius cruised silently towards her. It slowed down and flashed its lights, and she was horrified to recognise Elaine behind the wheel.

Iris shrank back against the shop door, which fell open. She stumbled in as it tinkled shut behind her, and stood there, baffled.

Suddenly, the lights snapped on, and the shop seemed to be full of about twenty people, who turned out to be Troy, Ignacio and his two children, and Sammy, with flowers twined in her hair, like a half-dressed extra from a Botticelli telepic.

'Surprise!' A bang like a gunshot rang across the floor. Iris landed on her stomach at Ignacio's sandalled feet, only to realise it had come from a bottle of elderflower champagne Sammy was pouring into a collection of recycled bottle glasses. 'You okay, Iris? You seem a bit jumpy.'

Iris looked up at them, standing round her in bemused concern. Troy leaned down and held out a hand. It was warm, and strong, and he looked into her eyes and smiled, as she scrambled up, asking: 'So – um, what are we celebrating?'

Iris had never felt less like celebrating in her life. But the glass Troy handed her began to melt the edges of her misery. Sammy took a swig. 'So you don't know? I told you, she's totally out of the loop. That guy you threw the pie at?'

'I DIDN'T THROW IT! Bloody Arlo threw it. Sorry, Troy. But really... And it was a cake, not a pie. And if I'd known what was going to happen to it...'

'But that's just it! Where's the paper?...' Sammy downed the rest of her champagne and scuttled into the back, reappearing with a battered copy of the Financial Times. 'Look, Iris! Look what happened yesterday!'

'Long Bonds Look Weak in Early Japan Trading?'

'No, schtoopid, look here!'

'Global food and fuels giant Zoom International today announced a joint venture with the government of Baratoria for all future agribusiness activities in the region. The deal gives the government of Baratoria fifty per cent of all proceeds from Zoom's local biofuel business, and coincides with the replacement of several key executives. The changes, with immediate effect, see London-based Carlos Liminosa'...

'That's him! The pie guy!'

'...released...'

'They fired his ass!'

'...along with several others intimately involved in the troubled operations in the Baratorian rainforest.'

No wonder he was so pissed off with me last night. He must have known. But, hang on...

'It says "a joint venture" – doesn't that mean that they're going to carry on tearing up the forest? Wouldn't it be better if they went somewhere else?'

Troy smiled, the worldly-wise adult to the innocent, idealistic child. 'Of course it would be better. But it's not about to happen. There's no way they're stopping now, not with the market red-hot. At least this way the Baratorians get the technology, and half the profits.'

Feeling a little confused, Iris read on. 'The change in direction is further highlighted by the hiring of a new head of Government Liaison and Corporate Social Responsibility, the Baratorian politician Ignacio...'

Iris stopped reading and turned, speechless, to where Ignacio was sitting on a sack of potatoes, hanging cherries on his children's ears. He looked up with a modest, yet triumphant smile. She stared back, baffled. 'Ignacio! He's going to work for Zoom International?'

Troy went over and put an arm round Ignacio's shoulders. 'Meet the conscience of the evil empire. He's got gazillions to spend. He'll be liaising with his old pals in the government, setting up free schools and clinics and who knows whatall else. Maybe an orphanage for all those displaced baby animals? What about it compadre? The public loves that fluffy big-eyed shit, it'll be great for the brand.'

He and Ignacio exchanged hi-fives over the children. Iris looked from one compadre to the other. 'But I thought - Didn't they ruin his life, and that of countless thousands more?'

'Well, here's their chance to make up. Anyways, better inside the tent pissing out, than outside pissing in. Plus remember, he's got the family to think of. Baratorian diplomats earn diddly-squat. Working for Zoom, he gets a giant pay check, health and dental for life, and an apartment big enough for the entire village.'

Ignacio grinned and spread his arms wide, as though to draw all those destitute indigenes into the comforting embrace of the executive lifestyle.

Iris was desperately trying to make sense of it all. The simple, stark battle of good vs evil wasn't so simple after all. It certainly wasn't something she could unpick on three hours of sleep.

Then Troy spoke again, suddenly warm and heartfelt. 'I hope you realise what a great thing you did there, Iris.'

'I did?'

He smiled, and rested one hand on her shoulder, like a saint blessing his acolyte. Iris, drained of everything but air and adrenaline, shivered at his touch.

'Thanks to you, thousand of kids will live happy, safe lives, they'll go to school, they'll eat well for the first time ever. And it's not only the kids; all the people of Baratoria will share the wealth. D'you know what that means, Iris? It means running water, electricity, pay checks for moms and carers. The indigenous families will be paid as custodians of their land. And with Ignacio in Zoom, it doesn't stop with Baratoria. Sempre mas, Ignacio!'

Ignacio smiled at Iris and whispered to the children, who wriggled for a moment, then shyly came over and hugged her. 'Gracias, Senora Iris!'

Could it be true? Had she – or at least her rum and caramel marjolaine - really changed their lives? It seemed a bit too good to be entirely plausible, but very nice to hear, just at this moment. Then she remembered something. 'Have you heard any more from the Planet, Sammy? Only I – um, I happened to meet somebody. And I had a word. I think it might help.'

'Not a beep. Maybe you scared 'em off.'

'But – well anyhow, about the happy children and stuff. To be fair, it wasn't really me, was it? It was poor Arlo.'

For a moment, the name seemed to rattle Troy. 'You are so right, Iris. This shit runs on teamwork. The passion of the people. The strongest force there is. And like I said, this is just the beginning!'

Iris wasn't at all sure she wanted it to be the beginning of anything; if it carried on, it seemed as though it could well be the end, at least of her family. There, in the shop, she felt so - supported, even loved. Safe. But at home, with her real family, she was defensive, marginalised. And terribly alone. How had it all turned upside down like this?

They stood around her, waiting for her to join the effusion of delight and triumph. All Iris could think was that, one way and another, Zoom International seemed to have destroyed her happy life for ever. A tear slid out of her eye.

'Oh babe, no! Here...'

Iris suddenly found her legs wobbling. Sammy led her over to another sack, and sat her down. 'It's just – I just found out my husband is working with them. With Zoom. Well, with one of their companies. It must have been going on for months, and I never knew.'

'Shit!'

'You don't say!'

'I mean, I don't even know what he's doing, but... Anyway, he's furious with me. And I can't stay at the house...'

Sammy flipped in a moment from loving concern to righteous indignation.

'Of course you can't, you'd never forgive yourself.'

'No, I can't, because I've locked myself out. And I don't know what I'm going to do. I'm so...'

Tired? Confused? Hurt? She felt as though she needed to be somewhere very calm and quiet, to think about what to do; about Malcolm and the children and her future. Calm and quiet were rare commodities in this part of town.

Troy stroked a wisp of hair off her face, and said, as though he'd read her mind: 'Why not come and hang with me for a couple hours? I know just the place. Peaceful, beautiful. No stress.'

Sammy looked at him sharply, and then at Iris. She rummaged in her pocket and came up with a packet of tissues. 'You be careful with her, okay? She's precious.'

Malcolm was about half way between Planet Plenty and his office, and no further towards solving his problem, when he turned to look into the window of Hamley's and found himself face to face with the solution. Half term! The perfect alibi!

Iris wouldn't be too pleased. But she owed him one. And she certainly owed Ted and Molly. He wasn't thinking of it exactly as a test, but it was about time Iris made up her mind whose side she was on. Obviously, she couldn't go on breaking the law and publicly trashing Zoom International if he was involved with them at a high level, as he might well be, for some time to come.

He'd better put it to her, before he said anything to Kateriina. He didn't want to do it over the phone, and anyhow, he was feeling vaguely guilty about the way he'd just run out on her this morning. God knows how distraught she might be by now, having come to her senses and realised what she'd done.

Still, his financial worries seemed to have gone away for the moment. He needn't go back to the office just yet. Best to go home while the children were out, get Iris on her own, and have a proper chat.

He arrived at the house and let himself in. The breakfast dishes were still in the sink, which was unusual; one positive side-effect of Iris' new habits was that she now raced to do the washing-up and the laundry, before he could get to it with proper detergent and hot water.

He called out: no answer. But her bike was outside, locked up in its usual place by the overflowing compost bin. And the egg was parked where he'd left it, after its full-body post-Hackney detox.

Where could she be? The only place he knew she went with any regularity was that shop, what was it called – that muddy place she was always raving about. He was curious, in any case, about what exactly its attraction might be. Perhaps she'd walked round there to have a moan about her evil capitalist running dog of a husband.

Malcolm walked quickly, and turned the corner just as the rain cleared. A watery rainbow arced over the council flats, and sunlight splashed the pavement outside the shop. As he approached, the door opened and two people came out; a tall, tanned man with shaggy blond hair, with his arm round...

Malcolm had never much liked surprises. For a moment his breath wouldn't come, as though a huge weight had dropped on him. All this time, with everything Iris had said and done, the one thing he'd never thought of - the one reason he'd never suspected for her sudden transformation... It seemed almost a joke, like some cliché out of East Enders. But it was unquestionably Iris. And presumably East Enders had to be based in some version of reality, or people wouldn't watch it so addictively.

Christ, what a tit he'd been. What a bloody fool. It was so obvious, even Molly had seen it – or hinted at it.

So much for that little heart-to-heart chat. Why bother? Seeing what he was up against, even at this distance, he'd a pretty good idea what the outcome would be.

from: Malcolm Richie, mrichie@richiewinterbottom.co.uk
  to: Kateriina Toivonen, ktoivonen@freeflow.org

Dear Kateriina

Thanks again for breakfast. What an interesting location for a meeting.

I've been thinking over your highly attractive offer. Naturally, I'm extremely interested in the challenge of facilitating blue-sky creativity, and it sounds as though once again you've lined up all the ducks and found the resources to make it happen.

My only slight problem is a practical one. As you know, I've two kids, and the proposed trip next week unfortunately coincides with their half term. However, if you're agreeable, I could bring them along – happy to pay their fares of course, and from what I've heard of Dubai, there'd be more than enough to keep them happy while you and I were working.

I hope that this isn't too much of an inconvenience. I'm afraid the days are gone when us fathers could just assume our wives would take care of that end of things (and I think I'm not being disloyal when I suggest that you'll understand why, in my particular case, I'd rather not rely on that).

Let me know either way. As I said, I'd love to work with you on it.

Malcolm

Malcolm read it through, deleted the bit about disloyalty which was, clearly, utterly disloyal, considered replacing it with 'and in this case, unfortunately I just found out that my wife is shagging someone else', but in the end just typed, 'Needless to say, given her views on air travel, my wife will be staying behind in England.'

Then he inserted a 'probably'. Miracles could happen. There might be an innocent explanation.

That would do. The children would be fine on their own for a day or two in whatever lavish resort hotel Zoom stumped up for. Whether he'd be fine with Kateriina was another question.

from: Kateriina Toivonen, ktoivonen@freeflow.org
to: Malcolm Richie, mrichie@richiewinterbottom.co.uk

Dear Malcolm,

Well, this is a bit of a surprise, I must say. But how can I condemn your devotion as a father, since I myself am coming from a country where fathers' rights are enshrined in many laws? And for me it will be a chance to get to know the children. Who knows, we may become very close in the future!

Of course there is no question of you paying for any of it. Consider it a little advance against your fees.

So I will send a car for you tomorrow morning, if this is not too soon. That way we can be fresh to begin the project on Sunday, which as you know is not a holiday there.

Now I must get back to work. Since today my responsibilities have grown a little. We poor working women have no time to think about children. Lucky for me that I may sometimes borrow other people's!

K XXX

By the way, here is the URL of the hotel, if you wish to show to your family.

www. royal-suites-dubai.com/aladdin-palace/honeymoon.htm

Iris sat on the back of Troy's electric super-bike, swaying with him as they glided silently northward. Past the shops and the school, through the street markets of Holloway and Tottenham, swerving round Brent Cross and looping round the north circular; Iris watched it all go by, not thinking, not trying to figure out where they were headed, just glad that for now, all the decisions had been taken from her.

Somewhere beyond Barnet, they stopped on the edge of a wood. A rudimentary fence ringed it, and a hand-painted sign informed them that it was private property, and asked them, very politely, to take as much care as they possibly could of this lovely place, but please wander freely and marvel at its wonders and delights.

She stumbled off and stood there, as Troy parked the bike and straightened the sign. 'It's been too long. Needs maintaining. This way!'

He stooped to remove his Birkenstocks and wiggled his toes on the young grass. Unlike the toes of Englishmen, Iris noticed, they were straight, hairless, and uniformly golden. The nails had been carefully cut, and buffed to a rosy gleam. In fact - could that be polish? Iris looked up and caught Troy watching her, puzzled.

The sky had cleared and the day had warmed into the delicious blood-heat of early summer. A thousand greens filtered the sunlight, dappling their feet as they walked over the soft forest floor.

'I bought this piece of woodland way back, when the kids were tiny. Haven't been for years. There's a neat thing I'd love you to see, if it's still here.'

Iris followed him silently, feeling like a little child again. Sunlight flooded a clearing in front of her. A sudden twirl of butterflies passed through it, and was gone. Iris noticed a tiny beetle, horned and iridescent, scuttling over the fallen leaves at her feet. The thick silence of the wood seemed to sharpen her eyes, magnifying everything.

As Troy passed the trees he was touching them, inspecting their bark, pulling off bent twigs and clearing the path. With his green eyes and tea-brown skin, he seemed almost part of the wood. Iris was wearing a pink tee shirt and jeans spattered with fabric glue, but she hadn't dressed this morning for a tryst in paradise.

'Hey. It's still here. Would you believe that? Let's see now...' He'd stopped in front of a huge oak, a tree on a different scale from anything around it. Down from the first branches and over its roots, it had been extended with other branches, with packed mud and hazel twigs, into a kind of giant burrow. He walked around it, Iris following, until they came to an opening. Peering inside, Iris saw a room, walls smoothed with mud, knotholes punched out into windows. It was a leaf-strewn, rather cobwebby version of Big Ears' house. A playhouse for a tree-hugger.

Troy stood aside to let her enter. She walked in and touched the wall, feeling the tree breathe around her. Troy followed her. 'Neat, huh? Years ago, I had plans to power it up, so we could stay overnight, and in winter. You can power a radio with a potato, so why not power a house with a tree? It'd be cool, huh?'

He turned and smiled, his profile etched in the light. Iris wondered why this idea, which Malcolm would have dismissed as pure insanity, sounded quite rational coming from Troy.

'Now, let's see if it's still...' He walked across to a a opening hollowed in the ceiling. A narrow plank staircase wound up from it. He gestured towards it. 'Go ahead.'

Iris climbed the stairs, resting her hand on the cool wood. Up, and out onto a thick, flat branch, polished by many feet. She looked up. Ladders led from one branch to the next, right up through the canopy.

Troy followed as she climbed. Finally, they emerged onto a big, square platform, built between high branches. Two hammocks were slung over it. Nothing else but sunshine and whispering leaves.

'Well, how about that! After all this time. Let's see if....' Troy pulled on the ropes of a hammock, testing them. He rolled himself in experimentally. The hammock swung gently from side to side, then he swung himself out and held out a hand to her. 'Come try this. I swear you'll never want to get out.' He held it steady while she tumbled in, then climbed into the other one.

They lay there, looking up at a pale sky through the tissue of leaves. Out on the branches, birds rustled for insects, and somewhere a pair of squirrels was having a furious flying dispute. After a few minutes, he spoke. 'I know how you feel. About your husband, and your kids and all.'

She opened her eyes and found him looking over at her. Did he? How could he? She had a sudden image of Troy turning up at 26 Hartland Gardens, and didn't know whether to laugh or cry. He carried on, almost whispering, his voice charged with understanding and sympathy.

'It's lonely, isn't it? It's damn hard and lonely, and mostly it feels like they just don't get it. Maybe don't even want to.'

Maybe he does know. Perhaps he's been through it too. I've never thought of that. Arlo certainly didn't seem like the product of a happy family home.

Iris brushed a wisp of hair behind her ear, and found herself scratching it. Oh, really. Not now. She definitely didn't need any help now.

Troy hadn't noticed. He'd put a hand over his eyes, as though to help him find the right words. 'Or they do get it, but you can't let them near it, because it's too damn risky. That was the deal with Arlo. I had to keep him away from a lot of shit, but I couldn't tell him why. He never got over it.'

'Poor Arlo'.

'He's a good kid underneath. But I can't bail him out forever. I guess you think I'm tough on him, but it's for his own good. He has to lead his life.'

He reached out his hand, and she realised he was about to take hers. Like a scene from a movie.

'Shhh.... It's okay.'

Why shouldn't he? It was a perfectly innocent gesture. She wasn't some schoolgirl, after all. She was Iris Richie, who had shaken the political foundations of a subcontinent without even trying.

But her hand went instead to her ear, which was now itching furiously. She turned away from Troy and muttered: 'Give me a break! I'll talk to you in a minute, okay?' Then she took a deep breath, turned back to Troy, who was looking rather bemused, and tried to relax into this timeless, weightless, worryless world. If only she could just stay here, and stop crusading. Just for a bit. Troy had been on the road, doing battle, for decade, and he didn't seem to want to stop. Maybe he'd have some advice.

'So why do you go on?'

'Go on?'

'With all this, all this travelling the world, campaigning, giving up everything for it. Being lonely, and not being there for your children, and stuff.'

'Why do I? What choice do I have? I see it the other way, I look at where we're headed, with the U.S. already on its knees in debt, printing more and more money for wars they can never win – I look at all that and I think, why doesn't everybody in the world drop everything, seeing how none of it will even be there soon, if we don't sort this shit out right now? Why doesn't every goddamn body on the goddamn planet shout out the message, every way they can?'

He looked over at her, and his voice dropped back to its velvet, empathetic range. 'But hey, I don't need to say this to you, do I? You know it's not a choice. People like you and me Iris – it's a calling, right? Does that answer you?'

A tiny animal, a vole or a shrew, darted out of a hole in the tree above Iris' head, and scuttled down the rope inches from her face.

She watched it, barely breathing, until it disappeared below her feet.

Troy's words swirled in her head. The future, which had seemed utterly bleak a few hours ago, started to sprout little buds of possibility, like the twigs around her. She needn't be alone; she had Sammy, Troy, their big, loose-knit web of friends and fellow idealists, whom she was only beginning to discover. Even people like Wayne; drab on the outside, but willing to endure prison for their beliefs.

She imagined Ted making friends with Ignacio's children, bonding over football with them – every kid in South America plays football, don't they? She pictured herself setting out with Ted and Molly on all sorts of adventures charged with excitement and surprise - two things Malcolm hated above all others, with the possible exception of outdoor living, and tree houses.

The mention of 'a calling' reminded her of another thing she could never discuss with Malcolm, and she had almost nerved herself to ask whether God ever spoke to Troy, when her phone rang. She picked it up, only to realise that this might be Himself, having failed to get through on any other channel. But the voice on the other end was reassuringly girlish. 'Iris?'

'Who is this?'

'It's Fern! Iris, I'm so glad I got hold of you; I've got a teeny favour to ask, except I don't think it's actually a favour, because I bet you'll be glad when I tell you.'

Iris made a mental note to turn her phone off more. 'And what is it?'

'Well, I bet you know Troy Hauser, don't you?'

Iris looked over at Troy, inches from her, giving his craggy temples an Ayurvedic finger massage. 'Sort of. A bit. Why?'

'Well, as you of course know we've got our Summer Conference starting in a couple of days and we'd be totally thrilled if he could come along and speak, you know. I mean, he'd be really the keynote speaker. We only just thought of it, when we found out he was still in the country, but we can easily, you know, juggle the programme. D'you think he might?'

'Maybe. Where is it?'

'Birmingham. And of course it's not all work, we've got a fabulous international evening planned, and oh I almost forgot, a special private tour of a new super hi-tech landfill.'

'A landfill. In Birmingham.'

'Yes. Really fascinating, we only just got that confirmed this morning. In fact – gosh, now I'm thinking about it, how about if he actually made his speech at the landfill! It would really make the point about waste and mindless consumerism, wouldn't it? The Press Office would love it! So could you possibly ask him, do you think? Or even give me his number and I could?'

'No, it's okay, I'll ask him. I've got to...'

'Oh, and if Ignacio Hermanos is still in the country, it goes without saying we'd be thrilled to welcome him too. God, the way the Baratorians have stood up against the U.S. and spearheaded the whole socialist revolution, it's so inspiring, isn't it?'

'Yes, of course – well, I'll do my best and call you back, okay?' She switched off the phone. Troy opened his eyes and looked over at her.

'There's an offer you'll find it hard to turn down.'

'Me? What's that?'

'The Greens want you to be a keynote speaker at their conference. In Birmingham.'

'Birmingham? Is that a neat place?'

'I can tell you that the highlight is a visit to a landfill. In fact, she wants you to make your speech there.'

'That's a first.'

'So shall I tell her you're not free? She said something about bringing Ignacio too.'

'Well, on that front, there's a bunch of stuff we have to go through, with his new job and how it interfaces with my issues. Working with Zoom he's going to have a hell of a lot of leverage in the region. I guess we can do that as well in – Birmingham as any place.'

'Are you sure? I mean I'm very fond of Fern and the other Greens, but they're not exactly the most dynamic bunch on the planet.'

'All the more reason to shoot 'em up with the old Troy adrenaline.'

Iris imagined Troy playing a conference hall full of Deborahs and Maries as he'd played the crowd outside Zoom International. If anybody could make the Greens electable, it had to be him.

He lay back in the hammock, thinking. Then he turned to her. 'Tell you what, Iris. I'll go if you go.'

'Me? They don't want me.'

'Sure they want you. Didn't you do that neat thing for them, with the text messages? You have to come. Plus...' He leaned over, reaching for her hand again. 'Plus, it'd be a heck of a lot more fun with you there. C'mon...'

She didn't hear his next words. Her head was suddenly full of several hundred watts of James Blunt warbling 'You're Beautiful! You're Beautiful! You're...'

'What the...?'

'Well, I tried everything else. People have been struck down by thunderbolts for less. You're lucky you've been Chosen, I can tell you. Though, if I weren't infallible, I'd have been having serious doubts about my own judgement in the last few minutes. Not to mention yours.'

'What do you mean?'

'What do I mean? Have you entirely forgotten the book of Exodus? The bit with Aaron and the golden bull?

'Troy is not a golden bull!'

'Not so far off. Once you've adjusted for cultural context.'

'And anyway, it's nothing to do with...'

'Nothing to do with the fact that he looks like Errol Flynn and he's coming on to you like a steamroller?'

'Look, this isn't some cheesy romance, all right? It's a meeting of minds. He's been through the same struggles, that's all.'

'You could have fooled me.'

'He needs to go to Birmingham. We all, actually, since you mention it, need him to go to Birmingham. I've seen what he can do to a crowd.'

'Like Savonarola, maybe? And if it's crowd-pleasers we're looking for, how about Hitler?'

'Hitler! Talking of thunderbolts, where were you with the thunderbolt when he was on the loose? You could have saved a few million lives without much effort.'

'If you want to have the conversation about free will, you'll have to make a booking. It can take a lifetime, and right now, you've got other things to address.'

'Anyhow, Troy isn't some psychotic megalomaniac, he's...'

'All right, have it your own way. You're going to Birmingham with this – disinterested near-stranger – purely to help him help the benighted locals to see the light.'

'Finally you get it.'

'Mind your tongue, young lady. Who needs thunderbolts when there are hammocks and rotting branches all around? Anyway, go if you must, but I'll be watching.'

'I was pretty much taking that as read.'

'And I'm not above a bit of razzle dazzle in an emergency. Ever been turned into a laurel tree?'

'I thought that was Zeus' speciality.'

'And Zeus's other name would be?... But, if you prefer, there's the pillar of salt trick. If you thought waiting in that police station was dull, just try being a human condiment dispenser for ten thousand years.'

Backed by a final crescendo of 'Beautiful.... To Me!' the irritable voice faded away. Iris found Troy leaning towards her, sincerity infusing every perfect pore. 'C'mon Iris, I can't do this without you.'

What was God talking about? Troy's track record spoke for itself. And he needed her help. The Old Testament was full of references to how jealous God was. Clearly, he just didn't like his chosen vessels listening to anybody else.

'Well, I – I haven't spoken to Malcolm really, since... I've no idea what he's got to say to me. I have two children who probably think I'm about to abandon them to an orphanage... Christ! The children! What time is it?'

She held her watch between her face and the dazzle of the sun, which had shifted a good way down the sky. 'Jesus, I have to go and pick up Ted!'

Molly had a few minutes before Ted was due to erupt from the Juniors. Who knew if Iris, or Malcolm, or nobody, was going to turn up for him. She'd better be there just in case. She got out her phone and started texting.

Hi J just chckd diary & ok 4 2morrow if u r still up 4 it? Nything 2 gt out of house 2 b honst. Parnts!!!*** Lt me knw whn & whr ok? M

She hit 'send' and looked up to see Iris hurrying towards her,

her expression more absent even than usual. She came within inches of Molly, and was about to go straight past.

'Hey! Mum?'

Iris stopped and swung back. 'Molly! What are you doing here?'

Her voice was different; softer. And there was a strange look in her eye.

'I was gonna collect Ted. I mean, after all that shit this morning, who knew if you'd be here for him or not?'

'Oh, sweetheart, how sweet of you, how awful it all is! I'm afraid we are - at a bit of a crossroads. I owe it to you to be honest, and I know - I know that one day, maybe not today, but one day, you'll understand.'

In Iris' head, bits of this, at least, sounded more or less how she had planned: brave, sad, full of loving concern, but determined on her course. Apparently that wasn't how it came across to Molly. 'You sound weird, Mum. Are you on something, is that what this is all about?'

'On something? Oh, for goodness sakes, of course not, honestly Molly, don't be ridiculous. It's about... it's about lots of things. But if you must know, it started with a cake. Shouldn't we go and find Ted? He always panics if I'm not there the moment he emerges blinking into the light.'

They set off along the razor-wire fence that separated the Secondary from the Primary School.

'Everything's about cake with you Mum, you are so sad.'

'Well this was a specially embarrassing cake, my darling, as it ended up being chucked all over the high powered executive of a particularly nasty multinational with whom, entirely unbeknownst to any of us, your father appears to be doing business.'

'What as in, a pie in the face? Hey! Wait – not...?'

Molly stopped, whipped out her phone and hit a few keys. 'Not this?'

There it was again, on MySpace this time: 'Pie in Face'. Iris wondered if it was worth contacting MySpace to let them know it was, in fact, a cake not a pie. Probably not. Molly hit 'Play'.

'Stop it there! Look. See?...'

'Fuck, Mum. But...'

She peered at the tiny image of the yelling, male person

throwing it, and then back at her mother. '...that's not you, is it?'

'No, that's my hand, see, just on the edge of the frame, trying to get it back off him, the bloody idiot. But it was definitely my cake. And unfortunately, I was close enough for the throwee to recognise me. Which he did, at that posh do we went to last night. God, was it only last night? Oh look, here he is. Ted! Ted, sweetheart, how are...'

The rest of her sentence was lost in a huge tumbled hug as he ran into her. 'Mum! I thought you weren't going to be here...'

'I know, I'm so sorry, but...'

'Ted, Mum's famous. Like, really mega celebrity level now. She's gone viral. Look.'

This time all three of them watched it, huddled cosily together. Why had she even thought of leaving them? It was so obvious they belonged together.

Iris noticed that today Molly's tee shirt said, 'What You Own Will End by Owning You.' It seemed unkind and unnecessary to point out that the tee shirt itself was, in one sense, something she owned. Molly had clearly had a major change of heart. And Ted would love the combination of animal orphanages and non-stop street footie.

All I needed to do, all along, was follow my heart. Who cares if Malcolm's stuck in the past, with his suits and his technology megadeals and his sleazy little affairs? Let him be embarrassed if he wants to. The children and I are moving on!

Malcolm pushed open the front door with his elbow. Each hand clutched several large, shiny carrier bags and his keys were between his teeth. 'Anybody home?'

'Why shouldn't we be? This is still our home too, isn't it? Or were you thinking of changing the locks?'

Iris came down the stairs with a bowl of water and a sponge, with which she had been trying, not very successfully, to disinter the decomposed phytoplankton from Ted's Chelsea bedside rug. Somehow, this had provided time and space for her rosy optimism about the future to be contaminated by memories of Malcolm's general unfitness to live anywhere near decent people, or indeed near any life form higher than blue-green algae.

Thirty seconds before, Malcolm had been almost willing to believe that what he'd seen outside Buzzybees was totally innocent, and that Iris deserved – after a proper period of grovelling – a second chance. Now, he dumped his shiny, rustling spoils right in front of her on the kitchen table, strode to the stairs without meeting her eye, and called up: 'Molly! Ted! Come down here, I've got a surprise for you!'

Molly's head appeared on the top landing, black hair tangled over her face. 'The surprise being you're working for international corporate criminals, and hanging out with some Icelandic tart half your age? Mum filled us in already. It's okay Dad, you're nothing special. Men have midlife crises all the time.'

'Ha ha, well I see she's made a real effort to give you a balanced view of the situation, so I won't bother sketching in the blank half of the page for now. No, the surprise is, I'm taking you to Dubai for half term. Tomorrow morning, in fact.'

'You are? Since when?' Iris wheeled round to ask this question, and getting no reply, poured the dirty water down the sink with such force that it sploshed over a large area of the floor. 'That would be the same Dubai where they're currently putting the finishing touches to a brand-new, six-runway airport? Where they chill the water in the swimming pools, and run indoor ski slopes year-round?'

'The very same. I could explain, but you seem to prefer to draw your own hysterical conclusions.'

Molly, heading back towards her room, turned to hiss: 'And you seem to have forgotten, Dad, that I'm a key member of Cool the Planet. It wouldn't look exactly great if I started flying round the world on holiday, would it? Duh?'

Ted crashed past her down the stairs, pulling a Chelsea Champions' League away shirt over his school clothes. 'Dubai? What on a plane? Can we watch videos all the way there and all the way back and all the time when we're there?'

He carried on towards Iris, skidded on the wet patch, and landed in a tangled heap with her on the floor. 'Sorry! What are we having for tea Mum?'

Iris looked up, sodden and reeking of old fish. 'Gall and wormwood.'

'Have we had that before? Do I like it?'

'You'll get used to it.'

She grabbed a cloth from the sink, swished energetically at the wet patch, hurled the cloth back, and banged over to the table with a tray. 'Excuse me, could you possibly remove all this... stuff. I need to set the table for tea.'

'Oh, that reminds me'...

Malcolm scrabbled in the bottom of one of the shiny bags. 'I popped into Somerfield on way back and picked up a couple of things. Here you go, Ted, Smarties Megamuffin.'

He tossed a big crackly packet, emblazoned with a giant Nestle logo, over to Ted. 'And there's a pineapple for Moll. I thought she'd probably be a bit fed up of that dried stuff by now.'

Beaming with expansive generosity, he handed the pineapple to Iris, the 'Air Freighted for Freshness' label about six inches from her nose, and asked: 'D'you want me to do the tea? I expect you still feel a bit rough.'

'On the contrary, I've rarely felt better. But then, I wasn't the one who stayed out until two thirty a.m.'

'Well, I had a bit of smoothing over to do, as you can no doubt imagine.'

Molly was still hovering at the top of the stairs, gripped by the drama below. Malcolm, appearing not to notice, opened up his laptop and set it on the table. 'Here Ted, d'you want to check out the hotel? It's pretty special, I'm told. The URL's right here...'

Ted went over and huddled beside his father. Malcolm hit a few keys and the screen filled with an image straight from Cecil B De Mille's Gomorrah; crystal fountains plashing in a vast mosaiced courtyard, surrounded by arcaded terraces, and backed by a deep plantation of date palms.

'Wow Dad, is that the Sheikh's palace?'

'No, Ted, that's your hotel. What else?'

The image dissolved into another, of a salon with Bokhara rugs, a ten-foot plasma screen, and more sofas than a DFS showroom. 'Here we go: "The suite contains its own cinema and mini-gym, a double bathroom with Jacuzzis, underwater massage jets, tap water scented in a choice of four exotic perfumes, and two bedrooms, each with a giant circular bed..." '

'You're wasting your breath.'

Iris, pouring tea in the background like an unpopular au pair, was once again amazed that she could still be amazed by the capricious opportunism of the young.

Malcolm appeared not to hear her.

'... hang on a tick, let's look at the other hotel amenities – here you go Ted... "Our four swimming pools between them offer snorkelling among actual reef fish transported into specially planted living coral, giant slides, submerged air beds, swim up snack bar, and SuperSurfTM kiddies surf adventure. In our 3.5 acre tropical forest playground, you can feed and interact with real monkeys and other rainforest creatures, or travel through it at warp speed on the world's longest rollercoaster..." What d'you reckon? All that, or a week shuttling between the Library and the Leisure Centre. Your choice, no pressure. I'm sure Mum'll think of lots of other exciting treats too, if she's not too busy dismantling the structures of modern capitalism.'

At the top of the stairs, Molly's phone buzzed. She looked at it, rushed back into her room and banged the door.

Malcolm turned to Iris, who was viciously scalping the pineapple. 'I won't have any tea by the way, I had a big breakfast.'

'I expect we can all guess with whom.'

She slammed down the knife and banged his mug and plate back into the cupboard. 'I think you'll find you've totally misread the children, Malcolm. While you were out having your "breakfast," we've had a really positive, intelligent conversation, and though I hate to break it to you so abruptly, you might as well know that they're both entirely with me on - everything. Including Ted, who is deeply concerned for the planet, and understands perfectly the interconnectedness of things. So the idea that either of them would even contemplate going with you, on a plane, to Dubai of all places...'

Molly came out of her bedroom, sniffed loudly, wiped her nose and eyes on her sleeve, and clattered down the stairs. 'And what am I supposed to do while Ted's having close encounters with his cousins in the rainforest?'

Iris stopped in mid-breath, and looked sharply at Molly. Molly avoided looking back as she slid into the seat beside Malcolm, who was smiling at nothing in particular. 'I expect we can turn up something – how about, ah, here we go, "Free twenty meg wireless broadband throughout the suite, three thousand digital videos on demand, twenty-four-hour complimentary room service, ayurvedic spa with free treatments including eighteen different massages, and the world's third largest indoor ski slope, complete with ice sculpture park and toboggan rides." Will that keep you going for a day or two, d'you reckon?'

Molly said nothing, but grabbed a slice of pineapple and sat beside him, scrolling through the site. Ted, his face smeared with every Smartie in the rainbow, looked down and saw the bags. 'Hey Dad, what's in them there?'

'Oh, just some bits and pieces I picked up for the trip - we can get anything else we need in the mall. Malls. Have a look, I think it's fairly obvious whose is which'.

'I haven't said I'm coming...'

'They're yours anyway, Moll. Let's just say I'm celebrating.'

'Tea's ready.'

He still hadn't said a word to Iris. She stood there holding the tray, ignored and forgotten, while Molly and Ted dived into the bags.

'Wow Dad - Billabong trunks! And a Speedo mask and goggles, look Mum it's the Steve Irwin Memorial special in camouflage print, look it gives me shark teeth look Mum!' He ran to her, festooned with designer logos and the scarily lifelike dentition of a Great White Shark.

Iris looked down into Ted's face, glowing with delight, and forced herself to kiss his BreathetasticTM camouflage forehead, as she addressed her husband.

'Did I miss something last night, or have you, by an extraordinary simultaneous coincidence, won the triple rollover on the national lottery?'

'Let's just say that some business breakfasts actually do result in business, shall we?'

He still hadn't looked at her. 'Now, Molly, it's a bit flashy, but with your colouring I thought...' He fished out a DKNY Sport swimsuit. Sleek, simple, shimmery gold.

'Oh Dad! It's....' Molly took it with trembling fingers, stroked it, held it out for another look, then against herself. It was utterly her. Likewise the Nike beach shoes, MiuMiu slip dress, Chanel sunglasses and the Moschino Cheap and Cheerful diamante-rimmed sun visor.

So much for solidarity in the glorious cause.

'The visor's got speakers built in, for your iPod. They're good ones, too, for a change. I had a listen in the shop. And look, Iris...' Finally, he turned to her, with every semblance of innocent goodwill. '...I even found some info on things you can be doing meanwhile. Seeing as this obviously wasn't going to be your bag.'

Suspiciously, Iris took the leaflet from him.' "One Week Sustainable Living Courses in the Beautiful Welsh Mountains"... '

'..."Straw Bale Building Techniques, Simple Sewage, Step by Step to a Plastic Bottle Greenhouse..." – right up your country lane, I'd have thought.'

'Ha ha. Very thoughtful. Does anybody actually want any tea?' The pain in her voice was so obvious that Molly got up to hug her mother with pineapple-sticky hands. 'He doesn't mean it, do you Dad?'

'On the contrary, it seemed to me they'd suit her perfectly. Anyway, as she says neither of you two will come either...'

'Hey, wait, it wasn't me said that!' Molly snatched the swimsuit and hugged it to her chest as she wolfed the rest of her pineapple. Ted, ploughing through the carapace of Smarties on his second muffin, looked anxiously from one parent to the other.

'Why can't we go? Mum, we can, can't we? Can you come too? It looks great doesn't it, will you come on the rollercoaster with me?'

'Your father knows very well, Ted, that...'

'I'm afraid it's not really Mum's sort of thing Ted...'

'She does like rollercoasters, don't you Mum?'

Malcolm stood up and began folding bags. No reason to live in a tip, just because his marriage was in crisis. '...Unless, that is, she regains her sanity and realises that her family is more important than the antics she's been getting up to lately. It's her call. God knows I'm a patient man, but enough is enough.'

The last words were apparently addressed to the recycling box, as he stowed the folded bags neatly into it. He didn't like fighting in front of the children. But it was hardly his fault. She'd flown off the handle the minute he'd appeared, without giving him a chance to explain. He was just defending himself.

He half-turned on his way to the stairs. 'I'm going to pack a few things for myself. If you two want to come up after tea, I'll help you with yours. We're off pretty early tomorrow.'

Molly locked the door behind her and pulled up the message again, like an itch she couldn't help scratching.

Hi got yrs srry wll b prtty bz nxt fw wks, kp in tch ok? c u J

How could he just turn round and do that? The slimy pox-ridden bastard? All that guff about how he admired me, and how cool Mum is! And why? Because I actually bought his stupid line? Well, he can rot in hell along with the other fuckwits at that crapulous school. I can't believe I made such a tit of myself. Thank Christ nobody else saw us. Oh God! I might as well have worn a name tag saying 'pathetic needy boy-mad loser.' Well I won't make that mistake again. No no nonononononono!

She looked over at the holiday bling on the bed, stomped over to her wardrobe, pulled out her baggiest, blackest tee shirt, pulled it over her head, and sat down at her computer.

Altarica felt like coming home, after far too long away. What was up today? The GloboDome was hosting a packed lecture on 'Fractal Scaling in Four-Dimensional Virtual Structures, with Special Reference to Altarican Dwellings' but she wasn't ready to set up house here – not just yet. Over in the Morphology Playpen a bunch of kids were swapping avatars, but she felt even happier than usual sticking with Blank Generic Female.

What she really wanted was to reassure herself that there was still sane, adult life in here. That last time, when Ubiquitur hadn't showed at all, had freaked her. Maybe he'd given up on Altarica, left it to run itself. Maybe she'd lost him for good. That would be bad. But where to begin looking?

She sat back and loaded Megadeth's Dethless Hits into her earplugs. Metal was good for thinking. Blocked out all the other crap, like whatever her parents were up to, which no doubt they'd be telling her all about soon enough, whether she wanted to hear it or not.

As she flew over the virtual parkland, a banner on the GameZone caught her eye. 'LAST FEW DAYS to claim your Early-Bird Special for GAME WORLD! DON'T MISS the GREATEST EVER MMOG and ARG CONVENTION. May 25-29! MINGLE with your favourite TV and game characters! WIN PRIZES on in-game sports and contests! LEARN easter eggs and micro tagging! WATCH demos of games in development, SEE mind-bending new graphics and TAKE PART in real-time, real-life ROLEPLAY'S every day on the convention floor itself "The most fun you can have with some other guy's clothes on!" (Jack Black). Exclusive all-in packages available now from...'

That sounded cool. But there was no way they'd let her go on her own. And anyhow, it looked like she was going to be in Dubai. She'd come back to school with like, a perfect tan and half a stone lighter, and walk right past – he wouldn't even register on her field of vision. Whatever his name was. She couldn't even remember, right?

Meanwhile, she was still looking for the High Master. Of course. He was Ubiquitur, right? Which means 'everywhere'. She didn't have to look. She just had to tunnel. She typed in a few words of code, and sure enough, the nearest surface she zoomed into, there he was, embedded and tiny, but very much active. He wouldn't understand anything about the whole ludicrous Janos escapade. Which was exactly what she needed. He wouldn't give a flying fuck.

Colin hit 'send', still not sure what Morphea had been so upset about, and rather overwhelmed with her protestations of eternal loyalty to Altarica and the pure beauty of knowledge. It was a pity there weren't a few million more like her, so he could actually make some money out of it. Intellectual curiosity was a devalued currency in the virtual world these days.

'So what would it take to turn you lot into a heartless genocidal fighting force?' Colin spent a good part of most nights talking to his bugs, in the belief that any kind of stimulus would make them grow. And, on this occasion, because he was genuinely interested in the answer. But the silence from the neat array in the centrifuge was as enigmatic as ever. You don't get a lot of small talk from bugs. He was about to embark on the next, top-secret element of the bio-nutrition programme, the nightly reading from 'Just William', when he noticed the mail icon his mail icon jiggling epileptically in the corner of his screen.

FROM: mrichie@richiewinterbottom.co.uk
TO: cwinterbottom@richiewinterbottom.co.uk

Col,
Hope things are rolling along okay at your end. This FreeFlow deal seems to be growing by the minute (good news!) but it means I'm

going to be off the scene for a few days, doing what my new colleagues are pleased to call 'Blue Sky Adventuring'. I've also made some rather alarming discoveries about the scale of Iris' recreational activities, which may need a bit of reining in if anything akin to normal life is to be resumed. I'll keep in touch. Back in a week or so, and phone if you need me.

M

Malcolm keyed in 'new message' and wondered what he should say to Kateriina. True, Iris didn't seem quite as penitent as he had hoped, but now he'd won the children over, she was more likely to come round, wasn't she? The more he thought about trying to effect a harmonious introduction between his two children and Kateriina in the check-in at Terminal Three, the more alarming it seemed. And every time he thought about leaving Iris alone here for a week, the image of whatever he'd seen outside that shop swirled back into his mind. If he left her now, God knows where she'd be when he got back. A family holiday in a lovely warm, luxurious place, with nothing to do but rest, talk and have fun, seemed exactly what they all needed to put things right. It wasn't as though Iris and Kateriina would have to spend time together. Maybe he could hold Kateriina at bay for an hour or two, until he'd had a chance to talk to Iris.

Downstairs, in the empty kitchen, Iris slammed the last of the washed-up tea things back in their places. She felt angry, and hurt, and after the faint sunbeam of false hope this afternoon, more than ever an outcaste in her own home.

But below all this stirred an intimation of something worse. If Malcolm still had his contract, whatever it was - and presumably he did, as he'd always been more cautious than a snail under a flower pot, and it was not the action of a cautious man to spend several hundred pounds on holiday tat without a substantial revenue stream in prospect – if this deal was still on, and she hadn't ruined his life after all, why was he still being so vicious to her?

Maybe he had genuinely thought it would be her idea of a treat. Everybody knew men didn't have any emotional intelligence. Or maybe he was offering it as an olive branch, a way for them both to put the children first, together. Either way, she must have hurt him really badly, to have goaded him into using the children as weapons.

She remembered the family holidays they'd had when the children were little. Paddling in pale water with a thrilled, pudgy Molly, shrieking as tiny fish slipped between her toes. Squinting into the sun with a vague, happy consciousness that Ted was about to leap on her and demand another ice cream. How had that blissful Eden turned into this?

I have to go. I can't let them go without me. Lots of people, thousands of people every day do it without even thinking about it, pack a bag and head for the sun. I haven't had a holiday for ages. What difference will one more person make, on a jumbo already carrying six hundred others?

She thought back to that afternoon in the tree house. Suddenly it seemed ludicrous. Just like God had said. Something out of some overblown fantasy, with Troy as Superman and herself as his loyal sidekick. That wasn't her reality. Her reality was here, with her family, making it work.

If I spend the time explaining everything to Malcolm, telling him what the demo has done for Baratoria, getting him to see how much happier we could all be, if they were all a bit more tolerant and I didn't have to be furtive and guilty all the time – if I use the trip for that, surely it's okay to go?

I can go. I have to go.

Iris paused outside the bedroom door, to gather strength. No doubt Malcolm would take full advantage of her apparent capitulation to heap coals of fire on her. She just had to think of the children, and wait for it to be over.

As she stood there, she heard his voice through the door. He seemed to be speaking to somebody on the phone. 'Right then... no, I'll know pretty soon, I'm sure... yes, I'll call. In any case, I'll see you at the check-in... Yup, they're pretty excited. And so am I. Of course... See you then, Kateriina.'

'Kateriina!' 'See you at the check-in!' Oh no. It isn't possible. All that sanctimonious drivel about how I'm – I'M - neglecting the children, and not thinking about MY family, and all along, he's... How could he stoop that low? To sneak his children – MY children – on holiday with that, that...

Iris threw open the door to find Malcolm returning the phone to his pocket, and resuming the orderly packing of a small suitcase with hot-weather clothes. Unlike those of any normal person, they'd been perfectly pressed and folded before being put away for the winter, so now they slid on top of each other as neatly as scales on a fish.

She stood there for a moment, but he didn't even look up. The man beggared all the vocabulary of shamelessness. Iris meant to say something that would scorch the blood in his veins, but what came out was: 'Why not just pack all your stuff while you're about it? You're clearly not coming back.'

He turned to look at her. 'For the millionth time, this is a business trip, okay? Or is nobody allowed to travel more than ten miles from where they live any more? That's really going to help with world peace and understanding.'

'Don't be stupid, that's why we have television, and the Internet.'

Malcolm stood up and opened a drawer beside the bed. Old habit made her add:

'If you're looking for your sunglasses, Ted borrowed them to be Dick Tracy in last year's show. I'm not sure they survived.'

He almost banged the drawer shut, opened another and began pulling out tee shirts and shorts. 'So we can do our work over the internet, can we? Does that include Greenpeace activists and Medecins Sans Frontieres too? Are they supposed to sink whaling boats and cut off gangrenous limbs over the Internet? Or maybe they can get to their battlegrounds in coracles from now on?'

'My God, do you still have those? There's no way you'll get into them now.'

He'd unearthed a pair of shorts patterned with Hawaiian hibiscus, from some unimaginably distant past. A past that was going to be the beginning of a life-long future, together. Iris managed what she hoped was an ironic sneer as she said: 'That's something you could usefully have bought, while you were on your spree. Or maybe your new friend likes her men with their hairy paunches hanging over their trunks?'

'What?' Finally, something had interrupted the orderly process of Malcolm's packing. He sat back and looked at her. Utterly calm, and cold as polar ice. 'I don't know what you think you're talking about. But whatever it is, I'd say it's a bit rich, coming from you.'

'Me?'

'Right now, I haven't time to worry about your pathetic shenanigans. Not that it's any of your business, but this deal of mine, which is purely a business deal, just as this trip is purely a business trip, has nothing to do with CleanTech, or Planet Plenty for that matter. But if it did...' He scanned the contents of the case, made a neat space in one corner, and began to fill it with underpants. '...if it did, it wouldn't have made a blind bit of difference. What d'you think makes the world go round, Iris? Motherhood and apple pie? Or should that be chocolate cake?'

'It wasn't chocolate. Anyhow, I'd rather believe in that, and be wrong, than believe in whatever cynical, hard-boiled "commercial reality" you're getting from that – Grendel monster and her cronies.'

'For God's sake, Iris. Please stop shouting. I don't want the children any more upset than they are already.' He got up and carefully closed the door.

The man wasn't human. How had she have failed to spot it for fifteen years?

She sat on the bed, exhausted. He came back and sat beside her, with an expression of calm forbearance more infuriating than the anger. 'Look. You had children, right? And at that moment, your first responsibility became your family. When they're grown up and gone, you'll have plenty of time to be a battling granny, and I can be somewhere where I don't have to spend my life bailing you out of your messes. Okay?'

'But if I wait till then, it will be too late! The crisis is now, the gas is building up now, the oil shock and all its nasty ramifications are now! They're not going to wait around for Molly to decide her parents are an even more unattractive option than paying rent! When Hitler - to choose a random example you'll recognise – when Hitler was pulling on his wellie boots to invade Kent, Churchill didn't say, "Oh dear, I've a rather pretty still life to finish just now, I'll fight the war in 1947". Did he?'

'But the bit you seem to be missing is that you're not Churchill. Or even Hitler, though you've done a passable imitation a few times lately. You're just a well intentioned, kind, rather anxious person with grandiose delusions about what childish exhibitionism can achieve in the name of politics.'

'Childish exhibitionism?'

'As I said, you'll have a week to think about it. I've said what I've got to say.' And he kneeled by the case, snapped it shut, twirled the combination lock, and carried it downstairs.

As soon as Ted was tucked up, his football-shaped clock set to shriek 'GOAL' at 05 45 next morning, Iris went up to bed too. This was partly because she was utterly spent, but more to bag the bed for herself. After all, if Malcolm was going to be lolling on ten-foot-square silk sheets for the next week, he could stand one more night on the sofa.

It had been perfectly clear that she wasn't welcome on this trip, and now she knew why.

Fine, then. Let him throw in his lot with somebody half his age and twice his height, like Rod Stewart or – Dudley Moore. But I'm not stooping to that level. No judge would give an adulterous husband custody. The children will be mine, safe from that Arctic vixen's influence. And maybe, in due course...

At that moment, the door opened and a familiar shape slid in beside her. She braced herself: had he come to hit her with some more home truths, or cajole her into a last-minute reconciliation? Neither, it appeared two minutes later, as the familiar mint-scented snores wafted across the duvet. How could anybody, even a robot with anti-freeze for blood, spend what could well be their last ever night in the marital bed, just – asleep?

Sheer fury at his cloddish insensitivity kept her wide awake after that, cramped on the edge of the bed. Ignored. Finally, as daylight glowed through the curtains, Iris got up, more dead than alive, to spend a precious last few minutes watching Ted sleep before the alarm went off.

'GOAL!!' She reached over, pulled the pillow off his head, and whispered lovingly: 'Ted, it's time to get up'

'GO AWAY!!!'

'No, you're the one going away, have you forgotten? There's a big fancy limo coming for you, and...' Before she could finish her sentence, he'd shot out of bed and was pulling his trousers on over his pyjamas. Automatically, she went over, pulled the trousers off again, and helped him out of the pyjamas, which was not made easier by his decision to rifle through his encyclopaedic mountain of football shirts at the same time.

Outside, she heard Malcolm come out of the bathroom and go

to bang on Molly's door.

Why am I helping him? Why am I making it easy for Malcolm? You're not. You're making it easy for the children.

She marched Ted into the bathroom, made sure his teeth were clean, packed the toothbrush and the washbag, unearthed the goalkeeper's gloves, and stumbled downstairs to put the kettle on. One big mug of strong builder's tea, one small mug of Earl Grey, one blueberry smoothie, one foamy hot chocolate. A graceful, economical time and motion dance perfected over years, and ripped apart in a moment. Such a pity. Such a waste.

All this, that she and Malcolm had made together. How could they just chuck it all away? Was that what he really wanted? Did she?

'Are you really going to save the world while we're having half term?' Ted looked up at her, his upper lip foamy.

'Did your Dad tell you that?'

Thanks Malcolm.

'Yeah right. "Heads of State paid tribute today to the achievements of Mrs Iris Richie, eighty-five" ' ... Molly, fetchingly draped in a Metallica farewell tour bomber jacket and a pair of Malcolm's old pyjama bottoms, slouched towards her smoothie ' "... for single-handedly saving the world from global conflict and environmental meltdown in seven days. Not since the creation of the world has so much been achieved in a such a short time, commented God. Mrs Richie, ninety-seven..." '

'Don't tease your brother, Molly'

'Well, what do YOU think, pinhead? This is our Mum you're talking about here'.

Iris stood behind Ted and wrapped her arms round him as he drank. 'I'll do my best, Ted, I promise. I'll be saving it for you.'

'But you will be here when we get back?'

She was aware of Molly watching, waiting for the answer.

'You're not getting rid of me that easily!' She smiled at him, and at Molly, who clattered her glass down, not smiling, and made for the door. 'I'm gonna wait outside, okay?'

'Bye Mol – give us a hug before you go...'

But the door banged, and Molly was gone, without looking back. Ted put down his mug, wrapped himself round Iris, and hugged till she could barely breathe. Then he pulled away to search her face with bright, puzzled eyes, 'Please come with us Mum. Please please!

Why don't you want to?'

Just keep going till the car comes. Any minute now.

Then the doorbell rang, and Malcolm appeared from upstairs with the bags. Ted turned to him. 'Dad, make Mum come, we want her to come, don't we?'

Malcolm handed Ted his backpack. 'Out you go and wait with your sister, there's a good lad.'

'It's okay, Ted. I'll be here. Now do as your Dad says.'

Ted hugged Iris once more, then made reluctantly for the door. Malcolm waited for it to slam behind him, put down the bags, and took Iris gently by the shoulders. 'I know you mean well. And I know domestic life gets tedious. But I think you know things can't go on like this, don't you?'

Something about his calm, reasonable, sanctimonious tone enraged her more than any insult. 'Do I? And how long were you planning to carry on your little joint venture?'

His hands dropped away as Molly shouted from outside. 'Dad! Dad you have to come like NOW, the man says it's blue murder on the Westway!'

'Coming!' He picked up the bags, paused for a moment and made for the door.

'I'll keep my phone on, okay?'

And that was it. He closed the door carefully behind him, and before she had a chance to kiss the children one last time, her whole life was gone. She wanted to call out 'Wait!' or 'Not yet!' or 'You're joking, right?'. But there was the car through the window, serenely turning the corner by Mr Slobodka's. Vanished.

What now? A sink full of washing up. A silent house. She ought to make the beds, finish the dishes, put the sheets in to wash. But wherever she looked, all she saw was their absence; all she heard was the awful echo of angry

voices. She had to get out. Anywhere. But this time she was careful to take her keys.

A milky sun was just hitting the park as Iris arrived. She locked her bike to the stump of a baby cherry tree, its splintered top spilling blossom on the pavement. Not even trees have happy childhoods any more.

The park was barely more than a giant outdoor lavatory for the local dogs, with a playground at one end and a skateboard loop at the other, bounded by a path dotted with broken metal benches. Iris began to walk, empty-headed, around the perimeter. Between the path and the fence, the tulips diligently planted by Parks and Leisure Services were swathed in cigarette film and ice cream wrappers. Mechanically, Iris bent to clear them, muttering encouraging words to the bruised petals and bent stems.

People will think I'm a nutter. And they're right. And Malcolm's right. What are my footling efforts, any efforts of some tiny straggle of middle-class do-gooders, against the giant forces pulling the other way? Recycled carrier bags at the supermarket. A few more people biking to work. Turn off the tap while you're brushing. Sales of long-life bulbs up a record twenty percent. Don't leave your phone charger on standby! Like that's going to make a difference.

Look at this place. They give us trees and flowers and grass, and what do we do with it? Dog shit and Magnum wrappers. What an idiot I am to let it get to me. Just live with it.

'Hello, Iris. Goodness, I don't know why you bother doing that, it'll only be right back to how it was by tomorrow. The kind of people who've started to move in round here...'

'Oh, hello Elaine. You're out early.'

And look at Elaine. Fern's gallant army struggles for weeks to collect a hundred pounds, while Elaine and thousands more like her chuck ten times that at a mini-break in Cambodia. It's hopeless.

Iris had collected a substantial pile of malodorous garbage on her walk, which kept Elaine at a safe distance as they walked along together, trailed by a bad-tempered ball of white fur. 'I'm just walking Snowflake, exactly as I do every morning. Leading my dull little life. Not like you, battling the forces of evil and getting yourself all over the TV.'

'I'm not battling anything any more, actually.'

'Well, thank goodness for that. Of course I'd never have said anything but, between you and I, anybody could see you were just making yourself look foolish to no purpose. Snowflake, no! Leave it alone.'

The dog had found a dirty nappy in a patch of wallflowers.

'Put it down, Snowflake!'

But Snowflake thought the nappy was the most delicious thing she'd ever smelled. Elaine pulled a neatly folded latex glove from her pocket, and with enormous distaste bent to pick it up. She stood there, the nappy dangling from her fingers, the dog yapping at her heels.

'I mean, what is the point of you and I doing our little bit, when the Chinese are building power stations hand over fist? You can't stop progress, Iris.'

'There's a bin over there, if you can bear to carry it that far.'

They walked on, each with her whiffy burden. Penance for a life of sinful consumption, thought Iris. Or, as Colin would say, a waste redefinition opportunity. Then Iris remembered the last time she'd seen Elaine. 'But hang on, wasn't that you in a Prius the other day?'

'Precisely my point. Iris. Progress, and wealth creation. As Ron is always saying, if you put the wealth creators' backs up, they'll just leave, and then where will we be? And it's a joy to drive, I can't think why we didn't get rid of that great big Porsche ages ago.'

Iris stopped, and stood there looking at Elaine, sleek with the satisfaction of being one up on everybody else. Floods, droughts and famine might be about to engulf the world in horror, but she was not about to give up her comfy car, her winter tan or her out-of-season raspberries for anybody.

Suddenly something almost like joy flooded through Iris. While there was one Elaine left in the world, she had a job to do. She knew it absolutely, and there was nothing to stop her now.

'Do you know, Elaine, I can't remember when I've so enjoyed talking to you.'

Elaine practically dropped the nappy.

'Really?'

'Yes, you know how sometimes you get chatting with somebody, and what they tell you just happens to be exactly what you needed to hear?'

'Oh well, I make no great claims, but if I do say so myself...'

'Unfortunately I have to run now, but thank you so much! Oh look, here's the bin. Bye!'

The phone rang and rang.

It's the wrong number. He's changed it again. He's left already. He'll think I'm weird, or a stalker...

'Yuh?'

He's asleep, Oh God...

'Oh Christ, Troy, I'm so sorry, I forgot how early it was.'

'Mmmm. Who's this?'

'It's Iris.'

'Hey. Iris. How're you doing?'

'I'm fine. No I'm not. I haven't really slept for the last two nights, to be honest, so I probably won't make a lot of sense, but...'

'Whoa. That's not good. You need to take care of yourself.' His voice dropped a few notes, and softened. 'Better yet, you need someone to take care of you.'

Yesterday, Iris would have been touched by his concern, but today, rather annoyingly, it sounded like a pickup line.

'I'm fine, really. But listen, did you mean what you said, before?'

The line went silent, as he groped for a response.

He's forgotten all about it. What a bloody idiot I am.

'Birmingham? Remember, you said, you'd go if I went...'

'For sure I remember! Birmingham. Let me get a hold of Ignacio. You and me, Iris. We're gonna rock their world.'

Malcolm felt a bit guilty about 'saving the planet over half term', which was probably why he found himself snapping at Ted the fifteenth time he mentioned it. Iris probably thought he'd said it just to set her up, which wasn't true. Though after that cheap shot about Kateriina... it seemed particularly unfair, given that this whole trip was just a giant exercise in fending her off.

But of course Madam hadn't given him a chance to explain any of that, she'd just jumped to her usual melodramatic conclusions. As, he had to admit, had he. Neither of them had done any explaining, and now they were about to be separated by thousands of miles, and God knows what temptations. He was sleepy, and exhausted, and wondering whether it had been quite wise to empty his bank account on the vague assurances of a woman who had probably learned all her business skills from Eva Peron.

That was the next horror facing him. Malcolm had an admirable hold over his emotions in most circumstances, and had managed to squirrel away the question of how he was going to introduce his children to both the concept and the reality of Kateriina, in a mental compartment marked 'en route to the airport.' Now he was en route to the airport, but when he opened the compartment, the question was still there, and without any conceivable answer.

Maybe he should start the conversation now, so they had a chance to get used to the idea before they met her. Or maybe that would just land him in forty minutes of pointless aggravation, objections and speculation that would be answered the minute she appeared – brisk, businesslike, obviously no threat – in front of them.

On the other hand, he really did hate the uncontrollable, and nothing more completely filled that description than Molly and Ted's potential response to the news that their half term week was to be shared with a seven-foot tall, extremely rich ice maiden in the grip of an unaccountable crush on their father. He was about to open the dialogue with some general remarks about how he'd be having to do a bit of business on and off during the week, when his phone rang. He recognised Kateriina's number.

'Hello?'

'Oh, Malcolm. I'm so glad I caught you. Is everything fine? Are you on your way?'

'Absolutely fine, yes.'

Except my marriage is in tatters, and my children don't know about you.

'That's marvellous. D'you know, something has come up, and I'm going to have to meet you out there, I'm afraid. But don't worry, a courier will meet you with the tickets, and somebody will take you to the hotel at the other end. It's a long flight, I'm afraid, but at least with business class you can be a little more comfortable. I should be with you later today or tomorrow at the latest. Such a bore! I hope they won't be too disappointed, I'm so looking forward to meeting them.'

'I expect they'll cope. I'll break it to them gently.'

Could she hear the dizzy relief in his voice? Ted was glued to the TV screen in the back of the seat in front of him, but Molly, who'd pulled one earplug out when his phone rang, looked at him sharply.

'Bye then, I'd better ring off, we're almost there.'

'Bye! See you very, VERY soon!'

Molly pulled out the other earplug, as the car swung into the terminal parking area. 'Who was that? Who's going to cope with what?'

'Nobody. Now, who can spot the person with our BUSINESS CLASS tickets?'

Iris was a few minutes late at the station. It had taken her much longer than usual to pack, initially through trying to arrive at a compromise between what was acceptable to wear in the company of several thousand Greens, and what might make her more attractive than, say, a pile of old newspapers left out for recycling. Attractive to whom, precisely? That she wasn't admitting, even to herself.

But the thrill of the adventure before her - whatever it might turn out to be - was tempered by the thought of what might happen if Malcolm came back unexpectedly, all ready for a touching reconciliation, only to find her gone.

He'd never forgive me then. He'd be bound to think the worst.I can't take that risk.

She emptied the suitcase on the floor and reached for her phone. Then stopped.

So then what? Even if Malcolm does 'forgive me', I'm back to where I started, bored out of my mind, sitting at home while the world descends into chaos, and waiting for the children to leave, so I can listen to my watch ticking for the next forty years. Bugger that. I'm not waiting around for Malcolm, ever again.

She piled everything back in, but with the precautionary addition, in case he did come back and change the locks, of the top half dozen items on her 'what would I take from a burning house?' list: the purple knitted koala that lived by Ted's pillow, a black tee shirt of Molly's, several rather heavy framed photos, and the piston rod from

Malcolm's first ever car, a Ford Capri, that he'd polished up and given her for an engagement present.

So she arrived at Euston Station to find the caravan already assembled: Ignacio trying to stop his children from ingesting the toxic fumes of capitalism from the WH Smith opposite the departure board, and Troy deep in discussion with somebody whom Iris did not immediately recognise but who turned out, when Troy waved to Iris over her shoulder, to be Fern, with blonde hair. This small change had transformed her from a fresh-faced young woman into a 24 carat babe. Before she could stop herself, Iris sang out: 'Hi Fern! Great hair colour, is it new?'

Fern looked at Iris, blushed, twirled a curl defensively in her fingers, and replied: 'Colour? Oh, I was out all weekend on that canal clean-up, you know? I must have caught the sun. Anyway, now that you're finally here, Iris, let's get on the train shall we?'

An hour later, they were all squashed into their seats. Troy had seemed slightly put out to find himself in Second Class, but was obviously not going to suggest outright that the meagre funds of the Green Party might have been expended on giving him a bit more leg room. As it was, he'd settled himself in a seat by the aisle, into which his sheeny, muscled calves spilled casually, in their unbleached cotton cut-offs.

Opposite him were Ignacio and Fern, while Iris was rather pleased to find herself with the children on the other side of the aisle. Fern, who turned out to speak fluent Spanish, and had obviously had time to hear Ignacio's life story while Iris packed and unpacked, whispered as they boarded: 'His wife died having Alejandro – awful! So he takes them with him everywhere.' Iris looked over to Ignacio. 'I'm so sorry.'

He was busy settling the children in their seats, and giving them each a pencil and a drawing-book. He said a few words in Spanish, and the children dutifully opened the books. Iris, already missing Ted and Molly, leaned over and said to Fern: 'I'm so sorry, I don't speak any Spanish. Could you ask them what their pretty books are about?'

Fern, with only a soupcon of smugness, leaned across the aisle and addressed Elena: '?Que libros mas bonitos! De que tratan?'

Elena giggled and shrugged. Fern turned to Ignacio, poised to repeat her question, when he broke in: 'They are picture story books we have made, about children's rights in our country.'

'You speak English!' Fern seemed rather put out, as though their previous conversation in Spanish had been one long practical joke at her expense.

'Very, very bad. Not good for a diplomat.'

'Not so hot for a top-level wheeler-dealer either.' Troy was still relishing the shift in his pal's fortunes. Ignacio smiled at Iris. 'So I try, if you forgive me. We in Baratoria think education is not only for books and facts. We must change many years of capitalist propaganda. So we teach them to be good citizens, when they think they are just making – dipintos?'

He turned to Fern, who jumped in eagerly. 'Pictures. So they're not just colouring in any old pictures, they're colouring in pictures with meaning. They just absorb it naturally. That's so cool!'

Ignacio, evidently realising that the conjunction of a captive audience and a willing translator was not to be squandered, carried on. 'And we have also educational programme for adults. For them, we print their dereches'... 'Their rights' ... 'on the – bolsas? Of food?'

'Food bags? Oh, food packaging. What a brilliant way to get the information out there!'

'..And, we have consilias populares...'

'Popular councils...'

'...so we give all the big decisions, all the power, directly to the – grass roots? Your government does not trust its people. It holds tight to the power, no?'

He clenched his arms to his chest, miming a bandit with his plundered hoard. Fern was bouncing in her seat with excitement. 'Wow, how totally galvanising that has to be! Imagine, Iris. Instead of all those ghastly bureaucracies and all those corrupt time-servers from the building industry and the Chamber of Commerce, imagine if every street, every block of flats had a committee, making all the decisions for themselves!'

Iris looked around, trying to imagine the pallid occupants of the Virgin Family Coach, currently snoozing, slumped over their Nintendos and flicking through magazines, extending an eager welcome to grassroots participatory democracy.

One or two of them had, it's true, turned to see what all the foreign shouting was about. By now, Ignacio was declaiming loudly enough for them all to hear. His whole body was animated by passion for the empowerment of the poor, the voiceless and the dispossessed. He gestured to Elena and Alejandro as he continued: 'We have taught our children to understand that publicidar'

'...advertising...'

'...is selling a lie that is not true, and only for the - fat dogs?'

'Fat cats. Or, um, running dogs?'

'...of capitalism to grab their money and...' He finished with an emphatic pantomime of a fat capitalist shoving the hard-earned pennies of the proletariat into a very deep pocket.

The children in question, meanwhile, were the only occupants of the carriage paying absolutely no attention. They buried themselves even more diligently in the pages of their notebooks, presumably because they'd heard it all before, and more than once.

At this point, the automatic doors from the next carriage sighed open, and the Roving Refreshment Service clanked through, its attendant uttering her monotonous dirge:

'CoffeeTeaSoftDrinksSnacksDrinksCrispsCakes?'

Immediately, Elena and Alejandro dropped their pencils and jumped on their seats to get a better view. 'Snickers!' exclaimed Elena. 'Mira, Alejandro! Mars Bar! Coca Cola!'

Iris couldn't help looking at Ignacio, while Ignacio looked at the children. His brows furrowed like a storm gathering over the high Andes. They fell silent, and cowered back in their corner. Then Fern half-turned to Iris, with the air of a UN mediator navigating a nuclear standoff. 'That really sums it up, doesn't it? No wonder the Bolivarian governments need to exercise strong controls. It's all very well for the foreign media to criticise, but look how suggestible even the most carefully protected children are! You can see why they need censorship.'

Iris, whom the sight of food had reminded that she had once again forgotten to eat anything since leaving her tea untouched that morning, had been in the process of fishing out her purse to offer elevenses all round. Instead, she put it back in her bag, and shared a smile of forlorn sympathy with the children as she, and they, watched the laden trolley clatter into the next carriage.

They arrived at New Street some time later, nourished only by uplifting discourse and bottled tap water from Fern's backpack. Fern produced a photocopied map and said, apologetically: 'All of us Greens are booked in to the Travelodge together, but I'm afraid they didn't have any more rooms. So – I mean, we could double up...'

Troy looked from her to Iris, new possibilities fermenting in his expression.

'...I mean, Iris and me, of course. I don't know about...' but Ignacio had frowned and leaned over to whisper in Troy's ear, and whatever he said apparently changed Troy's mind. 'Hey, no problem. We'll sort something out. It's just a bed for the night, right?'

Unfortunately, Troy's enquiry at the station's accommodation bureau revealed that the only beds for the night were at the Endymion Park Plaza, the most expensive hotel in town, and the only rooms available at no notice were two top floor suites. Iris' alarm as she found herself waving goodbye to Ignacio and the children was somewhat dissipated when she discovered that the several rooms of the other suite contained several beds, one of them the largest she'd ever seen. Troy kicked off his sandals and threw himself down on it, spreading his arms generously. 'This is more like it, huh?'

Iris wasn't sure whether he meant the hotel itself, the suite, or her presence in it, alone with him. It certainly seemed an odd choice for an environmental activist: the place was bristling with electronics and blasted with air conditioning. A giant fridge-freezer behind the wet bar churned away making ice nobody would use, and God knows how many gallons of hi-pressure hot water it would take to fill even one of the twin jacuzzis.

She stood there, wondering how to frame a response that wouldn't imply the wrong assumptions. Troy saw her bemusement, and laughed:

'Not that I'd stay in a place like this from choice. Shit, no. Give me a mattress and a million stars and I'm happy. No, this is all for Ignacio. A guy in his position's gotta stay in the pack, or he loses face. So you and I pretty much have to go along.'

He yawned, stretched and looked around the vast, padded

room. 'Still, you can kind of get how they're suckered into it, huh?'

He went to investigate the fruit bowl, and helped himself to a peach that had certainly not been grown in West Bromwich. 'Plus, you know, it's the last place the spooks would look for me.'

'The spooks?'

'Sure. After what we did to Zoom, I put a foot wrong and they'd be all over me like hives. Always keep the cops guessing, Iris. And always let 'em know you've friends with money.'

He sat on one end of a giant sofa, and patted the billowing cushion beside him.

'But that's enough about me. C'mon over here, Iris.' His voice dropped to a swoony velvet whisper she'd have to get closer to hear. 'It's time you and I got to know each other a little, huh?'

Throughout his speech, Iris had fought a growing unease at Troy's evident comfort in these lavish surroundings. She remembered the Rolex, and the iPhone. And now all this about hiding out from the Secret Services by not doing what they'd expect.

She didn't need the voice in her ear to know what it would be saying. Instead of yielding to the promise in his voice and the tug of his hand, she found herself dashing for the door. Troy sat up, amazed, as she banged on the door of Ignacio's suite opposite.

'Hey, Ignacio, I had a thought. Wouldn't it be better if I stayed here with the kids, and then you and Troy can do all your, you know, business stuff and we won't be disturbing you? I'll just get my things, and then we'd better get to the Landfill!'

Fern had been having a difficult afternoon. Having Troy deliver his last-minute keynote address at the local landfill site had seemed a masterstroke when it had first occurred to her, and one certain to attract all of the local press and, who knew, the national majors. Well, at least the Guardian Unlimited. After all, this was the national conference of the party whose central concern had suddenly become that of the entire planet. Admittedly, in the last year or so all the other parties had somehow managed to shoplift these concerns and arguments, and re-package them to their own advantage. But there wasn't much the Greens could do about that. It would look, to say the least, petty, to stamp their feet and shout, 'We said it first!' with civilisation's fragile ark rapidly approaching an irreversible Niagara.

The main thing was that people were finally listening. She had arrived at the Arnold Bennett Waste Processing Facility full of enthusiastic anticipation, and set off happily enough with Mr Goodbody to check out the plant's recommended backdrop for the speech.

'I think you'll be very pleased with what we've come up with, Ms Armitage'

'Oh, please, I hate titles, they're so antidemocratic aren't they? Just Fern is fine. Alastair.'

Mr Goodbody rather liked being called Mr Goodbody, antidemocratic or not, but as he'd only been drafted in for a day from Facilities Management, he decided not to make a point of it. They walked past a couple of large, hangar-like buildings, and at the third he punched in a code, pushed open the door for her to go in first – probably also undemocratic – and followed her in.

'Well, here we are' he announced, with gruff satisfaction. 'What do you reckon?'

It was hard for Fern to put into words what she reckoned, but what she felt was mostly surprise, verging on panic. Mr Goodbody added, helpfully: 'It's the most highly engineered plant in the whole Three Counties, this. Brand new technology, cleanest there is.'

That was the problem, right there. They were standing in a vast vault of sparkling tubes, pipes and boilers, with not a bit of rubbish in sight. This was not at all what Fern wanted as the backdrop for Troy's towering, Mosaic denunciation of the ugly face of greed. She'd dreamed of something smelly and disgusting, a desert of foetid trainers, bubble pack and old cushions, as high as the Pyramid at Giza, as endless as the Sahel, as malodorous as Shrek's swamp. Not this.

'Oh. Goodness. What a surprise. It is clean, isn't it? I thought - isn't there a place where it all arrives? All the unprocessed stuff, you know that people have just shoved in their bins?'

'There is, but it's not a place you'd want to go, believe you me, miss.'

'Oh no really, I would. I mean...' She thought carefully about how to win him round. 'How about we do a sort of "before and after" bit? If we go first to the place where it's all dumped...'

'That would be, bulked up, cell-tipped and compacted, I presume?'

'Of course. That's just what I meant. If we sort of go there first, just to you know, show people how bad it can be, the truly garg – gig – giant scale of what you're faced with, you know, what people expect you to deal with...'

She looked sideways to see if sympathy worked on Mr Goodbody. It's hard to tell with engineers. '...and then you know, that way they'll be even more impressed when they see the solution, how amazingly you deal with it!'

Mr Goodbody looked more mystified than inspired, but being only on secondment, he had little experience to help him out. 'Well, it's your call, I'm just here to mek sure you people get what you want. But I have to warn you, it's not very salubrious out there. Not at all.'

'That's fine! That's absolutely fine, not salubrious is exactly what they'll be expecting, isn't it? And everybody's been warned to wear wellies, haha.'

Mr Goodbody set off towards the exit. 'And it can tend to get a bit noisy. I hope he's a good pair of lungs on him, your man.'

Troy and Iris arrived at the main entrance to the plant five minutes before he was due to speak. He had no notes and had made no obvious preparations, but Iris assumed that he was so used to this sort of thing he didn't need to bother. He had also said not a word to Iris ever since she'd fled into the other suite, but this turned out to be something of a relief. Everything else going on in her life seemed to be making it quite complicated enough, for the moment.

Ignacio had decided to forego the landfill, on the basis that having dedicated his early life to escaping from a favela entirely built out of garbage, it might well trigger devastating flashbacks. Plus, the children needed protecting from the myriad temptations of the hotel.

'You're wanting Active Cell 343' said the man in the guardhouse. 'It's about a ten minute walk. Straight down, you can't miss it, and watch out for the lorries.'

They set off, Troy loping easily in his rugged boots, Iris slithering on the muddy path as she tried to keep up gracefully. Every few seconds a sixteen-wheeler would attempt to run them off the road, and from time to time their faces would be brushed by a wisp of slimy clingfilm that had stubbornly resisted the bulking-up process, preferring to take its chances on the chilly eddies of the truck's slipstream.

A light drizzle, too listless to fall as rain, hung in the air as Troy and Iris arrived at the little huddle comprising Fern, Mr Goodbody, and half a dozen Green Party honchos. As far as they could see in every direction were giant rectangular rubbish tips, some covered with earth, others being added to. They could barely hear Fern's frantic yell of greeting over the sounds of compacting, tipping, and earthing over. A Safety Officer lurked around, disapproving, and chivvying people away from the crumbling edges of the tip.

Fern scrambled over to them, her face glowing with excitement. 'So what do you think?' she yelled into Troy's ear. 'Pretty gross, isn't it?'

Troy, who'd been huddling away from Iris like a sullen child, was suddenly all charm and energy again. 'I should say so!' he yelled back at Fern. 'You think they'll be able to hear me?'

'What was that? Shall we give it a few minutes for the Press to get here?'

'Sure'. He turned up the collar of his Patagonia jacket and got out his phone.

Five minutes passed. Then ten. A few more party faithful straggled up. Iris was almost beginning to feel sorry for Fern, when suddenly Fern's face lit up and she scrambled across to greet a girl even younger than herself, wearing a determined air, a huge puffa jacket and an implausibly large head of ginger bubble curls, and carrying a tape recorder and a gun mic.

'Katie! You made it! Everybody, this is Katie, she works for Midlands Today. Katie, can I introduce Troy Hauser? Should we wait for the crew? Are they on their way?'

Katie smiled briefly at Troy, took Fern's elbow and steered her a little way away, rather needlessly in view of the ambient noise level. Iris watched Fern's cheery face melt into disappointment. Then she said something back to Katie, and returned to Troy with a look of gritty resolve worthy of the Normandy landings.

'So, apparently there's been a bit of a mix-up and today she's just here on her own initiative, sort of thing, but she did just stress that if it's a good story, the Editor will definitely go for it...'

'Except with no camera, it'll just come over like a radio interview in a freight yard.'

Fern looked like a kitten who's just had a rock chucked at her. Troy smiled his thousand watt smile and put an arm round her. 'Hey. No big deal. We'll do the speech some place else. Give us more time to organise the publicity, get your friend a camera, huh?'

She smiled back up at him.

Oh god, thought Iris. Maybe I'd better warn her... No, she's a big girl. Going blonde doesn't necessarily wipe out your brain cells, does it?

But Fern did seem alarmingly smitten. 'Oh, really?... Okay then, but since we're all here...' Fern raised her voice to include all eight people who were still huddled around the tip. '...and as Mr Goodbody has kindly agreed to answer questions, does anybody have any?'

Mr Goodbody stood there, helpfully. Fern stood there, hopefully. Katie stood there, journalistically, recorder primed. Troy was inching his arm further round Fern's waist. Nobody else moved or spoke.

Iris just wanted to make everybody feel better, but she couldn't think of a question. All these weeks she'd been thinking of little else but rubbish, its causes and consequences, and now her mind was totally vacant. Then she remembered something she'd spotted in the local paper in their suite.

'Excuse me!' she shouted, waving her hand like a schoolgirl. 'This mall that's opening tomorrow – the one that's going to be the biggest in Europe – what are they going to do with all the waste from there?'

Mr Goodbody's face brightened. 'Well, young lady, that's a very interesting question, I'm glad you asked me that, because it's one I'm in a position to answer as fully as you require.'

He launched into a long and detailed description about combined heat and power schemes and on-site composting technologies, to which Iris listened dutifully, with lots of encouraging nods and smiles. Meanwhile the other Greens drifted silently away, while Fern held a whispered summit with Katie, in which she appeared to be urging her oldest pal to give it one more shot, while her oldest pal wondered when, if ever, it would be payback time.

Iris was suddenly aware of a whisper in her ear. This time it wasn't God but Troy, who had deferred his sulk to ask a question. 'What's this about a mall opening?'

Iris whispered back without breaking eye contact with Mr Goodbody, whose equilibrium in the face of all the changes of plan appeared to be sustained only by her loyal attentiveness. 'I think it's tomorrow, and it's going to be the second biggest in the world. You know, acres and acres of shops and restaurants and playgrounds, all under a giant glass dome. Non-stop playground of consumer capitalism, etc. Very, very un-Green. In fact...'

She forgot Mr Goodbody for a moment, as the thought struck them both at once.

'...it'd be...'

'The perfect goddamn place for my speech!'

Iris had had surprisingly little difficulty persuading Troy to accept her absence from the Salsa Evening. Allured though she obviously was by the prospect of the indigenous music of the High Andes, performed by representatives of the Global Women's Strike and stoked by a medley of vegan canapés, the prospect of an entire night of uninterrupted sleep, on her own, between crispy sheets with a sumptuous thread count, allured her even more. And though she was fairly confident of being safe, from now on, from Troy's attentions, who knew what the heady rhythms of the tango and the bossa nova might not unleash in him?

So she waved him and Ignacio off, got undressed, and went to check on the sleeping children before tumbling into oblivion.

But the minute she saw the children she thought of her own, and the minute she thought about them, she couldn't help also thinking about Kateriina – Kateriina lolling beside Malcolm in a white teenykini, Kateriina tutting over Ted's sunburned neck and soothing it with cream - that hand, touching her child! Somebody else kissing it better! That - giant elk - tucking her own children, Iris' children, into bed, and singing Finnish lullabies to them in a voice no doubt trained at Scandinavia's finest conservatoire.

She was more exhausted, yet more wide awake, than she'd ever been in her life.

Oh God. Oh please, just let me sleep.

'No point asking me. It's not me stopping you from sleeping. It's that perfectly good brain you've addled. You got yourself into this mess, and you're going to have to get out of it.'

Both ears were buzzing this time, and the effect was a weird kind of SurroundSound seeming, at first, to be in the room, not in her head. Iris sat up, and scrabbled for the light. A sigh crackled through her head. 'We've been over this before. I'm not some cheesy spiritualist apparition, you know.'

'Why are you here, if you're not going to help me?'

'We've been over that, too, if you remember. I'm always here, more or less. Besides, there's a fundamentalist bishop in Kentucky I'm trying to avoid. Why these people think they have a special claim on my attention, just because they give themselves fancy titles and dress up in frocks...'

'Well, I'm happy to be your alibi, but please may I go to sleep now?'

'If you can, by all means. But I think you'll find you're far too confused. I blame myself, or at least I would if it weren't ontologically impossible. I give you lot the opportunities and the intelligence to make yourselves safe and comfortable, and look at you! Moaning and whingeing if you're not happy round the clock, and so dim you need the days of the week printed on your underwear. Once upon a time it was worth my while to manifest in church. Even deliver the odd miracle. People used to thank me then, just for getting through another week. These days it's all grumbling and wanting. What you need is a few plagues, deformed children, wasting illnesses, natural hazards, feral animals and internecine wars. Then you'd be a bit more grateful for the crumbs of ordinary domestic happiness you manage to claw out of the chaos. But no, it's all got to be a fairy story. The odd minor disagreement, and all the toys go out of the pram.'

Minor disagreement? Was that what He called it? It hadn't felt minor – was it only this morning? Was it a minor disagreement whether your family or the wider world had first claim on your fleeting passage through life? What had Malcolm called her – a childish exhibitionist? But Troy and the others said she was a heroine, a saviour. That didn't sound like a minor difference either.

If only there was somebody to mediate, some neutral third

party who could explain them to each other. For a moment she wondered about asking God to smooth her path with Malcolm, till she remembered her husband was existentially incapable of believing in voices, and would probably try to banish the Deity with eardrops.

Anyhow, the voice was fading. 'If you'd take my advice, you'd go and live in a nice empty cave for a bit. On your own. But you're not going to do that, are you? You've barely got rid of those encumbrances of yours, and here you are, wanting them back...'

from: Kateriina Toivonen, ktoivonen@freeflow.org
to: Malcolm Richie, mrichie@richiewinterbottom.co.uk

Malcolm!

I'm certain you and the kids are having loads of fun, and I'm sick as a dog that I'm missing out. Unfortunately a situation has developed in one of our processing facilities in Colombia, and I've been asked to help strategise it through. It looks like I may not make it out there just yet.

But that's no reason for me to hold you up. So I have arranged a car and driver to take you to the Genius Centre location, where you can soak up the atmosphere and get inspired. Then we can talk it all through together when we meet up.

I'm so envious! Don't you just love it out there?

Till VERY soon

XK

Two days into the trip, Malcolm was feeling rather like a chocoholic celebrating the end of a prolonged fast; not as happy as he'd expected, and distinctly nauseous. Already, he and Ted had fed sardine lollies to the penguins at the SnoDome, jogged along the Great Wall of China, and ridden a rollercoaster through a giant spitting cobra, only to be spat out like undigested lunch. The relief he felt at Kateriina's message was not just that she and the children would be kept apart for a bit longer, but also that he could finally do something sensible for an hour or two. He picked up the hotel's 'What's on Today1' guide and went to find Ted, who was lying on his back in the bedroom, watching cartoons on the TV in the ceiling.

'I've got to go out for a bit – what d'you fancy doing meanwhile?'

Ted kept on staring at the screen. 'What is there Dad?'

'Well – let's see: go karting, paintballing...'

'No.'

'...Space Shot, camel racing....'

'Boring!'

Malcolm threw the Guide onto the bed and started to make things up. '...ride a rocket to Mars, take a flying carpet to Aladdin's cave, meet the mermaids in the coral reef, learn to talk animal with Dr Doolittle...'

'Boring Boring Boring!!'

Ted drummed his fists and feet on the bed, adding, perhaps superfluously: 'I'm bored!'

'Why's that then?'

'It's not real! None of it's real! I want to do something real!'

'Okay well, when I get back, I promise we'll do something completely real. Meanwhile you just hang on here for a bit, there's a good lad, don't go anywhere, and if you're hungry just call the nice people at Room Service, okay?'

Molly was also flat on her back, on a heart-shaped lilo in the middle of the Hollywood Starlet pool. It wasn't the text from Janos that was bothering her. Within a day, it had turned into an embarrassing blip, and she was just grateful not to have made more of an arse of herself, and more publicly. It was this place. She'd worked her way through the Wadi Pool, the Cote d'Azur Pool and the Rat Pack Pool, all of which turned out to be excuses for yet more blue tile and palm trees. She'd tried the on-demand video library, but the problem with having three thousand films at your fingertips is that it's all too easy to switch the minute the action falters. In two hours she'd watched the beginning of seventy films, all of which she remembered loving last time, but none of which now seemed any good at all.

Maybe her problem was being too clever. Maybe she'd overfed her intelligence, and now it was having like, withdrawal. What was the best way to kill off spare brain cells? It was bound to be around here somewhere.

'I've got to go and do a work thing. It might interest you. D'you fancy coming?'

Malcolm was looming over her. Hot weather didn't suit him; he was pink and shiny, and he'd never really had the legs for shorts. Molly paddled her hands in the water, drifting slowly towards him. 'I s'pose so. There's fuck all else to do here.'

'I'll take that as a heartfelt yes, shall I?'

The car drove them silently between twinkling glass towers and low-rise condominium complexes. Finally it swung in through a metal gate, and drove down a drive as smooth as a knife blade. On either side was a perfect strip of emerald turf, and beyond the turf, blocks of office units in a variety of familiar styles: Hacienda Style, Adobe Style, Colonial Style, French Style and Mediterranean Style. All identical in height, layout, acreage and amenity. All unblemished, and apparently unoccupied.

The driver halted the car at the end of the drive, in front of a large square of unmarked sandy earth. 'Here is site. Please sir madam, get out and look around.'

Malcolm looked out, hoping that the square of earth would miraculously appear more inviting close up. 'Coming, Mol?'

Molly stared out of the window, then back at him, as though the sun had turned his brain. Reluctantly, he opened the door, clambered out, and walked slowly onto the patch of earth. He looked around him at the bland, silent offices, and beyond them at the bland, sheeny structures of the city. How was genius supposed to find inspiration in surroundings like this? Shakespeare would have struggled to write a postcard here. He tried to think what had inspired him in other places he'd visited; he remembered watching tuna nets being folded, hay being winched up to winter barns, spices weighed in complex balancing scales. He wiped his neck, turned back to the car and leaned in to the driver.

'Is there somewhere I can see people actually doing things? You know – working?'

'Working people? You want to see working people. Here, in Dubai?'

'Er – yes?'

The driver looked baffled. He had been asked for many things in this job, and was proud never to have drawn a blank. But this one had him stumped. Malcolm continued: 'You know – whatever people do here. Did here. Crafts? Traditional activities?'

'Ah!' The driver's face cleared. His reputation was safe. 'I know place. Hop in please sir!'

An hour later, Malcolm and Molly emerged from the Old Dubai Theme Park, where they had indeed seen people working: animatronic fishermen swaying in fibre glass boats, animatronic pearl divers opening mechanical oysters, and animatronic Bedouin feeding authentically bad-tempered holographic camels. They climbed back into the car, where the driver turned to them eagerly.

'Lots of working people, sir?'

'Indeed. Thanks. I think we can go back to the hotel now.'

Malcolm sat back, feeling no more inspired than when he'd set out. Here was a place where anything was possible: archipelagoes in the shape of the world, underwater hotel rooms, the Eiffel Tower re-conceived for modern comfort, as a luxury apartment block. But when you can have everything, and do anything, what do you want? How do you decide?

'The problem with this place is, there's no here here.' Molly turned from gazing blankly at the shop-fronts gliding by. 'It's like Second Life, actually. It even looks like Second Life. Only it's all so like, literal. I mean, why bother making a fantasy place out of like, actual concrete and stuff, when you can make a virtual fantasy place, and save all the energy and shit. Like, imagine what the carbon footprint of this place is...'

'Carbon footprint? You're sounding just like your Mum.'

'So? Is that so bad?' She turned to stare at him. 'She's still my Mum, you know. Plus she's still your wife, from what I understand. She'd hate it here.'

'Just as well she's somewhere else then, isn't it?'

Molly didn't say another word for the rest of the trip, and as soon as the car came to a stop she slid out and disappeared into her room. Malcolm went to look for Ted, and found him exactly where he'd been, only the other way round on the bed, watching Spongebob Squarepants upside-down.

'I'm...'

'Let me guess – thrilled? Excited? Grateful and happy to have been brought five thousand miles to a cornucopia of every luxury and extravagance the human imagination can conceive?'

'...BORED!!! You said we could do something real, what can we do that's real Dad?'

Malcolm craned his neck up to the TV screen. Spongebob's bathing trunks gave him the idea. 'We can go to the beach. This place has acres of beach. Is that real enough for you?'

By the time they'd collected their bathing things and ascertained from the concierge that there was indeed a beach, and only ten miles away, the car had gone. Eventually, another car arrived, and drove them to the beach, where one of the thirty very helpful lifeguards on duty informed them that the beach was closed, owing to a 4cm swell observed half an hour ago, which according to the terms of their public liability insurance meant that no bathing could be allowed, even supervised.

Ted's face fell as he and Malcolm stared out at the perfect glassy expanse of the ocean. The lifeguard took pity on them. 'But only a few miles away we have Wild Wadi Theme Park. There you can find artificial thunderstorms, artificial surfing waves and many other attractions! Very safe for children! Computer controlled!'

Ted didn't even look at the lifeguard. He turned, trailing his Chelsea beach towel from one hand and his Steve Irwin shark mask from the other, and made for the car. As Malcolm got in after him, a tear dribbled down Ted's face.

'I want my Mum. I want to go home!'

FROM: mrichie@richiewinterbottom.co.uk
TO: cwinterbottom@richiewinterbottom.co.uk

Col,

Things have wrapped up a bit sooner than anticipated here, so it looks as though I'll be heading home tomorrow, though may not make it into the salt mine until the day after. Have not been in direct communion with the Queen of Green, nor have her activities since our departure made it onto CNN, so not exactly sure what awaits on the domestic front.

Hope you've been lighting fires under our friends in the shires, and look forward to hearing all about it.

M

At the moment the email pinged into his in-box, Colin was squashed in a shuttle bus heading from Birmingham City Airport to the Convention Centre. In Malcolm's absence, he had completed an overdue report on anaerobic digestion of non-hazardous matter, made several faint-hearted calls to the unattended phones of local council waste reduction czars, finished reading 'William and the Currant Bun' to his bugs, and, thus stimulated, launched them successfully on the next stage of their experimental activities, which involved a mixture of engine sludge and photocopier ink, at a considerably higher temperature than they'd had to put up with before.

Their performance had exceeded even his expectations, and, as it was not possible to reward them directly – bugs not having, so far as he could ascertain, pleasure centres, as we would recognise them – the next best thing seemed to be to reward himself. The Gaming Convention was in full swing; he could easily whiz off there for a couple of days, and be back long before Malcolm, who would never need to know anything about it. Malcolm had no idea that Altarica even existed, but if there was some way Colin could turn a penny on it, he might – just might – free himself from his current grim servitude to Waste.

The bugs nestled, in their vacuum sealed travel pod, in the breast pocket of his Terylene sports jacket. In the bag at his side were his overnight things, his promotional materials and the robe and hat his Mum had sewn him the Christmas after Altarica was launched. They weren't exactly high fashion items, but they hid his face and body almost completely. He felt much more comfortable when people couldn't see much of him, and it helped him get into character.

He stared out of the window as the shuttle bus looped off one motorway onto another. It certainly wouldn't be Malcolm's idea of a holiday destination. But then, nothing would have dragged Colin to Dubai...

from: Malcolm Richie, <u>mrichie@richiewinterbottom.co.uk</u>
to: Kateriina Toivonen, <u>ktoivonen@freeflow.org</u>

Hello Kateriina,

The kids and I have had a wonderful time here, thanks to you and your generosity, and I very much enjoyed the site visit. The possibilities are certainly wide open, and I look forward to discussing them all with you very soon. In fact, the moment I saw the location, I just wanted to get back to work, so I've taken the liberty of catching an earlier return flight than scheduled, on the assumption that your other concerns would prevent your joining us here.

I can't thank you enough for introducing me to Dubai which has, as you foresaw, given me much food for thought. Give me a bell when you're free and we can get going on the Distribution Centre.

Yours,
Malcolm

Composing an email that made it sound as though a plan for the Genius Centre was even now bubbling away in his head, without actually lying outright, had been the hardest part of the change of plan. Malcolm had considered adding some expression of regret after the sentence about Kateriina not making it out to join them, but decided in the end that the last thing she needed was more encouragement. He'd had no problem changing their flights, and even less getting Ted and Molly to pack their bags.

For his own part, although he wasn't especially enjoying Dubai, he wasn't much looking forward to what they might find at home – or more to the point, might not. But he obviously couldn't hide away for ever, and it was always possible that a miracle had brought Iris to her senses, and they'd open the door on 26 Hartland Gardens restored to conditions that a few months ago he'd have described as 'fine', but now, in retrospect, appeared Arcadian.

The flight had gone perfectly until the point, towards the end, when their doze was punctured by the chirrup of the co-pilot on the tannoy, announcing that, owing to an earlier suspected terrorist incident at London Airport, they were going to be diverted elsewhere.

Molly stirred in the seat next to Malcolm and muttered: 'Wassat?'

'We're landing somewhere else, I think. Birmingham? Sorry about that, we'll have to get a train, if we land at any kind of reasonable hour. What's the local time in England, any idea?'

Birmingham. Sorry. Sorry? What was that about Birmingham? A faint bell rang in Molly's head ...Game World! It would still be going on! That was like, the most amazing piece of luck, ever.

'Don't worry Dad. I expect we'd better stay over. Don't want poor Ted getting home totally knackered from his holiday, do we?'

Iris was woken by the sound of a vacuum cleaner in the corridor outside. She must have fallen asleep while God was still lecturing her. Jesus was reported to have had harsh words for Peter under similar circumstances, but human endurance, as He'd reminded her, had degenerated considerably since those days.

She opened her eyes. The vacuuming sound was not reassuring. How long had she slept? She could hear a tinny babble coming from the other room. The children must be starving. She stumbled out of bed, padded over and opened the door.

Elena and Alejandro were lying on the floor, inches from the plasma TV, each slurping happily from a can of Coke. Cushions were scattered round them, and empty chocolate wrappers and crisp packets spewed from the gaping minibar.

Seeing the door swing open, they jumped to switch off the TV, hid the Cokes behind it, and attempted to shove the incriminating wrappers out of sight. Elena pulled two notebooks and two pencils from under a cushion, and they were about to bend their heads into studious attention, when they simultaneously realised that Iris was not their father. 'It's okay, he had to go to a meeting, so I said I'd look after you. Would you like some breakfast?'

Two dubious, baffled faces looked back up at her. Iris patted her tummy and poured an invisible hot chocolate down her throat. 'Come on, let's get you dressed. I don't know about you two, but I'm ravenous.'

The coffee shop was packed with men in suits and lapel badges, gulping down filter coffee and cardboard croissants. But Troy and Ignacio weren't in the coffee shop. Troy, Ignacio and – ah, Fern!

were the last occupants of the hotel's hushed, chandeliered dining room, where they sat at a large central table, surrounded by the rout of what had clearly been a vast and enjoyable breakfast, courtesy of the onerous requirements of trans-national corporate convention.

Seeing their father, the children rushed to his side. Ignacio looked up, smiled and waved Iris to join them. A waiter appeared with three more chairs. Iris slid in between Elena and Troy, who had Fern on his other side. Iris pulled a menu from beneath the crumbs, feeling much more able to face her future than she had twelve hours ago. 'Morning. Did everybody sleep well?'

'Muy bien, gracias.'

Fern looked up with a brief smile, before bending her head in again towards Troy's. Troy didn't even look up.

Iris put down the menu and scrutinised them. Fern was looking somewhat the worse for whatever it was, and appeared to have lost all interest in Ignacio. Troy, on the other hand, might have slept for a thousand years and then done a hundred laps of the pool. He'd never been more handsome, charismatic, vivacious, or attentive. To somebody else.

Iris felt a twinge of humiliation – just because she hadn't jumped into his arms and his bed, did that totally annul all her other achievements? Wasn't he supposed to be about saving the world, and hadn't she done quite a bit more than Fern on that front, despite a total lack of training, or time served minuting committees?

In fact, she was more disappointed about that than his priapic leanings. That was the sort of guy thing nobody took seriously. But unless he made his speech, and unless it was a history-changing triumph, everything she'd risked by coming here was pointless. And, worse, she'd look like exactly the naïve idiot Malcolm had accused her of being. Whatever Troy thought about it, she was staying on his case until after the speech.

And the least he could do, after dragging her here, was stand her breakfast.

Iris picked up the menu and addressed the waiter, busy clearing the mountain of glasses, bowls, plates and cutlery scattered over the sparkling acres of linen. 'I'll have the full English, please, with soft scrambled eggs and two fried slices.'

The waiter barely glanced at her. 'No cooked food. Only continental.'

The others had had bacon. She could see the remnants. There was even something on Troy's plate that looked distinctly like a crumb of black pudding. So much for only eating meat you've killed yourself..

She was almost hungry enough to face the indignity of an argument, but not quite. The waiter paused for a microsecond to give her one last chance. Iris whispered: 'Oh, okay. Sorry. My fault for being late. Continental it is, then. Oh, and could the...'

But the waiter had vanished before she could order for Elena or Alejandro, bundled on Ignacio's lap. Meanwhile Troy was mesmerising Fern with an impassioned monologue, barely punctuated by huge bites of toast.

'...and sell 'em on the big picture story. A wholesale, top to bottom, one hundred ten per cent value switch. Like, for instance...'

Maybe he was trying out his speech. It seemed to be going down well. Iris just missed the last triangle of marmaladed toast as he seized it, gesticulating to a vast audience in the fire-retardant drapes behind Fern's chair:

'...imagine a world where the wealth of nations is measured not by the junk that passes between them - a thousand tonnes of pig iron one way, a million Barbie dolls and patio lamps the other - but by the good they do each other, and the happiness of their people. There's a radical paradigm shift, huh? The ChimQumKwat in Northern Manitoba derive their status not from what they get. No!' He leaned in to share the secret with Fern. 'They get more status, the more they give away! He, or she...' his free hand squeezed Fern's on the tablecloth '...who gives the most, ends up gaining the most; in respect, in affection, in all the ways that really count. Their lives are simpler. They sleep easy at night. And we have their example right before us. So why the hell can't we learn from it?'

Whatever his faults, the man certainly knew how to string words together. Iris tried to imagine Pie Man and his colleagues evaluating this particular paradigm shift, and decided that Troy must be betting on the simpler emotional reflexes of the masses.

Who cares, in the end, how much of a scumbag he is? So long as he does his stuff at the mall.

Fern seemed quite faint with rapture, though it could have been hunger, as she seemed to have been too excited to eat at all.

At that moment the waiter reappeared with a cup of thin, grey coffee and a single, weary croissant on a gleaming plate. Iris couldn't even remember how many meals she'd missed, and she was about to shove the entire thing down her throat, when she noticed Elena and Alejandro staring at it too. Maternal training is hard to set aside. And it was her fault they'd also missed the full English. She tore the croissant into three pieces, just as Ignacio's phone rang.

He stood up, displacing the children, and moved away to answer it, revealing the waiter wheeling off a trolley piled with mini-packs of Frosties and Cheerios. Elena and Alejandro saw it too, but it was Iris who sprinted after it, returning with three boxes for each of them, which they tore into like jackals after a fifty-mile hunt.

Ignacio came back, swearing under his breath as he put away the phone, then speaking very quickly, in Spanish, to Troy. Fern listened, her mouth falling open. 'Oh – oh that's awful – really?'

'What's that?'

Troy was apparently not planning to translate for the benefit of a person who had spurned his advances less than twelve hours before. Iris gulped down her croissant and nudged Fern instead. 'What? Is everything okay?'

'No, it's awful, apparently these gangsters, like paramilitaries you know, have invaded CleanTech's plantations and taken them over. At gunpoint.'

Ignacio had turned to talk to the children, their faces blurred with sugar and chocolate.

'He says he has to go, now, and sort it out.' explained Fern. 'Thank goodness they got hold of him!'

'What, so he's going to send in CleanTech's gangsters, to chase the others away?'

Ignacio shot Iris a thunderous look, and shouted even more loudly. Fern looked mortified. 'Iris! How could you? CleanTech doesn't employ gangsters. They employ guardians of the sovereign rights of the people and the land.'

Iris pondered this distinction. 'And do they have guns too?'

'Of course they have guns, this is South America we're talking about! Anyhow, he has to leave and sort it out, and...' Ignacio was gesturing at Elena and Alejandro. '...and it's far too dangerous to take the kids.'

Thank God. This was the first sensible thing Iris had heard all morning. Fern continued: '... and he's never left them before. So....'

Troy leaned over and ruffled Alejandro's hair. 'That's cool, leave 'em with us. We'll show 'em a good time, won't we - Fern?' His nose was practically in her ear, and he twirled a lock of questionably blonde hair between two bronze fingers. These two were hardly ideal babysitting material. Ignacio looked from them to his children, parental concern fighting public duty in his expression.

Iris got up and sat Elena on her knee. Since her own overnight demotion from heroic role model to cast-off fellow-traveller, she had all the time in the world. 'I'll look after them. We're old friends already. Aren't we?' She ruffled Alejandro's hair. Ignacio looked hugely relieved, pumped her free hand, and kissed her on both cheeks, before bending to smother Elena and Alejandro in farewell hugs.

Iris looked on, suddenly filled with a dreadful ache of longing. At least he was leaving his children for a legitimate reason. Why on earth had she left hers? And when - if ever - would she get to hug them again?

For reasons Malcolm was too jet-lagged to question, the moment Birmingham had been revealed as their destination for the night, Molly had taken control, with an air of cheerful command reminiscent of her mother at the supermarket in the good old days. While they waited for the baggage crew to decide which items of luggage weren't worth rifling, she had already got on to the Hospitality Bureau and sorted out a couple of hotel rooms for the night. Unfortunately, she reported, the only hotel able to accommodate them at this short notice turned out to be by the Convention Centre, and miles from the city itself. But, Molly pointed out, they were only going to be there for the one night, so it didn't really make any odds, right?

But they woke, rather late, the next day, to discover that the closure of Heathrow had backed up not only all the flights, but all the other transport in and out of London, and it was going to be mid-afternoon before they'd a prayer of getting on anything.

'Never mind.' Molly offered Malcolm a consoling kiss. 'I'm sure you and Ted can find something fun to do round here while I... um, catch up on my homework.'

She pulled open the pleated beige curtain, to reveal a huge, half empty car park, dotted with puddles and fringed with wheelie bins. Beyond loomed the vast blank hangars of the Convention Centre. Ted came padding out of the next room in his pyjamas. He looked out of the window, a mutinous frown appeared on his face, and he said: 'I'm...'

'Hungry? Let's see if we can get you some...'

'Not hungry. Bored!' He padded past Malcolm to the television, grabbed the remote and switched it on, to reveal an over-lit studio studded with primary coloured sofas, on one of which sat a man with stiff hair, saying: '...our roving reporter Katie Champion, who'll be out and about as usual, bringing us the hot local happenings. What have you got for us today, Katie?'

The picture cut to a girl in a big puffy jacket with a ball of curly red hair, holding a microphone and standing by a fountain in a glass hall.

Katie had decided, despite Fern's manic sales pitch, to stick with the 'Local Economy to Benefit from Biggest One-Day Retail Expansion in History' line, in selling the mall opening to her editor. It might be that the Green protest angle would come good, and it was clear from Fern's frantic babble that she believed this guy could walk on water, but frankly, after dragging her arse to that landfill, Katie wasn't taking any chances as she waited for the cue light. 'Well, Mike, if I were you I wouldn't be lolling on that sofa, I'd be emptying out my piggybank, arming myself with a very large shopping bag – but no plastic, please! – and putting on my comfiest shoes. Because, as I'm sure I don't need to remind anybody, today sees the opening of SilverFalls, set to be Europe's biggest shopping mall. And the credit crunch might as well not exist, because after only two hours it's already absolutely packed. As you can see looking behind me, it's got...'

Ted was jumping up and down on the bed, a treat absolutely forbidden at home. Somehow, in the last few days, Malcolm had lost all control over his son's behaviour. Not for the first time, he remembered how easily Iris had managed Ted, who was yelling: 'I want to go! I want to go! You promised! You promised I could have a football shirt for my coming home present if I was good, and I was good and we never...'

Between Ted's yelling and Katie's gush, Malcolm was getting a headache. He went to grab the remote from Ted. 'Look, we've just spent four days surrounded by bloody malls, and this one is no doubt miles from...'

As he went to hit the 'off' button, Katie trilled: '...right next door to the Convention Centre, with brand new dedicated transport links and...'

Malcolm shut off the TV. Ted glared at him. Molly was lounging on the other bed, calmly deleting texts. 'There you go, it's right here. Don't worry about me Dad, I'm fine. Go on Ted, get your shoes on, you can find a newsagent and bring me back a New Scientist.'

Molly had totally intended, the minute Ted dragged his reluctant father out of the door, to make straight for the Convention Centre. It hadn't seemed worth the hassle of raising the subject with Malcolm. At the first mention of the words 'Online Gaming' she could imagine exactly what would come into his mind: a toxic swarm of paedophiles and poker addicts just waiting to pounce on her nubile flesh, unprotected by the solid walls of Hartland Gardens. All in all, it would be easier to say nothing, nip over to check it out, and be back for a blameless family lunch in the Salad Court.

But now they'd gone, she was suddenly shy. After all these months sustained by the brilliance and creativity of Ubiquitur, unsullied by any real-world limitations, did she really want to put human features on him? And what would he think of her, in the flesh, after knowing her only as Morphea, a blank-faced, dark haired Generic Female with an A* scientific brain?

He might not even be there. There was no wi-fi in this dump of a hotel, not even an internet café. She had no way of knowing if it was even worth her while forking out whatever rip-off price they were charging.

They'd be hours yet, wandering around looking for this shirt or whatever it was. She'd just hang for a while, and then see.

Iris had spent an enjoyable morning entertaining the children in the international languages of hopscotch and noughts-and-crosses.

Babysitting duties provided her with an excuse to miss Fern's Green Plenary at the Travelodge, and Troy's speechwriting preparations on the emperor-sized bed, which he had graciously insinuated she still might have a chance of sharing, if she happened to think better of the previous day's foolishness.

With fulsome expressions of regret on both fronts, she'd taken the children for a substantial lunch on CleanTech's tab before joining Troy and Fern outside the hotel. Regrettably, there appeared to be no public transport between the hotel and SilverFalls, so they were all obliged to pile into a massive taxi. They set off out of the city centre, round myriad clover-leafs and subways, until they emerged onto a brand new overpass signposted 'SilverFalls Expressway.' It flew them over an endless grey jigsaw of industrial estates, vehicle depots and new housing developments, until suddenly Fern pointed out of the window: 'Look! That must be it!'

Troy and Iris followed her pointing finger. Blades of sunlight punctured the blanket of cloud, and one of them shone on a distant mass of glass and steel. There they were: the shops, cafes and restaurants, fountains, trees, chapel, funfair and Botox Box, each encased in its own glittering, solar-panelled all-weather dome. Like a giant's bubble-bath, or the Eden project with cancer.

'Stop the car! Just pull over, right here!' Troy was having an idea. Iris knew the signs. The driver reluctantly pulled over, muttering about CCTV cameras and public liability, and Troy leaped out onto the hard shoulder. 'C'mon all of you, I want you all to see this. Look at it. What is the one thing a place like that absolutely cannot be without for one moment?'

Fern and Iris climbed out too, leaving the children safely inside. Iris fished for an answer. 'Er – customers?'

Fern shot up her hand, then put it down again, looking foolish. 'Money?'

Troy paused for effect, then said, raising his voice over the traffic: 'Juice. Electricity. Electricity is the blood of these places. The aircon, the doors, the escalators and elevators and walkways, the tannoy, the coffee machines, the hand-dryers and vending machines and cookie ovens. And don't forget, the cash registers. Without power, they're dead. The whole place just - stalls. Are you following me?'

In what sense? Iris wanted to ask. She had no trouble following the plan, if this was really what Troy's major media event was going to be, but she was beginning to have serious doubts as to the advisability of following Troy into a cage at Guantanamo, or wherever else people who hacked into the power supplies of brand new retail complexes were liable to end up.

Fern appeared to have no such doubts. All she saw were tomorrow's headlines, and more coverage than the Green Parties of the world had achieved in the whole of their history. She gazed up at Troy and said: 'You can - you would - do that?'

'Sure. Why not? Think big, Fern. The other guys do.'

Iris stared out at SilverFalls, then back at Troy, trying to read his face for clues as to which side of the hair-thin line between genius and criminal lunatic he properly belonged. Did he actually believe he could do this, or was it just a new EcoWarrior variant of the male courtship ritual, with all the splendour of a peacock's tail, and all the practicality? Was it even possible? If it was, she needed to warn somebody. It was her fault Troy was here. It was her duty to make sure he stayed on the rails.

Molly would know. If only Molly were here. Then Iris remembered Molly had her phone with her in Dubai. She couldn't call just to chat. That would make it too obvious she was missing them, that her fabulous new life had a few rough edges. They might even suspect her - God forbid - of spying on them, and on the Elk.. But now that she had an excuse, the thought of hearing her daughter's voice again, however petulant and foul-mouthed, was like champagne. Just as soon as she could get away for a minute. 'Come on then, Troy', she said, scrambling back into the car. 'Let's see you do it.'

A few minutes later, they were at the mall. Evidently not just one, but several new motorways had been constructed to converge on it, hacking apart quiet neighbourhoods, old high streets and playing fields. They debouched into a dozen car parks, most already full. The car dropped them off at the main entrance, a seventy-foot wide concertina of automatic doors, unblemished by handprint or bird dropping.

As the doors parted and they walked in, Iris felt a tug on each of her hands, as the children stopped, rooted in incredulous wonder.

The floor was marble, inlaid with intricate mosaics of toys, clothes, cakes, even an intaglio marble MP3 player. To one side and the other fountains danced, and beyond them the atrium opened up into dizzy vaults, with jungle plantations and glazed walkways to the various retail sectors. There was an arcade, and a little girl dancing up and down in front of a karaoke machine. Vending stalls were dotted about, selling chocolate-dipped doughnuts and ice cream.

Elena and Alejandro trembled either side of Iris, unable to believe that such a paradise could exist, still less that they were actually allowed in. She squeezed their hands and smiled down at them. 'This looks like fun, huh?'

Troy strode ahead, scouting for high moral ground. Iris and the children hurried up to him. Finally he stopped, right between the fountains, the karaoke bar and the games arcade. As a location, it was, if possible, even noisier than the Arnold Bennett Waste Processing Facility.

'Right here. Perfect.' he yelled over his shoulder. Fern, no doubt remembering yesterday, looked just fractionally dubious. 'ISN'T IT A BIT NOISY?'

'NOT FOR LONG!' he yelled back, and winked. Fern looked puzzled, then delighted, reading his prankster intentions.

Now that the caravan seemed to have halted for a bit, Iris was desperate to make her call. She hurried the children up to Fern. 'Could you possibly look after them, just for five minutes? I have to call somebody. Urgently.'

She put one little hand firmly into each of Fern's, gave them a reassuring smile, and left.

It took her a while to find somewhere quiet enough where she could still get a signal, so she was outside, perched on top of a pristine rubbish bin, when the phone finally rang through. It had only been days, but it felt like a century. Pray God Molly hadn't turned hers off.

Molly had more or less talked herself out of going to Games World at all, when her phone rang. She looked at the number as it flashed up.

Christ. Mum.

She felt a familiar, pleasant irritation, mixed with something like homesickness. Iris was probably checking up, to see if they were eating okay. Or more likely, if they were having a better time than she was. 'Hi Mum. What's up?'

The moment Molly picked up the phone, Iris realised she couldn't possibly mention Troy. Her family knew he'd been at the same demo as she, but no more than that. There was nothing she could say about recent developments that her family would take at face value.

'Oh. Hi Moll. Nothing much. I'm just here, holding the fort. At home. Feeding the hungry maw of the compost bin, ha ha. Um – how's it going out there? Are you having a fabulous, sun-soaked time, you lucky girl?'

Molly realised there was no way she could let Iris know where she was. How sad would it sound, to admit they'd come home early because Dubai was less cool than Birmingham? 'It's pretty fab, actually. I'm you know, having like a cool drink in the pool. I mean...' She padded over to the bathroom, ran a tap and crouched down beside it '...one of the pools. There are like, four or five? It has like, this free swim-up bar? And underwater iTunes, you can just program in you know, whatever, and like, listen to it while you swim?'

'That does sound lovely. I feel like a real womble, stewing back here at Hartland Gardens. Anyhow, I won't keep you, but I did just have this techie question and I knew you'd be able to answer it, if anybody could. I was reading you know, one of my dreary green mags, and there was this totally bonkers idea about crashing all the computers people like TKMaxx and Primark and so on use for their ordering. All at the same time, in a sort of chain reaction. To stop anybody buying anything. Bring the machinery of capitalism to a juddering halt, sort of thing. I mean, could it be done? Would it work, d'you think?'

This was the last line of questioning Molly had expected, but it was an intriguing one. She stopped paddling her fingers under the tap while she pondered the answer, then remembered where she was supposed to be, and held the phone right next to it.

At the other end, Iris cried out in alarm. 'Are you all right, darling? Did you fall in?'

'What? No I'm fine. I guess – if they all fed into the same place at the other end, like in the same giant factory, which they probably do – you could probably seed it with motes, and make like a speckled net, or a bit torrent, distributed over...Yup, I guess. Pretty smart. Where'd'you hear about it, again?'

Iris craned over the thin plantation of ficus trees blocking her view of Troy and his entourage inside. Fern's reaction to the children did not inspire trust. She needed to get back. 'Oh, um – some you know, freesheet? Anyhow, I'd better hang up, this must be costing a fortune. But you're fine, are you? All of you?'

Molly was still pondering the previous question. It was a cool idea; given that all these guys did everything over the Web, and that the same few factories must supply them all... Suddenly she realised who would know. 'I could probably find out and call you back. I mean, if it's important. Is it?'

'Oh, yes. I mean, no. Well, of course it's just you know, idle curiosity. But if you could find out... I'd better run now, there's something about to, um - boil over. Love to Dad and Ted, okay?'

Malcolm and Ted had had no difficulty finding SilverFalls, given the thousands of people thronging towards it, and the deafening music of the various local cultural ensembles hired to celebrate the occasion at every entrance.

Once inside, all they had to do was locate a mall map, then locate on the map the Sports and Leisure Pavilion, then work out where they currently were in relation to it, and then fight their way through the crowds to get there. It was therefore only a matter of an hour or so before Ted found himself at the entrance to the biggest branch of SportsWorld he'd ever seen. It was no mere world, it was a constellation. Twenty cash registers funnelled customers from thirty initial aisles, behind which more aisles, pods, zones and bargain corners opened out to infinity.

Ted bounded through the door thrilled and clear-headed. The entire way here had been occupied by a painstaking and detailed mental evaluation of all the shirts he might possibly choose, and their relative rankings in terms of desirability to himself and, more crucially, to Jack and his cronies. Finally, as they stepped off the last travelator, he had decided on the Middlesboro' goalie's winter practice strip, which was less local than something from West Brom, but much more objectively hot.

But the minute he saw what else was here, the shirt was forgotten. In its place was a vast, jumbled pile of possibility, where one ball, or sweatband, or bat, would thrust itself on his attention for a moment, only to be swept aside by something else. All his clarity was gone, and what he felt was panic, confusion and a kind of terror that somewhere in this vast space, something was hiding, more wonderful than anything he'd ever seen in his entire, whole life – and he wasn't going to find it.

Malcolm followed his son around the shop while Ted picked things up, looked thrilled for half a minute, stopped looking thrilled, and put them back. He tried, with no success at all, to persuade Ted that each thing in turn was definitely, finally, the right choice. Then he tried suggesting that it didn't really matter. After all, it was just something to remind Ted of the holiday. Then he tried putting a time limit on the decision, which just sent Ted into an even wilder frenzy. Finally, Ted turned to his father and burst into tears. 'I don't know! I can't decide!'

Malcolm bent down and hugged him while he sobbed it out. 'Tell you what, I think you and I had better do some GCSEs in Advanced Consumerism before we come in here again. We'll pop up to that place on the High Street on Saturday, I bet they've got the Middlesbro' strip, and if they don't they'll get it for you. It'll be just the same. Meanwhile, I think I saw something not too many miles from here that might just cheer you up...'

He took Ted's hand and led him back along the travelator,

down the escalator and through the tunnel and along the walkway, until they saw in the distance the bobbing pods and flashing lights of a fun fair; no battered row of coin-operated fire engines and motorbikes, but a proper funfair, with a whirling carousel and a hoop of aeroplanes soaring and swooping to the tinny strains of 'Puppet on a String'. Malcolm stopped at the entrance. 'There you go, how about that to cheer you up?'

Ted stared at the rides, and just saw more Dubai. 'No thanks Dad, can we go and wait for the train now? Will Mum be there when we get home?'

The minute Iris left, the children had begun tugging at Fern's hands like mustangs at a rodeo. She'd never been specially good with children, despite her sister's assurances every Christmas that it was just a matter of practice, and it was probably about time Fern started getting used to them, because she couldn't put it off for ever, could she? These two were very cute, but they were also noisy and obviously needed to run off their energy. Plus, Katie was due any second with her camera crew.

It wouldn't hurt to leave them for a few minutes, just till the speech was over. The smaller one, the boy, knew exactly where he wanted to go. It was amazing that he'd spotted the funfair from two feet above the ground, and through a thousand other people, but he'd been right; there it was, with a big banner saying 'Free Rides All Day'.

Before she knew it, they were both off, dodging legs and shopping bags in their excitement. She called hopefully after them in Spanish: 'Just stay there, okay? Don't talk to any strangers. I'll come back for you in a few minute.'

But they were gone. Still, no problem. There was no way they'd be off anywhere else.

Molly had decided at the last moment that if she was really going to meet Ubiquitur for the first and more than likely the last time, she might as well give it her all. So, as she pushed through the turnstile and up the escalator into the main exhibition hall it was not only as a female in about a one to a hundred ratio to males, but a female in high heeled Roman sandals, big hoop earrings, the jewelled sun visor, and the tangerine Top Shop miniskirt.

A line of Trekkies swivelled from the bar to gape as she passed by; she understood enough Klingon to blush and speed up, past the huge booths crammed with Facebook salespeople, Slobodvian dealers in virtual real estate, and the silent, mysteriously uninteresting denizens of the Eternal Forest.

Behind these big, flashy showcases, a grid of smaller and smaller booths receded all the way to the back of the vast hall, with no obvious map to indicate where, if anywhere, Altarica might be found. She knew it had to be something of a niche, thanks to a fatal combination of intellectual complexity and zero profit opportunities, but she hadn't expected it to be right at the back, with Gamers Anonymous and Mothers Who Care.

But there it finally was. No banners, no flashy graphics, not even a flat-screen demo. Just a desk, a few dog-eared flyers and somebody who didn't seem to have dressed this morning. Could that somebody be he? Molly hung back for a minute, hot and cold all at once, longing for a big tee shirt, and frantically trying to stay calm.

Come on, lighten up. There's no way he even needs to know who I am, right? I could just be like, some random person getting lost on her way to Bebo. Plus I've got a specific question, in fact quite a cool and interesting question, to like, break the ice.

She went a bit closer, until she had a clear view of the desk. The person behind it did not improve with proximity, and – Jeez, was that a wizard's hat? There was no way, in this or any world, he could be Ubiquitur. But if he wasn't, did she seriously want to get into conversation with some creepy, bearded freak, in thick glasses, and with nobody else in sight?

He turned to her as she approached, with a myopic expression of generalised welcome. She looked at that face, and the beard, and...

Oh. Holy. Shit.

It couldn't be.

But it was.

Iris hung up the phone, jumped off the rubbish bin, and ran back into the mall. Fern was deep in conversation with Katie, who this time had arrived with a camera operator and a satellite uplink, which had clearly cheered Fern up a lot. Troy was off to one side, no doubt rehearsing his lines. But where were Elena and Alejandro?

'I'm back now, Fern - where are the children?'

Fern turned her head fractionally in Iris' direction. 'The children? Oh, the children. They're fine they're at the fair just over there. Honestly, Iris, they've travelled all over the world with Ignacio...'

And that was it, as she returned to reassuring Katie that the background noise would definitely not be any kind of problem once

Troy got going.

Iris felt like the school prefect asking the Friday night disco to keep the noise down. Maybe Fern was right; after all, if these children had survived evacuation at gunpoint, homelessness and a revolutionary socialist diplomat for a Dad, they'd probably live though half an hour in a shopping mall. So why was she feeling so uneasy?

Maybe because there was suddenly nothing for her to do, and no reason to be here. She'd come on this trip, letting Troy persuade her that she was a vital support to his campaign, a unique role model and example to the women of Britain, and all of that seemed to have been written out of the script, in favour of some lunatic stunt that would make Molly's look like a schoolgirl prank. What did that have to do with her, Iris, and her promise to Soren?

Troy jammed a finger into his ear. He could barely hear the guys on the other end, but they'd assured him all the code worked fine, and at this point he just had to take their word for it. He turned away from the crowd, checking his reflection in the mirrored glass beside him.

He was famous for not giving a damn about appearances; it would hardly do for somebody with his public image to be seen dallying with make up artists or cosmetic surgeons. But, having been born with that hair, those eyes and these cheekbones, it would be plain foolish not to take care of them. Time had weathered him, but in a good way, like a French chateau or a pair of hand-made shoes; if they helped to sell the world the message that it was cool to care, where was the harm in that?

'You there, or what?'

The voice on the other end was peevish with fatigue; it was central to the geek honour code only to work in the middle of the night.

'Sure am, dude. Hang in there, huh? We're real close now.'

Katie positioned herself with Troy in the background to record her second introductory piece to camera. Her earlier link out of the studio would do if they decided to go with the pro-SilverFalls line; a new benchmark in recreational shopping, somewhere to escape the god awful local weather, and a giant asset to the local economy, already set to record its single biggest day of growth since records began.

But she needed the anti-mall, Green angle now, so she'd be

covered however the story panned out. She checked her mic, patted her hair into place, re-configured her spendaholic smile to a frown of environmentalist concern, and began:

'Hello from SilverFalls, where as you can probably hear, the background noise is of scarce resources being used up, and yet more carbon spewed out, to feed our modern-day addiction to consumerism. I'm sure I don't need to remind viewers that, according to some, places like this are symptomatic of all that is wrong with our society. And one of those worried is the famously formidable eco-warrior Troy Hauser, who has travelled thousands of miles – no doubt by hot air balloon ha ha – to put the British Green Party back at the head of the bandwagon of climate concern. And I think in fact, we're just about to hear from him now...'

With practised grace, she turned to reveal Troy, who muttered into his iPhone, stepped up to Josh's camera, and held up one powerful, implacable hand. As if by magic, the fountains behind him leaped twenty feet higher in the air, a dramatic introduction which had the unfortunate side-effect of soaking Katie and Josh, as well as Fern and Iris next to them. But while Katie was still shaking the water from her curls and Josh was checking his lens, something more extraordinary happened.

The fountains sank back, then dribbled into silent stillness.

Then everything else stopped. The escalators ground to a halt. The plasma displays pinged into blackness. The whooshing elevators froze in their glass tubes. The dancing spotlight vanished from the karaoke floor, and the nasal yelp of the singer with it. The tills clattered out, the cacophonic swirl of a hundred competing Muzak tracks trickled away, and the machine gun bursts and revving engines died in the arcade. For the first and last time in its history, SilverFalls was silent, and still.

For a moment the whole place froze, suspended in disbelief. Shoppers, grazers and customer assistance personnel stood and gaped at each other. Then, before the puzzled crowds had a chance to move or react, a voice from nowhere and everywhere, like the Almighty himself, began to speak. Somehow Troy had organised his own power supply. Just as he'd promised, he was going to make damn sure, this time, that the whole world heard what he had to say. He checked his reflection in Josh's lens – cheekbones attractively high-lit by their fine mist of water – and began:

'People of Great Britain, thank you for welcoming me here today. And when I say Great, believe me I could not be more sincere. You are the people who, alone, fought back the tide of Nazism for the whole of Europe...'

The Brits could never resist that line about their yellow-bellied neighbours...

'...and you are the same people who celebrated that victory with the founding of the world's first Welfare State, showing the whole word where its priorities ought to be; taking care of its people – all of its people.'

They also loved to hear they were more compassionate than anybody else, no matter how blatantly untrue it had become. He had their attention, if only because there was suddenly nothing else to do. He made the prearranged off-camera gesture to Josh to zoom in for a close-up, and notched up the passion as he continued:

'Today, the world is facing a crisis every bit as grave as Nazism. And once again today, you Britons are in the forefront of this new battle. Climate catastrophe will bring grief, and murder, and darkness in its wake. Raw material prices are spiralling, food shortages are already spreading famine around the world. There are not enough resources on the earth to satisfy our greed. And our compulsion to spend what we don't have, to have ever more even when we need nothing, has brought the world's financial system to its knees.

So I have a question for you; a question I ask you to consider in all sincerity, as you stand here today. Are you the same people – is this the same nation – that once sacrificed all comfort, all safety, all thought of self, to defeat a deadly, implacable enemy?'

It was a risk, but with that stupendous dollop of flattery he might just get away with it...

'...Your fathers turned back Hitler then; can you turn back the tide of greed and devastation, today?'

Katie could barely contain her elation. Finally, one of Fern's overheated promises had come good. She'd been warned to expect something dramatic, but this was beyond anything she'd believed possible. The man was like Jesus, or Richard Gere in that courtroom thingy. The gravitas of Al Gore, the charisma of Bill Clinton, the glib sincerity of Tony Blair. He stood there, rock-like, letting his words sink in, as crowds flocked towards him from every corner of the mall, if only to find out what the bloody heck was going on.

It had not been easy, persuading the Editor to let her do this, with the uplink. But she'd finally more or less put her job on the line to get the satellite bike and the live feed. Which looked like it was really paying off. And the good part about Fern's failure to persuade any other channels to turn up - with which, of course, she'd been all sympathy when Fern had confessed it to her - was that it gave her, Katie Champion, a world exclusive.

She exchanged thumbs ups with Josh as Troy continued:

'In the words of the great Leonard Peltier, a modern-day Native American hero: "One good man or one good woman can change the world, and their work can be a beacon for millions. Are you that man or woman?

The crowds exchanged baffled glances. It was all very well being congratulated on the Dunkirk Spirit by some Yank; after all, everybody knew his lot had waited till the last possible minute to creep into the war on our coat tails. But where did he get off, quoting Red Indians as role models?

He hurried on to his conclusion, giving Josh the Extreme Close Up signal, so the world could read the ultimate question straight from those gorgeous green eyes:

'Today, you're all here for one reason: to hand over cash you probably don't have, for junk you surely don't need. You're here because that's what your lives – our Western lives - have become. But, as of now, you can't do that. The cash registers are all dead. So, what do you do now? Huh?

For a moment after he finished speaking, the silence held; thick, like glue, or milk-shake. It was the moment of high drama Troy, and Fern, and Katie had been planning and working for, as the reality of his last words sank in.

All over the mall, people stopped to think. Then they looked at each other, as a hundred thousand minds simultaneously had the same thought.

Then a hundred thousand pairs of legs turned to rush the shops, and a hundred thousand pairs of arms and hands swarmed the unprotected racks. Grabbing at garments whose security tags could no longer protect them, at sports bags and brand new bicycles, and even at white chocolate chip muffins, two and three at a time.

Screams and yells overwhelmed Troy's voice, as he recovered from the shock to remonstrate with them. Nobody could hear him any longer; and nobody cared.

Molly's first and only thought was to get away. Her visor fell unnoticed to the floor, as she dodged between the presentation booths and gawping gamers, making for an exit. Any exit.

Every certainty she'd ever had lay behind her in crumbling ruins. Her hero, the person she'd chosen above everybody else in the world as a role model, turned out to be her Dad's creepy friend. The genius who'd designed and built a dazzling masterpiece of virtual architecture, way beyond the scope of most human imagining, was a repulsive creep, who bagged up leftovers and rambled on about poo power. It didn't add up. Or if it did, then the arithmetic of human relations delivered all the wrong answers.

She kept running until she was slowed by a jam of people queuing for a Party Gaming strip bingo contest. A TV yammered on a bracket above her head; she ignored it until she heard the word 'SilverFalls', followed by the word 'riot'. SilverFalls! That was where Dad and Ted were. She stepped out of the crush and punched up Malcolm's number.

At that moment, Malcolm was in the bath at the hotel, warbling the crass and tuneless fragments that were all he could recall of a pop song Iris particularly loathed. If he had to begin a new life as an overburdened single parent, he might as well make the most of the few upsides.

Next door, the phone rang and rang in his jacket pocket, drowned out by 'Big Kids' keeping Ted entertained on the hotel's cable TV.

Colin wasn't quite sure what had just happened. When the girl had appeared, he had been deep in conversation with his bugs, debating whether it was safe for him to leave the stand to visit the men's room, and if so, whether he'd feel more or less vulnerable without the rather eye-catching robe. It had taken him a little while to recognise her as Malcolm's daughter, especially as she seemed to be dressed like some sort of teenage pop star. And by the time he had recognised her, she was rushing off again.

He had no idea what she was doing there; it seemed unlikely that Malcolm had sent her to spy on him, especially as she had made no effort to conceal her presence. If anything, the reverse. But no other explanation came to mind.

There was something on the mauve carpeting where she'd been standing. He got up and came out of the booth to look. It seemed to be some sort of mask or headband. Colin had very little idea about women's fashions, and for all he knew it might be vitally important. Anyway, she seemed quite distressed. She was very young to be alone in a place like this. Unlike Malcolm to do something so irresponsible, if that was indeed what had happened. He'd better go after her, to make sure she was all right.

With a few reassuring words to his bugs, he stowed them in the pocket of his robe, picked up the headband, and hurried after her.

Molly stood by the TV for what felt like forever, as people pushed past her and the phone rang at her ear.

Oh god. What if they're trapped inside? They'll never hear a phone in all the chaos. I'd better get down there.

She turned, looking for another way out, and her blood froze. He was coming after her! She turned, pocketed her phone, shoved between two Wookies jostling at the head of the escalator, and ran.

Iris' first thought, when the riot started, was that Troy's question had pretty much answered itself. And not in the way he'd been expecting. Once again the idealism of the Green message had stubbed its toe on the intractable reality of human nature.

Immediately afterwards, she thought of the children. The mall had erupted into chaos. The security people, even reinforced for opening day, were no match for the tidal wave of rampaging looters. She turned to Troy, who was rooted to the spot, pale with shock beneath his all-season tan, and Fern, gazing up at him in open-mouthed grief. 'Where are the kids again, Fern?'

Fern just stood there. Iris grabbed her by the shoulders and shook her. 'The kids, Fern. Where did you leave them?'

Finally, Fern heard her, and mumbled: 'The funfair. They wanted to go to the fair. Over there.'

'For Christ's sake! Come on!'

Iris ran, into the into the sea of people. She had no idea where the funfair was, until she heard the children's voices, screaming and yelling at the other end of a glass walkway lined with toy displays. People were already beginning to smash the glass as Iris hurtled past.

Maybe they were having a lovely time, enjoying the free rides. Then she remembered that the rides would have stopped, along with everything else. Well, that was all right then.

There it was, right ahead of her. There were dozens of children, milling about, clambering off the carousel, running to their parents to whine about the interruption to their fun. But no Elena and Alejandro.

Then she looked up. And up.

And then she saw them. Huddled side by side, in the cockpit of the highest plane on the tallest ride, clutching on to one another. The plane was sticking out almost vertically above its metal spoke, so the two children had to cling on with all their little fingers not to fall. She saw their gaping faces, imagined the terror in their eyes while Elena tried to be the big sister, to calm Alejandro into sitting still. There was no way they could get down from there, and who knew how long they could hold on?

Somebody would have to go and get them. Troy could do it. If he'd scaled ancient redwoods barehanded, he could certainly manage a fairground ride.

She turned, but Troy was nowhere to be seen. He and Fern had simply vanished. She was vaguely aware of the TV girl puffing towards her, with her camera guy trailing cables, but they were no use.

Oh God. It's all my fault. I got Troy here. I promised Ignacio I'd look after them. He trusted me to keep them safe. And I had to bloody leave them with that idiot...

She shouted up to Elena: 'It's all right! Hang on there!'

But the children couldn't hear her above the chaos. Any minute now, one of them would fall, thirty feet or more, right onto the sharp metal edges of the machinery. And it would be on her conscience, for ever.

There were bolts and screws sticking out of the supporting arm. They'd make hand and footholds, at a pinch. Iris kicked off her shoes, ran towards it, and began to climb.

When Troy's speech ended in unforeseen humiliation, Katie felt a moment's pang of sympathy, especially for poor Fern, who with lifelong consistency had once again backed the wrong horse. The horse himself seemed to be in shock. Clearly, they were no longer the story. The story was unfolding out there, in the mall. This was gonna kick the opening, and specially the bloody Green Party, way into the long grass.

Other reporters, faced with a hundred thousand berserk looters, might have decided to wait for reinforcements, or retired to a safe distance. Not Katie. This was the big chance she'd waited for, ever since joining Midlands TV. This was her moment of glory. She was going in.

And then she heard the woman beside her say something to Fern about children and funfairs. If there was going to be a hot angle, it would be there. Sobbing kiddies, distraught parents guilt-ridden at having abandoned their cherished darlings just so they could binge-shop unimpeded. The FunFair From Hell. So when Iris ran, Katie ran after her, and Josh, as well as he could, ran too.

When they caught up with Iris, the scene was even worse – or should that be better? - than she had hoped. If Troy had wanted the perfect illustration of mindless hedonism in meltdown, he couldn't have asked for more. She manoeuvred herself to where Josh would get a good head shot of her, with the carnage visible, but not too distracting, in the background, and began:

'Well, this is one publicity stunt that has definitely gone very badly wrong. The mall has collapsed into chaos, with shoppers looting and fighting one another, and no sign of any kind of order being re-established. But possibly the most horrendous scenes are right here, where...'

What was Josh playing at? The camera was wobbling about all

over the place as he gesticulated, yelling something inaudible at Katie. She finally made out that he was saying 'BEHIND YOU!' She turned to where he was pointing, and realised why.

There, high up in the air, were the two kids Troy and Fern had arrived with earlier. And climbing up towards them, maybe thirty feet above the ground without a rope or anything, was the rather dull, housewifey woman whom she'd written off as Troy's minder. This story was getting more amazing by the minute.

Katie turned back to the camera and continued, justly proud of her controlled professionalism: '...where as we can see, an act of extraordinary heroism is being played out right before our eyes here. The inexplicable power cut that has brought everything to a standstill has also halted the fairground rides, and two tiny children have been trapped way up in the air. It seems that all the security people have fled, but here behind me is a woman, who so far as we know is entirely unrelated to the children, climbing up to rescue them. This is an act of unbelievable bravery, risking her own life for the sake of – oh my God, the children are trying to climb out – they're shaking the whole ride – any minute now the whole thing is going to come crashing down, and there are literally dozens of helpless children and hysterical parents beneath – I have to tell you, this is very very hard to watch. Is she going to make it? Stay with me to find out...'

When the riot first started, most people's impulse was to join in. After all, if everybody else was having stuff, it was a free for all, right? But when it began to get ugly, and people began smashing display cases, the party spirit vanished, and the majority opinion began to favour going home.

Which was when the real problem began. Somehow, Troy's instruction to the hackers in Albuquerque to immobilise all the retail computers in the mall had been interpreted as 'all the computers'. Or maybe they just got carried away. However it happened, when Troy and Fern, along with several thousand other overburdened looters, arrived at the exit doors, they found them firmly sealed. Outside, the police, the Fire Brigade, and the representatives of SilverFalls management were all ready to swarm into action and bring everything under control. But they couldn't control it if they couldn't get to it. More and more people were gathering at the doors, pushing against the people in font of them. Pretty soon, something truly nasty was going to happen.

For the first time in his life, Troy regretted being half a foot taller and way more attractive than almost everybody else. Here he was, arguably – though luckily, not provably – the cause of all this, and instead of reigning triumphantly over a mass change of heart, he was sticking out like a jackass's hard-on, in a crowd of smelly, overweight morons, as more and more people crushed in behind him. Where did those assholes get off, jamming the doors? With some difficulty he freed up his hand and dialled the number. After a couple of rings, a voice slurred: 'Dude. We need to sleep now, okay?'

Troy bent over and hissed into it: 'You need to re-activate the exit doors you fucked up, that's what you need to do.'

'Hey.' There was offence, almost emotional pain, in the tone. 'Dude, we did like you said. We crash things, man. We are not in the restoring business, capisc'?' and the line went dead. He called back, but the jerks had switched it off.

Standing beside him, Fern looked up, all doe-eyed sympathy, and reached for his hand. 'You were great', she said. 'They're just not quite ready to hear it yet.'

The hand was snatched away from her. Troy's patience had finally run dry.

'Give me a fucking break!'

As Molly ran from the Convention Centre across the vast acreage of parking lots, the conversation with Iris popped into her head. Iris had been talking about Primark and TKMaxx and jamming computers, right? And it sounded like that was what had happened here. How was Iris mixed up in this? Anyhow, meanwhile she might be of some use.

As she got nearer the doors, she could see emergency service vehicles, and ribbons of yellow tape with which a junior police constable was trying, with only limited success, to cordon off the area.

Molly dodged under the tape and headed right for the big,

pudgy guy in firefighter's gear who seemed to be in charge.

'Excuse me, young lady...'

'It's okay. I can help. I'm good with computers.'

'Are you indeed?'

He looked the bling-wrapped ladette in front of him up and down, took a moment to share the joke with the half-dozen uniformed men around him, and continued into his phone: 'Hello? I'm told I need to get onto IT, would that be you? We've a bit of a situation on hand here, and...'

In front of him, his colleagues, and Molly, was a wall of squashed human faces and bodies fifty feet wide. As she watched, more and more people were piling up behind them, and the faces by the glass were filling with panic.

She tugged at the bearded guy's sleeve. 'You need to find the override pad. It'll be somewhere by the door here. There'll be a...'

He hunched away over his phone. 'Sorry mate, it's bloody mayhem here. What's that? I need to look for the what?'

Molly tried to move to where he could read her lips. 'Right by the door, there'll be a pad, you need to ask them for the code...'

He shooed her away and bellowed more loudly into the phone: 'Pad, was that? It's where?'

'Oh, for fuck's sake...'

Molly slipped under the tape and ran to the door. There it was, under a flap just to the left of the furthest panel. There were only so many combinations they'd have used...

After a couple of minutes of frantic tapping, she heard the hiss and sigh as the door seals began to give. At that moment, the bearded man came up behind her. 'Young lady, if you don't mind, you're right where I need to be.'

He barged her out of the way, holding a scribbled scrap of paper in front of him. As his finger touched the pad, the hissing stopped and the doors whooshed open, all at once. He stepped back as the first wave of shoppers stampeded past him, still with the phone at his ear. 'Worked a treat, boys. Well done.'

As Iris climbed, no tetchy voice itched her ear, either to help her along or slag her off for an idiot. He knew when He was beaten. Even Elvis, in fringed lame, singing 'It's Now or Never', would not have pierced her focus. As she climbed, she wasn't thinking about where to put her feet, or whether the beam would hold. Nor did she hear the screams and yells of the baying crowd, half-hoping, deliciously, that she'd fall, bringing the children down with her.

All she saw was those children, those white, open-mouthed, terrified faces. Only here because of her. Scared voiceless because she, Iris, had had some insane delusion that only she could get Troy to Birmingham, and that Troy could work some miracle.

And when she looked away, she saw Ted's face instead. His face when she shouted at him about the Nikes, or when he was buying carbon credits in the desperate hope of getting his proper mother back; when he couldn't bear her to come to school because of what Jack had been saying to him, because of what he'd been put through in the playground.

All she wanted was to do something, anything, that would be enough to wipe away those memories. With a tougher skin, Iris would have shrugged it all off as good for Ted: character-building, inevitable. But with a tougher skin, she wouldn't have risked her neck to put things right.

It is said to have been Nancy Reagan who first opined that a woman, like a teabag, never shows her true strength until she's in hot water. If Iris had been asked in a rational moment to carry two hysterical children down a thirty-foot vertical iron girder, she would pretty much have backed away as fast as her heels permitted. And if Katie had had a chance to ask her how she'd done it, as she finally lifted Elena and Alejandro down onto the platform, she would have barely understood the question. As it was, as the flushed reporter stepped forward to thrust the gun mic in her face, what Iris said was: 'For God's sake, not now. These children need to be got out of here.'

She took a child's hand in each of hers and marched away from Katie and Josh, down the glass tunnel towards the entrance.

But as they emerged into the main atrium, they were met by a straggle of people fleeing the other way, coughing and covering their mouths. Unfortunately neither the Fire Brigade nor the SilverFalls IT crew had ever experienced an electrical re-activation on this scale, and the sudden power surge had started wires smouldering all over the mall. The heat, in combination with the large quantity of synthetic materials in what remained of the mall's stock, was rapidly filling the air with toxic fumes. The doors were now open, but the doors were several hundred yards away, and clouds of smoke were coming at them like a wall.

Iris looked down at Elena and Alejandro, then over at the smoke, already filling the tunnel to the main entrance. She turned the other way; upstairs to Sports and Leisure, and downstairs to the Food Court. The Food Court... What had Mr Goodbody said the other day, about waste disposal at SilverFalls?

Meanwhile, Katie's composure had finally begun to fray. There they were, she and Josh, and the woman, and the kids, and about a hundred other people; they'd witnessed Iris' amazing feat, they'd got it on tape and checked the sound. And now, after all that, it looked like they were all about to succumb to toxic fumes. Children were whimpering, adults shouting: determined to die having the last word.

As Katie stood there, wondering how Josh could possibly be checking his batteries at a time like this, she saw Iris grab the children's hands more firmly, and yell to the panicky crowd around her: 'This way, everybody! I know another way out!'

Molly stood by the door, watching the crowds pour out, speeding up past the police just in case somebody had a go at separating them from their loot. She scanned the faces, hoping against hope to see Malcolm's and Ted's. God knows what horrors were unfolding in there. She'd been calling every couple of minutes, but still with no luck.

Finally, the stampede thinned to a trickle, and the fire fighters barged in past her, shouting instructions. She could see clouds of smoke. Maybe Malcolm and Ted had got caught somewhere, miles from an exit, and been overcome by the fumes? A row of police spread out along the doors. She daren't try slipping in past them.

She pulled out her phone and hit 'redial' one last time. She was so convinced Malcolm wouldn't answer that she was about to hit 'cancel' when a voice said into her ear: 'Moll? Is that you?'

'Oh Dad! Thank fuck! Finally! Where are you?'

'Where are we? We're here, where are you? I've been packing, and Ted's been gorging himself on junk TV, just for a change. Were you thinking of rejoining us any time soon?'

Malcolm never heard Molly's answer. Ted was yelling at him from the next room: 'Dad! Dad! It's Mum! On the TV! And with pasta in her hair!'

He turned back to the phone. 'I think we may have located with your mother.'

Once she'd remembered Mr Goodbody's detailed explanation of how the waste from the Food Court was funnelled directly down a large metal chute, into a custom-designed compost bin outside the mall building, it had been a relatively straightforward business for Iris to lead her party out. She'd taken a calculated risk that not much would have been sent through in half a day, and indeed they had emerged from the blessedly fresh air and empty space of the service area, and thence the almost pristine membrane of the compost pit, only sparsely adorned with iceberg lettuce and stir-fry noodles.

For about half a minute, Katie was just grateful to be safe. Then she realised that the story had got bigger than ever. This mousey woman had not only saved the lives of the two kids, but very possibly of the hundred or so other people even now hauling their swag up out of the pit. This could go national, and prime-time; maybe even international. And it was Katie Champion's exclusive story. Nothing was going to take it from her now. There was no way anybody was leaving before she had her interview in the can.

Her headset was still in place. She found her phone and hit the speed dial button for the news office. It was picked up almost at once. She had to sound calm, yet urgent so they'd take her seriously. 'Get me the national editor. This is Katie Champion. I need to be patched through, live.'

After a minute a weary voice rasped: 'Champion! Where the bloody hell have you been?'

'It's a bit complicated, but anyway I've found a woman who's saved these two kids' lives, and now she's saved about a hundred more of us, and we've just come out of a garbage chute, so we got the signal back, and I think you're going to want to see this.'

'Am I indeed? Well, there's fuck all else on. But it'd better be good.'

Live! And national! She debated taking a couple more minutes to call Mum and Dad, but decided that was not what Kate Adie would have done. She waited for Josh to clean the ketchup off his lens and frame her up, before wedging herself between Iris and the service gate.

'Well, this has been the wildest, weirdest afternoon of my life, and I'm betting of thousands of other people's, too. And of all the extraordinary events that have unfolded, by far the most dramatic has to have been the astoundingly heroic rescue by this ordinary woman – a woman I haven't even had the chance to ask her name...'

Iris was barely aware of the gabbling person in front of her. For the last hour she'd been running on pure adrenaline, powered only by the need to rescue the children and get them to safety. Now that they were out, the shock began to hit her. She felt the arms that hugged Elena and Alejandro shaking, and her legs felt floppy. She looked down into two frightened, confused little faces, and suddenly she was overwhelmed by terror. Where were her own children? What if something had happened to them? What if their plane crashed on the way home?

All she wanted was to have them back again. She'd never leave the house, she'd never answer the phone, she'd never move a muscle without asking permission, ever in her life, if only – if only...

'It is her! I told you it was! Mum why are you wearing a salad?'

'You know Mum, Ted, she'll do anything to get on TV'.

From either side of her, Ted and Molly tumbled into Iris's arms, right in the frame of Katie's camera.

'Oh Ted! Oh Molly! Watch out – this is Elena and Alejandro, they're – I think they might be coming home with us. Just for a bit. Where's your...?'

But she could see him now, there behind the annoying woman and the man with the camera, hanging back until the children had had their hugs. He was beaming at her. And, best of all, there was no sign of Grendel.

It was a long time since Iris had had such an enthusiastic reception from her family, and she wasn't especially interested in sharing it with a bunch of strangers. She was about to tell the bubble-headed reporter to shove off and leave her in peace, when her ear began to tickle in an all-too familiar way.

Oh please. Not here. Not now.

She shook her head vigorously, hoping that it might be some residue from the waste chute, but the itch persisted. And the voice. 'And just what do you think you're doing now?'

Maybe he was about to beatify her. Iris had no objection to sainthood in itself, but she'd a nasty suspicion that it could only happen after you died. It seemed peculiarly unfair to have survived today, only to be assumed up to heaven before she could bask in the recovered affections of her children.

'I'm trying to have some quality time with my family. Do you have a particular objection to that?'

'In principle, no, but I am here – reluctantly, as you can imagine – to remind you that you've already had fifteen years of quality time, which for some reason you've failed to appreciate. Right now, on the other hand, there's a captive audience of probably half a million or so highly suggestible people watching you, in every corner of the country, all ready to take to their quivering, sentimental hearts every word you say. I tell you, if my boy'd had that sort of audience for the Sermon on the Mount...'

The Sermon on the Mount? What did that have to do with...? Oh.

Katie's smile was beginning to sag a little at the edges. They weren't going to keep the feed going for ever, on some have-a-go heroine hugging her kids. But at least she'd had a minute to get a name and a few details from the husband. 'Mrs Richie – Iris – you have just done a truly remarkable thing. You're an ordinary housewife, and from what I've been told, have no history of doing anything like...'

Iris seemed to be trying to protest, but Katie was damned if she was stopping now. This had better bloody be good, after what she'd been through to get it. Or she might as well not bother going in to the studio tomorrow. The woman looked as though she might faint any minute. Come on. Just give us a line or two to wrap the story up. '...What makes somebody do what you just did? How does it feel?'

Iris was suddenly very, very tired. How nice it would be just to go to sleep with her arms round her children again...

'GO ON, WOMAN – SAY IT!'

It wasn't the woman, it was the angry old man in her head. Oh. Oh God. Yes. Sorry. Okay.

She hugged Ted and Molly closer, smiled her most innocent

smile at Katie, and replied. 'Well, obviously I just randomly happened to be there this afternoon, when Mr Hauser made his speech...'

'Just to fill our audience in, we're still trying to find out whether Mr Hauser himself was responsible for the collapse of the electrical systems – do you have an opinion on that?'

'Oh, I really wouldn't know. Surely not? And if he was, I mean obviously I'm not advocating anything like that, as a way to make a point, but...'

It was very hard to remember what she wanted to say, with that woman nodding dementedly beside the camera. Iris turned from Katie to look down the lens, and suddenly it came to her. She imagined all those people on the other side of it, all hoping that in the same situation they'd do the same thing. All wishing it was them being celebrated, and showered with attention and praise, instead of sitting in front of the TV yet again, trying to recover from another day, just to face the next. People like her. Frightened, confused, terrified of the doom-laden future they heard about every day. Lots and lots of them.

Just forget the reporter. Speak to them.

'All I meant is – even if he chose a rather um, high-risk way to say it, what he was trying to tell us is real, isn't it? And important. I may have helped these - these two children just now, but he is trying to save all of our children, millions of them, isn't he?'

The voice in her ear almost chuckled. 'Good, very good. The old innocent children line. They're loving it. Carry on.'

Katie was, indeed, beaming with relief behind the mic, and the man with the camera had his free thumb in the air.

Iris took a deep breath; months of frustration poured out in one last plea. 'I don't know about you, but when I think of the future, I'm terrified. Wouldn't it be great not to be? We can turn it around. I know we can. I'm only one person, I'm certainly not special, and luckily most people won't ever have to do what I just did. But we can all shove things in the right direction, can't we? It doesn't matter if what you do seems tiny, so long as it makes the world a tiny bit better, not worse. One small thing at a time. That's all it takes, isn't it?'

She stopped, still looking right down the lens. Katie counted to ten in her head before turning to Josh's camera and opening her mouth to wrap up.

But Iris wasn't done. First she wouldn't start, and now the

bloody woman wouldn't stop.

'So that's really all I want to say. It's simple. Listen to your hearts, take it one small thing at a time, and never, ever, think you don't...'

Nobody heard the rest, because at that moment a bearded figure in a red polyester velvet robe embroidered with stars and wizard wands, tripped over Katie's cables, and pulled out her plug.

Malcolm had stepped back a few paces to give Iris her well-earned moment of glory. The man in the robe fell right into him, nearly losing his glasses.

'Here you go,' said Malcolm, catching them just in time. 'My god. Colin. What's with the dressing gown?'

Colin turned round at the sound of Malcolm's voice, got even more tangled in the cables, and was about to fall with them into the empty compost pit, tugging Katie and Josh behind him. Which would not have made a good end to anybody's day.

'Maybe you should lose the fancy dress, what do you think?' Malcolm grabbed Colin just in time. It reminded Malcolm of that Rag Week in their second year, when he'd had to disentangle Colin from a Mother Goose crinoline, in not entirely dissimilar circumstances. He righted his friend, carefully unwrapped and coiled the cables, handed them to the long-suffering Josh, and yanked the robe off Colin by the shoulders. Katie was talking on the phone to the editor, who had rather liked the unexpected drama of the piece's conclusion, and Josh was getting useful shots of the compost pit and the chute.

Malcolm turned to Iris and the four children. 'Hey everyone. Look who I've found! What are you doing out of captivity, Col?'

It had taken Colin the whole afternoon to catch up with Molly. He'd been getting on all right as she left the Convention Centre and set off across the parking lot towards SilverFalls. But it was difficult to run in the robe, and he was reluctant to remove it, as there was no other convenient place to keep the bugs close to his body.

So by the time he reached the Mall she was nowhere in sight. All he saw was a sprawl of emergency vehicles across the open doors, and a trickle of fire-fighters in decontamination suits and gas masks, moving in and out. As he got closer, one of them was saying to a bearded man who seemed to be in charge: 'Well, that's the fire out, but what the bloody heck are we going to do about the slurry? It's chucking gas into the place by the gallon, there's no way we can pump it out – the sodding place is full of it.'

Colin felt the badly-trimmed stubble on his neck stiffen. He'd brought his bugs along just because he always did; after the years he'd spent engineering them, tweaking the molecules, altering the reproductive regime, he wasn't going to risk something going wrong in the lab in his absence. But this was like a miracle. Just at the point where he was pretty sure they could handle anything, an opportunity to test them out on a proper scale literally – so to speak - fell into his lap.

He ducked behind the row of ficus trees shading the entrance, reached into his pocket for the test tube, and crept unseen to the other end of the row of doors. It took only a minute to dash in far enough to smell the gas, and find the puddles of molten wire and polyester leaching it into the air. Luckily, he hadn't had time to feed the bugs since this morning. They'd be ravenous enough to eat anything, and so long as the food lasted, they'd multiply unstoppably.

He opened the tube, muttered a few words of encouragement, and tipped a few drops of goo out onto the first puddle. Then he scampered back out again, before anybody could ask what he was up to.

He had actually been looking for a discreet place to monitor his experiment when he found himself at the food service area; it was pure happy accident that he'd now bumped into the very person he'd set off to find. He just needed to hand over the headpiece, and then he could go off and check up on progress.

Somehow it seemed to Iris entirely typical of her relationship with Malcolm that Colin would be there, smirking and shuffling, to witness their reunion, in a garbage pit outside Birmingham. He seemed to have rationalised his normal habits, and decided to wear his bed.

'Hello Iris. Actually, it was young Molly I was after. She left – oh there you are, you dropped...'

He was holding out the eyeshade, but for some reason young Molly seemed reluctant to take it from him, or even to look at him. She'd buried her face in her mother's shoulder, which Iris seemed to be enjoying.

Colin felt more than usually foolish, especially when he realised Malcolm had obviously not sent his daughter to spy on him, had not even known he'd be here. And now, no doubt, the daughter was about to reveal everything about his extra-curricular activities. He had no idea how much she knew about Altarica, or how she'd found him at the Convention, but he didn't feel ready to explain himself right here.

He reached out, whisked his robe from Malcolm, and backed away, muttering about being expected somewhere. In a sense, it was true. To the extent that a hungry family of several billion micro-organisms, on their own in the big wide world for the first time, could be said to expect anybody. He waved generally to the little group, turned and fled.

He had to know how they were getting on. He hurried back to the main entrance, and peered between the ficus trees. The fire chief was now engaged in an earnest conversation with SilverFalls' head of property management, who was none too happy about the situation.

Suddenly, a fire fighter ran out, pulling off his mask to reveal a puzzled face. 'Chief, there's summat rum in there.'

'What now, Badgerwick?' The fire chief turned to his minion with a demeanour not especially welcoming to the interruption of a confidential summit on the ins and outs of insurance claim finessing.

'Looks like a miracle to me, chief. I know what you'll no doubt say, after...'

'Oh, for pete's sake, Badgerwick, not again. Remember last time with the dog? The dog did not undo the deadbolt, Badgerwick. Remember what we said then? We leave Jesus and his miracles at home, okay?'

'I know, Chief, but if you'll just come and see for one minute... All that gas in there? It's gone!'

The bemused fireman grabbed his boss's sleeve, trying to drag him bodily inside the Mall.

'For the love of Mike...'

'Excuse me?'

Now there was somebody pawing at his other arm. The fire

chief turned to find himself staring at a wild-eyed, bearded lunatic in thick glasses and a dressing-gown, waving a test tube in his face with barely-contained glee. 'Excuse me, you don't know me but, um - he is absolutely right. I think you'll find the air in there is, in fact, considerably purer than the atmospheric norm for an urban area. I was just er, performing a small experiment with these micro-organisms here... it's my, it's just a little hobby of mine. For now.'

'Oh it is, is it? That's how you spend your Sundays? Randomly infiltrating public spaces with your micro-organisms? Does the word 'bioterrorism' mean anything to you?'

Before Colin could respond, the Chief had pulled a whistle from his oilskin, and was blowing on it frantically. Heavy footsteps pounded in from all sides, and even Colin could see that things were looking grim, when the whistle was suddenly snatched from the Chief's mouth.

'Hang on a tick.' It was the man from SilverFalls. He turned to Colin. 'Are you telling us you make bugs that eat toxic fumes?'

'Well – that is a bit of an over-simplification, but – if you wanted to put it in lay terms, I suppose you could say – yes.'

'And no nasty by-products?'

'Well, that's the whole beauty of it. Given the right molecular manipulation, there's no reason why they couldn't deal with more or less any toxic waste, and just leave behind oxygen, or sometimes water vapour. That sort of thing. Of course, I haven't had the chance to...'

The property manager turned to the fire chief. 'Forget insurance fiddles, George. We've just stumbled on a gold mine.'

Once the first thrill of reunion had passed, Iris began trying to find out what had happened to Troy and Fern. Apparently Troy's willing cooperation with the police had turned up absolutely no clue as to the reason for the mysterious power failure. However, he had thought it wise, in the interest of possible future relations with the forces of international law and order, to set environmental principle aside for once, and take the first flight out. So it was Fern, in the end, whom Iris reached.

For similar reasons, the final plenary of the conference had been cancelled, but it would have been hard for even the Principal Speaker to top the afternoon's events. Fern could barely contain her excitement at the apocalyptic demonstration of the horrors of mass consumption that Troy's stunt had, albeit unwittingly, unleashed. 'If you hadn't found the way out, Iris, all those people would have died of looting! Imagine that!'

'That's not a very nice thought.'

'Oh no, of course not. I mean, it would have been awful. Totally. But... You're amazing, Iris. I always knew it. Right from that first evening, with the envelopes.'

'So what am I going to do with Elena and Alejandro?'

'Oh, well Ignacio called just now, he's just wrapping up the terms of the joint venture with the Colombians...'

'The gangsters?'

'Well, it turns out they were being funded by the government, so technically that's who Ignacio's dealing with now. Ex-diplomat to diplomat, and all that. Anyway he said he'll be coming back through in a couple of days, so if you could maybe just look after the little ones till then...'

Iris gazed out of the window at Ted and Alejandro, playing a frenetic game of Wembley Touchdown between the hotel's recycling bins.

'They'll be fine with me. I can't promise to shield them absolutely from the evils of capitalism. Not with my family around. But I expect they'll live.'

She put down the phone to find Molly staring at her from the doorway, having left Elena learning English from Tracy Beaker on the hotel TV.

'That was actually pretty cool today, Mum. It's freakish how every time you mess up, somehow it turns out okay.'

'Excuse me, but that mess in the Mall was definitely not of my making. The worst you can say is that I could have been a bit more discriminating in the company I kept. But I'm not exactly alone in that, either.'

This last sentence may or may not have been addressed to Malcolm, who had been quietly packing the children's bags. He looked up at her, opened his mouth to speak, closed it again, then said: 'We all make mistakes.'

He snapped the last bag shut, stood up, and came over to Iris.

They looked at each other for a moment. Then he wrapped his arms round her in a very fond kiss.

'Ugh, Dad! You might warn us when you're going to do that. So does that mean Mum's coming home then?'

'I hope so – is she?'

They looked at her. She gave it a second's thought. 'Oh, I expect she is. Somebody's got to make those poor kids up a bed for the night.'

Iris spent the next few days more or less besieged at 26 Hartland Gardens, while letters, emails and phone calls poured in with suggestions for parlaying her new-found status as national treasure and Homespun Heroine into solid cash. At first it all seemed very exciting, but when it emerged that the three front runners were an invitation to take part in 'The Green Apprentice', a rather modest offer to endorse Sainsbury's new carbon-neutral ready-meals, and another from the makers of a revolutionary idiot-proof barbecue specifically targeted at women, Iris began to realise that the life of a minor celebrity was not the perfumed water-bed the credulous tabloid reader might suppose.

Then, after a few days, a Cabinet minister was caught in flagrante with twin trapeze artists, the phone went quiet, and Iris was almost relieved to resume her former life.

But one bit of her moment of glory stuck in the public imagination, like gum on a shoe. One Small Thing became the next day's headlines. Then a buzz-word in the Sunday think-pieces. Then, mysteriously, it turned up on flyposters at Camden Lock, from a sad girl group re-branding itself for the zeitgeist. Apparently, the idea that anybody at all could change the world, if they just did one good thing at a time, had brought the public's vast, amorphous terrors down to a manageable scale. It was hardly original, and it was only a slogan. But it was a slogan with legs.

And it was One Small Thing that caught the attention of the Women's Institutes. One day, just as the rivulet of publicity was finally trickling dry, a call had come in, asking if she might possibly have any interest in serving as the W.I.'s Campaigns Officer. Iris, whose life in an inner London borough had not, until now, included any direct contact with the W.I., had been on the point of detailing her total lack of relevant skills or qualifications, with particular reference to ownership of twin-sets, Labradors or relatives in the Armed Forces, when her attention was caught by one tiny, but resonant, word: 'cake'.

The WI had tracked the history of her activities, and intuited that it might find in Iris a sympathetic ear for the horrors the Health and Safety Executive was visiting on all its blameless members up and down the country. Until now, they had been brightening the lives of old people in care homes with a weekly visit, accompanied by home baking of famously impeccable quality. Not any more. Baked goods of untraceable provenance were no longer allowed over the doorsteps of any institution in receipt of public service support. No more cake for old ladies.

It was, of course, outrageous; petty cruelty, pointless bureaucracy, and the irrational terror of an infinitesimal risk to institutions, outweighing a clear and present benefit to the vulnerable and lonely. It needed to be fought, and defeated, with every weapon in the W.I.'s formidable arsenal.

But, more significantly to Iris, that arsenal included money. Money for a regular salary. And one thing Iris had learned in the past few months was that money, even in modest amounts, was an indispensable lubricant to the engine of domestic harmony.

So she had put down the phone without actually committing herself either way. Elena and Alejandro had been so thrilled by the prospect of an excursion with Malcolm to the supermarket that it had seemed cruel to deprive them of its forbidden delights.

Waving goodbye, she climbed on her bike and set off to Buzzybees, trying to imagine herself riding into battle with a cookery book in one hand, and a bound volume of European standard protocols in the other.

The door was locked, but a sign saying 'In the Garden' led Iris down the passage at the side, and up a rickety fire escape to the roof. She emerged onto what had been bare tarmac, to find it thickly turfed, and bordered with pots of herbs and tomatoes. Pepita, abandoned after Arlo's forced departure, was coiled round a sunny chimney-pot.

Sammy turned from watering some late basil. 'Hey you.

Welcome to Extreme Smallholding. Look, we'll have meadow all the way to King's Cross before you know it. Plus, it halves the heating bills.'

Iris looked out over the rooftops. There was, indeed, a surprising amount of cultivation up here. In all directions, on top of shops, flats and offices, people were pottering in the summer sun, and bemused birds and butterflies dipped between patches of green. It was nice to see Sammy, if it was indeed she; not much of her was in fact visible.

'Did you make that?'

Since they'd last met, Sammy had apparently inched even closer to the outer limits of sartorial self-expression. Despite the heat, she was wearing thick trousers, biker boots and gloves, topped by a bamboo coolie hat, all swathed to the waist in a bridal veil. 'It's my bee suit. Can't be called BuzzyBees and not have bees, can we? I'm feeding them up. You'd better stay over there.'

The two wooden crates in one corner of the roof were emitting a hum, which swelled to a low roar as Sammy opened a lid and tipped in the contents of the watering-can. A few bees floated out. She waved them vaguely back inside, then reached into a pocket, pulled out her mobile phone, and put it in with them, before replacing the cover on the hive. Iris stared from the hive to Sammy, and back. 'Um – was that your phone you just put in there?'

'Oh, no, just Arlo's he left behind. All the bees in Europe are getting lost because of phone signals interfering with their homing instincts, so I thought, better bow to the inevitable, and train 'em to glom onto this one.'

Iris squatted on the soft grass, twirling her fingers in the daisy stems. 'Does it work?'

'Who knows? It's not like we can tag their little bottoms. But judging by how many of them turn up here, either it's working or this out-of-date maple syrup is bee crack cocaine.'

Sammy put down the jug, took off her gloves, and lay down in the sun. 'So what are you going to do now?'

Iris lay down beside her and looked up into a sharp blue sky. She shaded her eyes with her hand and muttered: 'I think I'm going to work for the W.I..'

Sammy bounced upright, and pulled off her hat to get a better view of Iris' face. 'The W.I.? Helen Mirren bouncing about with cherries on her tits? You're insane, they lynch people like us. You'd be a bladder on a stick before you could say Morris Dancing.'

Iris rolled away. 'Actually, it's a high level executive post. Policy and campaigning, that sort of thing.'

'So it's a desk job. Better yet. You'll shoot yourself inside a week. I've got a much better idea.'

Iris allowed herself to roll back and squint up at Sammy, fanning her rosy face with the hat. 'You have?'

'Yeah, it's wild actually. The Planet came back and offered me a huge lump of money to keep everything exactly like it is.'

'What? What's the catch?'

'None, from what I can see. They finally worked out people here like stuff that looks like, ramshackle and home-made. Make that "lovingly hand-cultivated by dedicated artisans." So they're still planning on buying out all these places like us, but now they want to keep them how they are, all different from each other. I'd just have to put up with them traipsing through from time to time to watch us sprinkle the fairy dust.'

Iris had been listening with half an ear, while looking for animal faces in the clouds, and wondering why she hadn't done this for so long. It took a while for the significance of the information to sink in. Then she half-sat up, propped on one elbow, and stared at Sammy, who looked back at her serenely.

'But that means – you'd be selling out. To the enemy.'

'Which is exactly why I told them to bloody shove it. Still, it gave me a much better idea. I've been talking to a bunch of the others, you know all the other indie shops they've been breathing over, and we're setting up a cooperative, like, you know, an UnChain. "We have nothing to lose but the Chains!" Geddit? We get economies of scale without all the centralising crap, and if we all say no to them, there's fuck all they can do. Which still leaves the problem of the lease, but there'll be another internet café going under any minute, they're like athlete's foot the way they come and go round here. So there's just one more thing...'

Once Iris had realised that the threat wasn't real, she'd gone back to watching clouds. Eventually, she noticed Sammy had stopped talking, and was staring at her, as though waiting for her to speak. 'Sorry, did I miss something?'

'Yeah well, with all the bloody custom we've been getting and with Arlo gone, I can't do it on my own. You're super-organised, and you can do all that horrendous money shit. And you spend half your life here anyway. So I thought you might want to come in on it. As a partner. I mean, with all the dosh the credulous public have been hurling at us, I could probably even pay you, in, like, cash.'

Cash? A salary? To hang out with Sammy and her crew all day long? And not have to go into an office, or read sub-clauses over a sandwich? 'Wow. That would be pretty cool.'

Except...'Only - well, the thing is, I made this sort of promise to Malcolm. When we got back. That there was this one person I'd never ever talk to again. And I can sort of see his point, given that she started the whole thing off. And unfortunately, she happens to...'

'Oh, if this is about Soren, she's far too busy to waste her sermons on us. She's got this new thing she invented called Carbon Watchers. It's like Weight Watchers, they help you keep your footprint down by monitoring what you do every week, and giving you allowances and shit. It's spreading like Japanese knotweed in the Home Counties, in fact if you took that WI job you'd probably bump into her all the time.'

'I think that settles it. When do I start?'

From: pwrynose@silverfalls.org
To: c.winterbottom@richiewinterbottom.co.uk

Dear Mr Winterbottom

It was good meeting you the other day and, again, my apologies if we started off on the wrong foot. I'm sure you can understand that, given our customer volumes, we have to be hyper vigilant in these matters. You can never be too careful, especially in this era of terrorism issues, unfortunately.

However, you may not have realised that we here at SilverFalls Holdings have an impressively diverse portfolio which we are always looking to extend into new ventures, and having done a bit of asking around at Group HQ, I think we can probably make up to you for our discourtesy with some pretty hefty backing for your research.

Needless to say I am not personally apprised in the cost of test-tubes and whatever, but we would be happy to invite you for a meeting at your earliest convenience to discuss terms.

Please telephone Mandy in the office here any time to arrange it.

Yours sincerely,
Peter Wrynose
General Manager, Business Development, SilverFalls Holdings, Inc

from: Kateriina Toivonen, ktoivonen@zoomtech.org
to: c.winterbottom@richiewinterbottom.co.uk

Dear Colin – I hope you excuse the informality, Malcolm has told me so much about you that I feel I know you as well as I have come to know him!

I suppose it's a no brainer that the oldest friend of such a genius should be a genius in his own right. Frankly, I'm kicking myself that all this time we at Zoom have been so close to work of the world class quality of yours yet quite unaware of it! You scientists are way too reticent for your own good, as I have told Malcolm many times.

But in any case I hope it is not yet too late for us to make it up to you, and take you into the Zoom International family. Malcolm will not have told you, as it has until now been a confidential project, but we have for some time been planning to set up a Genius Centre to promote exactly work such as yours, and give you whatever facilities you might need to bring it as swiftly as possible to production status.

It goes without saying that everything about the Centre will be the best, and of course we would include a handsome compensation package, to include a generous percentage of royalties. As you may know, we have interests in the production and distribution of many types of biochemicals, so your work would synergise perfectly into our portfolio.

I am sure you can ask Malcolm anything you need to know about his experiences since we began our enjoyable and already productive collaboration. So far he has not uttered any complaints!

I look forward very much to getting to work on this. Do not hesitate to respond with any question, and meanwhile I am your good (new!) friend

K XXX
Kateriina Toivonen
Deputy Worldwide CEO
Zoom International, Inc

Colin scraped out the last of the bioactive strawberry yoghurt with his plastic spoon and licked it absently as he read the email through again. The rapid developments of the last few days, on top of the unwonted change of environment and exposure to outside air, had given him a nasty cold, which he was hoping the yoghurt might treat. One of the many things he envied his bugs was their freedom from the complexities of the human metabolism, with all the tedious upkeep it entailed. Still, the strawberry flavouring was quite palatable.

He put down the pot and spoon, rolled his chair up to the desk, closed Kateriina's mail and then scrolled back to the one from SilverFalls. It was gratifying, after a professional career of obscurity leavened only with moments of ridicule, to have not one, but two major conglomerates begging to open their coffers to him. But, as Malcolm had cause to know and regret, money had never been Colin's motivation.

A couple of spaces further back in the in-tray was an emailhe'd been re-reading every few minutes since its arrival the day before. To Colin, it might have come directly from heaven, which given the reach of the Web was entirely possible. He opened it and read it again:

FROM: hvd@optogen.org
TO: cwinterbottom@richiewinterbttom.co.uk

Hey Colin
I don't believe we ever had a chance to meet, but I heard about your little demo the other week (yup, news travels even here in the Galapagos). And I guess you probably know who I am.

We'll be quartered here in Vanuatu for a while yet. I have no idea what your commitments are but I figured if you had the time, you might like to join our research trip. We're finding some mind-blowing DNA in the deep oceans. Plus, I don't know how the weather is your way – is Kilburn a neighborhood of London? But I can tell you it's pretty good here, right now.

If you can free yourself up, we'll send transport from the mainland. You won't need much by way of gear but if there are special dietary needs, just mail our chief steward Rick (bigboat@optogen.org)

Looking forward to it. One thing about cruising the oceans, you get plenty of time to chat!

H

Horace Van Dieck! The man who'd unravelled the human genome, tweaked ruminant DNA to rid their farts of methane, and was now developing his vision for an entire post-human planet, re-engineered from the molecules up. Colin had never even dreamed of sharing a conference session with Horace, and now he'd been invited for an indefinite sojourn on Horace's personal yacht.

He opened up a new mail and addressed it to Kateriina.

Dear Ms Toivonen,

Thank you for your very flattering words in your email. I am pleased that my colleague Malcolm Richie has spoken well of me.

Unfortunately I am not available to take up your attractive offer as I shall be travelling for the foreseeable future. However, if you go to the library in my Second Life experimental lab, Altarica, at

www.secondlife.org/altarica/archive.htm

I believe you will find most of the documentation you're after. As it's already on the Internet, of course it's in the public domain, as I would hope any future work of this sort would continue to be.

Good luck with your Genius Centre. It sounds very ambitious.

Yours,
Colin Winterbottom

PS I may be hard to reach for the next few months.

He copied the body of the text, sent an identical email to Peter Wrynose, passed on the news of the upcoming adventure to his bugs, and opened their book at 'William Gets His Feet Wet'.

'So that's what he's gone off to do? Sail round the world with a Nobel prize winner in a hundred foot yacht, dipping test tubes in the water to look for bits of wacky DNA? Jammy bugger.'

Iris was standing beside Malcolm in Free-Flow's Person-Centred Distribution Centre, which had been opened half an hour ago by Kateriina to the thunderous applause not only of FreeFlow's entire management team, but all the people working in it. Malcolm had been coerced into delivering a modest but quietly entertaining speech, which made only oblique reference to having had to travel half way across the world, nearly losing his wife in the process, in order to find inspiration in Woking.

Iris stood at his side, pink with pride, in an extremely smart and expensive outfit, which she justified to herself on the basis that the more money you spend on something, the longer it will have to last. Which has got to be a good and sustainable result. One thing her brief twirl in the spotlight had taught her was never to go anywhere public in flat shoes and a boy's tee shirt, because, you just never know.

Afterwards, Kateriina melted away to finesse the executives, and Malcolm escorted Iris down the long aisle between the packing hubs, at each of which a man or woman sat, pressing buttons and speaking into microphones, as boxes and crates travelled between them down ramps and along belts.

'You see, in most places like this it's the other way round. The stuff just comes tumbling in on them, whether they're ready or not, at whatever speed the people at the other end send it. They have no control, they can't do it their way. They have to keep up with the machines. Just like Charlie Chaplin in 'Modern Times'. It's a disgrace, and totally unnecessary these days. Or at least, that's what I thought. So all I did was turn the system on its head.'

'Imagine, all those mornings I thought you were just reading the Weetabix packet! You're so clever, I'm so proud of you. Still, I'm going to have to get used to it now aren't I? Wife of top-level creative exec, hireling to the faceless conglomerate, etc.'

'You don't sound very proud of that bit.'

'Well...' Iris struggled for a way to express what she felt without either perjuring herself or heaping insult on her husband's new bosses. He let her suffer for a minute before whispering: 'Anyhow, it's not going to happen.'

'It's not?'

'If you remember, I didn't do too well the last time I had to play office politics. Anyhow, this Person-Centred stuff is my baby. I've been nurturing it for the best part of a decade now, and it's a bloody good idea. See how well it's working? I'm not about to abandon it for some airy fairy job as Kateriina's lap dog. Though I didn't put it quite like that when I told her. Still, it's curtains for the luxury executive lifestyle, I'm afraid, and back to consulting, at least until I sell this idea to a few more people.'

As he said this, his hand slid round her waist. Iris turned to him. He was still Malcolm, after all. What a wonderful discovery, and how extraordinary that it had taken all this to make her realise how wonderful it actually was.

Malcolm realised, with sudden alarm, that she was about to make a public display of emotion. He allowed her lips briefly to brush his cheek before adding: 'Still, I got her and Zoom to pay for the proof of concept. Anybody who doubts that it works only has to come here.'

'Indeed. Clever you.'

'Anyhow, she's after Colin now. She wants him to put the Genius into the Genius Centre.'

'Colin? Has she ever actually met Colin?'

She stood, watching the silent rhythm of machines and people, working together. Having a better life, because Malcolm had quietly decided to do something about it. 'But he is actually sort of a genius, isn't he? Maybe that's what geniuses are like. You know, those BBC nature films with the insects scurrying around the forest floor, looking very dull and boring and being stepped on by bigger creatures, barely even showing up on the camera. And all the time being the ones everything else depends on. Not making any fuss, or drawing attention to themselves, or needing huge forests to roam around, like the bears or the tigers. Getting on with it. Sorting out messes for the rest of us.'

'Oh, I don't know. If it weren't for the tigers and bears, there wouldn't be any point. Come to think of it, you look rather tigerish in that outfit. Let's get out of here, I've definitely earned my fee for today.'

He wrapped an arm around her waist and led her out into the sun. As he unlocked the egg, he looked over it and added: 'You know, there's no need to worry about all this stuff.'

'What stuff?'

'Everybody knows that nobody ever predicts the important things. Like the Internet, or Starbucks. When Ernest Rutherford discovered nuclear energy he thought it had no practical application. The pioneers of radio never thought of broadcasting. Thomas Watson started IBM to make a few adding machines. Et cetera.'

She opened her door and slid in, as he climbed in the other side. 'So?'

'Well then, if everybody all over the place is predicting the end of civilisation as we know it, it's not going to happen is it? And meanwhile the Austrian postal service has found a way to put ice-cream flavour into stamp glue. Human ingenuity never fails.'

'Ice cream flavoured stamps? I'm supposed to stop worrying because of that?'

She glared at him, calmly fastening his seat belt. He looked up, saw her face, and smiled. 'Or maybe not. You seem to have developed a knack for snatching victory from the jaws of public humiliation. Just try to avoid getting arrested when I've a big meeting on, would you?'

One hand reached out to move the hair away from her face. 'But meanwhile, if you ever manage to fasten your seat belt, we can go home and make the most of our afternoon off in an empty house.'

Later, she took Ted to the park, having changed out of her posh frock into Molly's present on departing for her orientation trip to Paris, a black tee shirt saying 'Stop Changing Sheets, Start Changing History'.

Ted, at least, had wrested some concrete benefit from his mother's adventures. A letter from an anonymous nine-year-old fan to the Chelsea Football Club might well have gone unanswered, but a letter from the son of Mrs One Small Thing was a different matter. The Board had been properly impressed by his suggestion that, as the roster of League mascots already included two other lions (the chocolate-coloured Yorkie and the feral, if mangy, Millwall Zampa), it would be a brilliant stroke of publicity for Chelsea to adopt, instead, the representative of an endangered species. Background checks on possible conflicts of interest with the Chairman's business activities had revealed that, although it might be embarrassing for the club to be publicly associated with the attempted preservation of either the Amur leopard or the Siberian tiger, Ted was quite safe trotting on to the pitch disguised as a polar bear.

And by an extraordinary coincidence, there just happened to be a polar bear costume, exactly the right size, all ready for his first game. So there he was, doing laps of the playground in full disguise for the Mascot Grand National, determined to better the record-breaking time set in last year's race by Cyril the Swansea Swan's narrow win over Peter Burrow the rabbit.

The park was looking almost idyllic in the light of the autumn afternoon. The local McDonalds' contribution to One Small Thing had been to sponsor a 'Grossest Garbage' contest, with weekly prizes for the biggest pile of repulsive detritus from the park's lawns and flower-beds. Although Iris wasn't totally sure about endorsing anything rewarded by a Happy Meal, it had certainly made the place look a lot nicer.

Iris sat on a bench, closed her eyes, and listened to the sounds of the city throbbing all around. Ever since she'd finally got the world's attention, her ear had stopped itching. Maybe He'd finally decided she was safe on her own. Or maybe He'd given up on her. Not tough enough for the long haul. She didn't feel like Joan of Arc any more. If she'd been Joan, she wouldn't have come trotting back into the bosom of her family. 'Back' was not a word in Joan's vocabulary, and certainly not 'Back to DomRemy for a nice Sunday lunch with the old folks; I owe it to them, after what I've put them through.' Joan had no children to worry about, but she did have parents. Her mother was so distraught after Joan died that she spent twenty years campaigning to have the death sentence overturned. Not that it would bring her daughter back, but no doubt it gave a focus to the anguish, a place to put it.

I can't do that, thought Iris. Maybe when the children have

left. Maybe if Malcolm shoved me out the door. But until then, I'm going to have to do what I can from here. While I'm here, with the rest of them.

What would it be like if we were all gone? All the concrete and rubber and coconut oil and plastic bags, the Barbie karaoke sets and knockoff LV luggage, all gone. Everything gone but the clouds and the mountains, the vast deserts and the spiky, persistent cactuses. And the odd worm or cockroach. No more gangsta rap, Capital Gold, jackhammers, muzak, taxi engines, sixteen wheelers, or ambulance sirens. No parks, no pets, no art, no opera, no gardens, no fishing, no football. No wars. No murders.

I don't want to leave this. I don't want to leave behind deserts and autumn colours, billowing roses and bluebell woods. But I shall. We all will. Fifty-four billion species have lived on our planet so far. Fifty billion are already extinct. Some things go quickly: snowflakes, mayflies and satin combat pants. Some things take a bit longer: the Great Auk, the dinosaurs, LPs. And us.

But something else will come along. Maybe something much less destructive; maybe something much more beautiful. And then, in about six billion years, whatever's left will vapourise in the heat of the sun.

And then there won't be anything more to worry about, ever again.

for the incomparable Kiki Constantinescu-Hayes, who made it look lovely

for Mr Fixit, who just goes on doing what he does, fixing...

and for Dorothy and Frank, who bear no resemblance, intended or otherwise, to any living person or animal

Sheila Hayman's parents were a Yorkshire Quaker activist and a German Jewish mathematician. She has been a BAFTA-winning filmmaker, Young Journalist of the Year, the official necrologist of the Oscars, and fiddle player in an Irish band in Los Angeles. Her two previous novels about family life, 'Small Talk' and 'Are We Nearly There Yet?' were surprise hits in countries with low birth rates. She hopes to do the same for environmentalism with 'Mrs Normal Saves the World'.

Mrs Normal is an ongoing project.
Join in, find out about the real Normals,
and strap on your own sword and shield at
www.mrsnormal.com

10509038R00187

Printed in Great Britain
by Amazon.co.uk, Ltd.,
Marston Gate.